"Miss? Miss?"

A hand on her shoulder brought Ariel out of the foggy state engulfing her.

Her gaze traveled over the masculine fingers, the large hand, to a dark coat that led up an arm, passed across broad shoulders to a very handsome face beneath a helmet.

"Stay with me," the man murmured.

That deep, rich voice brought her focus back to the moment. Memory flooded her on a wave of terror. The horror of rolling down the side of the cliff, hitting her head, landing in a bramble bush, and the fear of moving that would take her plummeting to the bottom of the mountain. She gasped with realization.

"Someone pushed me!"

Terri Reed
and
USA TODAY Bestselling Author
Maggie K. Black

Deadly Alaskan Pursuit

2 Thrilling Stories
Alaskan Rescue and *Wilderness Defender*

LOVE INSPIRED
INSPIRATIONAL ROMANCE

Special thanks and acknowledgment are given
to Terri Reed and Maggie K. Black for their contribution
to the Alaska K-9 Unit miniseries.

LOVE INSPIRED®

INSPIRATIONAL ROMANCE

Recycling programs
for this product may
not exist in your area.

ISBN-13: 978-1-335-42732-8

Deadly Alaskan Pursuit

Copyright © 2022 by Harlequin Enterprises ULC

Alaskan Rescue
First published in 2021. This edition published in 2022.
Copyright © 2021 by Harlequin Enterprises ULC

Wilderness Defender
First published in 2021. This edition published in 2022.
Copyright © 2021 by Harlequin Enterprises ULC

For questions and comments about the quality of this book, please contact us
at CustomerService@Harlequin.com.

Love Inspired
22 Adelaide St. West, 41st Floor
Toronto, Ontario M5H 4E3, Canada
www.LoveInspired.com

Printed in U.S.A.

CONTENTS

Terri Reed's romance and romantic suspense novels have appeared on the *Publishers Weekly* top twenty-five and Nielsen BookScan top one hundred lists, and have been featured in *USA TODAY*, *Christian Fiction* magazine and *RT Book Reviews*. Her books have been finalists for the Romance Writers of America RITA® Award and the National Readers' Choice Award and finalists three times for the American Christian Fiction Writers Carol Award. Contact Terri at terrireed.com or PO Box 19555, Portland, OR 97224.

Books by Terri Reed

Love Inspired Suspense

Buried Mountain Secrets
Secret Mountain Hideout
Christmas Protection Detail
Secret Sabotage

Rocky Mountain K-9 Unit

Detection Detail

Alaska K-9 Unit

Alaskan Rescue

Visit the Author Profile page
at LoveInspired.com for more titles.

ALASKAN RESCUE

Terri Reed

Now the God of hope fill you with all joy and peace
in believing, that ye may abound in hope,
through the power of the Holy Ghost.
—*Romans* 15:13

As always, it was such a pleasure to work with the other ladies, Maggie K. Black, Sharon Dunn, Laura Scott, Jodie Bailey, Heather Woodhaven, Dana Mentink, Shirlee McCoy and Lenora Worth. You all make the writing fun.
And a big thank-you to our editor, Emily Rodmell, for guiding us along the way.

A special thank-you to Patricia Whitesell for all the lovely photos of your Siberian huskies and interesting details that helped to bring Juneau alive.

ONE

"Ariel, hurry up."

"Coming. Are we sure we should be doing this?" Ariel Potter glanced behind her. Nothing but trees and thick underbrush covered in layers of April snow.

When Ariel's best friend, Violet James, had called her this morning to announce they were going on yet another wedding party excursion, which included Violet's fiancé, Lance Wells, and his best man, Jared Dennis, Ariel had anticipated maybe they were going sledding or even skiing. Certainly not hiking in Chugach State Park through the snow-covered forested mountains, one of the many natural wonders of Alaska.

Their tour guide, Cal Brooks, had led them off the marked trail despite the signs clearly stating all hikers were to stay on the path. Anxiety fluttered in Ariel's stomach. They were breaking the rules, which wasn't cool.

"It's fine." Violet adjusted her sky-blue knit cap over her medium-length blond hair. "You worry too much. We're going to lose the guys if we don't hurry."

Shaking her head, Ariel trudged on, thankful for the waterproof insulated boots on her feet. A shiver traipsed down her spine despite the warmth of her bright pink feather down jacket.

The area was so wild and remote, reminding her of the time when she was six and wandered from her family's campsite. It had been hours before she'd found her way back. Her parents hadn't even noticed her missing.

Her fingers curled against the memory. She was thankful for the hand warmers inside her gloves. The Nikon D7500 camera hanging around her neck had grown heavy. The thing only weighed a pound and a half but could be more like twenty if the pain tugging at her neck was any indication. She lifted it off her chest and snapped some pictures of Violet's retreating back and of the three men even farther ahead as they crested the rise and then moved out of sight.

With a sigh of resignation, Ariel continued to trek through the snow. This was not how she had wanted to spend her Saturday. She should be training her sled dogs for next weekend's last fun run race of the season. As well as seeing to the next breeding schedule, which was her main source of income.

And there was the puppy to consider. Poor Sasha was no doubt confused to be sent to the neighbors for the day again.

Not to mention, this week Ariel was going to be accepting an award for her skill at breeding champion dogs. The Iditarod had recently ended and many of her champion Alaskan husky sled dogs had placed in the top positions with their respective mushers, and she hadn't even started on her acceptance speech.

The only thing she could come up with was thanking her nomadic parents for teaching her everything she knew about dogs, mushing and breeding. Not that they would be in attendance. Her parents lived out of a travel trailer and rarely stayed in one place. It had been six months since the last time they'd stopped through Anchorage on their roamings.

Ah well. It was her own fault for letting Violet convince her that she could take a day off. Actually, another day in a long line of days off.

As the maid of honor, Ariel could hardly refuse Violet, who was so excited about her upcoming nuptials. Lance Wells, the groom-to-be, had planned all sorts of wedding events over the past week. First it had been whale watching, next an escape room adventure, then line dancing, and now hiking on unmarked trails.

Lance had insisted on this excursion and Violet seemed to want to do anything that Lance said. Because she was in love.

Ariel didn't like the sour grapes twisting in her chest. At twenty-nine, she kind of despaired she'd ever find her Mr. Right. She wasn't looking, mind you. Love seemed like a risky endeavor. Especially after the fiasco of her last boyfriend, Jason. A mistake she truly regretted. He'd seemed so sweet and kind at first, but then she'd realized it was a facade. She didn't care for the man he really was and had broken off their relationship.

But still, she liked the idea of a grand romance.

Up ahead, Violet crested the rise and disappeared.

With a grunt of frustration, Ariel stepped up her pace. She was honest enough with herself to realize she was a tad bit jealous, and sad, because she was losing another friend to marriage. Violet and Lance's wedding would be the fifth one that Ariel had been involved in over the past year and a half. What was it about nearing thirty that made people decide it was time to marry?

But Ariel really was happy for Violet. She was her best friend. And this was the first time she had been asked to be the maid of honor.

However, Ariel couldn't banish the deep sense of unease niggling at the back of her mind.

There was nothing specific that had her on edge lately. Just this strange sensation that something dark lurked, waiting to strike.

Giving herself a mental head slap for her silly imagination, she crested the rise onto an outcrop that ran along the mountainside. As her boots crunched over the rocks beneath the layer of hard-packed snow, she noticed her hiking mates were already starting up the next incline, and that she'd lost sight of Violet among the thick forest. Uh-oh.

The altitude pulled at Ariel's lungs. Her breath came out in ragged puffs. Shielding her eyes from the overcast sky, she contemplated the next mountain. Really? They were going to hike up *that* now?

Making a face, she turned to look out over the vista, needing a moment before she hurried after her friends. From this vantage point she could see the majestic Denali mountain, the tallest in North America, and the sprawling city that was Anchorage. The place she called home.

Movement in the sky caught her attention. A bald eagle soared, its wings spread. The white tail and head were so bright in contrast to the bird's dark body. Though Alaska was home to the bald eagle, Ariel never tired of them.

Seeing the majestic bird reminded her of the verse in Isaiah that said, *"Those who hope in the Lord will renew their strength. They will soar on wings like ea-gles, they will run and not grow weary, they will walk and not be faint."*

She scrambled to lift her camera to take pictures. The eagle dipped lower. Ariel hurried along the outcrop to the very edge, where it narrowed, snapping off images as the bird dipped, clearly looking for dinner.

The loud bang of a gun echoed across the valley. Startled, Ariel shivered, but chalked the noise up to hunters. She deplored that the state park allowed the hunting of one black bear per hunter from September through May.

Refocusing on the eagle, Ariel continued to take snapshots as the bird dove below the tree line and out of sight. Staring down the side of the cliff made her dizzy. It was a long drop to the bottom with many trees and rocks dotting the landscape and jutting out of the side of the steep cliff.

A moment later the eagle swooped toward the sky with a hare dangling in its mouth. The bird turned in a big arc and headed right toward Ariel. Her heart stalled in her chest. These were going to be fabulous photos.

From behind her, the rush of footsteps made her wince. No doubt Violet coming to retrieve her way-ward maid of honor.

As the eagle flew overhead, a hand on Ariel's back shoved her forward. Her feet lost traction. She slipped off the edge of the cliff, her arms flaying, the camera banging against her chest. A scream escaped her and echoed in her ears.

Lord, please help me!

She tucked herself into a ball and hit the side of the

cliff, her body rolling over sharp debris. The back of her head slammed against something hard. Pain exploded through her. She cried out, terrified that she was going to die.

Alaska State Trooper and K-9 handler Hunter McCord stepped into the conference room of the Alaska K-9 Unit headquarters late Saturday afternoon. Why had his boss, Colonel Lorenza Gallo, called a team meeting today? The unit typically had team briefings multiple times during the work week because Lorenza deemed it important that the team stay connected to one another and to the cases that were happening across the state of Alaska. But coming in on the weekend was unusual.

"All right everyone, settle down. Take a seat." Lorenza, wearing a tailored navy pantsuit sporting one of her signature elaborate gold and jewel-studded broaches on the lapel, stood at the front of the room. Beside her sat her senior dog, Denali, a handsome white-and-gray husky with bright blue eyes.

Tall and commanding with short silver hair, the colonel had been one of the state's first female state troopers to work with a K-9 and had formed the Alaska K-9 Unit ten years ago as a specialty team comprised of K-9 state troopers to supplement the state's law enforcement reach, especially in rural areas without resources for any K-9 dogs.

Lorenza had recruited state troopers from across Alaska and provided a requisite twelve-week instruction course at the K-9 training center that the state troopers shared with the Metro police department, which was located directly behind the Anchorage headquarters.

Planting himself in the nearest chair, Hunter noticed

Trooper Helena Maddox leaning against the wall. She and her partner, a Norwegian elkhound named Luna, specialized in suspect apprehension.

Rising quickly, Hunter offered her the chair. When the whole team was assembled, they usually were short a couple of seats. "Here you go, Helena."

With a grateful smile, she slipped into the chair. "Thank you, Hunter."

"Of course." He noticed the dark circles under her green eyes. "You doing okay? You look stressed."

She shrugged. "I'm just worried about my sister. I haven't heard from her in a while and she's not returning my texts or calls."

Concerned, Hunter put his hand on her shoulder. When one team member hurt, they all did. They were a family. "Let me know if I can help."

"Thanks," she said. "I will."

Hunter moved to rest his shoulder against the wall beside Trooper Will Stryker. He was passionate about stopping the drug trade in the state and his partner, a border collie, excelled at detecting the illegal substances. "Hey."

Will, roughly the same height and build as Hunter, gave him the chin nod.

"Do you know what this is about?" Hunter asked, his voice low.

"No idea," Will replied, his brown eyes looking more serious than usual as he focused on their boss.

Trooper Sean West glanced over his shoulder from his seat next to Helena. "Something big must be happening."

Hunter hoped Sean and his cadaver-seeking partner,

an Akita named Grace, wouldn't be called upon today. Recoveries were hard on all of them.

Lorenza held up a hand, quieting the room. "I know it's a Saturday and some of you are technically off. But crime does not rest."

There was a murmur of agreement through the room.

"Earlier this afternoon, the tour company, Unexplored Alaska, called Metro police when one of their tour guides and his group of four didn't return to base as scheduled. They were headed into Chugach State Park for an 'off the beaten path' hike. The police, accompanied by the owner of Unexplored Alaska, searched the area that was on the tour guide's agenda."

Lorenza taped up a photo onto the glass wall behind her of a young man lying prone in the snow. "The guide, Cal Brooks, was found dead from a single gunshot wound to the chest."

She put up four other images, which looked like driver's license pictures, onto the glass pane.

"The hikers were all part of a wedding party, consisting of the bride-to-be, Violet James." Lorenza pointed to a photo of a blonde woman with big blue eyes and delicate features. "Violet is the daughter of the late Alaskan oil baron Samuel James and his wife, Marie."

She gestured to the two men's images on the wall. "Her fiancé, Lance Wells, owns and operates an import-export business, and his best man, Jared Dennis, is a commercial fisherman. And the maid of honor, Ariel Potter, is a local Alaskan husky breeder." The last photo was of another blonde with pale brown eyes and a generous smile. "These four are missing. No trace of them. The local PD has requested our help."

"Could this be a kidnapping?" Trooper Brayden Ford

asked. "Was the deceased found near one of the lakes in the park?"

Brayden and his partner, a Newfoundland named Ella, handled the team's underwater searches.

"No body of water nearby. As for kidnapping, that remains to be seen."

"Have there been any avalanches reported?" Trooper Gabriel Runyon asked from the other side of the conference table. Gabriel and his beautiful Saint Bernard, Bear, were proficient in avalanche detection.

"None reported in that area, but if you would work with the state's avalanche technician and see if there has been any activity in the park, that would be helpful," Lorenza said. "At this point we don't have enough information to know the motive for the murder. We need to know what happened to these four civilians and who killed the tour guide and why." Her gaze swept over the room and landed on Hunter. "Hunter."

Under Lorenza's scrutiny, he straightened from the wall. "Yes, ma'am."

"You will lead a search team. Maya and Poppy will go with you."

Grateful for the opportunity to take point on the search, Hunter kept his satisfaction in check. He would do his colonel proud.

"See Katie on your way out," Lorenza continued. "She will give you the details." Her steel-eyed gaze returned to the room at large. "The rest of you, I want in-depth background checks on all five of these people. Was Cal Brooks involved in criminal activity that followed him up the mountain? Or was one of the others the target? And we will work with the James family in case this is a kidnapping and ransom demands are made."

Mentally going through his checklist of equipment needed, Hunter headed for the conference room door, along with fellow troopers Maya Rodriguez and Poppy Walsh.

In the hallway, he paused. "I'll meet you two and your partners at Katie's desk," Hunter said. "Gear up. We're in for more snow."

"Roger that." Poppy pushed back her auburn-colored bangs. "I wonder if the tour group happened upon poachers?"

"A valid question considering the state park's hunting restrictions," Hunter said.

Which was probably why the colonel assigned Poppy and Stormy, an Irish wolfhound, for the initial deploy. Stormy was highly cross-trained to detect weapons and people, while Poppy was also an experienced wildlife trooper. Maya and her partner, a Malinois name Sarge, were experts at sniffing out all types of weapons and explosives. Even infectious diseases.

After retrieving his partner, a red-and-white Siberian husky named Juneau, from Hunter's assigned small office and gathering the equipment necessary for a mountain search, Hunter headed to the colonel's administrative assistant's office. He stopped in the doorway.

"Good afternoon, Hunter. Come in," Katie Kapowski, a petite redhead with sharp green eyes, was the consummate professional. She rose from her desk with a file folder in her hand.

As Maya and Poppy and their respective dogs joined Hunter and Juneau, Katie gave Hunter the folder. "Here's everything I could gather quickly on the missing wedding party. I've already been fielding calls from Mrs. James and her representatives, wanting answers."

"We will do our best to bring home the four missing people," Hunter assured her. He never made promises he couldn't keep, and he knew from experience that sometimes search and rescue missions ended up as recoveries. He sent up a prayer that wouldn't be the case here.

Following the directions in the file folder, Hunter drove his vehicle to the Glen Alps trailhead parking area. Poppy and Maya brought their own SUVs to a halt alongside his.

A Metro police cruiser sat waiting with its motor running next to a van with the logo of the tour company, Unexplored Alaska.

Hunter climbed out of his SUV and breathed in the crisp, cold air. Overhead more clouds gathered, giving credence to the predicted coming snowfall.

A tall police officer climbed out of the cruiser and jogged over to him. "Trooper McCord?" the officer asked.

Hunter stuck out his hand. "Yes. Hunter McCord. Officer—" Hunter glanced at the name badge on the other man's jacket. "Brand."

"Call me Everett. My chief wanted me to let you look at the Unexplored Alaska van before we have it taken to the state crime lab."

"I appreciate it," Hunter said. "Were there any signs of foul play in or around the van?"

"Not that we saw," Everett said. "But I'm sure Tala will find anything if there is something to find."

Hunter knew the forensic tech, Tala Ekho, from the Alaska State Crime Lab, was top-notch, and he had confidence that what Everett said was true.

"Open the van, will you?" Hunter instructed. "We'll let the dogs take a good sniff."

Everett complied, opening the side door to the ten-passenger cargo van.

After releasing Juneau from his compartment in the SUV, Hunter had the dog explore the van. Then Hunter and Juneau moved aside to let Maya and Sarge take a sniff. Then Poppy and Stormy had a turn. Though Sarge and Stormy weren't necessarily trained for search and rescue, their noses would be assets out in the field.

Everett locked up the van when they were done.

"We're going to head up the mountain and search for our missing wedding party," Hunter told him. "If we find anything, I'll alert dispatch and they can alert you."

"Copy," Everett said and jogged back to his cruiser.

Consulting the notes provided by Katie, Hunter said to Poppy and Maya, "We take the main trail, and then we'll branch off to an alternate route for the top of Flattop Mountain."

"Where was the tour guide found?" Maya asked, looking over his shoulder at the map.

"Here." He pointed to a red dot that had been marked on the paper topography map. "A few yards above what looks like a crag in the mountainside."

"Let's do this," Poppy said as she adjusted the strap on her climbing helmet.

Hunter tucked the map into the front zippered pocket of his winterized jacket. He put his climbing helmet on his head, making sure his goggles had a good seal before jamming his hands into his gloves. Then he hefted his internal frame pack loaded with everything he could possibly need for this mission onto his back.

Maya and Poppy also had similar packs. And the

dogs were outfitted with winter coats marked Alaska K-9 Unit and long leads.

Hunter and Juneau led the way up the marked trail at a fast clip. When he gauged they'd traveled the right distance, he checked the map again, looking for where the tour guide had taken his party off the path.

Maya and Sarge moved ahead of Hunter. "Here." She gestured to where a yellow cone had been set in the snow, revealing the route many feet had recently tread, which appeared to lead toward Flattop.

With Maya now leading the way, they followed the intermittent yellow cones as they traversed the man-made footpath. The terrain was rough, the forest thick and the incline steep.

"We're coming to the crag," Hunter said loudly.

The outcrop was approximately ten feet wide where they stood but extended farther along the face of the mountain until it narrowed into a short ledge, barely wide enough to stand on.

More yellow cones led up the next incline. Hunter paused to assess the area. There were footprints in the snow all over the outcrop. No doubt from the tour group and the police department.

"Let's spread out," he said. "Maya, search where the body was discovered. See if you can find the weapon or any other evidence that might be useful."

Maya nodded. Then she and Sarge proceeded to follow the cones.

Hunter stood facing the mountain. "The others had to go up, right?"

"Or around," Poppy said. "There was nothing to suggest they went back the way they came."

"You take a path up to the right," Hunter suggested. "I'll go to the left. Check in frequently."

"You got it." Poppy and Stormy headed off.

Hunter unhooked Juneau from his lead. "Search."

The dog cocked his head, sniffed the air, then put his nose to the snow. Rather than turning toward the trees as Hunter expected, the dog took off toward the place on the outcrop that was narrow. Juneau stared over the side of the cliff, let out a series of sharp howls, then hurried back to Hunter before circling back to the edge of the cliff.

Hunter rushed forward. He peered over the side but couldn't see anything through the thick forest and snow covering the side of the mountain. He shrugged off his pack and retrieved his binoculars. Once he had them adjusted properly, he swept his gaze looking for what had Juneau alerting.

His gaze snagged on a flash of bright pink.

There was someone caught on a large bramble growing out of the side of cliff face about twenty feet below where he stood. He was going to have to rappel down the mountain.

He prayed this was a rescue and not a recovery.

TWO

Heart beating a chaotic rhythm in his chest with his gaze locked on the still figure sprawled in the snow-dusted bushes below, Hunter grabbed the radio from beneath his jacket. Thumbing the mic, he said, "Poppy, Maya, I found one of the wedding party over the edge of the outcrop. I need to get down there."

"Headed back now," Poppy's voice came through the device.

"Copy," Maya said. "On our way."

Hunter took another look through the binoculars and stared down at the motionless form. The bright pink of the jacket suggested a female. Her blond hair was matted with blood on the back of her head. The bride or her bridesmaid?

The grooves in the snow suggested she tumbled down the side of the cliff.

Dead or alive? His gut twisted. It had been three hours since the wedding party had gone missing. If the woman below was alive, she had no doubt sustained injuries and was probably slipping into hypothermia.

Hunter had to get to her.

Using the radio again, he called dispatch, asking

for EMS. He gave them the location. Then he searched through his pack and unloaded the rappelling gear, which consisted of ropes, a climbing harness, and a carabiner brake rig. Spying a nearby tree that would be a sturdy anchor, he looped the ropes around the tree trunk, then made a bowline removal knot. He tugged on the rope, assuring the knot would hold, then stretched the ropes to the edge of the cliff. Once he had his harness secured around his waist, Hunter threaded one end of each rope though his Rollnlock, an ultra-light pulley and rope clamp/brake.

Poppy and Stormy came out of the trees, dislodging clumps of snow from the branches, and hurried over. Poppy gave the command for Stormy to sit. The big Irish wolfhound's head almost reached her shoulder.

"I called for EMS," Hunter said, handing her the binoculars.

Poppy went to the edge of the cliff, then hustled back to his side. "I see her."

"I tied off to the tree as an anchor," he informed her. "I need you to keep the lines from tangling and make sure the ropes don't get caught on anything."

"Will do."

Within moments, Maya and Sarge joined them. Snow clung to Sarge's fur. Hunter explained his plan to rappel down the side of the mountain to assess the woman's injuries.

"Maya, can you be my beta and navigate me down?"

"With pleasure." Taking the binoculars, Maya hurried to the cliff's edge and lay down so she could peer over the side. Sarge went on his belly beside her.

Hunter secured his goggles, slipped on his heavy-duty climbing gloves, then double-checked his harness and rigging.

After a moment of scanning the trees, Maya said, "Okay, you're going to go straight down from here. Then you'll need to go twenty degrees to your left to miss a boulder. It appears to have a smear of blood on it."

"Got it," Hunter replied. "That explains the blood on our victim's head." He didn't like the idea of a head injury.

"Ropes look good," Poppy said.

To Juneau, Hunter said, "Down." The dog went onto his belly. "Stay."

Hunter knew his K-9 partner wouldn't break until given permission. There was no reason to take Juneau down the face of the cliff. "Poppy, can you send word to Sean that a search around the base of the mountain is in order in case any other wedding party members also went over the side of this ledge and weren't as blessed to have a bush break their descent?"

Sean and Grace would recover whomever hadn't survived the fall because the base of the mountain was a good sixty or so feet down. Hunter sent up a prayer that the victim he was about to rappel to would be alive.

At the edge of the crag, after one last safety check of his harnesses and then locking the carabiner clip that would act as a brake, Hunter clutched the rope and put his booted feet on the lip of the ledge, bracing himself as he leaned back and stretched his legs out. Slowly he walked his way down the cliff face, allowing the rope to slide smoothly through the device. His boots slipped on loose rock and debris beneath the layer of snow, but thankfully, they were equipped with crampons that provided traction.

With each step of his descent, his heart stuttered. Questions ran through his mind. Who shot the tour guide? And why? Was this a kidnapping gone wrong? Or something else? Was the woman below alive?

He paused a moment to glance upward as the first few flakes of snow began to fall, quickly melting against his jacket.

A sense of urgency hurried him on, and he quickened his pace.

"Stop!" Maya called. "Shift left."

Praying the rope didn't fray on the sharp edge of the outcrop, he walked horizontally along the sheer cliff face.

"Perfect," Maya said. "Good to go for ten more feet."

Moving swiftly yet carefully, Hunter glanced over his shoulder. He was almost to the woman. Her blond hair was tangled in the branches of the bush she'd landed on. He grimaced at the up close sight of matted blood on the back of her head.

Thankfully, the thicket had prevented her from falling farther down the mountainside. Hunter sent a quick praise to God for big blessings.

When he reached the woman's side, he planted his feet to brace himself, locked his brake mechanism in place and then stripped one glove off.

He gauged the woman's height around five feet, six inches. She wore hiking boots and snow pants and gloves.

Careful not to dislodge her, he rooted beneath her hair and the collar of her bright pink coat for her neck, praying he would find a pulse.

There was a definite thump against his finger. A pulse. Weak, but there. "Yes!"

Where were her friends? Was this the bride?

Hunter thumbed his mic on his radio. "The woman is alive. As soon as EMS arrives, we need a litter down here," he said. "I don't want to move her until we have to."

Poppy's voice crackled on the radio. "EMS is on their way to us. I will let them know the status of our rescue."

A *rescue*. Hunter once again sent up a praise to God for another blessing on this bleak day. The irony that he was thanking his Heavenly Father wasn't lost on Hunter. There had been too many prayers that had gone unanswered over the years.

A groan echoed in Ariel's ears. Was someone hurt? She needed to help them.

She heard another moan and decided she was the source of the noise. Nausea rolled through her stomach as the world seemed to spin. What was happening?

Somewhere in her mind, she realized she was being turned over onto a hard surface. Dull pain pounded the back of her head.

"Miss? Miss?"

A hand on her shoulder brought Ariel out of the foggy state engulfing her. Opening her eyelids proved to be a struggle. Snow fell from the sky, stinging her cheeks, falling into her eyes. Then a hand shielded her face from the elements.

Her gaze passed across broad shoulders to a very handsome face beneath a helmet. Dark hair peeked out from the edge of the helmet and a pair of goggles hung from his neck. Was she dreaming? Who was this man?

She'd never seen this guy before in her life. This had to be a dream, right? Yet how could she dream about a man she'd never seen before?

The pull of sleep was hard to resist. She closed her eyes. Maybe the man in her dream would help her. But help her with what?

"Stay with me," the man murmured.

His voice coaxed her to do as he instructed, and she forced her eyes open.

Where was she?

Awareness of aches and pains screamed throughout her body, bringing the world into sharp focus. She was flat on her back and her head throbbed.

Ariel started to raise a hand to touch her head, but something was holding her arm down. She tried to sit up, and when she discovered she couldn't, she lifted her head to see why. Though doing so created more pain. Straps had been placed across her shoulders, her torso, hips and knees to keep her in place on a rescue basket. A metallic silver Mylar blanket had been tucked around her, insulating her body's warmth.

"Hey, now, I need you to concentrate on being still and staying awake."

That deep, rich voice brought her focus back to the moment. Memory flooded her on a wave of terror. The horror of rolling down the side of the cliff, hitting her head, landing in a bramble bush, and the fear of moving that would take her plummeting to the bottom of the mountain. She must have gone in and out of consciousness before being rescued. She gasped with realization. "Someone pushed me!"

The handsome man's piercing blue eyes widened. Then his eyebrows drew together. "*Pushed* you?"

"Where's Violet? Lance and Jared?" She struggled not to freak out. Why had someone shoved her off the edge of the cliff?

The man winced slightly. "You're safe now. No one's going to hurt you."

Her dream man's voice soothed her. But why wasn't he answering her questions? She swallowed, her mind rebelling at the possible answers. "Who are you?"

"Trooper Hunter McCord."

Definitely not someone she'd previously met. Ariel rolled the name around in her head. She liked the sound of it. Strong consonants, masculine and powerful. Was he someone she could count on? Trust?

Doubtful, her cynical side chimed in. There was no one she could rely on in life, except for God. She knew this, but still that dream of a grand romance lingered at the edges of her consciousness. Hmm. She must've taken a hard hit to the head if she was romanticizing her rescuer.

A beam of light shone bright in her eyes. "Can you tell us your name?"

She flinched against the light. "Ariel Potter."

When the light was turned off, she realized the first man wasn't alone. Two other men were with him, both dressed in snow coveralls with the Anchorage Emergency Medical Services logo on the breast pocket and across their helmets.

The men talked in a low tone with the trooper. She couldn't make out the words though she strained to hear.

Hunter moved closer. "Okay, Ariel, we're going to lift the rescue basket and take you up the side of the mountain."

"What?" She writhed against the restraints.

"Don't move," Hunter said again. "It'll be a lot easier on everybody if you lie still and let the EMS do their job."

She settled down, trying to keep her body still. She hated the helpless, vulnerable reaction stealing over her.

Hunter straightened. He made a whirling motion with his hand. And then she was moving. First, she was elevated to only a slight incline, and then she was almost vertical as the basket was pulled up the side of the cliff. Her stomach lurched, and her heart slammed against her ribs. She watched the world through narrowed eyes, too afraid to close her eyes but too afraid to open them all the way.

Beside her, Hunter climbed alongside the basket.

It seemed like forever before she was horizontal again.

Once the basket was no longer moving, a wet, rough tongue licked her hand. She jerked, her gaze locking eyes with a dog. A beautiful rust-and-white-colored Siberian husky with amber-colored eyes that seemed to express worry. *For her?* Why would a dog she'd never met be concerned about her? Was the dog even real?

A woman squatted down next to her. She had auburn hair and a kind smile. Her jacket was similar to Hunter's with the words Alaska State Trooper K-9 Unit. "I'm Poppy."

"Where is Violet? Please, you have to tell me."

"We're working on finding your friends," Poppy said. "Right now you need to concentrate on you. You took a nasty spill. Let us worry about them."

Ariel's mouth dried as the trooper's words sank in. Something was wrong. Panic assailed her, and she bucked on the litter beneath her. A strong hand gripped her shoulder, forcing her to turn her head away from the woman. She met Hunter's piercing blue eyes once again.

"You're going to injure yourself," he said, concern

etched in the lines of his face. "Your friends are our priority. We'll keep searching for them, but we need to get you to the hospital."

She shook her head, wincing at the cascade of pain that rippled over her. "No, you need to find them now. Find Violet. You don't understand, she's—" Ariel clamped her lips together. That wasn't her secret to tell.

Hunter frowned. "She's what?"

Ariel hesitated but then decided they needed to know. "Violet's pregnant. Please, you have to find her."

Surprise flashed across Hunter's face. He turned to Poppy. "Can you update the colonel?"

"Of course." Poppy moved away to talk on her radio.

Hunter refocused on Ariel. "You said somebody pushed you?"

"Yes." She took a shuddering breath. "I was taking pictures of a bald eagle. Oh, no, my camera!"

Hunter held up her Nikon. The outside casing was cracked with pieces missing, and the lens had fractured into a spiderweb of lines. "I found it. It's pretty banged up. Sad to say you'll need a new one. I'll put it in my bag."

She sighed, part frustration, part relief. "Thank you."

"You were saying...?" he prompted.

Refocusing took effort. "I heard a noise, like someone running toward me, and then—" Her voice broke. "Someone pushed me."

Her heart sank. Had one of her friends done this? No. She couldn't believe that. *Wouldn't* believe it. Someone else must've come up behind her at the edge of the outcrop. She should have stayed with her friends. Why hadn't they come looking for her? "Did Violet call you?"

She couldn't keep the hope out of her voice. "Is that why you came to find me?"

Hunter shook his head. "I'm sorry, no. Do you know where your friends went?"

She turned her head toward the mountain. "Up there." When she looked back at Hunter, she caught the glance he exchanged with a dark-haired woman who was rolling up a length of rope.

Three dogs sat in a line, staring at Ariel. She blinked, half afraid they would disappear, but the dogs remained. The beautiful Siberian husky, an Irish wolfhound and a Malinois. Each wore a vest with the words Alaska State Trooper K-9 Unit stitched into the fabric. So well trained.

Ariel missed her own dogs. The need to return to her pack brought tears to her eyes.

"Did the tour guide lead your friends up the mountain?" Hunter's question brought her focus back to him.

Unease traipsed down Ariel's spine. "He did. He said we were going on an untraveled trail. The tour guide was supposed to keep us safe. Is he missing, too?"

Hunter's expression darkened. "There'll be time enough for all of this later, but right now we have to get you to the ambulance waiting at the parking lot."

The two EMS men moved to the front and back of the basket. "We'll carry her."

Hunter straightened. "The snow is packed well enough we can hook the basket up to the dogs. They can transport her to the parking lot."

"Are your dogs used to sleds?" Ariel asked. Having trained sled dogs her whole life, she knew it wasn't as simple as hooking a dog to a sled and expecting the animal to know how to safely pull a sled, or rescue basket, in this case.

Hunter's head tilted. "All our dogs are properly trained."

She bit her lip to keep from directing him as he and the other two troopers attached lines to the basket, then produced the proper nylon harnesses for the three canines. She couldn't fault their work.

Within a short time, the dogs were hooked to the basket with the Siberian husky up front taking the lead position, then the Malinois doing double duty as the swing and team dog with the Irish wolfhound as the wheel.

Hunter gave the command prompting the dogs to pull. "Let's go."

With the humans walking on each side of Ariel, the dogs carted her down the mountain. While the going was mostly smooth across the snow, the occasional bump sent pain stabbing through her head. When they arrived at the parking lot, an ambulance waited and she was transferred to the bay of the vehicle. The two emergency medical service men consulted with the ambulance personnel before heading to their own rig.

"How did you find me?" Ariel asked Hunter as he and his dog stood by the ambulance doors.

Hunter put his hand on the dog's back. "Juneau found you. He's a—"

"Siberian husky," she said at the same time he did.

Hunter smiled. He had a nice smile. "Yes."

"Sir, we need to go," the paramedic said as he climbed in beside Ariel.

"Wait! Please, Hunter, tell me what happened to my friends."

There was a brief hesitation before he said, "They're missing."

Ariel's heart clenched. "What about the tour guide?"

Hunter's gaze darkened. "He was shot and killed."

The breath left her lungs.

"Do you know why someone would want to kill you?"

"I don't know." Tears burned her eyes.

"We'll have to assume that whoever did this will try again once they learn you're still alive."

His words sent terror streaking through her heart. But why would someone want her dead?

THREE

Hunter hooked his thumbs in his uniform utility belt and paced outside the emergency exam room of Alaska Regional Hospital, waiting for the doctor to finish his examination of Ariel Potter. Juneau sat by the door as if guarding the entrance.

Why had someone pushed Ariel off the edge of the cliff? Where were the other wedding party members? Who shot the tour guide?

The questions bounced around Hunter's head, unanswerable and not nearly distracting enough.

Everything about hospitals made him twitchy. The beeping of the monitors shuddered through him like alarm bells, and the smells of disinfectant and sickness turned his stomach. Anxiety clawed its way up his spine, an all-too-familiar sensation that brought back dreadful memories. Memories he'd rather not relive.

Yet with every passing second, he was taken back to age twelve. His mother had been diagnosed with stage IV pancreatic cancer. There'd been many doctor visits, trips to the ER, and hospital stays. Hunter had considered those days would be the worst he'd ever have to face, crying out to God to save his mother.

God hadn't saved his mother. She had passed with her husband and son by her side.

His father had done the best he could as a widower raising a rambunctious teen on his own while serving the community as a Metro police officer. Hunter had followed in his father's footsteps by going into law enforcement.

Then, five years ago, Kenneth McCord had been retired and restless until he'd met Celeste Roper, who, it turned out, was involved with a scam ring. Celeste had fleeced his father of his life savings. With some good detective work, she and the ring had been brought down and now were in prison.

And God had denied Hunter's request to save his father from the danger of a ruthless woman, which left him wary of God and His promises. Why had God let his mother die and his father lose his life savings?

The swish of the sliding glass door opening yanked Hunter from his spiraling thoughts, and he straightened as the doctor walked out. Juneau stepped inside the doorway as if to see what was happening inside the exam room. Hunter let out a short whistle, bringing the dog back to heel.

Hunter strode over to Dr. Chen. The doctor had been working at the hospital for as long as he could remember. He was a tall, lanky man with a headful of thick salt and pepper hair and dark eyes.

"How's the patient?"

Dr. Chen said, "Miss Potter is a little banged up, though nothing is broken and there are no major internal injuries. She did take a blow to the head and will need to be monitored closely for the next twenty-four hours. I didn't see anything abnormal on the CT scan, and she's lucid. I've made her promise to follow up with her primary care doctor."

"I'll make sure someone is with her around the clock," Hunter promised. Surely Ariel had family who would be willing to come to stay with her overnight.

Curiosity burned in the doctor's eyes. "You don't normally wait around to check on those you bring to the hospital."

"Miss Potter is part of an active investigation," Hunter replied.

Ariel had to know something that would help the Alaska K-9 Unit uncover what had happened on the mountain. That she was pretty and vulnerable and had sent all of his protective instincts surging really wasn't the point.

He had learned the hard way that pretty and sweet didn't always reflect what went on inside a woman's heart.

Though he'd never questioned his mother's love for him, she'd been a hard woman to please. Combined with what happened to his father and Hunter's own dismal track record in the romance department, he had determined romance wasn't something he intended to pursue again. He had his faith, his father, Juneau and his family within the K-9 Unit. They were all he needed.

"It's not usual to see you taking an active interest in your witness," Dr. Chen said.

Hunter cocked his head. "Why assume she's a witness?" Had she said something to the doc that he needed to know?

Dr. Chen smiled. "You didn't put her in handcuffs. So either she's a witness, or—" His dark eyes assessed him. "You're worried about her."

There was truth in the doctor's words even if he didn't want to admit he was worried. "Someone hurt her. I want to make sure they don't succeed a second time."

"Very commendable."

"Just doing my job. I still need her official statement," Hunter said. "Can I see her?"

"I'll release her to your care," Dr. Chen said. "The nurse is helping her dress now. We gave her a pair of scrubs because her clothes were so tattered. And I figured you might want them for trace evidence. Though we did give her dry socks and put her boots back on to keep her feet warm."

"Thank you. That will be helpful. I'll have someone come retrieve them."

Dr. Chen shrugged. "You work emergency room trauma long enough, you know the drill. I'll have her discharge papers ready in a moment." He walked away.

A few seconds later the door to the exam room opened again and the curtain was pulled back. A young nurse wheeled Ariel from the room. She was dressed in green scrubs and cocooned in a thin blanket, clutching a brown paper bag in her hands. Hunter's gaze zeroed in on the bandage wrapped around Ariel's head, her blond hair sticking out like golden pieces of straw. Her cheeks were rosy, but her skin chalky, and the pupils of her pale brown eyes were dilated. She was still recovering from the shock of the fall. Juneau moved to walk beside Ariel's wheelchair.

When the nurse brought the chair to a halt, Juneau put his head on Ariel's knee. She stared at him while gently stroking his head. Hunter wasn't surprised that Juneau was offering her his comfort. The breed was highly intelligent, friendly and gentle. Juneau's gift of being in tune with the emotions of humans matched well with search and rescue work.

"She can take some Tylenol for the headache," Dr. Chen said, drawing Hunter's focus as he joined them and handed him paperwork with instructions. "If she worsens or blacks out, bring her back to the ER."

"You have my word," Hunter assured the doctor.

Shrugging out of his jacket, he gave it to Ariel. "Here, put this on."

She slipped her arms into the sleeves. The jacket was huge on her, but it would be warmer than the blanket.

"You're very kind," she murmured.

The nurse wheeled Ariel out to Hunter's SUV parked in the spot near the entrance reserved for law enforcement. The night was dark, broken only by the glow of the streetlamps. Snow continued to fall steadily, coating the world in pristine white.

Ariel glanced up at him, blinking away the snowflakes landing on her eyelashes. "You don't have to take me home. You can just put me in a cab."

"Not happening, Miss Potter," Hunter said. "Someone tried to kill you. Your friends are missing, and a man is dead."

Her shoulders slumped. "I know. You don't have to remind me. You should be out looking for my friends."

"People are searching for them now."

"Why are you helping me?" The genuine puzzlement in her tone had him frowning. Why did she find it strange that he'd want to assist her?

"Because you need help and it's my job."

"Ah. Well, thank you."

Her words made Hunter bristle. Yes, he was being paid to do his job, but he was also helping because she needed it and he could offer it. He assisted her into the front passenger seat, tucking the blanket around her and securing the seat belt in place. His jacket was big and bulky on her, making her appear young and vulnerable and in need of his protection. Part of his job was to protect, but what stirred the soft places in his chest had more to do with the woman than his duty as a law enforcement officer.

Uncomfortable with that notion, he put Juneau in his compartment, then jogged around to the driver's side and climbed in.

Ariel had opened the brown bag and retrieved her cell phone, which appeared intact. A frown pulled at her eyebrows. Her lower lip quivered.

"Everything okay?" he asked.

"Just texts asking to buy one of my pack dogs," she said.

He understood the value of canine companions, but he wasn't well versed in the monetary gain to be had from sled dogs. "Does that happen often?"

"I have at least three or four requests a week. I've told this particular person no several times, that I'm not interested in selling my breeding dogs, only the puppies," she said. "I was hoping maybe Violet had contacted me. I'm going to send her a text." She typed on the phone's keyboard.

The need to sooth away her troubles tugged at him, but at the moment, the most he could do was get her home and settled comfortably.

After starting the engine and turning the heat to high, he brought up the navigation system on his dashboard. "I need your address." Though he had it in the information Katie had given him, he'd rather engage Ariel.

She seemed to shake off whatever she was ruminating about to give him the street name and number. He typed it into the system. She lived on the outskirts of town. It made sense for a dog breeder to have a bit more space. The drive through Anchorage was quiet this late in the evening. The falling snow required the wipers to go full blast, the swishing noise grating on his nerves.

"Do you have someone to stay the night with you? Family I can call? A friend?"

She shook her head and winced. With a beleaguered sigh, she said, "No."

"No?" How could she not have family or friends?

"I'd say Violet, but… I suppose I could ask my neighbor if she'd be willing." Ariel blew out a breath. "I just hate to ask more from her. She has my puppy right now."

"Just one puppy?" Hunter loved all dogs. "I remember the joy, and misery, of taking care of a puppy. When I was a kid, my dad brought home an eight-week-old Lab. I loved that dog."

"Is that why you joined the K-9 Unit?" Her voice was soft and wrapped around him within the cab of the SUV.

"Yes. Raising Kato was the catalyst to me becoming a K-9 handler."

"I imagine Juneau was a ball of fluff as a pup."

"I received Juneau as my partner when he was a year old. I missed out on the early development stage. And the sharp puppy teeth."

She laughed, the sound pleasing and melodic. "Yes, that is one of the hazards of raising puppies. Sasha, the puppy my neighbor is watching, was the runt of my most recent litter and sickly. I had to nurse him to health. Most breeders would've let nature take its course or sold him as a pet. But I just couldn't do either. I fell in love with him."

"Puppies have that effect," he commented.

"I need to call my neighbor and check on Sasha. And make sure that Trevor fed the dogs. They are on a very regimented diet."

She rubbed at her forehead, clearly suffering a headache. Then she dialed and waited a moment. "Mrs. Nelson, it's Ariel. Everything is fine now. I took a fall on a hike today."

Hunter raised an eyebrow at her. Way to sugarcoat the incident.

"A little bruised," Ariel hedged. "How's Sasha?" She listened for a moment, then said, "I wouldn't want to burden you. Could you have Trevor bring him over to the house in about ten minutes…?" The conversation went on for a little while longer, and then once she'd confirmed that Trevor had in fact fed the dogs their dinner, she said goodbye and hung up.

"Who's Trevor?" Hunter asked.

"Mrs. Nelson's college-age son. Trevor's a responsible young man who will one day be a great musher and dog trainer. A few years ago he asked me to teach him how to mush. We worked out an agreement. I'd mentor him, but he also had to learn how to train dogs and help me around the kennel. A musher is only as good as the dogs pulling the sled."

He admired her compassion and commitment to her dogs. "Are you sure you're up for dealing with a puppy tonight?"

"Sasha is my responsibility," she said. "I'll be fine."

"Tell me about your breeding business."

She leaned her head back, then abruptly sat forward. No doubt putting pressure on the wound reminded her of her injury. Her hands twisted in her lap. "I breed Alaskan huskies. I took over the business from my father after college. My parents had run a smaller operation. But it was enough for us to get by on."

"Aren't the Alaskan huskies part Siberian husky?"

"The Alaskan husky isn't its own distinct breed but rather a mix of various northern breeds such as the Siberian, greyhound or German shorthaired pointer, and bred primarily to be working sled dogs. Most of my dogs were sired by one of my father's original dogs, Thorn. He was a mix of malamute and saluki. He was the best dog and sired a lot of champion sled dogs over the years. He passed not long after this last litter was born. I kept Sasha as a tribute to Thorn."

"How many dogs do you have?" Hunter asked.

"At the moment, nine including the puppy. I compete in smaller races with them in an effort to show off their abilities. People see how well they do and want their offspring. We have a race coming up the Sunday after Violet's wedding." She gave a sigh filled with despair. "You will find her, won't you?"

"We won't rest until we do," he assured her. "Tell me about your friends."

"Violet and I were college roommates. She became my best friend even though our lives are so very different. She's kind and generous."

"What do you know about her fiancé?"

"He owns his own business. Violet met Lance at the golf club. Violet's mother doesn't exactly approve of Lance."

"Interesting. What's your take on him?"

There was a moment of silence before she said, "Violet is happy with Lance. That's all that matters to me."

Hunter had the sense there was something she wasn't saying. Did she not approve of Lance, too? Did Violet know this?

He brought his vehicle to a halt in front of her house. A ranch-style with two outbuildings and a large pasture rimmed by dark woods.

Ariel popped open her door. A cacophony of dogs howling echoed through the night.

In the dome light of the cab of his vehicle, her panic was visible. "Something's wrong!"

"They probably heard the crunch of the tires on the drive," Hunter said, praying that was the case.

"No. This is not normal." She jumped out.

Hunter hurried to her side and let Juneau out. The dog sniffed the air and then growled. He took off at a fast run toward the closest outbuilding.

They rushed after Juneau.

A light glowed through the high windows along the side of the structure.

Ariel grabbed Hunter's arm. "Someone's in the kennels. My dogs are in trouble." She ran past him toward the building.

Adrenaline pumping through his veins, Hunter quickly caught up to her at the entrance door and kept her from touching it. The lock had been jimmied.

Tugging her behind him, he commanded, "Hang back."

He withdrew his sidearm and held the piece in a two-handed grip at the ready as he toed open the door. His ears were assaulted with the ferocious barking of the dogs.

At the far end of the kennel, a person dressed all in black had muzzled a dog and was attempting to drag the canine out of its kennel.

"No!" Ariel yelled and tried to push past Hunter, but Juneau blocked her.

"Halt, police!" Hunter shouted.

The intruder swung the beam of a flashlight in their direction, momentarily blinding Hunter, but not before he glimpsed the glint of a silver handgun tucked in the thief's waistband.

Abandoning what was clearly an attempted theft, the perpetrator turned and bolted for the back door of the kennel building, escaping into the night.

Hunter pivoted with Juneau at his side and ran around the outside of the building. Then he abruptly stopped, unwilling to leave Ariel alone to chase after the suspect. He could barely discern the dark figure running away from Ariel's place through the open field toward the woods beyond. A few moments later an engine turned over. The armed suspect had escaped.

"Quiet," Ariel shouted as she quickly flipped on the overhead light switch. Her heart thumped in her chest so hard she hoped she didn't crack a rib. The fatigue she'd suffered in the car on the way home had evaporated to be replaced with anxious adrenaline.

The dogs immediately ceased their howling at her stern command. Each sat in its kennel, ears back and tail high. A quick glance at each assured her all but Dash in the last crate appeared unharmed.

She raced to the far end of the building and dropped to her knees inside Dash's open crate. He was a beautiful Alaskan husky with a blue-gray and white coat. A muzzle had been strapped in place over his nose and mouth. He lay on his side.

"Shh," Ariel soothed him. "It's okay. I'm here." She undid the muzzle and stroked his thick coat. "What did that bad person do to you?" She ran her hands over the dog but found no obvious injuries.

Hunter and Juneau returned. Juneau whined and sat down next to Ariel.

"Is he okay?" Hunter asked as he crouched beside her.

"There's no physical injury that I can see," she said. "But he's groggy." She rose. Hunter followed suit.

"I need to call Cora," she said. Worry for her dogs made her limbs quake.

"Dr. Madison?"

"Yes. Do you know her?"

"She's the veterinarian the K-9 Unit uses."

Ariel wasn't surprised. "She's the best in the area."

"I have her on speed dial," Hunter said. He made the call and Cora promised to come right away. "She advises not moving Dash in case there are internal injuries. She said the best you can do is keep him quiet and still."

The thought of Dash hurting brought tears to Ariel's eyes.

Grateful to know help was on the way for her dog, she said, "I take it the intruder got away."

Hunter nodded. "I've called for backup."

Ariel shivered and burrowed deeper into the trooper's jacket as the cold seeped through the thin scrubs. The scent of his spicy aftershave clinging to the fabric was pleasant and soothing. But still, a lump rose to her throat and she sniffed back tears in an attempt to keep them from spilling down her cheeks.

"Hey, now." Hunter gathered her in his arms. "You're safe. Your dogs are safe."

She found solace in the comfort and security enveloping her. Trooper Hunter McCord had a charisma and energy about him that filled the building, making the space seem somehow smaller, yet she didn't mind.

Must be the head trauma.

"Thank you for being here," she said, not at all inclined to step away from the warmth of his embrace. "I'm sorry to be such a burden."

"No apologies necessary." He rubbed her back. "And you're not a burden. This is my job. It's what I do."

Logically she understood he was doing his job. And for some reason a bubble of disappointment floated through her. Odd. There was no reason for her to wish this man wanted to be here because he cared about her. They didn't even know each other. It had to be the upset from the day causing her to be an emotional mess.

So much had transpired in a short space of time. Had it only been this morning that she'd left to go hiking with Violet?

Worry for her friend crowded her chest. *Please, Lord, let Violet be okay.*

In the distance, the whirling red-and-blue lights of more law enforcement coming meant this night wouldn't be ending anytime soon.

She eased away from the trooper and found his dog was leaning up against her leg as if he too wanted to offer her support.

Hunter smiled. He had a nice smile that crinkled the

corners of his blue eyes and made her heart do a little skip. "He likes you."

She tangled her fingers in Juneau's fur. "And I like him."

Ariel had to admit she was thankful for Hunter's and Juneau's presence. If she'd returned home to find the intruder on her own, what would have happened?

She swallowed back the bile rising to burn her throat. A question tore through her mind, making the pounding at her temples increase. "Could the intruder have anything to do with what happened on the mountain?"

Hunter's eyes met hers. "We can't rule anything out."

Exactly what she'd been afraid he'd say.

FOUR

As the Metro patrol cars stopped side by side in the driveway of Ariel's house, Hunter stepped out of the kennel building, followed by Ariel and Juneau. She'd returned his jacket and had put on a barn coat. The dog seemed glued to the woman. Considering her traumatic fall, he was sure the dog sensed she needed comfort, and he respected how well she was holding up after everything she'd been through.

Another vehicle pulled in behind the officers, and there was no mistaking the Alaska K-9 Unit logo on the side of the SUV. His boss, Colonel Lorenza Gallo, had shown up, as well.

Hunter's surprise gave way to a heavy breath of frustration. He'd let the perp get away. But he'd been more concerned about Ariel and the dogs. He didn't know if whoever had tried to take her dog was working alone or not. Chasing down the suspect would have left Ariel vulnerable and exposed to another attack. And he wasn't going to let anything happen to her on his watch.

This case was proving to be confusing and worrisome. First Ariel was pushed off a cliff and then, later that same night, someone broke into her kennels. Coincidence? Or was she the intended target on the mountain to begin with? But where were her friends? Why kill the tour guide? The questions spun through his mind, turning his brains into cotton candy.

Focusing, he said to Ariel, "I'll be right back." He jogged to Lorenza's side but kept Ariel in his peripheral vision. She stood near the kennel building door with Juneau at her side. "Colonel Gallo?"

"Trooper McCord," Lorenza replied with a sharp nod. Her silver hair peeked out from beneath the edges of her dark blue wool hat. Over her dress suit she wore a calf-length warm coat. "I heard the call come in."

"Any news on the other hikers?"

She shook her head. "Unfortunately, no. Sean and Grace searched the base of the cliff and found nothing." Her gaze zeroed in on Ariel. "This is the victim from the mountain?"

Was no news good news? He wasn't sure in this case. "Yes, ma'am."

"Does what happened tonight have anything to do with what happened on the mountain?"

Hunter blew out a breath. Ariel had asked the same question. "Possibly."

"Two random attacks on one person seem unlikely."

He tended to agree. "Except this wasn't an attack, per se. The suspect attempted to steal her dog."

"Maybe someone followed her up the mountain and tried to get rid of her so they could steal her dog," Lorenza said.

"It's an awful lot of mayhem just to kidnap a dog when they could've easily done the deed while she was out on her hike. As far as I can tell, there's no security system." Something he would have to make sure Ariel remedied.

"Except a pack of dogs," Lorenza said with a glance toward the kennel building, where the sound of dogs howling and vocalizing emanated. Huskies didn't bark but they sure tried to talk.

"Yes, they would definitely sound an alarm," he admitted. "However, Ariel lives alone. A neighbor kid cares for the dogs when she is out. The intruder must have waited until he'd gone home before breaking into the kennels."

"The nearest neighbor is a mile back up the road I drove in on." Her gaze shifted back to the house. "I'd like to meet Miss Potter."

Ariel hung back with her arms wrapped around her middle as if holding herself together. Juneau remained close, his gaze alert on the police officers climbing out of their cars.

The bandage on her head was a stark reminder of the danger that had come close to ending her life. Something primal tightened in his gut. He never liked to see anyone hurt.

"Ariel," he called to gain her attention. When her gaze swung to him, he waved her over. She moved purposefully to his side.

"Ariel, this is my boss, Colonel Lorenza Gallo. She put together the Alaska K-9 Unit here in Anchorage."

Ariel lifted her chin and stuck out her hand. "It's nice to meet you, Colonel," she said. "I appreciate all that the K-9 Unit has done for me today. Everyone has been so kind and helpful."

Lorenza smiled, her eyes glimmering with approval

at the praise of her team. "It's nice to meet you, Miss Potter. You've had quite the day."

Ariel's lips twisted. "That is an understatement. Has there been any word on Violet and the others?"

"No, but we are doing everything we can to find them. Have you given your statement to the police yet?"

Hunter answered, "No, ma'am. We haven't. Everyone arrived at the same time."

"You two need to speak with the officers," Lorenza instructed and gestured toward the officers. "Shall we?"

"Yes, ma'am." Hunter put his hand on the small of Ariel's back and guided her forward.

Recognizing Officer Everett Brand from earlier in the day, Hunter introduced his boss and Ariel before explaining the situation. Everett took notes as they talked. It was important that both Hunter and Ariel give their own statements, because perspective was everything. He perceived things through the lens of a cop, while she viewed things through the eyes of a civilian and victim. She might've seen something he hadn't and vice versa.

Two officers fanned out to look for evidence with their flashlights.

"We'll have a crime scene unit come out in the morning when there's daylight," Everett said. "We wouldn't normally pull in CSU for a simple breaking and entering, but since Miss Potter had been so violently assaulted earlier today, we're giving this a more serious response."

"Thank you. I heard an engine start up off in the distance, so the suspect is long gone now," Hunter said. But that didn't mean the intruder hadn't left something behind, like a shoe print or tire print, that might lead them to identifying the would-be thief.

"On the far side of the property line there is a fire road for the forestry service," Ariel explained.

Lorenza looked at Hunter. "Did you get a good look at the suspect?"

He shook his head. "It was dark. The person was dressed in all black. Average height, slender. It could have been a man, a woman or even a teenager," he replied, wishing he'd been quicker and not let the perpetrator escape.

"We'll have someone check the area out there," Everett said. He focused on Ariel. "Why would someone want to steal one of your dogs?"

Hunter wanted to know the same thing. "Are the dogs chipped?"

"Yes, they are," Ariel answered. "My dogs are worth several thousand dollars apiece. They are all from champion lines and champions themselves."

"That sounds like motive," Everett said.

"But if the thief had succeeded, what were they planning?" Hunter asked. "To claim ownership of the dog? With the chip, passing a stolen dog off as their own would be a risky endeavor."

"Dash, the one the thief tried to take, is slated to sire my next planned litter, which would provide for my first quarter operating expenses. If I'd lost him…" She shivered. "I should check on him and the other dogs."

The sound of tires crunching on the gravel drew their attention. The veterinarian brought her vehicle to a stop and climbed out.

Dr. Cora Madison hustled over. She was a tall, regal woman with short, dark hair. She wore a thick shearling-lined coat, jeans and snow boots. In one hand she carried a black medical bag. "Hello, everyone."

"Cora, it's good to see you," Lorenza said. The two women shook hands.

"Hey, Doc," Hunter said. "Thank you for coming out."

Cora adjusted her red-framed glasses. "Of course." She moved to Ariel's side and put an arm around her shoulders. "Let's go see our patient."

He noticed the shadows under Ariel's eyes and how her shoulders drooped. She was exhausted and barely functioning. He wanted to alleviate her burden. "I can take you," Hunter said to Cora. "Ariel should go inside and rest."

A flare of surprise widened Ariel's eyes briefly. Then her eyebrows drew together and her gaze narrowed. "I'll rest once I know my dog is okay."

Her affronted tone doused his concern and grated on his nerves. "Ariel—"

"Hunter, let them go." Lorenza's clipped command kept him from saying more. "You and I are not finished."

That sounded ominous. Was she going to bring him to task for letting the suspect get away?

Keeping his frustration in check, he nodded. With a wary look at him, Ariel walked away with Cora. Juneau appeared torn between following Ariel or staying at his partner's side. Hunter gestured for the dog to heel. Juneau moved slowly to his side and sat, but the dog's gaze remained on Ariel. Hunter didn't blame him. He didn't want to let Ariel out of his sight, either, which was strange. She was safe now. There was no reason for him to be so protective.

"I'll go with the ladies," Everett said, taking off after Ariel and Cora.

Hunter couldn't protest, though he wanted to. He wanted to be the one to stick close to Ariel's side. It was his job.

"No need for you to be overbearing. It won't win any points with Miss Potter."

His boss's words jolted through Hunter like a rut in the road. "Excuse me?"

"That young lady seems very independent." Lorenza glanced around and then her gaze landed back on him. "She lives here alone with her pack. I'd imagine she's the one used to giving orders, not taking them."

Hunter's jaw firmed. "Her safety is my responsibility."

There was a slight curve to Lorenza's lips. "Duly noted." Her expression sobered. "And in that vein, Trooper McCord, I want you to see to Miss Potter's continued safety. Utilize the Metro PD. This woman needs to be guarded 24/7 until we figure out what happened on that mountain."

"Yes, ma'am." Having his boss confirm what he'd already surmised, Hunter's resolve solidified into place. No one would get to Ariel while he was on the case.

When Ariel and Cora entered the kennel building, the dogs all stood. Skye, a beautiful three-year-old agouti Siberian husky, was Sasha's mom. The dog's alternating band of color along each individual hair shaft made her markings unique and sought after as a mama dog. She let out a string of noises that made Ariel wish she could understand the story the dog was telling her.

"I know, girl," Ariel said.

The rest of the dogs watched her, tails wagging. A couple paced, clearly agitated by the chaos.

Empathy for her pack twisted in her chest. Normally when she returned from an outing she'd open each kennel and love on each dog. But at the moment, Dash was the priority.

She led Cora to his kennel at the far end of the room, grateful to see that Hunter had secured the back door.

"Hey, boy," Ariel greeted him.

Dash rolled from his side, getting his paws beneath him, but that seemed to be as much movement as he could muster. Ariel's heart broke for how close she'd come to losing him. If she and Hunter hadn't returned when they had, Dash would be gone. Stolen. What had the person planned to do with him?

The possibilities made her shudder with dread.

Cora set her black bag on the ground next to the kennel housing Dash before she moved to the sink to wash her hands.

Ariel opened the latch and sat on the floor inside the kennel. Dash lifted his head, his blue eyes nearly black with the pupils so dilated. "I'm here. You're safe now." She stroked his fur. He laid his snout on her knee.

Cora returned to their side and put on latex gloves. "I'll need to get in there."

"Of course." Ariel scooted out so that the vet could take her place inside the kennel.

Cora rubbed her hands over Dash's body. "I'm looking for any obvious signs of injury," she explained. The veterinarian stretched his legs and palpitated his abdomen, took his temperature and other vitals, and checked his eyes, ears, mouth and paws. "Nothing out of the ordinary for him." She combed through his fur, pulling the hair back to view his skin beneath. "Ha. A puncture wound."

"What?" Ariel crowded close to see a small spot crusted with dried blood beneath his fur.

"This puncture is larger than a hypodermic needle would leave behind," Cora said. "I'll take a blood sample, but my best guess would be someone used a tranquilizer dart to subdue him. Something I've seen used on moose and caribou."

Anger at the unknown person churned in Ariel's gut. "Doping him would be the only way anyone he didn't know could get close to him. Is he going to be okay?"

"Yes. How long ago was it that you and Hunter chased off the intruder?"

"Maybe forty minutes or so."

"That's good," Cora said. "Then whatever substance was used is fast acting but wears off fairly quickly. I'll know more once I run his labs." She patted Dash. "He'll be good as new before long."

"Thank God above." Relieved by the prognosis, Ariel backed out of the kennel.

Cora followed her, stripping off her gloves. "I'll call you as soon as I have the results from his blood work and to check on how he's doing. If he shows signs of worsening or refuses to eat or drink, call me and I'll come back out."

"I'd appreciate it." Ariel stood. The world wobbled. She grabbed onto the side of the kennel to let the dizziness pass.

"You should do as Hunter suggested," Cora said with concern lacing her words. "You need to rest. Head injuries are no joke."

"I will." Ariel stood upright and braced her feet apart. "Hunter's words weren't a suggestion but more of a directive."

Cora smiled and pushed her glasses up higher on her straight nose. "He obviously is worried about you."

"He's just doing his job," Ariel said. "He and Juneau were the ones to find me today."

"What happened?"

"Someone pushed me off a cliff." Even saying the words brought a sense of terror slamming into her. "I'd be dead now if a bush hadn't stopped my fall."

Cora drew her in for a hug. "I'm glad God protected you today."

Thankful for the show of kindness and the words of support, Ariel hugged her friend back. "Me, too."

Letting her go, Cora said, "Do you need me to stay with you tonight?"

Nearly brought to tears by the thoughtful offer, Ariel shook her head, then winced at the movement. "No. I'll be fine. You go home to your family." Cora had two school-aged sons and a firefighter husband.

"You shouldn't be alone," Cora said. "I'm worried about you."

"She won't be alone."

Hunter's deep voice made both women turn toward the trooper and his dog striding toward them through the kennel building. Her heart skipped a beat. The pair were so commanding and handsome together. Hunter had put his jacket on, the one he'd let her borrow that had smelled so good. His dark hair was mussed as if he'd run his fingers through the thick strands. A five o'clock shadow darkened his strong jawline, and his eyes appeared more vivid in the overhead fluorescent lights. Juneau also walked with purpose. He obviously wasn't bothered by the animals in their kennels. His focus was on her.

Ariel glanced at her dogs. Though each canine watched with interest, none of them seemed to mind Juneau or Hunter in their space. Interesting. Did the animals have some way of knowing what heroes Juneau and his human partner had been today?

Belatedly, his words sank in, and Ariel wasn't sure she understood exactly what he'd meant. Of course she'd be alone. She didn't have anyone she was comfortable enough with to invite into her house. Plus, wouldn't that put someone else in jeopardy if her attacker decided to come back?

She met his serious blue gaze. "Excuse me?"

"Juneau and I are staying with you," Hunter said, his voice firm. "Tomorrow I'll contact Metro PD to see if they can spare a patrol to keep watch. But for now, you're stuck with us."

Heart rate ticking up, Ariel barely refrained from shaking her head. She didn't want to cause another wave of pain shooting through her brain. "You don't have to do that. I'll be fine."

"It's our job to make sure you're safe," Hunter returned. "So, yes, we do."

Cora touched her elbow, drawing her attention. "Let Hunter protect you It's the right thing to do."

Stifling a groan, Ariel had to admit the truth in her friend's words. But that didn't mean she had to like the fact that a man would be keeping watch over her. Invading her space. She was very private and used to solitude. The last thing she wanted tonight was to have company.

Taking a calming breath, she decided the smart thing to do was acquiesce. She could handle the intrusion into her life for one night. "I appreciate your offer. I will accept."

A soft smile played at the corners of his mouth, drawing her attention. She liked the shape of his lips and the angular lines of his face. Her gaze drifted to meet his.

Attraction tugged at her, catching her off guard.

He'd saved her life, she reasoned with herself. Of course she'd be drawn to him. And he *was* handsome. There was no denying the obvious. Any woman with a pulse would notice. But none of that mattered.

She wasn't looking for a repeat of her last relationship, nor was she looking for Mr. Right now. Hunter was only temporarily in her life for a specific purpose. To keep her alive.

Because someone had tried to kill her.

The reality of what had happened settled around her like a dark cloak, blocking out all other thought. Her vision tunneled and a buzzing sounded in her ears. Her head pounded behind her eyes.

"Steady there," Hunter's deep voice murmured close to her ear, his hands holding her shoulders, creating hot spots on her biceps.

When had he moved?

Her mouth went dry. "I should sit down."

"Yes, you should," he said. "Let's get you in the house."

"Wait." She struggled to keep her mind from blanking. There were chores that needed to be done. A routine to follow. Things she had to take care of. "I have to let the dogs out one last time."

"I can handle that," Cora said.

"I can't ask you to do my chores," Ariel protested.

"Your dogs know me," Cora replied. "We'll be fine."

"I appreciate the offer, but I want to do it." She

needed to reclaim some normalcy, and caring for the dogs would calm her.

A commotion outside the kennel doors had Ariel spinning toward the noise. She yelped with surprise as Hunter tucked her behind him, his hand reaching for his weapon.

"Hey! Stop!" Officer Everett Brand's command jolted through Ariel.

Fear gripped her and she instinctively moved closer to Hunter, gripping the back of his jacket. She reached for Cora to draw her behind Hunter's solid back.

"Okay, okay. I'm looking for Ariel Potter."

Trevor! Ariel had forgotten he was bringing Sasha home. She pushed at Hunter. "It's my neighbor."

"Right." He strode out of the building and returned a moment later with Trevor Nelson and a squirming puppy.

Ariel rushed forward to take Sasha. The puppy licked her face as she hugged his little body close to her racing heart.

Trevor's eyes were huge in his narrow face. "Ariel, what's going on? Why are the cops here?"

Ariel looked to Hunter, hoping he'd field the questions.

"Miss Potter had a rough day," he said. "Did you notice anyone lurking around the property?"

Trevor shook his head. "No. All was quiet. I left after the evening feeding and exercise time."

Ariel sent a quick prayer of gratitude that the young man hadn't been here when the intruder broke in. "Thank you, Trevor, for caring for the dogs."

She kept a very regimented schedule. Routine was important for the dogs and her. If only she'd stayed with her original plan for the day instead of going up the mountain, maybe none of this would have happened. She wouldn't be hurt, her friends wouldn't be missing and someone wouldn't have tried to steal her dog.

A small voice in her head reminded her she wasn't in control of every aspect of life. She did what she did and now she had to figure out a way forward. "If you'd come by tomorrow I'll pay you."

"Uh, sure." Trevor hesitated as if not sure he should leave. Ariel appreciated the young man's concern.

"It's okay," she assured him. "Everything's fine."

But would everything be fine?

Hunter quietly explained the situation to the young man, telling him to be on alert whenever he came over to help with the dogs.

Hearing the warning sent a shiver of dread down her spine.

Would the assailant come back? And this time succeed in taking Dash and killing her?

FIVE

Hunter appreciated the care and attention Ariel lavished on each dog as she let one canine out at a time into the cordoned-off dog run behind the kennel building. She'd insisted on performing her nightly routine without any help, which had given him the opportunity to feed Juneau from the stash of kibble he kept in his rig while keeping an eye on Ariel in case she needed him. His boss had pegged her correctly. Independent. Used to being the one in control. And Hunter would add stubborn.

Now that all the dogs were back in their respective kennels, Hunter and Juneau escorted Ariel and the puppy to her house. "I still don't understand why you wouldn't ask Trevor to stay and help you," he said as he closed the side door leading into Ariel's kitchen behind him and secured the lock. Once again, he was struck by the coziness of the ranch style home. The kitchen was clean yet looked lived-in with a shining chrome toaster on the granite counter, a fruit basket in the corner filled with apples and pears, and a nice set of cutlery in a wooden block.

Juneau sniffed around the light-colored luxury vinyl

flooring, a good choice for a woman with nine dogs because of its scratch-and water-resistant properties.

Ariel placed Sasha inside a medium-size crate in the dining room. The rectangular dining table and four chairs had been pushed up against the wall to allow room for the puppy's crate.

"I just couldn't ask any more of Trevor. He and his mother have already done so much for me."

Hunter leaned against the counter. "What about Cora? She offered to stay and help."

Ariel made a frustrated noise and spun away. She went into the kitchen and grabbed the tea kettle before moving to the sink to fill the pot with water. "The dogs are my responsibility."

He wanted to still her movements, to make her slow down and take a beat. He jammed his hands into the pockets of his jacket instead. "You have a hard time letting others help you."

She set the kettle on the gas stove and lit the flame, then remained with her back to him for a heartbeat.

His observation must have hit a sore spot.

She faced him, her chin jutting out slightly and her light brown eyes sparking. "I learned a long time ago I can only rely on myself. Asking for help is something I do when I have no other option."

That seemed like a hard way to live. What life event had taught her such a harsh lesson? "You could have used the help tonight," he countered. "You sustained a head injury today and should be resting."

"Taking care of the dogs is my pleasure. And routine. I just want some normalcy." She grabbed two cups from the cupboard, shutting the door with more force than necessary. Then she huffed out a breath. "Plus, it seemed safer to send Trevor home." She met his gaze, her expression softening. "I do appreciate your help."

He hadn't done anything other than stand back and watch. The bond between Ariel and the animals was obvious. Each dog was eager to please her while she lavished the same amount of affection on each of them. He'd experienced a strange sort of yearning that had confounded him. What was that about?

"Your dogs are very well behaved."

She smiled, her gaze going to Juneau and back to him. He liked the way her eyes crinkled at the corners when she wasn't worried or upset. "Thank you. I would imagine you train with Juneau as much as I train with my pack."

"Yes, but I'm only working with one dog, not eight. How do you do that much training and give them each enough attention?" He sometimes suspected he short-changed Juneau when fulfilling his other duties.

"This is my job. 24/7," she said. "Just as policing is yours. You have to train when not out catching bad guys. Or rescuing people off the side of mountains. These dogs are my only obligation with the exception of the bookkeeping."

The puppy gave a bark and pawed at the door. Ariel opened the crate door and the puppy scampered across the floor, heading straight for Juneau.

Ariel scooped him up before the little guy could reach the bigger dog. Juneau stared at Sasha with his head cocked.

"Juneau wouldn't hurt the puppy," Hunter said.

Ariel smiled at Juneau. "I'm sure you'd be the perfect gentleman. However, this little scamp knows no boundaries. And I would hate for his still-sharp teeth to rip Juneau's ear or cause a wound on his legs or tail. The most likely places Sasha would attack."

Hunter appreciated her concern and her care for Juneau.

The tea kettle whistled. She deposited the puppy into his arms as she moved past him to deal with the boiling water.

He struggled to contain the wiggling ball of fluff in his hands. Juneau rose from his spot by the side door and moved to sit in front of Hunter, his amber eyes on the puppy.

Sasha's little mouth latched onto Hunter's finger, digging his razor-sharp teeth into Hunter's flesh. "Oh, no you don't." He pried Sasha from his hand and set him on the floor but stepped in the puppy's path to block him from charging Juneau, who rose and dropped his head as if ready to bat away the little dog if need be. "Does he need to go out again?"

"Maybe. Do you mind?"

Shooting her a glance and noting the twinkle in her pretty eyes, he lifted an eyebrow. Apparently, she didn't mind asking him for help taking the puppy out for a break. "Do you have a leash?"

"In the top drawer of the vanity dresser by the front door."

Picking up Sasha in a football hold, Hunter found the bright green leash and harness. He slipped the harness over the small body and latched it. Holding on to the lead, he allowed the puppy to pull him back into the dining room. With Sasha on a leash, Hunter let the scamp sniff Juneau, while the older dog sat and watched, but Hunter tugged Sasha back when the puppy went after Juneau's tail.

"Juneau is very patient," Ariel observed.

"That he is." Hunter couldn't have asked for a better partner. He trusted Juneau more than he trusted most people.

Ariel opened a cupboard. "Would you like chamomile tea, peppermint tea, spicy tea, black tea, lavender and lemon..."

Half afraid she was going to rattle off every flavor and blend she had in that very packed cupboard, he said, "Okay, hold up. You really like tea."

"I do." She paused with the box of chamomile in her hands. Her delicate eyebrows drew together. "You don't?"

"It's fine. I'll have what you're having."

She nodded and closed the cupboard. "You're a coffee drinker, right?"

"Most days. A little jolt of caffeine proves helpful now and again." He'd started relying on strong black coffee to keep his wits about him while helping his father through the dark days of betrayal by the woman he'd fallen in love with after his retirement from the police force. A decision that had cost his father not only money but his self-respect. A fate Hunter would never allow in his own life. Falling in love was a dangerous endeavor. One he hoped to avoid. He never wanted to be so imprudent as to let his heart rule his head.

"Well, just so you know, there are some teas that have a very high caffeine content."

What kept her up at night that made her seek out caffeine to get through her day? He tucked in his chin. "Good to know."

"But tonight, we'll go with a nice herbal blend. I'll

let the teas steep while you let the dogs out." She put a tea bag in each cup.

He chuckled at her pointed instructions. "All right, fellas, you heard the lady, outside." He unlocked and opened the side door. Juneau waited for Hunter to release him before he trotted through the open doorway into the glow of the outside lights.

Hunter and the puppy followed. The frigid April air stung Hunter's lungs. He searched the area for signs of any threats while the puppy sniffed the grass. Juneau disappeared around the corner of the house and came back a few minutes later.

Satisfied that all was well on the property, with no dogs howling to signal an intruder, he urged the puppy back into the house. Juneau slipped inside and lay down beside Sasha's crate as if he knew that was where the puppy was headed.

After removing the harness from the puppy, Hunter tucked him inside the crate and set the latch on the door. Sasha lay down with his black nose sticking through the wire holes, nearly touching Juneau.

Hunter returned to the kitchen, where Ariel handed him a cup of chamomile tea. The fragrant scent of the chamomile flower wafted up with the steam rising from the mug. He wrapped his hands around the ceramic and let the heat seep into his cold fingers.

He followed Ariel into the living room. She sat on an overstuffed wingback chair, tucking her feet up beneath her. He took a position on the couch facing the large picture window that looked out over the drive. Juneau left the sleeping puppy to lie down in front of Ariel's chair.

She glanced down at him. "Do you train him to do that with all your rescue victims?"

"Only the pretty ones," he quipped, then inwardly cringed. Where did that come from?

Her eyes widened and then lowered to look into her tea as if the world's secrets could be found in the soothing depths of her mug.

Great, she probably believed he was flirting with her. He was usually much better at keeping his thoughts from escaping. Hoping to alleviate the sudden tension between them, he said, "Tell me more about your business?"

Lifting her gaze, she said, "My dad was a champion musher until he had an accident that left him with a bum knee. But he loved the sport so much that he decided to start breeding dogs and training them for other mushers."

"And he taught you?"

"Yes, I kind of learned alongside him," she replied. "We had dogs traveling with us for as far back as I can remember. My mother and I would go with my father on the race circuit around the US and Europe."

"Did he compete in the Iditarod?"

"He did, and usually placed in the top fifty."

"That must have been a very interesting childhood," he remarked.

"It was lonely," she admitted. "Just me and my parents."

Empathy twisted in his chest. "I don't have siblings, either."

"Being an only child does lend itself to loneliness, doesn't it?"

As did losing his mother at a young age. A subject he didn't want to talk about. "So, you traveled with your parents during the racing season. I assume you went to school the rest of the time?" He wasn't sure of the time frame for the racing season beyond the famed Iditarod, which started in Anchorage at the beginning of March and ended fifteen days later in Nome.

She shifted in the chair and leaned her head back and then winced, sitting straight up. "No, my mother homeschooled me."

Which meant she hadn't had school friends. "Were there other children on the race circuit?"

"Some. But there wasn't ever time to form any real attachments." She shrugged. "We traveled to places that some people only dream about. The excitement of race day was always something I looked forward to and, truth be told, still do."

"Hard to show off champion dogs without putting them to the test," he said.

"Exactly. Plus the purse money helps with my operating expenses."

"You do it all. Impressive."

"Training the dogs is my passion." She made a face, her nose scrunching up in an adorable way that had his gut clenching. "When I was old enough for high school, my parents decided it was time for me to enter the public school system. They dropped me off with my grandparents here in Anchorage."

"Difficult adjustment, I would imagine." He remembered his high school days. All the jockeying for popularity. The dramas between classmates. Everything seemed so much more important and life-altering until stepping onto a college campus.

"I got through it. College was better. That's where I met Violet." Ariel's gaze dropped to her tea. "I can't believe she hasn't been found yet." She lifted her gaze, her eyes filled with worry. "Do you think she's okay?"

He wished he could reassure her but there was no reassurance he could formulate. He answered honestly, "I pray so."

"I do, too."

"Tell me more about Violet." Maybe something Ariel knew about her friend might help them understand where she was or what had happened to her and the other two hikers.

"Violet came from wealth, but she doesn't flaunt it. She's kind and generous. Big-hearted. She recently become a Christian and dedicated her life to the Lord. And then she found out that she was pregnant with Lance's baby…"

"How did Lance feel about the baby? Is that why they were getting married?"

Ariel made a face. "Lance didn't know. She planned to tell him, but I don't know if she worked up the nerve to do it."

Hunter's mind turned this information over in his head. "Could she and Lance have eloped?"

Ariel perked up. "Now that's an idea." She frowned, her shoulders slumping. "But it doesn't explain who killed the tour guide or why somebody would push me off the edge of a cliff. And where's Jared?"

"Good questions." This case was certainly a mystery. He noticed her stifling a yawn and glanced at his watch. It was well after midnight. "I should let you get some sleep."

He took their mugs to the sink and rinsed them out. When he returned to the living room, she had collected a blanket and pillow for the couch.

"Would Juneau like a pillow, too?" she asked.

"He'll be fine. Most likely he'll plant himself by the front door." Hunter checked that all the window and door locks were secure.

Ariel retrieved Sasha from his crate and snuggled him to her chest. "Thank you, Hunter, for everything," she murmured and headed down the darkened hallway to the room at the end.

When he heard the soft snick of the door closing, he dimmed the lights and stretched out on the couch. His utility belt dug into his hip. He debated taking it off, then decided it was best to leave it in place. Juneau flopped down on the entryway tile by the front door.

Hunter closed his eyes but kept seeing Ariel balanced precariously on the bush jutting out from the side of the mountain. He prayed until he drifted off to a light sleep.

His phone vibrating in his front shirt pocket brought him fully awake. He glanced at his watch. Three in the morning.

"McCord," he rasped into the phone.

"Hey, it's Gabe." Fellow Trooper Gabriel Runyon's voice filled the line. "Dispatch received a call from our missing groom. Lance Wells and Jared Dennis used a satellite phone to report that they were injured and holed up in a cabin in Chugach State Park."

"Is Violet James with them?"

"They didn't say. The colonel asked me to mobilize a search team. She wants you with us."

Hunter sat up and wiped a hand over his jaw, the rough whiskers scratching his palm. He couldn't leave Ariel unguarded. "I'll meet you at the state park entrance as soon as I can. I need to arrange for Metro PD to send over a patrol officer."

"Copy that," Gabriel said.

Hunter hung up, dialed the precinct and asked for Officer Everett Brand. A few moments later dispatch connected him to the officer.

"Brand here."

"Everett, this is Hunter from the Alaska K-9 Unit. I'm hoping you can help me out. I'm at Miss Potter's, but I've been called away. I need you to come stand guard until I can return. She'll be more comfortable with someone she's already familiar with."

"I'm on my way. I'll arrange for someone to take over in the morning if you're not available by then."

"I'd appreciate that." Hunter hung up. He didn't relish waking Ariel up to tell her what was happening, but he knew if he left without saying anything she would be upset. Besides, she deserved to know that Lance made contact.

He walked down the dark hall and softly knocked on her bedroom door. It opened almost immediately. The soft glow of her bedside lamp backlit her as she stood in the doorway.

"I heard voices," she said.

"It was me on the phone. Lance Wells sent out an SOS message saying he and Jared need rescuing. Juneau and I need to go help in the search."

"Violet?"

"No word yet."

She made a distressed noise. "Where could she be?"

He hated seeing the anxiousness in Ariel's expression. "She might be with them. Don't lose hope."

Ariel took a shuddering breath. "I'm trying not to."

She pushed past him and headed for the living room. "You should go. I'll be fine here."

"Not quite so fast. Officer Brand is coming to provide you protection."

Her lips pursed. "Okay. I appreciate all you're doing for me. For Violet and the guys. Please bring them back, Hunter."

He knew better than to make a promise he had no guarantee of keeping. "I will do my best."

Ariel cuddled Sasha to her chest and stared out the front window as Hunter's taillights disappeared down the drive. The darkness enveloped his vehicle, leaving her somehow bereft of his and Juneau's presence.

Officer Brand sat in his car, parked near the front porch. He shouldn't be out in the cold like that, but he refused to come inside, stating he was used to long overnight stakeouts.

Needing something to do, she went to the kitchen and made a thermos full of hot cocoa. Then she put on her barn boots and jacket, and she and Sasha went out to deliver the thermos to the policeman.

Officer Brand rolled down his passenger side window. "Miss Potter?"

"Hot cocoa." She handed him the thermos. "It's the least I can do."

"Thank you. That's very thoughtful of you."

"I'll be sleeping in the kennel room with the dogs," she told him. "The house is too quiet." Not usually a problem for her. But she had to admit she was a little freaked out and nervous about this whole ordeal. She wanted the comfort of her canine companions. "I appreciate you being out here."

"Doing my job, ma'am."

A refrain she'd heard already once today from

Hunter. Were all law enforcement types so dedicated to their jobs? What else was Hunter dedicated to? Did he have a wife waiting for him at home? Guilt pricked her conscience. Had she kept him away from his family? And now here was this nice officer also sacrificing his time to protect her.

All because someone had tried to kill her.

With a shiver of unease, she went back inside. There was no way she'd fall asleep. Her insides were twisted in knots of worry for her friend. Grabbing the blanket and pillow from the couch, she stopped at the entryway closet for the baseball bat she kept there. Then she and Sasha headed out to the kennel room.

The dogs perked up as she entered. She checked on each dog before settling down next to Dash's kennel. She made herself a little nest and lay on her side in a position that didn't bother her wounded head. The pillow smelled like Hunter, spicy and masculine. Sasha turned circles in front of her before settling down and scooting up next to her belly. Dash put his paw through the wire grating, and she held on to him. As she worked to calm her racing thoughts, she whispered, "Please, Lord, bring Hunter and Violet back to me."

SIX

Once again traversing the fresh-snow-covered trail leading up to Flattop Mountain, Hunter's mind was half attentive to where the search party was headed. The other half of his brain was focused back at Ariel's house.

Was she safe?

He pushed the question aside. Of course she was. Officer Brand would see to her safety.

Yet Hunter couldn't deny that trusting others to do their jobs the way he wanted the job done didn't come easy.

One of his many flaws, as his father kept telling him.

He expected too much of people.

But no more than he expected from himself.

Was she scared?

Well, duh. Someone tried to kill Ariel. He'd hated seeing the fear in her eyes when he'd left her standing in the doorway of her home, holding the puppy, looking so sweet and vulnerable. He didn't understand why she got to him in such a visceral way.

He shook his head. Best to get his brain in gear and focus on the task at hand.

The early morning air clung to his breath every time

he exhaled. Tension twisted his gut into knots. They didn't know what they were going to find or what they would have to deal with once they reached the coordinates for the cabin where the groom and the best man were holed up.

Gabriel and Bear led the way, paused and pointed off to the right side of the mountain, away from the place where they had found Ariel and the tour guide. "That way."

"How did they double back down the mountain and go this direction without anyone seeing them?" Hunter asked. Was this some sort of ruse to draw them away from Ariel? The muscles in his shoulders bunched as the overwhelming need to return to her gripped him, making him misstep, nearly taking a header into the snow. Juneau glanced over his shoulder at him, his eyes bright in the dawning light.

"Maybe they went over the top of the mountain and down the other side," Maya said. "I saw no indications of them doubling back when we were up there earlier yesterday."

"That makes sense," Gabriel agreed.

"There's no way we will get an ambulance back here," Maya observed.

Hunter's flashlight swept over the path ahead of them. The rough terrain, especially with the new fall of snow, was perfect for the snow machines. "I'll call EMS and request snowmobiles."

"It's a good idea." There was a hint of mocking amusement in Gabriel's tone, his kind way of reminding Hunter who was leading the search party.

Hunter let out a breath. He liked to be in control.

Another of his many flaws. One he shared with Ariel. He shrugged. "Sorry. After you."

Gabriel clapped him on the back as he stepped past him and led Bear into the snow.

Hunter and Juneau followed, while Hunter made the call. The snow was deep and required effort to plow through, but the dogs were agile and easily navigated the drifts, occasionally stopping to shake, sending snow flying.

As the dark gave way to twilight, the outline of the cabin tucked beneath a grove of spruce and hemlock trees became visible. They fanned out and approached the A-frame structure with caution. Hunter and Juneau headed to the left, Maya to the right, and Gabriel straight to the front door.

Hunter edged around the side of the cabin and peeked inside through a chest-high, rectangular window. Dirt and snow covered the glass pane. Through the streaks of dirt, he could make out someone lying on a cot. But Hunter didn't see anyone else. Gabriel's loud knock on the front door broke the silence.

"Alaska K-9 Unit. Open up."

The creak of the door opening sent a chill over Hunter. Light filtered in through the open doorway, il-luminating the person on the bed. He wasn't sure, but it looked to be Jared Dennis.

Hunter and Juneau circled the building, meeting up with Maya and Sarge in the front. Gabriel and Bear had stepped inside the cabin. Hunter, Juneau, Maya and Sarge crowded inside behind Gabriel and Bear, shut-ting the door to keep the cold out.

Lance Wells, holding a rag to his head, shuffled backward. He was tall with short, dark blond hair, and his green eyes watched them warily. He was dressed in black snow pants, marred with dirt, and a dark jacket that had a rip down the side. He gave his head a shake, winced, then said, "I'm so glad to see you."

Jared Dennis lay stretched out on the cot with what looked like a bloodied T-shirt wrapped about the upper biceps of his right arm. His brown hair had leaves sticking out like ornaments on a tree.

Lance sat down on the cot and jostled his friend. "Jared, wake up. Help is here."

The man came to with a moan, his eyelids fluttering open. He licked his lips. "Water?"

Maya hustled forward with a small bottle of water from her pack. She helped the man drink some of the liquid, then handed Lance another small bottle of water.

Lance downed the contents in a few gulps. He wiped his mouth with the back of his hand. "Thank you."

Hunter took out a notepad from his jacket pocket and a pen. Knowing how worried Ariel was for her friend, he asked, "Where's Violet James?"

"She's not here," Lance said. "That woman is crazy."

Hunter's chest tightened.

Gabriel stepped forward. "Tell us what happened and how you came to be here."

Lance put his hands on his knees and bent forward as if he was going be sick. He took a few deep breaths before he sat back up. "It was Violet. She did this to us. She shot Jared."

"Where did she get the gun?" Hunter demanded.

"How should I know!" Lance raised his voice. "She conked me on the head. I lost consciousness. Jared tried to wrestle the gun from her, and she shot him."

Maya moved forward to evaluate the man's injury.

"It's a through and through. Doesn't look like it hit the bone." She glanced at Lance. "You did a good job of stopping the blood flow."

When she moved back, Jared rolled to prop himself up on his uninjured arm. "Violet shot the tour guide and she pushed her friend over the side of the cliff."

"Poor Ariel." Lance hung his head. "To be killed by your best friend."

Only she wasn't dead as they assumed.

"We found the tour guide, Cal Brooks," Gabriel said.

"Please, you have to find Ariel's body. She deserves a good memorial." Lance's eyes teared up.

"We have found Ariel," Hunter added, unwilling to reveal more just yet. The need to protect her burned bright within him. "Why would Violet shoot the tour guide and push Ariel over the cliff?"

Lance scrubbed a hand over his face. "Violet was having an affair with that man."

Tucking in his chin, Hunter stared. Really? Did Ariel know this? Had she kept that information from him? Hunter jotted down what Lance had said.

"With Cal Brooks?" Maya said. "How do you know they were having an affair?"

"He told me." Lance's wild-eyed gaze bounced between Hunter, Gabriel and Maya. "That's why she shot him. In cold blood. Just pulled out a gun and shot him."

"You saw her do this?" Gabriel questioned.

"Yes," Lance answered as he jumped to his feet.

Hunter put his hand on his weapon. All three dogs emitted a low growl.

Eyeing the dogs with concern, Lance said, "She took our phones and marched us here. She knocked me out and left us to die."

Hunter had trouble wrapping his mind around this information. This didn't sound anything like the woman whom Ariel had described. But then again, he should know how easily fooled some people could be. His father, a seasoned cop, had been duped by Celeste. Hunter would never make the same mistake. Maybe Ariel was keeping secrets. If so, Hunter would ferret them out just as he had with Celeste.

However, someone had pushed Ariel over the cliff and tried to steal her dog. Those were the facts that couldn't be denied. And his gut said Ariel was innocent. Ugh. His mind was going in circles. He needed to focus.

Had Violet suffered a psychotic break? Hunter made a note to have Katie check with the James family about the missing woman's medical history.

"How were you able to call for help?" Maya asked.

Lance pointed to the card table in the corner of the cabin. "We found that satellite phone here." He sucked in air, his agitation growing. "Violet has lost it. You have to find her before she hurts more people."

"I'll call this in," Maya said, and she and Sarge stepped out of the cabin.

Gabriel focused his gaze on Hunter. "We'll take a look around outside. You okay here with them?"

"Affirmative." He wanted a few aspects of the men's story clarified. As soon as Gabriel and Bear exited, he stared at the two men. "Walk me through the day. Start at the beginning."

Lance sat back down as if his legs couldn't hold him any longer. "It was supposed to be a wonderful, prewedding adventure. Violet loves adventures. I thought she'd enjoy going on an off-the-beaten-path hike." He pinched the bridge of his nose. "Next thing I know, Cal's saying,

I'm telling him. She hissed at him to be quiet. Then Cal said they were having an affair and she wasn't going to marry me." His voice broke on the last word.

Hunter took notes, his mind going back to what Ariel had said about Violet being pregnant. Was that a lie? Or was the bride-to-be actually pregnant, but the identity of the father was in doubt? He decided to keep that information to himself until he determined exactly what the truth was.

"Then she pulled a gun from her jacket pocket and she—" Lance covered his face with his hands.

"She shot the tour guide point-blank in the chest," Jared said. "There was no remorse, no nothing in her eyes. She has the coldest blue eyes."

"We ran." Lance dropped his hands back to his knees. "She shot at us. When she missed she turned and ran for Ariel."

Hunter cocked his head. "You saw her push Ariel over the cliff?"

Jared nodded. "I did. When Violet took off, Lance went to help Cal to see if he was alive. And I followed Violet, intending to help Ariel, but I was too late. She shoved the poor girl off the cliff. I ran back and got Lance and we started running."

"And Violet came after you?" Hunter tried to envision how this played out.

"Yes, she did." Lance's voice shook. "She caught up to us. Took our phones and marched us here. Once we got inside she shot Jared but it was her last bullet, so she knocked me over the head with the butt of her gun. She left us here to die. No heat, no water, no food. Nothing. If we hadn't found that satellite phone—" His breathing came in big gulping gasps.

"Right," Hunter said. "If you hadn't found the satellite phone, we wouldn't have been able to find you. But how did you know where you were?"

"There's a brochure," Jared replied. "This is a public-use cabin. Apparently, nobody reserved it for this weekend."

"And when I came to, I used my T-shirt to dress Jared's wound," Lance said.

Was what they were saying true? If so, this would devastate Ariel. Hunter didn't have a reason to suspect they were lying, which meant they had an armed and dangerous woman on the loose.

Where had Violet gone?

The sound of snowmobile engines coming closer alerted Hunter of EMS's arrival. "You two stay put," he said and walked out the cabin door with Juneau at his heels. He tucked his notebook into his pocket. Something about this whole situation had his hackles up, yet he had no reason to doubt the two men. Why would they make up such an elaborate scenario?

Gabriel and Bear joined Hunter and Juneau on the front porch.

The headlights from the snowmobiles stopping ten feet away mixed with the rising sun illuminated the shiny object dangling from Gabriel's fingers. "What's that?"

"I assume our suspect's bracelet," Gabriel said. "Look at the initials on the charm. VJ."

Violet James's bracelet. Proof that she'd been in the area? Hunter's stomach clenched. Was she close by? His gaze scanned the shadowed trees surrounding the cabin. "While you get these guys loaded onto the snowmobiles, Juneau and I are going to search the area." He knew if there was even a trace of Violet's scent left on the piece of jewelry, Juneau would detect it. "Let him sniff the bracelet."

Gabriel lowered the charm bracelet to Juneau's nose.

"Find," Hunter said to the dog.

Juneau lifted his nose to the air and then down to the ground, then back to the air before looping away from the cabin. Hunter went after him, praying he found Violet and she would come peacefully. For Ariel's sake.

Morning turned into afternoon and still no word from Hunter. Ariel had gone about her daily chores, very aware of the police car sitting on the front drive. Officer Brand had been relieved by a younger officer named Bruce Grayson. Throughout the course of the day, Ariel had checked on the officer, offering him hot coffee and use of the facilities.

Dash was back to his old self, though Ariel noticed he was more protective of her and stuck close by while the other dogs were released into the fenced yard for some much-needed recreational time with the plethora of toys that she kept for them.

She'd removed the bandage from her head hours ago and barely noticed any residual pain where she'd sustained a laceration on the back of her scalp.

After putting the dogs through their exercises and training for the day, Ariel returned them to their kennels with their evening meal.

Taking the puppy with her inside the house, she fed Sasha and put him in his crate so she could prepare her own dinner. Anxiety twisted in her chest. Why hadn't Hunter called? There had to be a reason. Maybe he'd found Violet, Lance and Jared. Worry chomped through her like a hungry beast as awful scenarios played through her mind. Were they all dead? Killed by a bullet or a fall?

"This is ridiculous," she groused aloud, eliciting a howl from Sasha as if in agreement.

With a quick twist of the knob, she turned off the burner on the stove that had been heating her spaghetti sauce and grabbed her phone. She was going to call the K-9 Unit and demand answers.

Unfortunately, the dispatch person who answered said there was no new information they could give her but promised to have Hunter call her soon as he checked in. Why hadn't he touched base? What was happening on the mountain? Was he hurt?

A different kind of concern arched through her, making her shiver with dread.

Please, Lord, no more tragedies.

She ate only a small portion of her dinner because her stomach was too tied in knots for very much food. Needing something to do, she took a plate out to the young officer.

"That's mighty nice of you, ma'am," Officer Grayson said.

"Are you sure you wouldn't rather come inside?" she asked. "You'd be so much warmer."

"Oh, no, ma'am. I'm fine here. I'm actually getting a lot of my computer work done." He flashed her a grin.

As grateful as she was that all was quiet and he was able to work, she couldn't shake the trepidation making her skin crawl. Her gaze roamed over the forested land rimming her property. Was someone out there watching? Waiting to strike?

What enemy had she made who was determined to hurt her?

Wrapping her arms over her middle she went back inside and dug into her own bookkeeping.

As darkness fell, casting shadows over her work, the frantic howls of her pack filled the air, causing the fine hairs at her nape to quiver with alarm.

The dogs sounded like they had the night before when an intruder tried to steal Dash.

Panicked, she raced out the door, her gaze going to the cruiser. She could see the deputy inside. But the dome light was off and all she could make out was his silhouette. Ariel debated going out to get him versus checking on her dogs. She knew what Hunter would want her to do—seek out the safety of the officer.

So she went with her gut.

As she ran for the cruiser, the sound of a rush of footsteps behind her chilled her bones. A sense of déjà vu struck her like lightning, her whole body vibrating with terror.

She spun to face the oncoming threat just as hands grabbed her around her neck and squeezed. A blur of dark clothing registered in her brain as she fought with every ounce of strength she possessed. Using her elbows and her heels, she kicked and screamed, eliciting a high-pitched yelp from her attacker. But the hands gripping her were strong, cutting off her air supply.

Bright lights swung across the driveway, stinging her eyes. Abruptly she was released. She crumpled to the ground in a heap.

SEVEN

Slamming the gear shift into Park, Hunter jumped from his vehicle while calling dispatch for EMS. His heart hammered in his chest. The image of someone with their hands wrapped around Ariel's throat etched into his mind in the brief flash of the headlights made fear, stark and cold, run through his veins. Using his key fob, he released the side door of the vehicle, allowing Juneau to leap out of the SUV. Then Hunter ran to where Ariel lay unmoving on the ground while a slim figure dressed in a dark hoodie sprinted away, disappearing into the darkness. Juneau chased the assailant, but Hunter whistled to bring the dog back. He wouldn't risk Juneau getting hurt.

Gently, Hunter rolled Ariel to her back and cradled her head to keep the pressure off the head wound she'd received when she'd fallen off the cliff. "Ariel. Can you hear me?"

Juneau licked her face and nudged her with his nose.

He checked for a pulse, fully prepared to begin life-saving measures. Her heart beat strong beneath his fingertips, easing the constriction in his chest a fraction. He leaned close, putting his ear near her mouth and nose. Her breath fanned over his face.

"Hunter?"

He turned to look at her face and found her big brown eyes watching him. He let out a silent prayer of thanksgiving that he'd heeded the urge to check on her. "You're safe. I've got you."

"There was a—" She coughed, her whole body shaking with the effort to expel air through what was no doubt a painful throat.

"Shh. Don't try to talk. An ambulance is coming," Hunter said. "I saw your attacker run away." He wanted badly to go after the perpetrator, but Ariel's safety was his first priority.

"A woman," she managed to say, her voice coming out raspy.

Acid burned in Hunter's stomach. *Violet.* Had she returned to finish what she'd started on the mountain? Was Violet the one who'd tried to steal Dash last night? Why? What motive had sent Ariel's best friend on a killing rampage?

His heart wrenched with the anticipation of having to tell Ariel what Lance and Jared had shared about Violet's horrific actions.

She gripped his arm and pulled herself to a seated position. "The officer."

Hunter's gaze whipped around to the cruiser parked off to the side of the entrance. When Hunter had turned into the drive and had seen Ariel being attacked, all of his attention had centered on getting to her and keeping her alive. Now he realized something was definitely wrong. Where was the officer? Had Violet gotten to him, too?

Hunter's chest tightened. He should've been here to protect Ariel. "Can you stand?"

She nodded and grasped his hand. He helped her to

her feet and put an arm around her waist. She leaned into him. The flowery scent of her shampoo clinging to her hair wrapped around him, a heady aroma that he would not likely forget. Together, with Juneau sticking close to her side, they approached the Metro police cruiser. The officer sat unmoving in the driver's seat. The interior of the car was too dark to ascertain if the man was injured.

Afraid of what they would find inside, Hunter leaned Ariel against the front bumper. "Stay put," he said. "Let me check on him."

With dread knotting his gut, Hunter approached the driver side window. It was down. The young officer sat slumped, his chin to his chest. The seat belt was the only thing keeping the officer upright. Hunter reached through the open window and pressed two fingers against the man's neck. He was alive. Hunter breathed out a relieved breath. But what had happened to him?

A siren growing closer heralded the arrival of the ambulance.

"Is the officer okay?" Ariel said, her voice hoarse.

Hunter went to her side. "He's alive."

He couldn't comment as to whether he was okay or not. Until they knew what had knocked him out, there was no guarantee that the young officer would survive this ordeal.

Hunter waved the ambulance forward and had them park near the cruiser. The two EMS personnel jumped out.

"We have an attempted strangulation victim," Hunter told the pair and gestured to Ariel.

One paramedic tended to Ariel, checking her airway and her heart rate, while the other checked on the unconscious officer.

"We need to get this man to the hospital," the paramedic said. "I don't see a wound. I'd hazard a guess he's been drugged."

Like Dash had been. Hunter was confident the doctors would find the same substance in the officer as the vet found in Dash. He turned to the other paramedic and Ariel. "How is she?"

"She should be seen at the hospital to assess damage to the vocal chords and have a CT angiogram to check if there's injury to the vessels in the neck."

Ariel made a face and shook her head. "I don't want to go back to the hospital."

"I don't like hospitals, either, but you need medical attention," Hunter said, then turned to both paramedics. "I'll take her. You take the officer. We'll follow."

Ariel tugged at Hunter's sleeve. "The dogs."

"I'll arrange for another guard to come out and watch over them."

"Trevor," Ariel said. "Call him, too."

"Where's your phone?"

She pointed to the house.

Once again tucking her close to his side and holding her about the waist, he gave the medics room to move the officer onto a gurney and put him into the back bay of the ambulance. Then Hunter helped Ariel into the house, where she directed him to her cell phone sitting on a charger. Juneau sniffed around the floor as she scrolled through her contacts, then handed Hunter the device.

He hit the send button.

Trevor answered on the third ring. "Hello?"

"Trevor, this is Trooper McCord with the Alaska K-9 Unit. We met yesterday."

"Yeah?" There was no mistaking the wariness in the younger man's tone.

"I'm at Miss Potter's place and she needs your help. I'm taking her to the hospital. Would you be willing to come and stay with the dogs?"

"Whoa. Dude, what happened? What's going on?"

Hunter figured the boy needed to know enough to be prepared. "Like I explained before, somebody has been targeting Miss Potter. She would appreciate having someone here the dogs know."

"That's messed up," the kid said. "I'll be right over."

Hunter then called Metro PD, explained to dispatch the situation and requested another officer to come to Ariel's property.

He hung up the phone and turned to Ariel. She sat on a dining room chair, holding her head in her hands. Juneau was perched at her feet, his amber eyes watching her.

Hunter knelt down before her. "You doing okay? Do you need to throw up?"

She shook her head and lifted her gaze to meet his. "Water."

He filled a mug and brought it to her. She took the cup and drank a few sips. After a moment she handed it back to him. She swallowed several times and cleared her throat.

"Thanks. I'm getting better already," she said, though the raspy tone of her voice hadn't lessened. "It hurts less. I don't need to go to the hospital."

"Right." He held out his hand. "Let's go."

She clutched his hand but didn't move. "You came in the nick of time. God sent you."

Hunter wasn't sure if God had prompted him to return to her place after leaving headquarters or not, but he was grateful he'd arrived in time. He'd finished up his paperwork and had seen the message that she'd called. If God was at work here, Hunter was thankful.

"Tell me about Violet," she urged. "What did you find on the mountain today?"

Not ready to delve into Lance and Jared's accusation, he said, "Let's get you to the hospital and checked out before we deal with that." He tugged her to her feet.

She wobbled, then steadied herself by flexing her knees and holding on to him. "No, I have to know."

He rubbed her hands between his, holding her gaze. As much as he knew the news would hurt her, he had to tell her at some point and if she insisted on hearing it now, then he would accommodate her. "We found Lance and Jared. They claim that Violet shot Cal Brooks."

"What?" She winced and yanked her hands from his to clutch her throat. "No."

"This is why I didn't want to tell you yet. You need to heal before you face all of this."

She lowered her hands and tilted her head slightly to keep eye contact. "I want all of it. Now. I'm not—" She swallowed and turned away to grab the mug. After taking a few sips, she set the cup back down, then faced him again. "I am not some fragile flower that can't handle the truth," she said between clenched teeth. "Tell me everything."

"Lance claims that Violet was having an affair with Cal Brooks and Cal wanted to come clean about it."

Ariel stepped back and shook her head. "That's not true."

Knowing his next words were going to cause her anguish, Hunter closed the distance between them, ready to steady her if needed. "Lance and Jared claim that Violet pushed you over the side of the cliff."

For a prolonged heartbeat, she stared with a stunned expression that had him fighting the urge to draw her to his chest and hold her. Ariel's sweet face registered shock, then denial as her eyes darkened, and she pushed past him to place her hands on the kitchen counter. Her shoulders sagged as she gasped for breath. Then she seemed to gather her composure. She straightened, lifting her chin, and turned to face him. "It's not true. None of it. They're liars."

He grimaced. "But what do they hope to gain by lying?"

"I don't know, but I intend to find out. I want to see them."

He could only imagine what it was costing her, both physically and emotionally, to be so strong. "We need to go to the hospital."

A stubborn light entered her eyes. "Lance and Jared first."

"Like I said, we're going to the hospital. That's where they are."

Her eyebrows dipped together. "Why didn't you say that to begin with? Let's go." She grabbed her wallet and keys off the sideboard next to where she had her phone charging. Then she stopped. Panic etched into her features. "Where's Sasha? I didn't put him in his crate."

Hunter grabbed her by the biceps as she swayed. "We'll find him. You sit down before you pass out." He helped her to the dining chair. "Could he be outside?"

She frowned. "I don't know."

She started to rise, but he held up a hand. "I've got this."

Deciding to start the search indoors, he called out, "Sasha!"

Hunter walked through the living room and down the hallway with Juneau at his heels. There was only one door opened. He and Juneau entered Ariel's inner sanctuary. The room was a burst of color with a bright flowered bedspread and a variety of pink, orange and yellow throw pillows piled high on the bed. A deep burgundy comfy chair in the corner near a bookshelf provided an inviting space to sit and read. Hunter could imagine Ariel sitting there at the end of the day with a book and a cup of tea.

His gaze zeroed in on the puppy. Sasha lay curled up on a fluffy round dog bed wedged between the side of Ariel's bed and the wall. The puppy lifted his head and gave a little yelp of joy as he bounded out of the bed and across the floor, jumping on Juneau. Juneau backed up a step, dropped his head and nudged the puppy backward. Sasha plopped onto his hindquarters.

"You little scamp." Hunter scooped the puppy up and cradled him close to his chest. "Your mom is going be very glad to know that you are okay."

When they returned to the dining room, Ariel had her hands folded on her lap and her head bowed.

Hunter stopped. The sight of her praying lit a fire in his heart. She'd suffered so many traumas in a short amount of time and yet she still believed, still looked to God for help and answers. She was an amazing woman. And he had better figure out a way to keep her from invading his heart. He wasn't interested in any type of long-term commitment beyond this assignment.

Aware of Hunter's gaze, Ariel finished her prayer, thanking God for saving her life yet again. And she also thanked Him for bringing Hunter and Juneau to the rescue.

She opened her eyes and her heart stalled in her chest

as her gaze landed on the big, handsome state trooper tenderly holding the little Alaskan husky in his arms, his beautiful K-9 partner at his side. The itch to photograph the man and dogs dug at her like a thorn. If only her camera hadn't been smashed in the fall.

Why wasn't she more alarmed at having Hunter in her space? Unaccountably, there was something comfortable about being with the man. He'd saved her life multiple times. It didn't mean anything beyond he was good at his job and God was watching out for her. She couldn't put any more importance on the emotions bouncing around inside her, not if she wanted to stay safe from heartache. Which she did. She'd learned long ago not to allow herself to rely on others for her happiness. It never worked out. Not with her parents. Not with Jason.

She rose and reached for Sasha.

"He was sleeping in his bed," Hunter said as he handed over the puppy.

As she nuzzled Sasha, his soft fur tickling her skin and his rough tongue scraping across her cheek with kisses, relief that he hadn't escaped out the door or gotten into anything harmful made her limbs quiver. The adrenaline ebbing from her body was making the pain in her throat and head throb.

"As soon as Trevor gets here as well as the other officer, we can go," Ariel said, not at all looking forward to what was to come. She'd need every ounce of strength to confront Lance and Jared. Why were they telling such vicious lies about Violet? "But I'd like to see the dogs now. Let them know I'm okay."

Hunter nodded and they walked out to the kennel room. She didn't believe a word of what Lance and

Jared claimed. Violet would not have shot anyone. And she definitely would not have pushed Ariel over the cliff. They had been friends far too long and had gone through too many dramas and heartbreaks and joyous occasions together. There was just no way. And there was nothing anyone was going to be able to say to make her believe that Violet had that kind of malice in her.

Inside the kennel room, she greeted each dog with a quick pat to let the pack know she was unharmed. And once again her dogs didn't seem to mind Juneau or Hunter. Which was odd considering every dog was an alpha in their own right.

A knock on the kennel building door jolted through her. Hunter looked at her and put up his hand, stopping her from going to the door.

She gestured for him to answer the knock, her stomach knotting with nerves. But she rationalized that a killer wouldn't announce their presence, would they?

A moment later, Hunter ushered Trevor in. He spoke softly to Trevor. The young man looked over at Ariel, then nodded. When they came forward, Hunter said, "The Metro officer is here. Your pack will be safe."

She stared into Sasha's eyes. He was going to be a gorgeous dog and would one day sire equally gorgeous Alaskan huskies. She handed him over to Trevor. "Thank you."

"Of course," he answered. "My mom wanted to know if you need anything."

"I'll call her later," Ariel promised.

Hunter cupped her elbow, and they walked out of the kennel building to greet the new police officer, a large, muscular man with a shaved head.

He made it clear he would not let down his guard. Hunter thanked him and then helped Ariel into his SUV.

On the drive to the hospital, she couldn't seem to sit still. Where was her friend? Where were Lance and Jared's accusations coming from?

Hunter's question—*what do they hope to gain by lying?*—bounced through her mind like a pinball ricocheting off one thought after another. "There has to be another explanation," she said aloud.

Hunter's jaw was set in a firm line. "You have to prepare yourself," he said. "Sometimes folks aren't who they seem."

She made a face. "I'm sure in your line of work, you see all kinds of horrible things from people. But I know my friend. We've known each other since our freshman year of college. There's just no possible scenario that would make me believe she did this."

"I *have* seen a lot of horrible things on the job. But I also know how hard it is when you love someone to see beyond what that person wants you to see."

Had someone he loved betrayed him? She was sad for him, but that didn't mean Violet was capable of such evil. "I'm sorry you were hurt by a loved one," she said. "But I'm sure this situation is different."

"Deception is deception."

"Just because someone deceived you doesn't mean that I can be easily deceived." Even as the words left her mouth, she recognized the pride in them. She winced. Was she fooling herself? Perhaps her ego was unwilling to entertain the idea of Violet's culpability, because it would mean Ariel had been a poor judge of character. She didn't want to contemplate that she was being obstinate out of pride rather than out of loyalty to her friend.

"Not me," Hunter said, claiming her attention. "My father."

She braced herself. "What happened?"

"Six years ago my dad fell in love. Head over heels, rainbow and unicorns, in love with a woman. He was too enamored to realize her true conniving nature."

"You did?"

"Yes. I had her pegged from the beginning, but my father wouldn't listen."

Which, no doubt, hurt Hunter and clearly made him wary of love. "She betrayed him?"

"Fleeced him of his life savings. And then planned to move on to the next unsuspecting mark."

Empathy bloomed inside her. She could only imagine how devastating that must have been for Hunter and his father. "*Planned?* I take it you intervened?"

Hunter glanced at her. His bright blue eyes reflected the soft glow of the dashboard lights. "Yes, I intervened. But not before the money was gone. I'll always regret that I didn't act sooner. She is now paying the price for her deception."

"But not everyone is like this woman," she argued. "That's like saying because one dog bites then all dogs are dangerous."

He brought the SUV to a halt in the parking lot of the hospital near the emergency room entrance. Then he turned off the engine and faced Ariel. "And if Violet is found guilty, then she will have to pay the price, too. Justice must be served."

A deep ache throbbed in her chest. "I agree that justice must be served. But Violet is innocent."

The look in his eyes as he popped open the driver side door made it clear he wasn't convinced.

EIGHT

When they arrived at the hospital, Ariel had to force herself to walk through the emergency room doors. Juneau brushed against her leg as if he sensed her hesitancy. She didn't want to be here. Not only because she didn't want to be poked and prodded again, but knowing she was going to face Lance and Jared and their accusations against her best friend had her stomach twirling like a weather vane on a windy day.

Hunter insisted that having her injuries checked out came before talking to Lance and Jared. She didn't protest, figuring it was better to get it over with. Hunter paved the way, dealing with the administrative process easily and pushing for a doctor to see her right away.

The doctor, the same one Ariel had seen the day before, scoped her throat and sent her off for imaging. When she returned, the doctor said, "It's a marvel that you're not worse off than you are. Whoever did this didn't quite know what they were doing. If they had, they would've been able to crush your larynx. As it is, they only managed to give you some mild bruising. Your throat will be sore and your voice a little hoarse for the next day or so, but you'll recover quickly enough with some rest."

Grateful for the prognosis, she said, "That's good news."

"For your sake, Ariel, I really don't want to see you again anytime soon."

"Believe me, I don't want this to become a habit."

After signing discharge papers and being given instructions on how to care for her throat, she and Hunter took the elevator up to the floor where Jared and Lance shared a room to recover from their ordeal.

An officer sat outside the hospital room door and stood as they approached. Hunter introduced himself and Ariel.

"Trooper McCord." He gave Hunter a chin nod of greeting. "Ma'am." He nodded to her. "My boss said I was to cooperate with the K-9 Unit."

The officer's gaze dropped to Juneau before he stepped aside to allow them to enter the room. The TV blared from where it was mounted on the wall. Jared and Lance each lay sitting up in their own bed. Lance, sporting a bandage on his head, had his smartphone out while Jared, whose arm was wrapped up in white gauze, stared at the TV. Both men's eyes widened and they sat up straighter when they noticed Ariel and Hunter.

"Ariel?" Lance exclaimed, barely audible above the noise of the TV.

Jared grabbed the remote control and turned the TV off. The silence was eerie as the men stared at her. Their faces drained of color.

Lance recovered from his shock first. "Ariel, you're alive!"

The two men glanced at each other, their expressions a mix of shock and disbelief, then looked back at her.

"This is so great!" Jared pushed himself up with his good arm. "We thought for sure you were dead."

A mix of anger at what they were saying about Violet and sympathy for the injuries they'd sustained swirled in her gut. "What really happened on the mountain?"

Both men looked to Hunter rather than Ariel. "We've already told the trooper, here, everything." Then Lance's gaze narrowed on her slightly. "How did you survive the fall? Jared saw Violet push you over the edge."

She shook her head and then decided that was not a good idea. Between the headache throbbing behind her eyes, the soreness of her throat and the ache in her heart, she really just wanted to leave, but this was too important. "It couldn't have been Violet."

"It was," Lance insisted, his face twisting. "She was out of control. She was having an affair with the tour guide and then she just went ballistic."

Ariel stepped forward. Hunter matched her step. Did he suppose that either of these two men would hurt her?

"She was *not* having an affair with Cal Brooks," Ariel ground out. A flush of outrage heated her face. "That's ridiculous. She didn't even know him until we met him that morning."

"Says you," Jared shot back at her. "We know what we know. She did this to us. And she did it to you. She's not a good person."

Ariel's fists balled at her sides. Her gaze zeroed in on Lance. "Did she tell you about the baby?"

Lance tucked in his chin and stared at her. "Excuse me? What baby?"

"She was pregnant with your child," she said as tears

gathered in her eyes. "She had planned to tell you on the hike."

Genuine shock registered in Lance's eyes. He shook his head, winced and leaned back. His gaze drifted to the ceiling. "I didn't know..." His voice broke. "It's not my baby. It's probably Cal's."

"No! She was not having an affair. I don't know why you're saying this horrible stuff." Ariel glared at Lance.

He met her gaze with sadness in his eyes. "Violet isn't the person you think she is."

Her breath caught. "Don't say that."

Hunter stepped past Ariel. "Hold up a moment. You really didn't know about the baby?"

"No, I didn't know about the baby," Lance said. "If there even is one." He looked at Ariel. "She could've lied to you."

A fresh wave of frustration crashed through Ariel. "She wasn't lying! I was there when she took the pregnancy test. It came out positive. She's carrying your child."

Lance scrubbed a hand over his face. "If that's true—" He looked at Hunter. "If that's true, you've got to find her. You've got to get my baby prenatal care and whatever else it is that babies need when they're still in their mom. You have to find her and put her in jail before she hurts anyone else." He leaned back again. "I have a child..."

"You'll have to fight Mrs. James for custody once the baby is born and Violet is behind bars," Jared said.

Lance looked at him. "Fathers have rights."

The two men nodded at each other.

Ariel couldn't believe that they were concerned about custody issues. Wasn't anyone worried about Violet's well-being? This just couldn't be happening. "You two are wrong. Why are you lying? What is it that you have to gain from lying about Violet?"

"I'm not lying. My heart is broken. I love Violet but she betrayed me. Please, get out." Lance turned away from her. "Just leave."

Hunter took her by the shoulders and drew her backward against him. "Ariel, it's time for us to go."

"They are lying!"

Hunter drew her out of the hospital room with Juneau protecting their backs, nodded to the officer, and then put his arm around her shoulders to lead her toward the elevator. Fatigue and despair settled around her. She slumped against Hunter as the doors of the elevator shut. Tears streamed down her cheeks. "I can't believe it. I won't believe what they said about Violet. I know my friend. I know you might think I'm being foolish, but I'm not. I know my friend."

Hunter turned her so that she faced him and put the crook of his finger under her chin to lift her head until their gazes met. The tenderness in his eyes brought a fresh wave of tears coursing down her cheeks.

"When we find Violet, we will find out the truth. Right now, my concern is you," Hunter said softly.

He sounded so sincere that she had a hard time remembering he was only doing his job.

"You heard the doctor. You need to rest," he continued. "I'm driving you home and you're going to take it easy."

A shiver of dread charged down her spine. "What if my attacker comes back?"

"I'm not leaving your side again," he promised.

As much as she wanted to take solace in his words,

her practical side had her stepping back out of his reach and bumping against Juneau. "You can't just abandon your job to protect me 24/7."

"You *are* my job until your attacker is caught."

She wanted to protest and tell him she'd be fine without him. But deep inside, the knowledge that he and he alone stood between her and doom kept her silent. Bottom line? She had to put her trust in Hunter and faith in God to keep her safe.

Juneau nudged her and she stroked his head, finding calm in the soothing gesture.

The doors of the elevator opened to a clamoring of voices. The lobby of the hospital was crowded with news reporters. Several stuck their microphones in Ariel's face. Surprised, she drew away and grabbed Hunter's arm.

He used his other arm to block the reporters surging forward. "Everybody get back."

Juneau positioned himself in front of Ariel, a barrier that wouldn't be breached.

"Is it true Violet James murdered Cal Brooks and pushed you off a cliff?"

Stunned, Ariel stared up at Hunter. How did the media discover Lance and Jared's accusations?

Anger crossed his features. "No comment," he said gruffly. "Make room."

The sea of reporters stepped back.

"Let's get out of here," Hunter murmured.

Juneau led the way to the door.

"Did Violet James do that to your neck?" a reporter called out.

Ariel pulled the edges of her coat closed to hide her throat.

"Violet James is a murderer who tried to kill her soon-to-be groom and his best man," another reporter stated.

"She tried to kill you, her maid of honor. Don't you have anything to say?" someone else called out.

Ariel stopped in her tracks. The injustice of what was being done to Violet boiled her blood. She couldn't let these people ruin her friend's reputation. It wasn't fair or right. "I don't know what happened on that mountain. Nobody really knows. But I'm sure of one thing. My friend, Violet James, is not guilty of what she's been accused of. We are all innocent until proven guilty. Don't you forget that."

Flashes went off, stinging her eyes. Hunter's arm snaked around her waist and urged her out of the hospital doors to his SUV. The reporters followed them. He got her into the passenger seat and Juneau in his compartment. She quickly buckled the seat belt, cringing as reporters crowded around the SUV. Hunter climbed into the driver's seat, started the engine and eased out of the parking lot.

Thankfully, the reporters moved out of the way, allowing them to pass. Ariel glanced into the side view mirror. The reporters dispersed, some heading back inside the hospital, no doubt hoping to interview Lance and Jared.

Her breath came in shallow gasps and her heart thundered as if she'd just crossed the finish line of a race. Then, embarrassment replaced the adrenaline that had surged through her. "I can't believe I did that." She groaned and dropped her head into her hands. "I never do stuff like that."

His warm hand on her shoulder offered comfort.

"Give yourself some grace, Ariel. You're upset. It's been a trying few days. You were defending your friend. And that is admirable."

She lifted her gaze to his profile. "But you suppose my loyalty is misplaced?"

"It's not for me to judge," he said. "My job is to protect you and to bring Violet in safely so that she can tell her side of the story."

She hoped and prayed that his commitment was real and that he wouldn't disappoint her. Who was she kidding? Disappointment was a part of life. Few people honored their word.

Hunter wouldn't be any different. And she'd be setting herself up for heartbreak if she allowed herself to believe in him. "Why don't you like hospitals?"

He slanted her a quick glance as if surprised by her question. "My mother died in a hospital. She was very ill for a long time."

Sympathy weighted heavily in her chest. "I'm so sorry."

"It was rough."

She could only imagine. And now here he was, taking her in and out of the hospital, which had to bring back the pain he'd suffered.

When they reached her house, Hunter hustled her inside. "I'll get Sasha and send Trevor home. You go do whatever you need to do to relax. We'll be in shortly."

Everything inside her rebelled at being told what to do. She wanted to deny that she needed him taking care of her, but the memories of her attacker grabbing her and squeezing her neck, trying to take her life, taunted her. She did need Hunter and she should be grateful he was willing to help her, even if it was only out of duty.

"Thank you, Hunter," she said. "It will be reassuring to have you here on guard."

Upon entering the house, she shivered at the quiet. Her attacker had robbed her of peace in her own home. She hadn't been this unnerved since Jason had lost his temper when she broke up with him. But thankfully, he'd left town and was somewhere in the continental United States or as Alaskans would say, the lower forty-eight.

She told herself to go into her room and change into her sweats, but she couldn't find the wherewithal to walk down the hall. So instead, she sat at the dining room table and once again bowed her head, folded her hands and prayed—for Violet, for herself and for Hunter. Unfortunately, she couldn't shake the dread gripping her.

The next morning, Hunter folded the blanket and stacked the pillow on the edge of the couch where he had slept the night before. He and Juneau went outside and released Officer Gorman, who had stood guard through the night, allowing Hunter to get some rest.

When Hunter and Juneau reentered the house, Ariel and Sasha came down the hallway. She wore well-worn jeans and a cable-knit sweater in a light pink that heightened the color of her cheeks and lips. Her skin was dewy from a recent shower and her blow-dried blond hair loose about her shoulders. Hunter couldn't deny how pretty and appealing he found her.

"Good morning," she said as she passed him to open the back door for Sasha. Her voice wasn't as raspy as the night before.

He hoped that was a good sign. "Morning."

The puppy clamored down the stairs and out to the

snow-cleared grass, compliments of Trevor. Juneau stayed by Ariel's side where she stood watching the pup. "So, I assume you'll be taking off now?"

He raised his eyebrows as he stopped on her other side. Did she forget what he'd said last night? "24/7. I meant it."

She bit her bottom lip, drawing his attention.

"That's really not necessary," she said. "The attacker has come only in the dark. I'm sure in the daylight, I'm fine. You should go do your job."

"We've been over this." He wasn't sure if he should be insulted that she wanted to get rid of him or not. He remembered what his chief had said about Ariel being independent. Ariel wasn't used to having a human in her space. He got that. It had taken him a while to get used to living with his dad when he'd moved in after the debacle with that woman. Deciding not to push Ariel, he said, "I'm going to grab my computer and join a team meeting via video conference call." He turned to the door.

"There's ground coffee in the freezer," she said, stopping him in his tracks. "I keep it on hand for when my parents come to town."

He grinned. "That's good to know. Do you have a coffee machine or am I doing a pour over?" He could use a jolt of caffeine, though he'd already decided he'd try her tea.

"There's a machine in the cabinet next to the sink. My parents would never tolerate a pour over."

"How often do your parents visit?"

She shrugged. "Whenever they feel like it or there's a race in the area that they are working. They were here for the start of the Iditarod. I suspect I'll see them next in the fall, despite the fact that there's a race coming up this week. It's too small for them."

The race. She'd mentioned she was competing. He hoped by then the danger would be over and she'd be free to participate. "I'll get the coffee going and some water boiling for your tea."

The spring sun made her hair glisten, but it was her smile that enthralled him. He forced himself to focus anywhere other than on her mouth. The trees lining the property were dusted with snow, but the green foliage created a beautiful backdrop against a blue sky with fluffy white clouds. Quiet serenity surrounded them. He liked it here. So different than the two-bedroom apartment he shared with his father in downtown Anchorage.

Maybe that's why he'd slept hard last night. He hadn't had much in the last forty-eight hours.

He went inside and found the coffee and the coffee maker. Once the coffee was percolating, the aroma filling the house, he put water in the kettle to boil. Then he set up at the dining table and fired up his laptop. When the pot whistled, he turned the heat to simmer.

Juneau stood by the door as if he wanted out again. "Already?"

Hunter opened the back door, but the dog stayed in place, waiting for the release command.

"Release," Hunter said.

Juneau flew down the porch stairs, across the divide that separated the house from the kennel building and entered the open door. Shaking his head, Hunter followed him. Ariel was feeding her dogs. Each kennel door was open with each canine waiting for their breakfast. One by one, she placed a bowl of food in front of them, then sprinkled a white powder on the food. He figured some sort of supplement. She glanced up at Juneau as he skidded to a halt a few feet from the first open kennel. The beautiful gray-and-white Siberian Husky inside cocked her head at Juneau. Though their colorings were different, both dogs had a similar look about them.

Ariel paused with her gaze on Juneau. "I've plenty of kibble if you'd like to feed Juneau."

"He's got his own food," Hunter told her. "I'll feed him soon. We don't usually eat this early in the morning."

Her curious gaze met his as she put down the last bowl. "What do you do this early in the morning?"

"Normally, we'd go for a run on one of the trails of Westchester Lagoon. It's only a ten-minute jog from my downtown apartment," he told her.

She faced the dogs. "Eat." The dogs dug into their bowls. Then Ariel turned to him. "We'll be fine here, if you two want to take a run up the fire road."

Not likely. Hunter wanted her inside the house, not out here alone. Even with the dogs ready to sound an alarm, he planned to stay close. He glanced at his watch. "My conference call is about to start. Are you coming in?"

Annoyance flashed in her eyes. "Are you going to be monitoring my every move?"

Her independent streak was showing. If he didn't get a handle on it, keeping her safe might turn out to be more difficult than he'd anticipated. Yet he had to admit to himself he liked her feistiness. There was much about this woman that he liked. And that might actually prove his undoing.

NINE

Hunter bit the inside of his cheek and held up his hands. He really had to get a grip on his attraction to Ariel. Treading lightly would be his best course of action. "Sorry. But I'd prefer to be in the same area as you."

She planted her hands on her hips. "I appreciate you being here last night. I'll admit I was freaked out. But in the light of day, I'm okay. I don't need a babysitter."

"Not babysitter. *Protector.* Big difference." Was she always this touchy or was she hangry? Neither of them had eaten breakfast. He could easily remedy that.

She shrugged, clearly unconvinced by his assertion.

"Let me make you some breakfast," he offered.

"I had a granola bar," she said. "You can help yourself to whatever you want in the kitchen."

Just prickly. Time to retreat, feed Juneau and get on the video call.

After grabbing Juneau's kibble and bowl, they went back inside the house. While his dog ate, Hunter snagged a granola bar from the cupboard and sat at the dining table where he had a clear view of the property entrance and kennel building.

Hunter logged into the video conference chat room and slipped his earbuds into his ears. Squares of live video popped up of each team member and his boss.

"Good morning, everyone," Lorenza said. "Now that we're all here... Hunter, why don't you fill us in on what happened last night."

He gave them the lowdown on the assault to Ariel and the drugged police officer, including telling the group about talking with Lance and Jared.

"Is Ariel okay?" Poppy asked.

"She is," Hunter assured his teammate. "A bit bruised and sore."

"Are the groom and his best man to be believed?" Lorenza asked.

Maya said, "There's no faking their injuries. But as to whether or not they were done by Violet James..." She shrugged.

"Hard to know at this point," Hunter agreed. "Eli, what can you tell us about the satellite phone that was left in the cabin?"

The small square frame filled with Eli Partridge, the team's tech guru, showed him frowning and not looking into the camera.

"Earth to Eli," Will Stryker said.

Eli jerked his gaze to the camera. "Oh, sorry." He pushed up the bridge of his dark round glasses that framed his blue eyes. "The phone belongs to the parks and rec department. They reported it missing a week ago. They aren't sure how it ended up in the cabin where you found the groom and his best man."

The team went on to talk about the situation, each of them giving their thoughts and opinions. Hunter's gaze was drawn repeatedly to Eli. He didn't seem his usual, affable self.

As the call was wrapping up, Hunter said, "Hey, Eli. Is everything okay? You've been awfully quiet. More than normal."

Eli made a face. "No, everything is not okay, Hunter. You see way too much."

The comment elicited knowing nods from some of the other team members.

"Care to share with us?" Maya asked, her dark eyes round with concern.

Eli hesitated, then said, "If it's okay with the colonel."

Lorenza smiled. "Please, whatever is on your mind Eli, you can say it."

"It's my godmother. She was my mother's best friend. And the reason I came to Anchorage," he said. "She's sick. Very ill. Stage III cancer. She's only sixty-five."

Hunter's stomach clenched. He knew the heartache of losing someone to disease. His mother's death had left a scar on his soul. "I'm sorry to hear that."

"Thank you," Eli said. "Bettina is in a cancer care home, but they've told me that the treatments will soon stop having any effect. I was with her yesterday. And her most fervent wish is to see her only son and his family again before…" Eli swallowed and turned away from the camera.

"What can we do to help?" Poppy asked, her green eyes glistening with sympathy.

Having collected himself, Eli faced the camera. "I need to find her son and his family. All I know is that they are survivalists and may be somewhere in Chugach State Park."

The same park where Violet James was hiding out. Considering the park was one of the four largest state parks in the United States, many survivalists and those who wanted to remain hidden had plenty of space to do so.

"It's a big area," Gabriel commented. "Lots of places where survivalists could camp out and not be seen, especially this time of year in the colder months. But with the summer months, it will be harder for them to stay out of the path of other hikers and campers."

"My ex-wife was raised by survivalists," Sean West volunteered. "She runs a mission in a remote area near Nome. I know that's far away, but perhaps she'd have some tips on how to find the family."

Hunter wasn't the only one to meet Sean's suggestion with raised eyebrows. It was well-known that he and his ex-wife, Ivy, were not on speaking terms.

"Are you willing to reach out to her?" Lorenza asked.

Sean nodded. "I am."

"That would be so appreciated," Eli said. "I'll owe you one."

"We all owe you, Eli," Helena said. "You've saved many of us countless hours and probably our lives numerous times."

There was a murmur of agreement among all the team members.

"That settles it," Lorenza said. "Sean, we'll wait to hear back from you. Eli, if you or your godmother need anything else, you let us know."

"I will, ma'am," Eli promised. "Thank you."

The meeting ended and Hunter clicked off. He put his computer away and then he and Juneau headed out to the kennel building, but the room was empty. All the dogs' bowls had been cleaned and put away. He and Juneau followed the sound of Ariel's voice through the back door and off to the side, where there was a large fenced yard. And a specially made treadmill that was wider than the normal exercise equipment found in a gym was hooked to a sled that had been bolted to a concrete pad. No doubt that was how she trained the dogs to run together in a two-by-two formation when not out on the trail. He was impressed by her business acumen and her operation. There was much about Ariel that he found appealing.

He turned his attention to her and the dogs. All of the canines were sitting six feet apart. Curious as to what she was doing, he stayed where he was so as not to interrupt. Ariel threw a ball and called out a dog's name. That dog would chase the ball and bring it back to her, then return to its place. She called the dogs' names randomly until each had had a turn chasing the ball.

Beside him, Juneau let out a plaintive howl. No doubt his partner wanted in on the chase. But he wasn't sure how the other dogs would react to Juneau in their domain. It was one thing to allow him near while they were still in their kennels, but off leash and loose? He wasn't going to risk it.

Ariel waved. She released the dogs and all eight trotted off in various directions to sniff around the pen. He noticed none of them played with each other but stayed apart.

"Everything okay?" she asked.

"Yes, everything's fine." He leaned on the slatted rails around the dog yard. "What's on your agenda for today?"

"The dogs and I need to prep for this coming week-

Alaskan Rescue

end's race," she said. "There are drills I plan to do. I was contemplating taking them out on the fresh snow—" Her voice had a distinct rasp to it.

He held up his hand. "Whoa. What did the doctor tell you to do?"

She made a face.

He waited, holding her gaze.

Blowing out a breath, she said, "Rest."

"Exactly."

She pinched the bridge of her nose. "Fine. I'll arrange with Trevor to come over and exercise the dogs."

"Good." He was glad she was willing to take it easy and let someone else do the work for her. "I could use some actual food. The granola bar was a nice snack." But certainly not enough to sustain either of them for long. If he made it seem that he needed the sustenance, then maybe she'd eat, as well. "And then I'm going to take Juneau for a run around the edge of the property. The crime scene unit will come back out here sometime today."

She grimaced and started walking back toward the house. "They came yesterday and didn't find any usable clues. They probably won't today, either. I feel bad dragging them out here a second time."

"They will come out here as many times as they need to," he said as he walked beside her. "That's their job."

Her nose wrinkled in a cute way. "I know. Just like it's your job to stay here to protect me and the dogs. But really, we'll be safe now. I can't imagine whoever attacked me would come back. And I don't for a second believe it was Violet."

"That remains to be seen," he said. "We don't know exactly what's going on. Better to be safe than sorry."

He'd made a promise to his boss and he was not going

to renege on that promise. Ariel Potter was going to be safe and he was staying put, whether she liked it or not.

Two days later, Ariel was about to jump out of her skin. Having somebody underfoot, in her space, wasn't comfortable. Add to that her growing attraction for this man who at every turn seemed to be there when she needed anything, whether it was feeding the dogs, cleaning the kennel and yard, locking up at night or preparing a meal. Though he'd slept on the couch the first night, she insisted he move his things into the guest room that her parents usually used when they visited. Much better than having him in the living room, should she want to get a drink of water in the middle of the night.

He was just so amenable and patient with her. She'd snapped at him on more than one occasion, mostly because she wasn't sure how to handle all the emotions he stirred in her. Gratitude, longing, frustration…affection.

Ariel couldn't help but smile at the image of him toggling his fingers at her and telling her to rest. She was tired of resting. Tired of the constant anxiety created by the threat of danger, waiting for the next time someone tried to hurt her. She kept telling herself the danger had passed, but Hunter wasn't convinced.

And to add to the pressure, she had a speech to write.

Tomorrow night was the regional awards banquet. The winners of the Iditarod and the runners-up would all be present, even though the official banquet celebrating the end of the Iditarod race had already commenced in Nome last month.

This banquet was for those who called Alaska home, and she would be receiving an award for the most champion sled dogs to come in the top fifty spots. She didn't quite know what she was going to say.

As she sat at the dining room table with a notebook and pen, Hunter came in and plopped down in the chair next to her, stretching out his long legs. He wore running pants and a thermal T-shirt that molded to his muscled and lean body. His hair was slicked back and his face glistened with a sheen of sweat. All that masculinity threw her off balance.

"What are you doing?"

Eyeing him, she wondered if he was always so curious. Must be a good trait in his line of work. "Trying to write a speech. The regional awards banquet is tomorrow night."

His chin dropped and his brow furrowed. "You are not going to an awards banquet."

She set the pen on the paper and faced him squarely. "Oh, yes, I am." She'd worked hard for this and nobody was going to deprive her of accepting that award. Not even this gorgeous lawman with control issues.

He made a noise in his throat that sounded suspiciously like a harrumph. "I need all the details."

"Like what?" she asked.

"Place, time, the organizers' info. I'll need to make sure Eli, our team's tech person, has access to the video surveillance cameras."

"If there are any," she said. "You don't know what you'd be looking for. And I am certain whoever attacked me wasn't someone from the sled dog community. I thought you believed Lance's tale that it was Violet who attacked me."

"I'm reserving judgment."

That was welcome and unexpected news. "So you think Lance and Jared are lying?"

There was consternation in Hunter's blue eyes. "I didn't say that. I'm not sure what to think. The only thing I am sure of is you're not going anywhere alone."

Though the temptation to argue with him was strong because she would be among friends and wouldn't be in any danger, she choked back the protest and said, "Super. You can come with me. Do you have a tux?"

She couldn't keep the smirk from her tone. Not many men had a tux ready at the drop of a hat.

His lips curved into a smile that sent her heart pumping as if she had just crossed the finish line at the Iditarod.

"Yes, in fact, I do have a tux. I've been in a few weddings over the years and will have my father drop it off." He grabbed her notebook and turned to a blank piece of paper. Then he picked up the pen and held it out. "Write down the details of this event, please."

Her mind turned from thoughts of his tux to the maid of honor dress hanging in her closet. A wave of worry crashed over her. Where was Violet? She missed her friend.

Taking a deep breath, she jotted down all the information that she knew off the top of her head about the award ceremony. Then she opened her laptop for any other details she'd missed while keeping half an ear on the one-sided conversation that Hunter was having with his father, asking him to bring the tux to her house.

It seemed she had a date for the banquet. She'd been on dates before so there was no reason for the flutter of nerves in her tummy. But she'd never had a date to something so public. Nor one she looked forward to with such anticipation.

The flutter died. So silly of her.

This wasn't a date. He would be on duty. Because someone wanted her dead.

The late afternoon sun cast shadows over the ranch. Was it a ranch? Hunter wasn't sure. Earlier in the day, he and Juneau had taken a few laps around the edge of the property on the lookout for anything out of place while keeping the house in view. Thus far they'd found nothing of interest. Nor had the crime scene unit when they'd conducted their search. "What do you call this place?"

Ariel sat in the recliner, reading a book with Sasha napping on her lap. Juneau lay next to the recliner and Hunter sat on the couch typing up his notes from the past few days. Or rather, revising his notes. Taking out his personal observations of Ariel. They had no place in his official report.

Looking at him over the top of her book, she seemed to ponder the question. "It's a ranch of sorts. But typically, when you say *ranch*, people assume you have horses or cattle. Most breeders say *dog kennel*. Then there's no question."

"Now that I believe."

His cell phone vibrated. He quickly scanned the caller ID on the cell before answering. "Hunter here."

"Hey." Will Stryker's voice filled the line. "We just got word from the hospital that Lance and Jared have barricaded themselves in an operating room."

"I'm on my way."

Ariel set her book aside and released the footrest on

the recliner with a slam. Sasha awoke and jumped from Ariel's lap to race to his water bowl. "What's going on?"

"Lance and Jared." He was up and moving toward the hall closet, where'd he'd hung the clean uniform and tux his father had brought over.

That had been a strange visit. His dad and Ariel had hit it off right away. And before Dad had left, he'd pulled Hunter aside and told him that Ariel was *the one* and he'd *better not blow it*.

Shaking his head to dislodge his father's words from his brain, Hunter grabbed the clean uniform and then headed to the bathroom to freshen up and change. When he returned to the living room, Ariel was standing by the door with her shoes and jacket on and her purse slung over her shoulder. Juneau stood beside her.

"What are you doing?"

"I'm going with you. You might need my help."

Hunter hesitated. He certainly couldn't leave her here unattended. The Metro police hadn't any officer to spare the past two days, and Ariel's safety took priority over whatever Lance and Jared were up to. "I'll call Metro to see if Officer Gorman is available for a few hours. Once he arrives, then I'll head out."

However, when Hunter started his SUV a half hour later, Ariel climbed into the passenger seat and wouldn't be dissuaded from going to the hospital with him and Juneau. Figuring that the situation would most likely be resolved by the time they arrived, he didn't bother arguing with Ariel.

However, when they pulled into the hospital parking lot, the place was on lockdown. He showed his ID, getting him, Ariel and Juneau inside. They met Lorenza and Will on the fourth floor, and both of his colleagues had a dog by their side. Denali sat proudly beside Lorenza and a sleek-looking, black-and-white border collie stood next to Will.

The colonel's eyebrows rose as her gaze bounced from Ariel to Hunter.

"Ariel thought she might be able to help," Hunter explained. "What's going on?"

Lorenza's gaze turned speculative. "We're not completely sure," she answered. "The officer who had been stationed outside Lance and Jared's hospital door had been knocked out."

"Lance and Jared are claiming that it was Violet James," Will stated. "They say she tried to kill them, but somehow they managed to escape and for some reason barricaded themselves in the OR by pushing some of the bigger equipment inside against the door. Maya is checking with the hospital's surveillance videos to corroborate their story."

Ariel made a distressed noise. Hunter's heart ached for her. This had to be hard to hear.

Gabriel approached with Bear. The big, strong Saint Bernard outweighed the other dogs by at least twenty pounds. "The operating room has no other entrance points."

"The hospital is being searched," Lorenza said. "If Violet is here, we will find her and take her into custody, hopefully without anyone getting hurt."

Hunter glanced at Ariel, who looked like she might throw up. "Here, you need to sit." He directed her to a plastic chair. Juneau nudged his way between them.

The last thing Hunter needed was Ariel taking a nosedive. Apparently it had been a bad idea to allow her to come with him. He'd let his growing affection for Ariel affect his judgment.

A mistake.

One he wouldn't repeat, because there was no way he wanted to end up like his father, duped by emotion into making bad choices. It was time to guard his heart and put some distance between him and Ariel.

Ariel hung her head between her knees and took deep breaths as the nausea rolled through her. Juncau's warm body pressed against her leg. But not even his soothing presence could calm the riot of anxiety beating through her veins.

Please, Lord, please, she begged silently.

She wasn't even sure what to pray. Violet couldn't have done this. There had to be another explanation.

She sat up and looked at Hunter. "Has the guard come to? Has he confirmed it was Violet?"

Hunter looked to his teammates.

The trooper named Gabriel answered, "The guard is conscious. He said somebody came up from behind him. He didn't see who it was."

Ariel couldn't wrap her mind around the information. She buried her hands in Juneau's fur. "The guard must have left his post for somebody to be able to sneak up on him."

From the grim expression on Hunter's face, he'd come to the same conclusion.

Inside the operating room, the jangle of a cell phone going off rattled Ariel's nerves.

"We're hoping Lance or Jared will answer their phones," Lorenza said. "But so far, they aren't picking up."

"Is there an intercom system?" Hunter asked.

Lorenza turned to the hospital security guard.

"Yes. At the nurses' station."

Lorenza and Gabriel walked down the hallway to the nurses' station. After a few minutes, Gabriel jogged back. "They asked for Ariel."

"I can try to talk to them." She rose. "Maybe hearing a familiar voice will help them to feel safe." She could only pray so.

Ariel moved quickly toward the nurses' station with Hunter and Juneau keeping pace. Hunter deferred to his boss. The colonel nodded. He flipped on the operating room intercom.

Ariel gripped the mic. Her heart pounded in her throat, making her already sore vocal chords protest as she said, "Lance. Jared. It's Ariel. Please, come out. The K-9 team is here. They will not let anything happen to you."

Ariel waited a heartbeat, then tried again. "Lance, you know me. I don't trust easily, but I trust these officers. You have to come out and let them help you."

There was a commotion down the hall as the doors to the operating room slowly opened. Lance and Jared stepped out, wearing hospital gowns and the gray hospital-issue socks.

Ariel hurried away from the nurses' station and skidded to a halt with a small gasp.

Lance had a scalpel in one hand and a bedpan in the other, held like a shield, while Jared had some sort of saw that he held like a bat. The white bandage around his upper bicep showed red seeping through from his wound.

"Violet's here somewhere." The green of Lance's eyes nearly disappeared behind his dark pupils. "You have to find her. She's evil, I tell you. She tried to kill us. Again."

TEN

A chill ran down Ariel's spine as she stared at the two men, who were clearly freaked out, claiming her best friend wanted to kill them.

It was so hard for Ariel to comprehend that Violet was some kind of maniac. But why would Lance and Jared make up such a story? She had to know.

Hunter's arm snaked around her waist and held her to his side. In a low voice, he said into her ear, "Let's get them disarmed first."

Juneau moved to stand in front of Ariel as if providing another line of defense. A warming sensation at the show of protectiveness from both man and dog chased away the cold that had filled her veins.

The three other dogs present stood beside their handlers and stared at the pair brandishing their makeshift weapons. An intimidating sight. Alaska State Troopers Will Stryker and Gabriel Runyon stood ready to move, with one hand hovering over their sidearms.

Lorenza stepped forward, drawing Lance's and Jared's attention. Ariel held her breath, praying for the other woman's safety as she dealt with the two men.

"Mr. Wells and Mr. Dennis, I'm Colonel Lorenza

Gallo of the Alaska K-9 Unit. We are here to help you, but I need you to put down those instruments so we can talk calmly, and no one gets hurt."

Lance and Jared shared a glance, then a nod, before putting down their weapons.

Will and Gabriel moved then, removing the scalpel and bone saw out of Lance's and Jared's reach before searching each man for any additional dangerous items.

Lance's gaze zeroed in on Ariel. He rushed to her side, his attention jerking to Hunter, then back to Ariel. "Ariel, we've got to go someplace safe. Come with us. We're leaving the hospital right now."

She pressed closer to Hunter. She didn't like the wild look in the other man's eyes.

"Hold on a second," Hunter said. "You two can't just leave."

Lance puffed up his chest. "We can do as we please. Jared and I are not prisoners or under arrest. We've stayed in the hospital because we thought we'd be safe. We're the victims here. My buddy and I are checking ourselves out and going where she won't find us."

"Yeah, that's right," Jared said. "We'll give you the location and a burner phone number once we're settled."

"Gentlemen." Lorenza held up a hand. "We can provide you a safe house."

"No offense, lady, but I don't know you," Lance said. "And I don't trust you. I don't trust *any* of you." His gaze settled on Ariel again. "Come with us, Ariel. It's the only way you'll be safe."

His fear was palpable, but there was no way she was going anywhere with him and Jared. Not only wouldn't she leave her dogs, but she wasn't going to forgo the safety of the K-9 Unit. "Lance, tell us what happened."

"I told you. Violet happened, that's what," he replied forcefully. "She came into the room with a gun in one hand and a knife in the other. She was going to kill us, but we managed to evade her. We barely escaped."

"That's right," Jared said. "Violet kept saying we had to die."

Ariel had a hard time wrapping her mind around the story the men were telling. Violet with a gun and a knife? No!

"I want my clothes." Lance spun away and made a sweeping gesture with his arm. "Where are my clothes, my shoes and my house keys?"

"Me, too," Jared said.

"Your belongings are bagged in your room." A doctor stepped forward, his forehead creased with a stern frown. "You'll be leaving against medical advice. We still have tests to run and that gunshot wound needs to be monitored."

"It's better than being dead," Lance retorted. "We're leaving."

Ariel didn't know how to fix this situation. She didn't believe Lance and Jared's accusation that Violet attacked them, but they were clearly afraid of someone. But who?

A moment later, K-9 officers Maya Rodriguez and Poppy Walsh joined them.

"We searched the whole building," Poppy said. Stormy, the Irish wolfhound, lay down at his handler's feet, but Ariel could tell the dog was on guard by the way his eyes surveyed his surroundings as if searching for a threat. "No sign of Violet James."

"The hospital security cameras are working fine, all except for the hallway outside of Lance and Jared's room," Maya stated. Her Malinois, Sarge, remained standing, his tail high, indicating he was also on guard. "Someone had pulled the cable from the camera."

"See, I told you, she's a criminal," Lance said.

The nurse returned with two large plastic bags filled with Lance's and Jared's personal effects.

"Will, escort these two men to their room where they can change," Lorenza instructed.

Will and his border collie marched Lance and Jared away. Ariel stared after them. Had she just stepped into an old episode of some crime TV show that her father and mother used to love to watch when she was little? This just couldn't be happening.

"Gabriel, put a tail on Lance and Jared," Lorenza said. "For their safety."

"Yes, ma'am." Gabriel went to make the necessary arrangements.

"Did the hospital's video surveillance show Violet James in the hospital?" Lorenza asked.

"I had the hospital send the day's video feed to Eli," Maya said. "If Violet was in the hospital, he'll find her with facial recognition software."

Ariel was confident this Eli person wouldn't find Violet. She touched Hunter's arm. "You have to believe me, Hunter, this wasn't Violet. I don't know what's going on or who is after Jared and Lance, but it's not my best friend." Anguish tightened her chest. "She's in trouble. We have to find her."

Ariel refused to squirm under the scrutiny of Hunter's team as she held his gaze.

His blue eyes searched her face. "No one's giving up on finding her," he said. "There's nothing more we can do here tonight."

Not liking that he didn't believe her, Ariel nodded. She was tired and just wanted to go home.

Hunter urged Ariel toward the elevator and out to the SUV. She shivered as a new blanket of spring snow fell from the sky. As they drove away from the hospital, she leaned her forehead against the cool glass of the passenger side door and closed her eyes. Her head throbbed and heart ached. Nothing made sense. Could she be wrong about her friend?

She shut down the doubt. No, she couldn't be. The authorities would have to present her with irrefutable proof of Violet's guilt before Ariel would ever concede that she was capable of such violence.

Ariel's hands shook as she applied eyeliner to her eyes. She paused and set the applicator down to shake her hands out. "Come on, you can do this," she muttered to herself. "It's no big deal."

Sasha lay on the bathroom floor near her feet. He lifted his head from the chew toy. She used her bare toe to nuzzle him.

But this night *was* a big deal. She was going to the awards banquet, where she would be honored for breeding championship dogs. And she would be on the arm of a handsome man.

No, a handsome state trooper.

This was not a date. This was him doing his job, escorting her to the banquet to protect her. Nothing more. And she'd best keep that in mind before she let herself pretend that Hunter might have feelings for her or let herself admit she had growing feelings for him. It was all too much.

Taking a steadying breath, she finished her eye

makeup, applied a light coat of pink lip gloss, and checked the mirror one last time to make sure the full-length black dress was okay with the colorful scarf she'd wound around her neck to hide the fading bruises.

Violet should be at her side tonight.

Ariel's heart clenched.

If her best friend was here, she would have done some fancy updo with Ariel's hair. Loose and straight was as fancy as Ariel knew how to do. If Violet was here, she'd probably lend Ariel one of her many ball gowns.

But Violet *wasn't* here. She was missing, possibly alone and hurt. Definitely afraid.

Ariel sent up a plea to God to keep her friend safe and to bring her home quickly. Ariel had to trust He was watching over Violet and her baby. Without her faith, Ariel didn't know if she could make it through each day, and she hoped that Violet was turning to God to see her through this ordeal.

Worry nipped Ariel as she picked up her handbag from the foot of her bed, slipped her feet into low-slung beaded heels and headed out to the living room with Sasha trailing behind. Her steps faltered as she caught her first glimpse of Hunter and Juneau. They stood side by side looking out the front window with their backs to her, like two sentries.

Juneau spun and trotted to her, wearing a cute little black bow tie nestled around his neck. Sasha jumped at him, trying to grab the edge of the bow, clearly wanting to play. Ariel scooped up the puppy and cradled him in her arms.

When Hunter turned to face her, his blue eyes flared with appreciation. Their gazes locked. Then her breath caught in her throat as she fully drank him in. His dark hair had been tamed back, his jaw was clean-shaven and his well-tailored tux emphasized the width of his shoulders. She couldn't help but sigh with delight when he came forward with a small square plastic floral box tied with a ribbon.

"Juneau's going with us?" Ariel asked in an effort to take the focus off the way her heart pounded in her chest over the fact that Hunter had bought her a corsage for the occasion.

"He is. There are very few places I go without my partner," Hunter said. "Hold out your left wrist." She tucked Sasha into her right side and extended her left arm. Hunter slipped the elastic band attached to a beautiful white gardenia over her hand and settled it onto her wrist.

He held her hand, his palm gentle and warm against her own. "You are beautiful."

Her mouth dried. She couldn't remember the last time a man, a handsome man at that, had told her she was beautiful. Certainly Jason never had.

Wariness reared in her chest. Could she trust Hunter's words? Or was he just being nice because it was part of his job?

"And you are quite handsome," she admitted, because she couldn't ignore the fact that she was drawn to him. She had to remind herself he was only accompanying her because he was doing his job. To protect her. To keep her safe. Not because he wanted to be with her.

The knowledge was like a drip of ice water down her nape, cooling her attraction and firmly putting her emotions on notice. *Do not fall for this man!*

Juneau nudged her leg, forcing her to break eye contact with Hunter. The minute she did she could breathe again. She crouched to scrub the Siberian husky behind the ears. Sasha squirmed, wanting to be set free. "You are quite handsome, too," she told Juneau.

"Are we taking Sasha?" Hunter asked.

She smiled and straightened. "No. I'll put him in a kennel with the others. Trevor will swing by to feed them later."

"I'll let Officer Gorman know," Hunter said and moved to open the back door for her. "Do you have a coat?"

Her cheeks flamed. "Yes, of course." She handed him Sasha and went to the hall closet, where she donned a calf-length down winter coat.

After settling Sasha in his mama's kennel and locking up, she found Hunter waiting for her.

He held out the crook of his arm. "Your chariot awaits." He led her toward his SUV.

The shrill jingle of the house phone grated on her nerves. Her steps lagged a moment, but she shrugged and kept moving.

Hunter tugged her to a stop. "Shouldn't you answer?"

"It's probably a solicitor or wrong number. Very few people have the house landline number. I only have it in case of emergency. Sometimes cell service out here can be spotty when there's a blizzard."

"Does Violet have the number?"

Her stomach sank, then bounced up into her throat. She hadn't considered that. "Yes. Yes, she does." Ariel hurried back inside the house. She picked up the landline's receiver, praying with all her might that she would hear Violet on the other end. "Hello?"

"Ariel, we saw you on the news," came her mother's worry-laden voice.

Her grip tightened around the phone. "Hi, Mom."

"I'm here, too, darling," her father said. "Are you okay? The news report said you were hurt. Should we come there?"

She closed her eyes against the onslaught of emotions pummeling her. "No. There is no need."

"It is true that Violet is a murderer?" her mother asked.

"No," Ariel ground out.

"But someone hurt you!" her dad exclaimed.

"Seriously, I'm fine. I have a protection detail keeping me safe."

"Yes, we read that, too," her mother said. "An Alaska State Trooper. We saw his picture in the *Anchorage Daily News*. You two looked very cozy together."

Ariel grimaced. "Mom, it's not like that." Great. She could only imagine how many other people had seen her and Hunter's photo taken at the hospital and would come to the same conclusion.

"Is the trooper there with you now?" her father asked.

Stomach churning with dread, she said, "Yes, Dad, one of the troopers is here." No need to mention it was the same one as in the photo.

"I'd like to speak to him."

"Oh, no. That's not a good idea." The last thing she needed was Hunter interacting with her parents. Why would they even be calling? They'd shown little to no concern over her well-being during her childhood and adolescence. Even as the thought tore through her brain, she could hear her therapist telling her that was unfair. That love was shown through actions as well as words.

They had fed her, clothed her and put a roof over her head. And they taught her about dogs. She would be nothing without that education.

"Dad, I'm on my way out the door," she said.

"Oooh," her mother chimed in. "Hopefully on a date?"

She could just see her mother clasping her hands in front of her in hopeful anticipation. Her parents had been on her for years to marry and have kids. But dating hadn't turned out so well for her, despite wanting a partner, someone to share her life with. She should resign herself to the fact that she was better off without anyone getting too close.

"No, not a date." Ariel glanced at Hunter. One of his dark eyebrows rose. Heat infused her cheeks and she looked away.

"Then what is it?" her father asked. "What have you gotten yourself into? You've always been a magnet for trouble, even when you were little. You'd wander off and get lost. I don't know how many times we had to go searching for you."

She bit the inside of her cheek to keep from commenting that she'd wander off because they weren't paying attention. And she couldn't remember them searching for her, only her being returned by some kindhearted person who had taken pity on her. Or her finding her own way home.

The only time her father took an interest in her was when she showed an interest in the dogs. Knowing they would badger her until she cracked, she decided to save the time and tell them, "The regional awards banquet."

"Ah. Good. I want to talk to the trooper," her father repeated in a voice that brooked no argument.

Ariel's lip curled. She didn't like when he used that tone. It brought back memories of her childhood. But whatever else she might think of her parents or how much she resented that she was never their priority, she was still the obedient daughter who loved her mother and father. Best to get this over with. She turned to Hunter and held up the phone. "They want to talk to you. Sorry."

His eyes were soft with empathy as he took the phone from her. She walked away to go stand in the place where he and Juneau had stood earlier, looking out the front window. The Siberian husky joined her, leaning against the side of her leg. Her fingers tangled in his soft fur, liking the fact that he was tall enough and she was short enough that she could reach him without having to bend down.

Behind her, Hunter's deep voice filled the room.

"Trooper Hunter McCord. Yes, sir. You don't have to worry. I'm good at my job, sir. Of course. Yes. Yes, thank you." Hunter held the phone toward her. "Ariel, your turn again."

With feet laden down by imaginary sandbags, she walked back to take the phone. "Mom, Dad, I really need to leave."

"Of course, dear," her mother said. "Remember we love you and will be with you in spirit."

"But we can be there in person to fix this mess you've gotten yourself into," her father interjected. "You just give us the word and we will hop on the next plane."

Confused by the worry in their tones—where was this type of parental involvement when she was a kid?— and curious as well, she asked, "Where are you?"

"Nova Scotia," her father said. "Helping to organize a race team for the next season. We have some really good mushers here. I'm going to train a few and bring them to Alaska next year for the Iditarod."

"Good for you, Dad. I'll call you if I need you. And I really do need to sign off now."

She stood there for a moment after hanging up to collect her emotions. Why did they always have the ability to rattle her? She'd spent many years working with a therapist and her pastor to let go of the hurts of her childhood. Apparently it was time to meet with Pastor Thomas again.

A gentle hand on her shoulder startled her, and she jumped.

Hunter held up his hands in entreaty. "Sorry, didn't mean to scare you."

"Lost in my own thoughts," she said, not wanting him to feel bad on her account. "We should go."

This time as they walked out the door of her house, she was definitely leaning on him and she couldn't make herself stop. She needed his strength right now because the next few hours were going to take every ounce of bravery she possessed to willingly get up in front of people she knew and give a speech.

The drive to the banquet hall was quiet. Hunter turned on the radio to soft classical music. He wasn't sure exactly why Ariel's parents' phone call had upset her. But he sensed that she needed this time of quiet to pull herself together before she faced the people in her sphere at the banquet.

Affection for this brave and capable woman crowded his chest, making him dread the day that he had to stop spending time with her. He'd promised her parents he would do everything in his power to keep her safe, and he intended to keep that promise.

He pulled into the parking lot and halted beneath a lamppost. Cutting the engine, he angled toward Ariel. The soft glow of light coming through the front windshield glinted on her blond hair. "I talked with the organizer of the banquet hall, and he tells me there is no video security inside, but he's hired some extra security guards to man the doors and be on the lookout."

She blinked at him, a small V appearing between her pretty eyes. "On the lookout for Violet, you mean?"

He threaded his fingers through Ariel's. "Until we know otherwise, we have to operate on the premise that she is armed and dangerous."

"Maybe you do." She tugged her hand from his. "But I don't."

Her loyalty to her friend was admirable. And he found himself yearning for Ariel to have that same sort of faith and confidence in him. Maybe he wasn't so very different from his father. And that was a terrifying revelation.

ELEVEN

Hunter climbed out of the SUV and rounded the vehicle to offer Ariel his arm. She hesitated. Was she so angry with him for doing his job that she'd refuse his help?

Her gaze softened and she reached for him. He blew out a relieved breath.

Thankfully, the parking lot and sidewalk had all been plowed so she didn't have to traipse through the snow in her heels to the door. Then he released Juneau and leashed him up, and together they escorted her inside.

The banquet hall was noisy and crowded as they entered. They handed off their coats to the young girl at the coat check. Hunter noted that several different booths with vendors were set up in the outer lobby.

"Do you want to look at anything?" he asked Ariel.

She shook her head. "Not tonight. The vendors will all be at the race this coming weekend."

He refrained from commenting about the race.

When they stepped into the hall, a bright spotlight was suddenly placed on them. For a split second, all conversations dimmed. All heads turned toward them.

Ariel tightened her hold on his arm and whispered, "This way."

Scanning the crowd, Hunter let her lead him, weaving through the large round tables toward a table at the front of the room by the stage. A podium had been set up with a microphone, and right behind it was a hand-painted wooden backdrop depicting a beautiful winter landscape of the Iditarod.

People called out hellos to Ariel, and she responded with a gracious smile and acknowledgment of the speaker by name.

A woman with short, curly red hair and dark brown eyes stepped in front of them. She wore a slinky emerald-green dress, and the color reminded Hunter of Ariel's college sweatshirt logo and how cute she'd looked wearing her school colors.

"Ariel, who is your handsome date?" The redhead eyed him with an appreciative gleam in her eyes.

Beside him, Ariel stiffened. "Carly, nice to see you again."

"Likewise," she said, but her eyes were on Hunter. "Carly Winters. And you are…?"

"Ariel's date," he said. "Excuse us."

They skirted around the woman, only to be stopped again by a stout, balding man. He grasped Ariel's hand in his. "Miss Potter, we are so glad you're here. We were starting to think maybe you weren't going to come."

The veiled chastisement for being late wasn't lost on Hunter, nor apparently on Ariel, judging from her grimace. She extracted her hand. "I am so sorry, George. My parents called just as we were headed out the door."

The man's eyes widened and he nodded. "Ah." Apparently just invoking her parents' names was enough to explain away her tardiness. Her parents really must be something within the dog sled racing circles.

George's gaze turned to Hunter and then to Juneau. "I didn't realize you were bringing guests."

"I signed up for a plus one," Ariel explained.

Waving a hand, George said, "We figured that would have been Miss James, but since—well—" He waved his hand again as if to swat away a fly.

The hurt on Ariel's face ignited a low burn of anger in Hunter. He didn't like to see her upset. Or the fact that the world already considered Violet guilty. Only the results of their investigation would prove one way or the other. And they didn't have all the pieces to the puzzle yet.

"We will add another chair next to yours," George assured her with a pat on Ariel's arm.

Hunter narrowed his gaze on the man. "Are you the event director?"

"No, that would be Willa and David Ford," George said. "They are around here somewhere."

"I'd like to speak to them."

George gave him a tight smile. "I'll send them over. This way to your table."

Hunter stayed close to Ariel as they continued to weave through the crowded tables to one with a single empty seat. Hunter sensed Ariel's agitation as they waited for another chair to be brought to the table.

Pasting on a smile, she greeted the other six people sitting there and introduced Hunter and Juneau. He held out the chair for Ariel to sit, then took the seat beside her while the dog settled between their chairs. Juneau crossed his paws and rested his chin on them. Hunter knew the canine was not resting but watching.

He trusted Juneau to have his back at all times. And now his partner would have Ariel's, as well.

Hunter leaned close to Ariel. "What's up with your parents?"

She unfolded her napkin and laid it across her lap. Bending toward him, she turned to speak into his ear, her soft breath tickling his skin. "What do you mean?"

Hunter glanced up to see if anybody was paying attention. Everyone had gone back to their own conversations. "I got the impression their call threw you into a little emotional chaos. And all you had to do was tell George your parents called, making us late, and all is forgiven? What gives?"

She leaned far enough away to meet his gaze. "Can we talk about this later?"

Her eyes held a plea and he couldn't refuse. He straightened. "Of course. But I'll hold you to that." He reached for his water goblet and took a drink.

Ariel did the same. She held her glass in front of her lips. "I have no doubt you will."

Ariel could barely choke down the deliciously prepared meal. Normally she liked these banquets because the catering company was stellar. But making small talk wasn't something Ariel enjoyed. She'd spent too much time alone as a kid with only the dogs as companions or later with a very small, select group of friends whom she was comfortable around. Most of her friends had either married or moved away. Violet would have been the last to get married. Ariel's heart ached. There would be no wedding to celebrate this coming weekend.

She was thankful that Hunter was adept at drawing out the other people at the table, though she speculated he was interrogating them with all his questions. If he was, he was very good at it. And when Willa and David Ford stopped by the table, Hunter stepped away to talk to the couple. She watched them until her gaze snagged on one of the catering staff. Surprise curdled her stomach. *Jason, her ex-boyfriend?* The man entered the kitchen and she shook her head, sure she was mistaken.

When Hunter returned to the table, his mouth was set in a grim line.

"Everything okay?" she asked.

He leaned to whisper in her ear, setting off a swarm of butterflies dancing a frantic jig in Ariel's stomach. She liked the way his aftershave mingled with his warm masculine scent. "Not as much security as I'd hoped."

"Are you worried?" Her nerves stretched taut, squashing the butterflies and making her limbs feel heavy. She doubted she could stand, let alone walk, even though she knew that very soon she was going to have to do both to accept her award.

"Irritated more than anything," he replied.

Hoping to calm her anxiety, she took the prepared speech from her handbag and looked it over.

Hunter stretched, putting his arm across the back of her chair, his fingers resting lightly on her biceps. Hot little spots of sensation fizzled her brain. The words on the page blurred.

Leaning in close, he murmured, "You're going to do fine."

She turned her head toward him and found herself not even an inch away from him. Her gaze dropped to his mouth and then back to his piercing blue eyes. A yearning she hadn't expected gripped her. She wanted him to kiss her.

Having his support meant the world to her.

Yet a tiny jaded voice inside her head mocked her. *Don't rely on this man. He'll only let you down as others in your life have.*

Besides, Hunter scoffed at love. And she wanted to believe that love was possible with the right person. She could only pray that God would reveal that person in time.

She shifted away from him, putting space between them. "It's easy for you to say. These people are not your peers. I'm going to make a fool of myself." Nervous tremors raced over her limbs.

His hand squeezed her shoulder. "No, not at all." He grinned. "Picture them all wearing party hats. I hear that works."

She rolled her eyes. "I'll have a hard time concentrating."

He chuckled. "Then just focus on me. I'm here for you, Ariel. I'm not going anywhere."

She swallowed as his words burrowed deep inside her, creating a longing that burst through her like a star erupting in the night sky. She didn't have anyone who was truly there for her. And while she trusted Hunter to keep her safe, could she trust him with her heart?

Unsure of the answer and horribly afraid to find out, Ariel turned to face the front stage as the award ceremony began. The first few awards were for the local mushers who had finished in the Iditarod.

As the seconds ticked by, Ariel grew more antsy. Her foot jiggled under the table. Juneau sat up and put his paw on her leg as if hoping to calm her agitation. Her heart melted. Dogs she could count on—they never broke promises or judged her and found her lacking. She reached down and ruffled Juneau's fur, taking comfort in the canine's presence.

Then they were announcing her name. Queasy with anxiety, she swallowed a gulp of cool water and laid her napkin aside to stand. Hunter's warm hand cupped her elbow, helping her to her feet. She gave him a grateful smile, fully expecting him to let go, but he didn't. Instead, he walked her up the stairs to the stage, making her feel cared for and special. She almost grabbed him to keep him at her side when he retraced his steps and took a position at the bottom of the short staircase, leaving her alone on stage.

With an inward groan, she chastised herself. This was all a sham. He was only in her life temporarily, doing his job. He wasn't her date, her boyfriend or even her friend. But her heart didn't want to believe that what they had between them was only about his job and the attempts on her life. Her heart wanted to connect to him, to bond and meld like a real couple. Once again, her desire to find Mr. Right reared, fierce and demanding. She squelched it. Hunter was not her Mr. Right.

But maybe for this moment, she needed to hang on to these feelings of being cherished, so that she could get through this speech without embarrassing herself. Then she would deal with the fact that she was letting herself get too attached to Hunter.

She stepped up to the podium and looked out on the sea of familiar faces. Yes, there were a few she didn't recognize, and it suddenly occurred to her maybe one of these people wanted her dead. She was certain, deep in her soul, that it hadn't been Violet James who had pushed her off that ledge, who had tried to strangle her and steal her dog. It could have been someone in this very room.

Panic sluiced through her veins. Her gaze jumped to Hunter. His reassuring smile and nod bolstered her courage. She could do this. He wouldn't let anything happen to her.

Her hands shook as she unfolded her speech. Juneau had moved to the bottom of the staircase beside Hunter. Ariel's gaze went to Hunter, and she mouthed *Juneau* and motioned for the dog to join her. Hunter's nod made her very happy. He whispered something to Juneau and the dog climbed the stairs and strode across the stage to stop next to Ariel, leaning into her side, offering her support. Her nerves calmed and she began to read her speech.

Hunter was so proud of how poised and articulate Ariel was as she humbly thanked the many people who had encouraged and supported her breeding business. She talked about the dogs from her kennel that had placed in the Iditarod and various other races throughout the last year, giving funny anecdotes about each of them. The room was warm and receptive to her, Hunter was glad to see her fear of embarrassing herself had only been pre-speech jitters. She had the audience enthralled.

A low, out-of-place noise underscored Ariel's voice. It took Hunter a moment to realize Juneau was growling deep in his throat. The dog had turned to face the wooden backdrop.

The hairs at Hunter's nape quivered with apprehension. He stepped up the first stair just as a sharp cracking sound jolted through the room. Juneau howled frantically, and then his teeth sank into Ariel's dress.

The dog backed up, trying to drag her away from the podium.

Alarmed, Hunter bolted onto the stage. He wrapped an arm around Ariel, drawing her close to his chest, then took a step toward the stairs.

The backdrop collapsed, falling forward.

With Ariel in his arms, Hunter dove off the stage, landing with a thud on the floor between the tables. Juneau jumped clear as the backdrop crushed the podium where Ariel had been standing. Splinters of wood and debris rained down on Hunter's back as he covered Ariel, protecting her head.

There were gasps and screams as people scrambled out of the way. Hunter lifted his head, smacking it on the very tip of the backdrop. He winced, then whispered into Ariel's ear, "Are you okay?"

"I think so," came her muffled reply. "What about Juneau?"

He rolled to the side to find Juneau standing guard, baring his teeth at anyone who tried to come close. "He's good."

Gathering her to his chest, Hunter said, "We're going to scoot sideways until we're out from under this chunk of wood."

She nodded. Together they shimmied free. He stood and helped her to her feet. She leaned heavily into him.

"I've got you," he said.

Her hands flexed on his arms in response.

He looked around, searching for the three security guards who had been hired to protect the venue. Several seconds passed before he spotted two of the men wearing black long-sleeve T-shirts helping the guests closest to the stage and assessing injuries.

The third security guard hustled out from the back of the stage.

Hunter reached into the breast pocket of his tux and pulled out his badge, showing it to the guard. "What happened? Why did the backdrop collapse?"

The guard, a tall, muscle-bound man with blond hair in a man bun, said, "The backdrop's wooden supports had been rigged with small explosive devices. It looks like it had a remote receiver."

Hunter's gut twisted and a burning anger ignited his blood. Someone in the room had triggered the devices to go off while Ariel was onstage.

Not an accident. Another attempt had been made on her life.

He sent up a prayer of thanksgiving that Juneau had sensed the threat and gave a warning. It had been a close call. If Ariel had been standing there a few seconds longer, she would have been crushed along with the podium. The killer was getting bold.

"Call Metro PD. Don't let anyone leave. I'm going to take Miss Potter to a safe location. I want you to search this whole building for that receiver. Start interviewing everyone. See if anybody remembers seeing somebody behind the stage who wasn't supposed to be there."

"On it." The security guard moved away with a phone in his hand.

Hunter helped Ariel toward the exit and realized she was wincing with each step on her right foot. He stopped. "You're hurt." Why hadn't she said anything?

"My ankle," she ground out.

He had her take a seat in the nearest available chair, then squatted down and lifted the hem of her dress to see that her ankle was swelling, the straps of her sandal pressing into her flesh. "We have to get that looked at."

He helped her to her feet, then swept her into his arms.

"Hey," she gasped, clutching his shoulders. "I can make it on my own."

"Not on my watch," he said. "We're going to the hospital. We have to make sure you didn't break your ankle."

She groaned. "I don't want to go back to the hospital. And neither do you. Can we just wait until tomorrow morning and I can go to my regular doctor at his clinic?"

"No," he said. "I'll be with you the whole way. We'll get through this together." A promise he intended to keep.

For a moment, she held his gaze, then nodded. "Hang on. I need my purse!"

Someone handed it to her. She murmured a thank-you and rested her cheek against Hunter's neck. Her vanilla scent teased his nostrils. He inhaled deeply. Something inside him shifted, and tenderness flooded his system. He liked having her in his arms. But the circumstances that had put her there twisted his chest into knots. He tightened his hold, wanting to take her pain away. To protect her for the rest of his life.

And that was almost as distressing as knowing he'd nearly failed to keep her safe tonight.

After retrieving their coats at the coat check, he carried her to the SUV and set her on the seat, tucking her dress and coat around her. Then he grabbed the seat belt and drew it across her lap, jamming it into the buckle. He paused as they were face-to-face. In the interior dome light he could see her eyes were wide, the pupils dilated.

"You're safe," he told her. "I'm not going to let anything happen to you."

She lifted a hand to cup his jaw. "I believe you. I believe *in you*."

His breath stalled in his chest. Ariel's words wound around him like a climbing strap around a tree, securing him to her in a way very little else could. Her faith in him was like an elixir to his jaded heart.

It would just take a slight movement for him to kiss her lush pink lips. Everything inside him wanted to give in to the attraction he'd been trying to ignore.

But she was fragile right now. Vulnerable. And he wouldn't take advantage of her. If he kissed her, he wanted her fully on board.

Yet he couldn't refrain from shifting his head to place a kiss on her palm where it had cupped his cheek. Her fingers flexed against his jaw and her eyes held his. The yearning, so bright in her eyes, enflamed the attraction arcing between them.

It took all of his willpower to straighten and step back.

"That's my girl," he murmured and shut the door.

As he rounded the front end of the SUV, his words echoed back in his head. Since when had he considered her his girl?

TWELVE

"Well, Miss Potter, you twisted your ankle."

Ariel breathed a sigh of relief at the doctor's announcement.

Dr. Chen looked at Hunter. "Will you be taking care of Miss Potter while she recovers from this latest injury?"

"I am," Hunter said.

The doctor smiled. "Well, that is very interesting."

Hunter tugged at the collar of his tux.

Ariel didn't understand what was going on between these two men, but whatever it was clearly made Hunter uncomfortable. If she weren't so exhausted and overwrought from tonight's ordeal, she'd tease Hunter. But all she wanted to do was go home. "Can I leave now?"

Dr. Chen looked to her, compassion in his eyes. "Of course. For the next twenty-four hours, ice and elevation."

She groaned. "*Seriously?* I am so tired of resting."

"Doctor's orders." Hunter gave her a stern look that was softened by the smile teasing the corners of his lips.

Her heart did a little flip. He was so handsome and

attentive, she wanted to bottle up this fuzzy warm sensation for later when he was no longer a part of her life.

"I'll have a wheelchair brought over along with your discharge papers," Dr. Chen said.

After the doctor exited the exam room, Hunter took her hand. His palm was warm against hers. She curled her fingers around his.

"Do you have any idea who would've tried to hurt you?" he asked.

Her breath hitched. "You aren't confident that the person targeting me is Violet?"

"I haven't ruled her out," Hunter said. "But it seems like there's more going on here."

The ominous tone in his voice sent a shiver down her spine. She tightened her hold on his hand. "I don't know. I can't imagine anyone in the sled dog community would want me dead. I mean sure, there's friendly competitions between mushers and breeders, but nothing that would warrant these assaults."

An image flashed before her eyes. She bit her lip with dread.

Hunter squeezed her hand. "What is it?"

"I'm sure it's nothing." She hoped it was nothing.

"It could be something," he insisted. "Tell me."

Anxiety gripped her and she said, "I thought, maybe, I saw my ex-boyfriend working for the catering company. But I only saw him from the side for a brief moment."

Hunter's expression hardened. "Tell me about this guy."

"Jason Barba." Just saying his named produced acid in her gut. "We met about five years ago. He worked for the bank as a teller and he asked me out. He seemed nice and stable." She blew out a scoff. "We dated for over a year. But he wanted more out of the relationship than I was willing to give. He became very possessive, which was irritating and unnerving. So I broke it off with him."

That was an unpleasant experience. She shuddered at the memory. "He didn't take the rejection well. He made a scene every time I went into the bank. They finally fired him and he'd left town. But now, apparently, he's back."

"All right. I'll have him brought in for questioning." There was a hard edge to his voice.

Ariel's stomach twisted. "Could he be behind these attacks on me?"

"Only time will tell."

Though she hated the idea that Jason could harbor ill will toward her, especially after all this time, having another suspect was far better than assuming that Violet was trying to kill her.

The doctor returned with a wheelchair and post treatment paperwork. He also gave her a couple of over-the-counter pain pills that she washed down with a cup of water.

"Call if the pain becomes too much," Dr. Chen said. "I can prescribe something stronger."

"I'm sure this medication will be fine," she assured him. "It's just a sprain. I've had worse."

When she was settled in Hunter's SUV and they were headed to her property, he said, "You don't have to be in pain. It's okay if you need something stronger. You've had a horrible, rough couple of days. A head injury, a throat injury and now your ankle. That's a lot for anyone."

"I'm tough," she said, half joking. Though she was exhausted and could sleep for a week, she kept her chin up.

Hunter laced his fingers through hers again.

She liked this. Liked him reaching out to her and holding her hand. It made her feel loved.

The word reverberated through her heart and settled like a flower petal falling on snow. Soft and gentle. If she allowed herself, she could fall in love with this man. He was tender, kind and protective. He seemed to get her. Understand her. Something very few people did.

But even entertaining the idea of loving Hunter was foolish. He had no emotions for her beyond the duty to his job. She glanced down at their entwined hands. Could she be wrong? And if so, what did she intend to do about it?

Hunter carried Ariel through the front door of her house, hesitating in the entryway. Juneau paused as well, looking up at him as if asking, *what now?*

Good question, buddy.

Ariel had slid her arms around his shoulders and rested her cheek against the side of his neck. The tender affection crowding his chest was becoming familiar where she was concerned. He didn't want to let her go. But he had to. She needed to change into more comfortable clothes and put her ankle up.

She lifted her head and, using the soft palm of her hand, turned his face toward hers. "Is everything okay?"

He glanced down the lighted hall toward her bedroom. "Yes. Everything is good," he said, his voice husky. He slowly lowered her onto a dining room chair.

"I need to check on the dogs," she said. "Trevor would have let them out for their last break, but—"

"I can do it."

"Thank you." She gave him a grateful smile. "You can leave Sasha with Skye."

"Okay. I'll be right back." To Juneau he said, "Stay with Ariel."

Juneau moved to her side in answer and made noises that sounded like he was trying to talk.

Hunter shared an entertained smile with Ariel.

Needing the cool air to bring back some sanity, he jogged over to Officer Gorman in his cruiser. After checking in and being assured all was well, he grabbed the crutches that Dr. Chen had insisted they bring with them out of his SUV.

Back inside the house, he helped Ariel to stand and adjusted the crutches beneath her armpits. "You need to get used to these for a few days."

Her light brown gaze snapped to his. "Twenty-four hours. Dr. Chen said twenty-four hours of elevation and ice. After that I am resuming my life. I can't keep sitting around doing nothing."

He got that she was a woman of purpose and liked to keep busy. He could only imagine how hard lying low was for her. But it couldn't be helped. "Off to your room to change into something comfortable. I'll get an ice pack ready."

She made a face. Then, using the crutches and her good leg, she hobbled down the hall to her bedroom. Just before she closed the door, he called to her, "Give a shout if you need anything."

Resting on the crutches, she turned to look back at him. "I will." Sparks danced in her eyes.

He shrugged, unwilling to apologize for his concern or his offer of help. That was why he was here and he'd best remember the reason.

She entered her room and shut the door behind her. Hunter scrubbed a hand over his face. He really should have asked Maya or Poppy to take over this assignment. He still could. If he were honest with himself, something he aimed for, he was growing attached to Ariel. More attached than he should, which was reason enough to find somebody else to take over this assignment.

However, he was loath to do so because, well, because he cared for the woman. There, he admitted it to himself. If anything happened to her and he could've prevented it…at least with him here, he would know that everything that could be done was being done to protect her.

His father's mocking voice inside his head jeered at him, *Arrogance is not going to get you anywhere, young man.*

Was he being arrogant believing he could protect Ariel? Maybe. But it was a small price to pay to keep her safe.

He found a large plastic baggie in a drawer and filled it with ice cubes from the freezer.

While he waited for Ariel to return, he called Colonel Gallo and gave her a full report of what had transpired that night.

"I'll have Brayden track down this Jason Barba," Lorenza promised him.

"Let me know if you find him," he said. "I want to be the one to question him."

There was a moment of silence before Lorenza asked, "Are you becoming personally invested in this case?"

Hunter sucked in a sharp breath, and he contemplated hedging the truth. But he knew the colonel would see right through him. "Yes," he said. "I am. But not so much that I can't do my job."

"Good to hear that. When we find this ex-boyfriend, we will let you know."

"Thank you, Colonel. I appreciate that."

He hung up and turned to find Ariel standing behind him, leaning on the crutches. She'd scrubbed her face clean of any makeup and tied her hair back into a loose ponytail, and she wore the college sweatshirt and sweatpants she had on that first night. So pretty his chest ached.

He cleared his throat. "You should sit." He held up the bag of ice.

She rolled her eyes and hobbled over to the chair. He rushed to help her sit, popping up the footrest. Then he grabbed two accent pillows from the couch, tucked them under her ankle and placed the ice pack on top of her swollen foot. The whole time her gaze tracked his movements like a physical touch.

"Would you like water or tea?" He pivoted toward the kitchen, but she snagged his hand, stopping him before he could move away. Her eyes were wide and full of trust and some other emotion that made his blood quicken.

A small smile on her lips drew his attention to her words.

"I know I've asked this before, but why are you being so kind to me?" She tilted her head. "It's almost as if you care."

His heart squeezed tight. He wouldn't lie to her. "I do care, Ariel. Someone's trying to hurt you. I'm not going to let them."

* * *

She tugged him closer so that he had to crouch down next to the side of the chair. Curiosity burned in his chest.

Releasing his hand, she twisted so that she could reach up and cradle his jaw, claiming his focus with her eyes. "I can't tell you how much your presence here means to me. How much you mean to me."

His mouth went dry. Her words and the sweet vulnerability in her gold-dusted eyes filled him with awe. His gaze dropped to her lips, then lifted back to her eyes.

"Hunter," she whispered.

There was so much in the way she said his name. A plea, a question, a demand. Did he dare kiss her? Did he dare refuse?

Who was he kidding? He could no more refuse her than he could stop breathing. Leaning forward, he pressed a kiss against her mouth. Her hands slid into his hair, gripping his head, pulling him closer.

The kiss deepened, and sensation rocketed through him, streaking along his nerve endings and making the world fade. Then her lips softened beneath his and tender emotions burned the backs of his eyes. They drew apart and he pressed his forehead against hers to let his heart rate calm and his breathing even out.

Eventually he leaned back on his heels, away from her, forcing her to let him go. "Ariel—" he began, not sure what, exactly, he intended to say. "I'm—"

She pressed a finger to his lips. "Let it be."

Let it be? Confusion clouded his brain. She didn't want to talk about that incredible kiss?

Sitting back into the recliner and turning her face

away from him, she said, "I'll sleep here tonight. Do you mind turning off the lights?"

"I'll turn all but the kitchen light off." He straightened. "You won't be sleeping out here alone. Juneau will be right here."

"I appreciate both of you looking out for my safety."

The trust in her eyes brought a lump to his throat. He swallowed and undid the constricting bow tie at his neck. "You should rest."

A soft smile touched her lips. "You looked very handsome tonight. Everyone—well—every woman in the banquet hall thought so."

He didn't care what anyone else thought. All he cared about was the fact that she found him handsome.

He spun away and strode to the guestroom. Okay, maybe his boss was right to question how personally involved he was getting in this case, how personally involved he was becoming with Ariel.

Was he losing perspective? Exercising bad judgment because he'd let down his guard and let Ariel in?

Ariel awoke warm yet stiff from sleeping in the recliner. A thick blanket had been put over her, but her foot was cold still. She glanced down to note that the ice bag had been refilled with new ice. Joy spread through her chest at his tender consideration.

Juneau sat beside the recliner, staring at her as if waiting for her to awaken. Her heart melted. Both man and beast were taking such good care of her.

She closed her eyes and relived the kiss.

So much better than she'd imagined it would be. And everything she'd hoped for. She hadn't planned on kissing him, but she'd been so emotional and had needed the connection.

Had it affected him as much as it had her?

She longed to talk to Violet right now. Her best friend would help Ariel process the overwhelming emotions swamping her.

She lifted up a prayer for Violet, praying she'd be found soon. Alive and well. It hurt to the core to consider her friend might be injured or worse.

Juneau whined as if wanting her attention. She scrubbed the dog behind the ears.

"Where is your handler?" she asked.

Juneau cocked his head, and then his gaze went to the back door.

Was Hunter letting her dogs out of their kennels?

Ariel tried to reach the crutches, but they were just beyond her fingertips, so she sat forward to remove the ice bag and set it on the arm of the recliner. Then, leaning down to release the footrest while keeping her injured ankle elevated, she scooted to the edge of the recliner and stretched as far she could to grab the crutches. It wasn't easy to maneuver them beneath her armpits, but she managed it and used her good leg to stand upright. Her ankle throbbed for a moment, then settled down.

She blew out a breath.

Between her head, her throat and her ankle, she didn't know what else anybody could do to her. Dread camped out in her chest. They could kill her.

She hobbled to the bathroom, and when she returned to the living room, Hunter was in the kitchen while Juneau ate his kibble.

"Are you doing okay?" he asked.

Seeing him making himself at home in her kitchen filled her with an odd and wonderful sense of contentment. "I am. The dogs?"

"I let them all out one by one so they could do their business and have a moment to chase the ball. And then I called Trevor. He'll be here soon to feed them. You need to get back in the recliner."

She growled, then regretted it as the reverberation hurt her throat. "You're going to take this twenty-four-hour thing seriously, aren't you?"

He grinned. "Of course. I found eggs in your refrigerator and some spinach. I'll make a scramble."

Her stomach rumbled, reminding her she hadn't eaten much of the dinner at the banquet. "There's bread in the freezer for toast."

"You keep your bread in the freezer?"

"I buy the organic, non-preservative kind. If I leave it out, it goes bad too quickly before I can eat it all."

"Makes sense."

She hobbled back to the recliner and got herself situated. Before she could blink, Hunter was there, tenderly lifting her ankle to slide the pillows under it. He grabbed the ice pack and gently laid it over the top of her ankle.

She'd embarrassed him last night with her thanks and her kiss. Or maybe he was overwhelmed, like she was? Either way she didn't regret kissing him. Ariel had never had anyone pamper her like this, making her feel special. She didn't care that it was part of his job. For now, he was here, and she was going to enjoy every moment of it.

THIRTEEN

Ariel sat on the edge of her bed and tested her injured foot on the third morning after the near miss of being crushed by the banquet hall backdrop. She chalked up her restless nights of sleep to the pain in her foot, but it was probably more the lingering fear. And no way would she admit to being kept awake by her growing affection for Hunter.

She was falling for him and there wasn't much she could do about it. Except keep the knowledge to herself if she hoped to prevent being hurt when his assignment to protect her ended.

Today, she was done sitting around babying her foot. After the first twenty-four hours had passed, she'd been unable to bear much weight on that leg. Hunter had insisted she continue to heal with rest. She'd grumbled but had to admit it was really nice to have him caring for her. Her head no longer throbbed, her throat was better and the swelling in her ankle had gone down so much that her foot looked normal.

It was time to resume her life. She had a race to prep for. Ariel had confidence that her dogs would do well. If she placed in the top four positions, she'd make a bit of money to keep things afloat until the next race or next litter of puppies.

First, though, she had to be able to stand and walk on her own, without the crutches or leaning on Hunter. Slowly, she put weight on her injured ankle. Tender, but doable.

Sasha nipped at her toes as she put on her socks. She tossed a small stuffed toy for him to tackle while she managed to put on a pair of sturdy hiking boots that would support her ankle. Determined Hunter was not going to thwart her effort to exercise her dogs, she squared her shoulders and left her room. However, Hunter and Juneau were not in the house. They must've gone for a run. Something that had become their routine each morning.

She made herself a cup of strong black vanilla bean tea and put it in a thermos. After feeding the dogs and giving them their supplements, she released them to the outside fenced area. She contemplated hooking the dogs up to a sled and heading down the fire road, but the recent events kept her from doing what she normally would. Frustration bit into her like a rabid dog.

Ariel wanted her life back to normal. She wanted her best friend home and well. And she wanted to not be afraid to go about her day. But the reality was, she had to be patient. A feat that seemed insurmountable at times.

An odd tingling at the base of her neck had her searching the trees beyond the fence marking the property boundary. Was someone watching her? A shiver of fear raced down her spine.

Movement in her peripheral vision jolted her heart rate, and a small gasp escaped her as Juneau came bounding around the corner of the kennel building. Her heart calmed from the momentary fright but sped up for an entirely different reason as Hunter came into view, striding purposely toward her. He had on running pants, a long-sleeve T-shirt and a beanie over his dark hair.

"You should have waited for me," he said, clearly displeased.

Glancing at the trees, she nodded. "Sorry. I was anxious to get out of the house."

"The ankle is better?"

She lifted her foot and rotated her ankle. "Yep."

Hunter's phone rang. He grabbed it from the pocket of his running pants. "I have to take this." He headed toward the house. "Are you coming?"

"Yes, I'll be right there." She allowed him a head start to give him privacy on his call.

He opened the back door and Sasha escaped the house, shooting past Hunter and Juneau to race toward Ariel.

Laughing, she squatted down to wait for the puppy to reach her. A sharp crack echoed through the trees, startling her. The wood railing next to her head splintered. For a heartbeat, she froze. Then realization stole her breath.

Gunfire. Someone was shooting at her.

She hobbled forward as fast as she could with her injured ankle, the pain a small price to pay. More shots were fired, the loud sound reverberating through the air. Bits of gravel, dirt and snow flew from the impact of the bullets hitting the ground close to her feet. She released the dogs from the pen and pointed to the house. "Inside!"

Sasha yelped, his little body quivering. Her heart leaped in her throat. She scooped up the puppy just as Hunter tore out of the house, running toward her.

She gestured wildly. "Go back!"

But he didn't. Instead, he wrapped her and Sasha into his arms, using his back as a shield, and hurried them inside the house behind the other dogs.

"Somebody's shooting at me." Her disbelief made her mind sluggish.

"You and the dogs get down!" He pushed her underneath the dining table. "Stay here."

With his sidearm in hand, Hunter and Juneau ran out the back door.

"No!" she protested, afraid they'd get hurt. But he was gone. She gathered the dogs close, burying her nose in Sasha's fur.

She waited for a long moment. Dread choked her. She couldn't let Hunter be out there alone. What if the person shot him? Or Juneau.

Terror sliced through her, leaving a bleeding trail. She needed to call for backup. Decision made, she crawled out from underneath the table, keeping the puppy close to her body like a football and herding the dogs to stay at her side. Then she grabbed the house phone, hurried into the bathroom and closed the door.

Dialing 911, she prayed Hunter would return to her safely.

Hunter ran in a crouch as he and Juneau headed off to the southwest corner of the property, where he was pretty sure the shots had originated. There was no cover for him or Juneau. He kept to the fence built on the property line. Then he took a breath, sent up a prayer for safety and bolted over the wooden fence. Juneau climbed underneath the rails. In the woods of spruce and aspens, the assailant crashed through the underbrush, not even trying for stealth. Juneau ran ahead of Hunter, leading the way toward the fire road.

The slam of a vehicle door followed by the roar of an engine ground Hunter's teeth together. The intruder was gone by the time he broke through the trees to the snow-packed road. And he noted that the barricade the police had erected had been dismantled. Hunter whistled to bring Juneau back; he didn't want the dog following the suspect's vehicle out onto the highway.

Now there was no question whoever had been targeting Ariel was using the fire road. He curled his fingers into fists.

Picking his way back through the trees, Hunter used his phone to report the incident and say that the shooter was gone. He learned Ariel had already made the call. Admiration for her spread through his chest. The woman had so much grit and spunk, compassion and kindness. She was also loyal and pragmatic. Stubborn. One of a kind. He was falling hard for her.

The realization made him stumble over a root.

Juneau's barking diverted Hunter's attention from his inner turmoil. He picked up speed, eating up the ground until he found the dog sitting next to a tree. On the ground at his feet lay a baseball cap. He removed a dog waste bag from his pocket and used the edge of it to pick up the hat so that he didn't contaminate the evidence. Then, searching the ground, he spotted three shell casings. He gathered those in the bag as well, careful to keep from handling them too much.

When he and Juneau arrived back at Ariel's house, he found her locked in the bathroom.

"Ariel, you're safe," he called to her through the door as he slipped on a fresh T-shirt.

The door flew open, dogs poured out and she threw herself into his arms. He held her against him. Emotions crashed through him. Affection. Joy. Relief. And then a fierce wave of frustration that this perp almost killed her pounded at his temples. He had to do a better job of keeping her safe.

She leaned away from him. "I was so worried. I was afraid that you would be shot."

He gave her a smile he hoped was reassuring. "I'm made of Teflon."

Her mouth thinned. "No," she said. "You're not. You're flesh and blood. And you're in danger by being here."

His arms tightened around her. "Danger is a part of my job, Ariel."

She dropped her gaze and leaned her head against his chest. "I know. And it scares me."

With the crook of his finger, he lifted her chin. "Ariel, I know you believe and trust God."

She nodded, her eyes never leaving his.

He cupped her cheek with his palm. "Then you have to trust that He will protect both of us."

For a moment, she stared at him. Then her hand slid around his neck and pulled him close until their lips met. She kissed him deeply, tenderly, and his heart swelled with more emotions than he could handle.

When she pulled away, she smiled. "Thank you for that reminder. I do trust God. And I trust you."

She let him go and walked toward the living room, leaving him standing there, stunned. He hadn't understood until this moment how much her trust meant to him. It was everything. *She* was everything. Boy, he was in trouble.

"I called for backup," she said over her shoulder. "They should be here soon."

That was just what he needed to galvanize him into action. He joined Ariel on the front porch. She'd put the adult dogs back in the outdoor pen and now cradled Sasha in her arms. Juneau sat beside her. Moments later, a Metro police cruiser arrived with lights flashing and parked, followed by an Alaska K-9 Unit vehicle.

Poppy Walsh and Stormy jumped out of the vehicle and hurried to confer with the police officers.

Hunter and Ariel met the trio in the driveway. Quickly he explained the situation as the officers took notes. "There are spent bullets here in the drive. And I have a baggie of shell casings I found in the woods."

"We'll find the bullets," the older of the two officers said.

As soon as the officers moved away, Poppy gave Ariel a kind smile. "Are you okay?"

"I am now," she said. "I shouldn't have left the protection of the house. When is this going to end?"

Hunter put his arm around her waist. "Soon."

Ariel glanced up to meet his gaze as she leaned against him. "You can't promise that."

No, he couldn't, but he wanted to. He wanted to keep this woman safe, to keep her close and to tell her—

Poppy cleared her throat, her eyebrows raised.

Hunter dropped his arm from around Ariel as a heated flush crept up his neck. "Let's take this inside. I have something to show you."

He led the way into the house.

"I've interviewed Mrs. James and the people who work at the estate where Violet lives with her mom," Poppy said.

"And they told you the same thing I did," Ariel said with confidence. "Violet wouldn't hurt anyone."

"Yes, that is the same thing I've heard from everyone who knows her," Poppy confirmed. "Everyone except her fiancé."

Ariel made a scoffing noise.

"I've also interviewed the groom's family," Poppy said. "Lance's parents, Ann and Carl Wells, say he's a wonderful son and are very concerned for his well-being."

"And the other people in his life?" Hunter asked.

"Here's where it gets interesting," Poppy went on to say. "His ex-girlfriend, Leah Orr, has a completely different story. She says he lies easily. She caught him in several over the course of the six months they dated, and he ended their relationship when an inheritance she was supposed to get didn't pan out."

"What kind of lies?" Hunter asked.

"She didn't go into specifics," Poppy said. "I had the impression the lies weren't anything big enough to cause her to break it off."

"Violet didn't know about the ex-girlfriend," Ariel interjected. "At least, she never mentioned her to me. Have you interviewed Lance's sister, Tessa Wells? She and Lance weren't on speaking terms. Violet was hoping to meet her before the wedding."

"She's out of the country. But I talked to a couple of her friends who said that she didn't think too highly of her golden boy brother. I will make sure to interview her when she returns."

"And what about Jared?" Hunter asked.

"Will's been looking into him," Poppy said. "The last I heard, he was having trouble finding anyone willing to talk to him about Lance's best man. Apparently he doesn't have family. Kept to himself when out on the commercial fishing boats."

"That's right," Ariel said. "I remember Violet mentioning that Jared grew up in foster care."

"Ariel, what did you think of Lance?" Poppy asked.

Hunter was also interested to know. She'd never spoken a bad word about her best friend's fiancé, though she'd denied their claims that Violet was violent.

Ariel made a face. "Well, to be honest, I have never really liked Lance. Or Jared, for that matter. But Lance made Violet happy so I had to be happy for her."

"What about Lance and Jared did you not like?" Hunter asked.

"There was nothing overt that I could put a finger on. Just little subtle things. Like when we would go out to eat as a group or go anywhere, really, Lance made all the decisions. He rarely consulted Violet or any of us for an opinion. I think Violet felt taken care of, maybe?" Ariel shrugged. "Her father was a commanding, run-the-show kind of man."

Hunter had no doubt that Lance's behavior would grate on Ariel. She was too independent to let any man choose for her. He liked that independent spirit. "And Jared?"

She shrugged. "Nothing I can articulate."

"You said you had something to show me," Poppy reminded him.

"Yes." He moved to the dining table and showed her the ball cap and bullet casings.

Ariel let out a little gasp.

Hunter narrowed his gaze at her. "You recognize this hat?"

"Not the hat specifically," she said. "That's Carly Winters's logo."

The name sounded familiar, but he couldn't place it. "And who is she?"

Disbelief shone in her eyes as she stared at him. "The redhead you met the other night."

An image flashed in his mind of a woman in a green dress. "Right," he said. "The woman who talked to us at the banquet hall. Is there a story there between you two?"

Ariel blew out a breath. "Not between us, per se. She moved here about a year and a half ago and started a breeding program."

"So basically, she's your competition?" Poppy asked.

"Technically, yes," Ariel said.

"Why didn't you mention her before?" Hunter mentally added Carly Winters to his list of suspects. Now they had three. Her ex-boyfriend, Jason, a competitive breeder named Carly, and Ariel's best friend, Violet. Which one of them wanted her dead?

"I didn't want to speak ill of her. It would sound like sour grapes," Ariel said with concern in her eyes.

"Is she breeding Alaskan huskies, as well?" he asked.

"She is."

Could this other breeder want to do away with her competition? Hunter wanted to talk to this woman. "Are her dogs as good as yours?"

"It's too soon to tell," Ariel said.

"Could she be jealous of you?" Poppy asked.

"I don't know." Concern lanced across Ariel's face. "We don't socialize."

Hunter doubted Ariel socialized with very many people because she was so focused on her dogs and her business.

"Carly has been wanting to buy one of my adult dogs since she arrived in town," Ariel said. "I've always said no because I'm not ready to retire any of my breeding dogs and I'm not going to sell a still viable dog to my competition. But, that said, I don't see her doing this."

Of course she didn't. Ariel tended to see the good in people. Hunter wasn't so inclined. "Poppy, do you mind taking the evidence to Tala and see if she can get any kind of DNA or prints that we could use?"

The forensic scientist was the best in the state. Hunter knew if there was anything to find, she'd find it.

"Of course," Poppy said. "Do you have a brown paper bag I could carry this in?"

Ariel found one, and then they walked Poppy outside. The two police officers held up an evidence bag containing three spent bullets. Poppy had them place the plastic bag inside the brown paper bag.

"Can you have Tala run the ballistics against the bullet we found in Cal Brooks?" Hunter asked.

"I sure will." Concern darkened Poppy's green eyes. "What are you two going to do?"

Hunter contemplated Ariel's comment that Carly wanted to buy a dog. "You mentioned before that you have people requesting to purchase your dogs."

Ariel nodded. "I have people all over the place who contact me about buying the puppies."

"We are going to pay Carly Winters a visit," Hunter decided because the woman was local, but was she out to hurt Ariel? "I'll ask the police officers to stay here until we return. Just to make sure no shenanigans happen while we're gone."

Surprise flared in Ariel's eyes. "I need to put the pack away. I'll be right back."

Hunter watched her walk away, glad to see she wasn't

limping. He spoke to the officers, who agreed to stay until he and Ariel returned.

"What should I tell the colonel?" Poppy asked.

"Tell her there's something else going on here. That these attacks on Ariel aren't being done by Violet James."

Poppy titled her head. "And what are you speculating about the attacks on Lance and Jared?"

"Two different cases," he said. "It could very well be Violet who is after Lance and Jared. But she's not the one targeting Ariel."

Poppy nodded. "I agree. Do you want me to accompany you to Carly Winters's place?"

Hunter didn't hesitate. "Actually, yes, that would be appreciated."

With Poppy following them and Ariel giving directions, Hunter drove to the Winters Kennels. The place wasn't as big as Ariel's property. A small two-story house stood off to the side of what Hunter suspected was the kennel building and a dog run. Hunter glimpsed movement at the window.

Someone was home. He knocked on the front door. A few moments later, the redheaded breeder opened the door.

Her dark brown eyes widened. "You were with Ariel at the banquet."

"That I was," Hunter replied. "Trooper McCord. I have a few questions for you."

She frowned, her gaze going over his shoulder. "What is this about?"

"We found a ball cap with your logo on it at a crime scene," Hunter said, watching the woman closely.

Surprise flared in her eyes. "Okay. That has nothing to do with me." She leaned against the doorjamb and crossed her arms over her chest. "Lots of people have my hats. I give them out at races and events. Is she accusing me of something?"

"No, ma'am," Hunter said. "We're just asking some questions."

Carly's gaze went to Ariel. "Right. You're just afraid that I'll take away from your business so you're making trouble for me."

Ariel climbed the steps to stand beside Hunter. "Carly, that's not it at all. We just want to know who might have left the ball cap behind on my property."

Her lips twisted. "I don't know."

"Were you giving the hats out the night of the banquet?" Ariel asked.

"Yes," Carly said. "That's not a crime."

Hunter exchanged a glance with Ariel. Could her ex-boyfriend have picked one up? "No, it's not a crime. Do you own a gun?"

Carly's eyebrows dipped low. "A rifle. I'm a woman alone out here. There's plenty of predators to warrant the caution."

Hunter couldn't argue with that. He'd have to run a license check to see if she had any legal handguns registered to her. If she had illegal ones…"You've been helpful."

Carly straightened, looking pleased. "I have? How so?"

"Thank you for your time," Hunter said, putting his hand around Ariel's elbow and leading her away.

As they joined Poppy, he said, "Jason Barba could've gotten one of Carly's hats at the banquet. We need to track him down. And find out exactly why he could be targeting Ariel."

FOURTEEN

Later that evening, Ariel scrubbed dishes to keep her hands busy while her mind raced with the idea that her ex-boyfriend could be the person behind the attacks on her. Why would Jason want to hurt her after all this time? And why try to steal Dash when he had never liked the animals?

Hunter's phone rang and she listened to the one-sided conversation, anything to take her mind off Jason.

"You got him?" he said. "That's good. Put him in the interrogation room."

Ariel's heart stuttered and her gaze swung to Hunter. *Got him?* As in Jason?

"I'll—" Hunter hesitated and glanced toward her. "We'll be there shortly."

She threw down the dish towel and hurried to his side. "What's happening?"

"Brayden found Jason Barba. I want to know what he was doing at the banquet hall last night and if he is the one trying to kill you." Hunter's grim tone sent a shiver down her spine. "We need to go."

Nerves jangling, she swallowed back the emotions clogging her throat. Was this nightmare finally about to end? All the ramifications crowded her mind. Her life could resume. Hunter would leave. But so many questions still bounced around unanswered.

If Jason was the one who was after her, then who was after Lance and Jared? And where was Violet?

Hunter drove them to headquarters. He hoped and prayed to put an end to the threat against Ariel's life tonight. She'd endured so much over the past week, he wanted to let her get back to her normal life. One that didn't include him.

Distress cramped his chest. A reaction he wouldn't have dreamed he'd have considering how much he didn't believe in romance or relationships. But the time spent with Ariel was showing him that maybe some relationships were worth taking a risk on. Was *he* willing to take the risk?

He wasn't sure.

Once inside, Maya and Poppy rushed forward to greet Ariel. He handed her off to the two females and left Juneau with them, knowing his teammates would take good care of Ariel while he was in the interrogation room with Jason Barba.

Brayden met him outside the door. "Barba's not very patient. He's been banging on the doors and on the table. This man has a temper."

Hunter bared his teeth. "Let him show me that temper." Was it anger that had prompted this man to try to hurt Ariel?

Walking into the interrogation room with Brayden on his heels, Hunter caught his first glimpse of Jason Barba. The sandy-blond-haired man glared back at Hunter, his gray eyes hard. He wore a plaid flannel shirt with the sleeves rolled up. Hunter stood towering over the sitting man. Jason started to rise but he held up a hand. "Stay seated," he barked.

Brayden took a stance in the corner, crossing his arms and his ankles. He was there only to observe. Or intervene if Hunter lost his own temper.

He turned the metal chair backward so he could straddle it, folding his arms over the top of the back. "Where were you this morning?" he began.

"Sleeping," Jason answered. "I worked until two a.m."

"Can anyone corroborate your whereabouts?"

"What's going on?" Jason gestured with his chin toward Brayden. "He wouldn't tell me."

Hunter wasn't inclined to enlighten the suspect yet. "Where were you Tuesday evening?"

"Working," Jason said.

"Working where?"

"What does it matter?" The irate man folded his arms across his wide chest. "I'm not saying anything more until you tell me why I'm here."

"It matters because your answer will determine whether or not you'll be sitting in a jail cell for the rest of your life," Hunter ground out.

Jason's face drained of color. "I work for a catering company."

"The same catering company that serviced the regional sled dog award ceremony?" he pressed.

"Yes. So?"

"Sabotaging the backdrop to try to crush your ex-girlfriend is a crime," Hunter bit out.

Jason held up his hands and shook his head. "I knew it. I knew you were going to try to pin that on me. No way, man."

"You were angry when she broke up with you," Hunter stated.

Lip curling, the other man said, "I don't know what story she told you, but I broke up with her. She was way more into her dogs than me. It didn't matter what we were doing, if the dogs needed her she dropped me like a hot potato. I didn't want that kind of relationship. I need somebody who's going to be there for me."

"Did you get rough with her? Want to hurt her?"

Jason frowned. "No way, man. Ariel would have turned loose those dogs of hers on me if I'd touched her. They're very protective of her. They wouldn't let anybody get too close to her."

Funny. Her dogs had let Hunter and Juneau get close to her. Hunter liked the dogs even more now. They were clearly good judges of character. "I want to know everything you did the night of the banquet from the moment you arrived at the banquet hall. In fact, I want to know everything you did that day as they were building the backdrop. Were you there?"

"I was not there building a backdrop. I don't belong in that world. Ariel made that very clear. I didn't even realize what the job for that night was till I got there." Jason fidgeted in his chair. "I couldn't watch her up there accepting her award."

"Where did you go?"

"Out back to have a smoke," he said.

Hunter narrowed his eyes at him. "That's a weak alibi."

"Hey, I wasn't alone," he stated. "You can ask my girlfriend, Sandy."

Girlfriend. Hmm. Interesting. Ariel had mentioned she thought the person who'd tried to strangle her was a woman. Could Jason's girlfriend be the one behind the attacks on Ariel? "You and Sandy were at the event together. Was she with you all day?"

"For most of it."

"You said you were sleeping this morning." Hunter drummed his fingers on the back to the chair he straddled. "Was Sandy with you?"

"I met her for breakfast before she went to work," Jason said. "What happened this morning?"

Hunter stood. "You better hope nobody saw you backstage because if they did, you're going down."

Sweat dripped down the side of Jason's face. "When can I leave?"

"Not until we talk to Sandy. Write down her full name, phone number and place of employment."

Brayden stepped forward with paper and pen.

Jason jotted down the information and slid the paper across the table to Hunter.

Grabbing the paper, Hunter and Brayden walked out.

"Do you believe him?" Brayden asked.

"Not sure." Was this Sandy person jealous of Ariel? Did she want to eliminate the competition?

Yet that didn't make sense. Ariel and Jason hadn't dated in several years. There was more going on here, and he couldn't see all the moving pieces. Frustration beat a steady rhythm in his head. His gaze went to where Ariel, looking lovely in a long wool skirt and amber-colored sweater, stood talking to Maya, Poppy and Helena. Juneau sat at Ariel's feet. Hunter guessed the other K-9s were in their handlers' offices, which would be where he'd have taken Juneau upon arriving at headquarters if not for Ariel's presence. He turned to

Brayden. "Would you be willing to track down Sandy Olsen?"

"I'm on it," his teammate said. "Looks like your lady has made some new friends."

Hunter's face heated. "She's not my lady."

Brayden winked. "Whatever you say." He strode away.

Shaking his head, Hunter joined the women. "Excuse me, I need to talk to Ariel." He drew her to the side while Maya, Poppy and Helena dispersed, going in different directions. "Tell me again who broke up with who?"

"Huh?" Ariel scrunched up her face for a moment. Then her expression cleared. "Oh, you mean with Jason?"

"Yes, with Jason."

"I broke up with him. I told you he was becoming possessive and he didn't like me spending time with the dogs. But he knew when we started dating that the animals are a big part of my life. He wanted me to choose between him or the dogs. Who does that?"

Hunter would never ask Ariel to choose between him and her pack. He pinched the bridge of his nose. Why had his mind even gone there? He was never going to get that far in this relationship with Ariel. He scrubbed a hand over his unshaven jaw. "We should head back to your place."

"What's with Jason? Is he the one?"

"We're still gathering information," he told her. "Until we have a definitive answer, we have to operate with the assumption that the perpetrator is still out there and you're not safe."

Ariel bit her bottom lip, and fear clouded her light brown eyes, emphasizing the gold flecks reflecting the station's fluorescent lights. "As long as you and Juneau are with me, I'll be okay."

Her confidence settled around his heart like a hug. And he prayed he wouldn't let her down.

"Do you mind if we stop for the mail?" Ariel asked Hunter as he turned into her drive. It had been days since she'd thought about the mail, and the bills that were no doubt stacking up. Her dwindling bank account needed a booster, exactly what the race the day after tomorrow would bring if she placed well and received the prize money.

He brought the vehicle to a stop, allowing her to climb out. The box was stuffed full.

Once they were inside the house, she sifted through the mail, and paused to stare at a plain white envelope addressed to her with no return address. Odd…

She opened the letter, pulled out a piece of paper and recognized Violet's flowing handwriting. Her breath hitched. Violet was alive! "Hunter! This is from Violet."

Hunter had changed out of his uniform, opting for worn jeans and a Henley-style T-shirt that made her very aware of the width of his shoulders. He closed the distance between them in a few long strides. "What does it say?"

Ariel swallowed against the trepidation robbing her of her voice.

Please don't let this be a confession.

Her stomach churned and she chastised herself for even going there. Her friend was not guilty of the crimes she was being accused of.

Taking a breath, she read aloud. "'Dear Ariel, I know what people are saying about me. Please believe me, I did not do what the media is telling the world. I didn't kill our tour guide. It was Lance. You have to believe me. I ran, because they were going to kill me, too. Whatever they've told you, it's all lies. You're my best friend. You know me. When it's safe I will return. Love, Violet.'"

Sweet relief lifted the heavy burden off Ariel's shoulders. "See! I told you." Her hands shook as she waved the piece of paper at Hunter. "Violet is innocent. It's Lance and Jared who are lying."

Hunter ran a hand through his dark, thick hair. "She could be just saying that to throw suspicion on them. We won't know the truth until we find her."

Ariel folded the paper and put it back into the envelope. "I don't care what you say. I will not believe that my friend is guilty of these crimes." She blinked back hot tears. "Tomorrow would have been her wedding day."

"Awww, Ariel." Hunter came closer, his nearness sending little shimmers of awareness over her skin.

The temptation to take comfort from him was almost more than she could bear. She stepped into his embrace. Wrapping his arms around her, he rubbed small circles on her back. She laid her cheek against his chest, the steady thump of his heart steadied her. She never wanted this moment to end. Never wanted to leave the safety of his arms. Here, all the fear and stress of the world evaporated.

"I need to bag that letter and envelope as evidence."

His gentle voice was like a hammer to her heart. Her lip curled. She couldn't keep the resentment out of her tone as she pushed away from him and held the letter out to him. "Of course you do. Here."

He held up his hands. "Hold on a second." He snagged a plastic bag from her kitchen drawer. "Slip it in here."

Blowing out a frustrated breath, she carefully slid the envelope containing Violet's letter into the plastic bag. He zipped it closed.

If only she could zip up her growing affection and attraction for this man as easily.

The next morning, Hunter worried about Ariel. Her mood was subdued, and she appeared to be on the verge of tears at any moment as she went about her chores of feeding the dogs, exercising them and cleaning out their kennels. Then she'd gone inside and started baking. The house smelled delicious and his mouth watered as he snagged a couple of oatmeal raisin cookies.

Ariel hardly glanced at him. He wished he could take her pain away. It hurt to see her hurting. But there was nothing he could do.

He set up his laptop at the dining table and was very aware of Ariel puttering around the kitchen. He put in his earbuds as Lorenza gave the team an update for the last week.

The search for Violet was going nowhere. She'd effectively found a place to hide and continued to elude the authorities. Speculation was her wealthy mother was helping her to hide while at the same time demanding law enforcement do everything they could to find her. But so far there was nothing to prove that theory.

Lance and Jared were also in the wind. The location of their "safe house" remained unknown. There had been no communication from the two men.

Meanwhile, Brayden was having trouble tracking down Sandy, Jason's current girlfriend. And the ballistic test done by Tala Ekho came back, showing the weapon used to murder Cal Brooks was not the same gun as the one used to shoot at Ariel. The disparity didn't prove or disprove whether the shooter who'd killed Cal or fired at Ariel here at the property were the same person.

Hunter was surprised when Lorenza gave the floor over to her assistant, Katie Kapowski.

Katie stepped into view of the camera as Hunter's earbuds died. With a grimace, he took them out and lowered the volume on the laptop.

The young woman's red-rimmed eyes tore at Hunter. Something was wrong. Her voice trembled as she said, "Team, I need your help. The Family K Reindeer Sanctuary Ranch, which rescues reindeer, has been robbed."

From the kitchen, Ariel let out a little gasp.

"How can we help?" Helena Maddox asked.

"My aunt is desperate," Katie replied. "A pen of reindeer was set loose. Two are missing. If she loses those reindeer it will devastate the ranch. It's barely functioning as it is. My aunt Addie has pared down to just two ranch hands."

Ariel moved from the kitchen to stand across the table from Hunter, out of view of the computer's camera. She waved to get his attention. He muted his laptop. "Yes?"

"I know Addie Kapowski. You and Juneau could find her reindeer. You found me."

Though Hunter appreciated her confidence in his and Juneau's abilities, he shook his head. "I'm not leaving you."

"Take me with you. I'll be safe with Addie while you two search for the reindeer."

"Not happening."

He unmuted the laptop and heard Lorenza saying, "Hunter, was there something you wanted to share with us? Can you hear me?"

Hunter gritted his teeth. "Sorry, Colonel. I'm at Ariel Potter's house and she—"

Ariel rounded the table and crouched down so that she could be seen in the camera. "Hello, Colonel Gallo. I was saying to Hunter that he and Juneau could find the reindeer. That's what they do, right? Search for missing people, or animals? I could go with him to see Addie. She probably needs a friend right now. We know each other from church."

Hunter held his breath, waiting to see what Lorenza would say. Several people nodded.

Lorenza nodded, as well. "That's actually a really good idea. I'm going to send you, Hunter. Take Ariel with you. I will also send Poppy because she and Stormy are used to wilderness searches."

Ariel patted Hunter on the shoulder and moved away.

"We're on it, Colonel." He shut his computer down and then stood with his arms folded, waiting for Ariel to return from her bedroom.

When she reappeared, she had on a pair of weatherproof pants and a sweater, wore a beanie on her head, and was carrying a puffy down jacket and gloves. "I'm ready whenever you are."

"Nicely done," he commented wryly.

She smiled. "You're not the only one who can make things happen when they want." She walked past him to scoop up Sasha. "I'll put him in with his mother and meet you at the car."

Hunter had no choice but to follow and was broadsided by the realization he would follow her anywhere.

FIFTEEN

At the Family K Reindeer Sanctuary Ranch, Hunter barely brought the SUV to a halt before Ariel climbed out and strode over the graveled drive toward the front porch of the red-cedar-sided house. Her knock was answered by Addie Kapowski, a tall and imposing woman with short graying brown hair. The older woman drew Ariel in for a quick hug.

Hunter released Juneau from his compartment just as Poppy Walsh arrived. He waited for Poppy and Stormy to join him.

"She has you on a short leash," Poppy commented with a cheeky grin.

He made a face. "Ha ha."

"In all seriousness, Hunter," Poppy said, "we like her."

Hunter's breath caught in his chest, and he shielded his eyes from the winter sun to stare at Poppy. "We?"

"Me, Maya and Helena. Ariel would be good for you."

Though he was glad to know his coworkers approved of Ariel, he needed to set Poppy straight. "There is nothing going on between me and Ariel."

"If you say so." She started walking. "Let's talk to Addie and find her reindeer."

Shaking his head, he grabbed an extra lead from the SUV and strode after his coworker, not liking the way Poppy's comments dug at him. Was he allowing his fondness for Ariel to show? Was he letting his attachment to her cloud his judgment? Was he making a fool of himself like his father had?

Irritated by his own musings, he stopped next to Ariel and Addie on the porch and introduced himself and Poppy.

"Thank you for coming," Addie said. "I've been beside myself. Katie said she'd send help. I hated burdening her with this, but I didn't know what else to do."

"Can you tell us what happened?" Poppy asked.

"Someone let the reindeer loose from the pasture pen where we'd kept them overnight. They are supposed to get their inoculations today," Addie said. "Took a long time, but we managed to corral them into the pen again, but there are still two missing. We can't find either of them. It's been several hours, and I'm worried about poachers."

"Could the gate have been accidentally left unlatched?" Hunter asked.

Addie shook her head. "No. It's a complicated latched system. It must have been deliberately undone by someone who knew the reindeer would be penned up. I fear that one of my ranch hands may have done it."

"Why would you say that?" Ariel asked.

"I had to cut their pay this past winter," Addie explained. She raised a defiant chin. "Times are tough right now. Donations for rescuing injured, orphaned and abused domesticated reindeer have diminished and

I'm barely keeping things afloat. And—" she shrugged "—I admit to being short-tempered of late. Gary got the ATV stuck in the mud by the river, which took time and money to get unstuck and I caught Blaze helping himself to my petty cash."

"We'll need to speak to Gary and Blaze," Hunter said. "But first we'll see if we can track down your missing reindeer."

"Do you have anything with the scent of the reindeer on it that we could use for the dogs to sniff out?" Poppy asked.

"Of course. This way." She led them to the reindeer pen.

Hunter kept a casual distance from Ariel but was ready to steady her if she needed. He still wasn't convinced her ankle was completely healed. In fact, he'd seen her slight wince a couple of times when she stepped on the injured foot.

Nearby was a barn where Addie retrieved two leather harnesses. "These belong to the two missing reindeer."

Hunter turned to Ariel. "You and Addie go into the house until we return."

Ariel nodded with a resigned yet understanding smile. "Of course." She threaded her arm through the older woman's. "Let me tell you what's been happening in my life…"

The two women headed back to the house. Hunter kept his gaze on Ariel. He didn't like leaving her unattended. But he was relatively certain she was safe here. He'd been on the lookout for anyone following them from her place and hadn't detected a tail.

Poppy nudged Hunter with her elbow. "Dude, you've got it bad."

"I don't know what you're talking about." He turned his attention to Juneau rather than let Poppy see the truth on his face. He did have it bad and had no idea what to do about it.

Hunter held the harnesses out for the dogs to sniff.

"Find," Hunter instructed Juneau. The dog lifted his snout to the air, then put it to the ground and took off.

Poppy gave her command to Stormy, as well. The Irish wolfhound let out a bark and raced after Juneau.

"Here we go." Hunter slung the harnesses over his shoulder and hustled alongside Poppy to trail the dogs' paw prints.

They passed a large fenced corral with over twenty horned reindeer milling about, their velvet noses snuffling beneath the snow for vegetation.

In the distance, the sound of the Frontier River drifted on the slight afternoon breeze. Hunter hadn't realized how close the sanctuary was to the multiforked body of water.

The dogs ran down a snow-covered dirt access road and disappeared into the forest surrounding the reindeer sanctuary.

"Look at these." Poppy pointed to tracks in the snow where the access road crossed the property boundary. "Snowshoe prints. And these deep grooves are from the reindeer."

"Not an accident," Hunter remarked. A human wearing snowshoes had released the reindeer. He put a hand on the grip of his sidearm. "Poachers?"

"Could be." Poppy's tone held a grim note.

He was sure she'd seen some horrible treatment of animals as a wildlife trooper in the Kenai Fjord National Park before coming to the K-9 Unit.

Up ahead the dogs barked. Something crashed through the underbrush and trees, coming toward Hunter and Poppy. Man or beast? Hunter braced himself.

A huge reindeer sporting tall antlers rushed at them. Hunter waved his arms. "Whoa, there, fella."

Poppy mirrored Hunter. The beast skidded to a halt, hot puffs of air coming from his snout, his dark eyes watching them warily as his feet pawed at the ground.

"Easy, boy." He slipped one of the harnesses from his shoulder and cautiously approached the animal. "We don't want to hurt you."

Poppy held out an apple. "Here's a good boy."

The treat seemed to do the trick. The reindeer snuffled her hand and sank his teeth into the apple. While the reindeer was busy chewing, Hunter managed to get the harness slipped over his head and attach the extra lead. He anchored the lead to a nearby tree.

"Good job with the apple," he commented to Poppy.

"I've got carrots, too," she said. "Grabbed them from the barn." She let out a whistle and Stormy came running.

Hunter called out to Juneau. The dog barked in response and raced to his side.

"Let's keep following the snowshoe tracks," Hunter suggested as he leashed up Juneau. "We should keep the dogs close to be safe."

Poppy agreed. They followed the snowshoe tracks to a clearing and a road where there were obvious tire tracks along with reindeer prints that ended where a vehicle was clearly parked.

"It appears as if someone had been intent on taking the two reindeer away but only managed to load up one reindeer," Hunter stated. "We better call this in."

As they collected the reindeer and headed back to the ranch, Poppy used her cell phone to inform the colonel of this development. Lorenza promised to send out a crime scene unit and the Metro police to see if they could trace the tire tracks.

Addie was beside herself when they returned with one of the reindeer in tow.

"I can't tell you how grateful I am," Addie said. "Each reindeer is special. I just hope whoever took my reindeer doesn't destroy him."

"I'm sure the K-9 Unit and the Metro police will do everything they can to find him," Ariel assured her.

Hunter appreciated Ariel's confidence.

Addie patted Ariel's hand. "After hearing what you've been going through and how well this young man has been taking care of you, I trust you are correct."

Hunter stared at Ariel. What had she told the older woman?

Poppy made a noise suspiciously like a covered laugh. Hunter slanted her a glance, to which she raised her eyebrows, the picture of innocence.

"I hate leaving you here alone," Ariel said. "Maybe I should stay with you."

"I'll stay until Katie can arrive," Poppy offered.

With that settled, Hunter escorted Ariel and Juneau back to the SUV.

"She's a widow, you know," Ariel said as he pulled away from the sanctuary. "She and her husband never had children. Katie is her only relative."

The melancholy note in her tone had Hunter's chest tightening. "It was very kind of you to stay with her while we searched for her reindeer."

Ariel unzipped her jacket. "It was the right thing to do."

"Yes, it was," he agreed. He'd half expected Ariel to insist on searching for the reindeer. His respect and admiration for this woman ratcheted up even more, which made his next words tough to say. "I need to take Violet's letter into headquarters."

Her shoulders drooped and she turned away from him. "Do whatever you have to."

That night after a lasagna dinner, Ariel headed to the kennel building with Hunter and Juneau tagging along. She fed the dogs and turned them out to the exercise yard so she could clean their kennels. Once she and Hunter removed all the beds, toys and dishes, she unwound the water hose to wash down each kennel. They worked well together. Ariel tried not to ruminate on how much she would miss Hunter and Juneau when the time came for them to resume their own lives.

"Let me do that," Hunter said, taking the hose from her hands.

Thankful for his help, she relinquished the hose and moved to grab a large duffel bag from a cupboard. She filled it with the items the dogs would need for the race tomorrow. Ariel had already had Trevor load the sled onto the back of her truck while she and Hunter were at Addie's today. She'd hitch the dog trailer to the truck in the morning.

Hunter turned off the hose and wound it back up. "What are you doing?"

"Prepping for tomorrow." She zipped up the bag. "We'll need to get an early start. I want to be at the race grounds to set up my station before it gets too crowded."

Hunter took her hands in his. "Ariel, I'm sorry but there's no way we can let you go to a race tomorrow. It's too dangerous."

She'd known this was going to be a battle. But she couldn't afford to concede defeat. Sighing, she squeezed his hands. "Hunter, I know it will be dangerous. And I know that every time I step out of the house I could be at risk. But I can't live my life ruled by fear."

A pained expression crossed his handsome features. "Caution. You'd be living your life ruled by *caution*. It's not the same thing."

"I can be cautious. And you'll be there to guarantee my safety just as you were at the banquet." Needing him to understand how important competing in this race was, she said, "The way I make money is by competing in races that allow small teams, and by breeding dogs that are showcased at the races. If I hope to pay Trevor for all that he has been doing around here, I need to finish in the top four slots tomorrow, as well as advertise my next pairing. I also need to line up prospective mushers for my puppies."

He remained silent for a long moment. "Let me run it by Colonel Gallo."

Did he not trust himself to make the call? "I can speak to her. She seems reasonable."

"She is," Hunter said. "I trust her judgment."

"And I trust yours," she told him. She did trust this man. With her life. And she was beginning to realize she trusted him with her heart. But he wouldn't want to hear that, not now, if ever. He'd made it clear that romance—love—wasn't something he believed in. "Hunter, she put you in charge of protecting me. She obviously considers you the right person for the job. I do, too. You'll protect me."

He didn't look convinced.

Frustrated with him, she said, "I'm going. You're here because I allow it. I don't have to accept your protection or your presence." She put her hand on his chest. His heart beat beneath her palm, solid and strong. Like the man. "Please, don't spoil this for me."

Hunter's gaze held hers, and his blue eyes glinted with an emotion that left her own heart racing.

He covered her hand with his. "What time are we leaving?"

Hunter could tell how excited Ariel was by the prospect of a race. Even the dogs seemed amped as they loaded them in the trailer, their energetic howls bouncing off the metal sides. Since Trevor was going to be coming with them to help Ariel with the dogs, Hunter decided to drive his own vehicle and followed them.

He didn't explain to Ariel the reason he chose not to ride with her was to make sure that she arrived at the location without mishap. He liked seeing her happy. And he understood how important today was for her business.

Her words about not living her life in fear had struck him at the core.

Too many times he operated out of fear.

He sent up a prayer that Ariel's confidence that nothing would happen today would be fulfilled.

The race venue was twenty miles north of Anchorage. She had explained that this was the last official fun run of the season. Afterward the snow would melt and training would be on dry land.

But thanks to the late spring snowfall, there was still enough of the white stuff on the ground for one last grand finale. She said it would be mostly mushers from the area since the majority of the Iditarod mushers and dogs had already returned to their homes all over the world.

Hunter parked his vehicle in the visitor parking lot, while Ariel drove her truck and trailer through the gate for competitors. He and Juneau hustled to catch up with them. He flashed his badge to the gatekeepers.

It was interesting to watch the way Trevor and Ariel got everything situated, hooking the dogs to the sled in a two-by-two formation. The dogs pranced in place and howled, but they didn't pull against the harnesses, though Hunter could see the muscles rippling in each dog with the effort to keep from prematurely taking off. Ariel slipped a race number over her red down jacket. Once they were ready to take the pack and sled to the start line queue, Ariel handed the young man a stack of flyers.

Hunter caught a glimpse of one that showed a picture of a litter of puppies along with Ariel's name and contact information.

"Make sure everyone gets one of these," she told Trevor.

She turned to Hunter. "Can you walk behind the sled and just keep it steady as we make our way to the start line?"

He was happy to oblige. Thankfully, he'd worn his heavy boots, warm jacket and gloves. He pulled the beanie on his head a little lower over his ears and positioned himself behind the sled. Juneau stayed close, but far enough back not to agitate the sled dogs.

Ariel moved to the front of her line, where Dash and Phoenix were harnessed as the lead dogs. She spoke softly to the dogs and then walked ahead of them. Without hesitation the dogs followed. Meanwhile, Hunter kept a steadying grip on the back bar of the brightly painted yellow sled and walked between the runners, careful not to catch his foot on the ski-like flat boards that would glide over the snow once the team started really pulling. She brought the dogs to a halt and lined up behind three other teams. Then she gave each dog a piece of salmon before joining Hunter at the back of the sled.

The howls of the multiple dogs filled the air along with a few barks by some of the various different breeds being used in the race.

The noise was nearly deafening. Ariel dug in her pocket and brought out two sets of foam earplugs. She handed a set to him and shouted, "It'll make things easier."

Nodding gratefully, he stuffed the little rubbery plugs in his ears, muting the cacophony of sound.

More racers lined up behind them. Hunter counted at least twenty-five teams. He'd never been involved in a race and could see why many enjoyed the adrenaline rush of seeing the dogs and mushers competing to get the best time on the course.

He caught a glimpse of a familiar face in the crowd standing behind the ropes and keeping the spectators from stepping into the path of the dogs.

Carly Winters.

Her gaze was trained on Ariel, and there was such malice in her expression that Hunter's senses went on alert.

He gestured for Ariel to take out an ear plug just as

he was doing. When she did, he said, "Is there a reason beyond just the competitive nature of breeders that Carly Winters would want to harm you?"

Ariel drew back with a frown. "No. As I told you, we're not friends. I've only spoken to her when she has asked to buy one of my adult breeding dogs."

Hunter's cell phone vibrated against his chest. It was Helena, his teammate. He motioned to Ariel that he needed to take the call. She nodded. He jogged away from the noise as far as he could while still keeping Ariel in view and held the phone to his ear. "Helena, news?"

"Yes, we found Sandy. She's been in Fairbanks visiting her sister."

"Why didn't Jason tell us where she was going?"

"Apparently it was her way of breaking up with him without having to face him. She decided that the night of the banquet he was still too hung up on Ariel. She left him the same night."

"Hung up enough on her to try to kill her? It doesn't make sense."

"No, it doesn't," Helena agreed. "Hey, another little tidbit. Tala got back to us on that baseball cap you found. There was a long brown hair in the hat, but couldn't get DNA from it or the hat."

Too bad there wasn't a hair follicle to provide DNA. Sandy, Carly and Violet did not have long brown hair. Was there a fourth female suspect?

"It's a synthetic hair."

Surprise gave way to frustration. "A wig."

"Yes."

"So our suspect could be anybody." Irritation fired along his nerves.

"Right. It could've been a man or woman," Helena said.

His gaze sought Carly Winters in the crowd, but she was nowhere to be seen. He needed to find her. "I've a hunch I need to follow. How quickly can you get here? I need someone to watch over Ariel."

"Ten minutes, tops," Helena told him before signing off.

Hunter hung up the phone. He needed to ask Carly some more questions. And time was of the essence because he wasn't going to let anyone hurt Ariel. Just the thought carved through him with the precision of a surgeon's scalpel, cutting away his resistance to allow her into his heart.

SIXTEEN

Ariel placed her feet on the boards along the edge of the sled runners and gripped the handle bar at the back of the sled. The seconds were ticking down. The team in front was amped up, the dogs dancing with excitement as the crowds cheered in anticipation of the start of the last of the season's fun run sled dog races. Teams would deploy in two-minute increments, and the team with the fastest time across the finish line would win. The next teams coming in after the winner would get a percentage of the prize money. Ariel needed that money.

She glanced around, trying to find Hunter among the throng of people gathered to watch. She spied him standing among the crowd, clearly searching for someone. A horn blew. Ariel frowned. It was the sound the judges used to let the mushers know there would be a delay. Like the other mushers, she stepped off her sled, setting the brake that would keep her team in place.

A disembodied voice came through the loudspeakers. "Ariel Potter, please come to the judges' tent ASAP."

Confusion and a prickle of fear slid down her back, creating a shiver that shook her body. She was aware of the gazes of her fellow mushers on her as she waved

Trevor over. He had earplugs in but popped them out. "What's going on?"

"I better go find out," Ariel said. "Can you stay with the dogs?"

"Of course." He traded places with her.

Once again, Ariel searched for Hunter. She couldn't see him as she jogged to the official judges' station. Just as she reached the enclosed ten-by-twenty tent, he joined her.

Hunter gave her a questioning look and she shook her head. They entered together. Monitors showing the crowd waiting for the start of the race and displaying the route along the Trozier Track lined one wall of the tent. Video cameras along the trail prevented cheating and alerted EMS if any mushers and their teams had problems.

Ariel took out her earplugs and approached the judging table, where four men and one woman sat. "I'm Ariel Potter."

A gray-haired man with bushy eyebrows steepled his fingers together and stared at her over his thick black-framed glasses. "It's come to our attention, Miss Potter, that you are doping your dogs."

Ariel's jaw went slack. No way could she have heard him correctly. "Excuse me? *Doping?* What on earth are you talking about?"

"We've had a complaint that you are giving your dogs performance-enhancing drugs," the woman at the table said with a disapproving tone.

Dumbfounded by the accusation, Ariel's gaze jumped to Hunter. "I wouldn't ever do something like that."

His troubled blue eyes held hers. "I've seen you giving the dogs some sort of powder in their food."

Disbelief knocked her back a step. "It's vitamins and minerals. Not only is it perfectly legal but good for them." She turned back to the judges. "I do not give my dogs anything to enhance their performance. I would never violate the rules, nor would I put my dogs' health in jeopardy."

"Until that can be verified, you are banned from any races," one of the other male judges stated.

"Banned?" Outrage heated her skin. "This is a fun run."

"It's still a race with a purse."

Ariel's fingers curled at her sides. "This is absurd!"

"The vet will need to take blood samples of your dogs to verify," the woman spoke again. "If the accusation proves false, we will reinstate you."

"Are you serious?" Ariel scoffed. "By the time that happens, the race will be over."

She looked to Hunter for help. He didn't come to her defense. Crushed by his lack of faith in her, she turned on her heels and walked out.

Hunter caught up with her. "Ariel, maybe this is for the best."

"For the best!" She rounded on him. "Did you do this?"

His eyes widened. "No," he said. "Of course not. I would never do that to you."

"Of course not," she mimicked him. "You didn't want me to compete in this race to begin with. Now you've sabotaged me. Thanks, Hunter. I thought I meant more to you than that." She stalked away from him.

"Ariel, where are you going?"

"I'm going to talk with the vet," she called over her

shoulder as he walked behind her. "I don't need you with me."

Tears blinded her as her heart caved in on itself. She'd almost considered herself in love with that man. Would she ever learn that was too much of a risk?

Hunter slowly followed after Ariel, keeping her in sight but giving her enough distance to cool off. It hurt to imagine that she believed he would do something so underhanded. He knew deep in his soul that she was a goodhearted woman who loved her dogs and she would never do anything to hurt them.

But somebody was obviously out to ruin her.

If it wasn't Jason Barba's ex-girlfriend, Sandy, who was in Fairbanks, then that left Jason, Violet James or Carly Winters.

Once Ariel entered the veterinarian's tent, Hunter picked up his pace. When he entered the tent, he found Ariel talking to Dr. Cora Madison. He was surprised to see the K-9 Unit's veterinarian working the race.

Both women stopped talking to stare at him.

He spread his hands wide. "It wasn't me, but I suspect I know who did make the complaint."

"Who?" Ariel's tone was filled with antagonism.

He wasn't ready to divulge his suspicion until he had it confirmed. "I'm going to deal with it. You stay here." He turned to Cora. "Please, don't let her leave this tent. And don't let anyone else in here. Helena is on her way."

Ariel blew out an exasperated breath. "Hunter, I'm done taking orders from you." She turned away, giving him her back.

A helpless sort of rage infused him. He didn't want her to believe the worst of him. Yet he had questioned her about the supplements she used for the dogs. And he hadn't wanted her to race, but not because of this.

He needed to make this right. He returned to the judges' tent and went to the young man sitting in front of the monitors. After showing his badge, Hunter asked, "Can you pan the crowd?"

"Sure." The man toggled a device on a keyboard sitting on the table in front of him.

Scanning the faces, Hunter didn't see Violet or Carly.

"I need you to send a copy of the last hour of video feed to this person." Hunter took out Eli Partridge's business card. "And then I want you to allow him to tap into the feed so that he can look at the crowd right now. There may be a killer on the loose."

A flash of alarm flared in the younger man's eyes. "You got it."

The gray-haired judge from earlier hurried over. "What are you doing?"

Hunter explained and the gentleman nearly convulsed with panic. The other judges rushed over, obviously realizing that something was going on, and nearly matched the older judge's distress.

"Please, don't make this public," the female judge said.

"Whatever you're going to do, do it quietly," another judge insisted. "We can't have pandemonium. People and dogs will get hurt."

"I'll do my best," Hunter assured them. "Who filed the complaint against Ariel Potter?"

The judges looked at each other.

"It was anonymous," the gray-haired man claimed, his gaze shifting away from Hunter.

Narrowing his eyes, Hunter said, "I don't believe

that. If you don't tell me the truth, I'll put an end to this whole race right now."

"You can't do that!" the woman exclaimed. "We're about to start the race."

Hunter ground his teeth together. "Then give me the information I need."

"Just give it to him, Tom," the woman said. "It doesn't matter in the long run."

Tom huffed out an agitated breath. "It was Carly Winters."

Just as Hunter suspected. Ariel's competitor wanted to discredit Ariel and hurt her business. He believed that Carly was behind the attacks on Ariel, as well. Without another word, he hustled out of the tent and nearly mowed over Helena.

"Whoa, slow down," she said, steadying herself. "What gives?"

In rapid-fire words, he gave her the highlights of the situation and where to find Ariel.

Secure that Helena would keep Ariel safe, he ran for his truck.

He was going to have it out with Carly Winters and arrest her for attempted murder.

Ariel's dogs checked out fine, just as she'd known they would. Cora marched off to give the judges an earful, for which Ariel was grateful, but she was too upset to even contemplate joining the race at this point. She wasn't sure why the officials had continued to delay the start of the race…though she suspected it had something to do with Hunter.

Maybe she'd been wrong to accuse him of sabotaging her. But the look in his eyes and his question about the supplements she gave to her dogs had made her see red. And ache with the pain of betrayal.

Just contemplating that Hunter could believe she'd do anything so underhanded and harmful made her insides twist.

And the question of who filed the complaint poked at her like a sharp stick, drawing bits of blood with every stab.

Hunter's questions regarding Carly played through her head. She'd been truthful that they weren't friends. But she didn't tell him that ever since the other woman had landed in the area and Ariel had refused to sell her a dog, she had made her dislike of Ariel very clear. Was Carly the one behind the complaint? Had the other breeder been so jealous of Ariel's business that she'd tried to hurt her?

A sinking sensation in her abdomen had Ariel needing to grab the nearest chair. Had Carly followed them up the mountain and acted on an opportunity to push her off the cliff? Then, when that attempt on her life hadn't been successful, had the woman tried to steal Dash, Ariel's most sought-after stud? Ariel was sure the person who had tried to strangle her was female or at least sounded like one. Could it have been Carly?

Her competitor had also been at the banquet. She could have easily been the one to orchestrate the collapse of the backdrop.

Heart hammering in her chest, Ariel jumped to her feet. She needed to find Hunter and tell him.

His teammate, Helena, and her partner, a Norwegian elkhound, walked into the tent just as Ariel was rushing out.

Helena's wide green eyes flared with recognition. "Ariel."

She stopped short, glad to see the trooper. "Helena, have you seen Hunter?"

"I just talked to him," she replied. "He left, though. He told me to stay with you and get you back to your place."

"Left?" Disappointment reared, mixed with the anger at his betrayal of trust. "Do you know where he's going?"

"He's following a hunch."

Ariel hesitated. Then determination straightened her spine and infused her muscles with energy. She tugged on Helena's state trooper jacket sleeve, pulling her and her partner into the judges' tent. "I need your help with something. We'll use your badge to get the information I want…"

"I'm here to help you in any way I can," Helena said.

Once inside the tent, Ariel marched up to the judges' table, where the panel sat. "My dogs are fine. But we need some information. Who told you I was doping my dogs?"

One of the judges rolled his eyes. "Not again."

Ariel narrowed her gaze on him. "What do you mean?"

"The other trooper was in here asking the same question," the gray-haired man told her.

Ariel's pulse ticked up. She shared a startled glance with Helena.

Helena stepped forward. "This is official business. What did you tell him?"

The woman sighed. "That the breeder, Carly Winters, was the one who made the accusation."

Helena gasped. "He's headed to Carly's!"

Ariel's breath stalled in her lungs. "I'm afraid she might be dangerous."

Helena's eyebrows dipped. "But just to you, right?"

"We don't know that for sure. She might do anything to keep from being caught." Ariel took her phone out of her jacket pocket. "I'll try to reach Hunter."

Her call went straight to voice mail. She sent a text, as well. Dread gripped Ariel like a harness belted too tightly around her chest. "He's not answering. We have to go to Carly's."

"I'll call for someone to go there," Helena said.

"There's no time. Carly's place isn't far from here," Ariel said. "We have to go ourselves."

"We'll take my rig, but you'll stay in the car."

Not about to argue, Ariel checked with Trevor to make sure he would take the dogs back to her place in the trailer.

With her dogs secure in Trevor's capable hands, Ariel got into Helena's SUV. She sent up a prayer: *Dear Lord, please protect Hunter.*

Hunter arrived at Carly's place, pulling up next to the red truck with the Winters Kennels logo on the side. He studied the house. A curtain moved in an upstairs window.

She was home.

Caution tripped down his spine. He checked his weapon. Then he radioed dispatch, giving them his location and informing them he was questioning a potential suspect in the Potter case.

He climbed from the SUV, keeping an eye on the front of the two-story house. Using the release button on his keychain fob, he released Juneau. The dog jumped out, landing silently on the plowed driveway.

Hunter attached a lead to Juneau's harness, and they approached the front entrance.

As he stepped onto the porch, a strange spitting sound raised the fine hairs at his nape in alarm. Beside him, Juneau let out a howl and then toppled over.

Heart jumping into his throat, Hunter dropped to his knees beside his partner. A blue-and-yellow dart protruded from the dog's side.

A tranquilizer dart.

Anger, swift and dangerous, flowed through Hunter's veins. He plucked the offending thing from Juneau, hoping to keep the full dose of the drug from entering his body. The crunch of footsteps on the porch stairs behind him had him reaching for his sidearm.

"Don't move," a gruff male voice demanded. "Get your hands in the air."

Slowly Hunter raised his hands and swiveled to face Jason Barba. The man held a tranquilizer gun.

"You." Regret for letting the weasel get the drop on him wound around him like an anchor rope to a tree. "Why aren't you still in custody?"

"Lawyer." Jason spit out the word. His face twisted with hatred. "You've gotten in our way far too much."

"Our?" Dread pinched Hunter's gut.

The front door opened and Carly Winters stepped out holding a .32 caliber weapon in her hands. She wore a baseball hat with her kennel logo over a long brown wig.

The pieces of the puzzle shifted. "You two are working together."

"That's right, handsome," Carly said. "Now put your weapon on the ground."

No way was he giving up his sidearm. "Why are you mixed up with Jason? Why are you trying to hurt Ariel?"

"Hey." Jason's voice rose to a higher octave. "What do you mean by mixed up with me?"

"Shut up, Jason," Carly said, her brown eyes glittering with malice. "Trooper, do as you're told or your dog dies." She shifted the barrel of her gun to Juneau.

Afraid she would follow through with her threat and kill his partner, Hunter rushed Carly. He'd rather be shot than let Juneau die.

She screamed and danced back. A sharp pain between his shoulder blades drew Hunter up short. Jason had fired a dart into his back. Another dart hit Hunter in the leg. He dropped to his knees beside his partner.

Carly pushed Hunter over with her foot. "Now, be a good boy and go to sleep."

Hunter fought the drug invading his system as the world went hazy, but it proved to be too strong and he succumbed to the darkness.

SEVENTEEN

With her heart in her throat and fear tingling through her, Ariel held on to the dashboard as Helena drove at a breakneck speed with the siren blaring toward Carly Winters's kennels. The two-story house and outbuilding came into view. There was no sign of Hunter. Carly's truck was not in the driveway, either. Helena brought the SUV to a skidding halt.

Ariel caught sight of a white tail sticking out from beneath the porch.

Dread and panic seized her breath. Juneau!

She sent up a litany of prayers and ignored Helena's directive to stay in the car. Jumping out of the vehicle, Ariel raced to the Siberian husky's side. Helena and her partner, Luna, were right on Ariel's heels. The howls of Carly's dogs inside the building to the side of the house raised the hairs on Ariel's arms.

She dropped to her knees, and her hands were shaking as she reached out to touch the soft red-and-white fur. "Juneau?"

At the sound of her voice, the dog lifted his head and gave a small howl of distress.

He was alive. Relief brought tears streaming down Ariel's face. "Thank God."

Helena tested the front doorknob. "Locked. We're going to check the back." She and Luna hurried around the house, disappearing from sight.

Ariel tugged Juneau out from beneath the porch, her hands roaming over the dog, looking for injury. But she had a sinking sensation she knew exactly what had happened. He had been tranquilized just as Dash had been the night the intruder tried to steal him.

Carly Winters. She had been the intruder. She was the one behind the attacks on Ariel.

She gathered Juneau's head onto her lap. "You're going to be okay. Where is your handler?"

Ariel's gaze swept the property, looking for any sign of Hunter or Carly. The dogs in the kennel building sounded distressed.

Helena returned. "There's no sign of Hunter or anyone else. The place is empty." She crouched next to Ariel and petted Juneau. "How is he?"

"He'll be okay. He's been drugged. Same thing happened to Dash the other night. Good thing he's a police dog, because taking him would be too risky. Especially once he woke up."

Luna nudged Juneau with her nose.

Helena nodded. "Yes, he'd be aggressive with someone he doesn't know."

"I'm sure Carly plans to dispose of him when she returns." Ariel's heart contracted at the thought.

"Let's get him in the SUV."

Ariel attempted to lift Juneau, but the dog resisted and managed to get his feet under him. He wobbled, and Luna moved to stand next to him. "Juneau must not have been dosed as heavily as Dash."

Helena's gaze went to the kennel building. "I'd better check that out."

"I'll come with you," Ariel said. Hunter could be in there injured. Or worse. Apprehension slithered along her limbs.

Walking at Ariel's side, Juneau let out a series of ear-piercing howls as they approached the building.

"Stay behind me." Helena had Luna sniff the door-knob before she tried it and found it unlocked. She pushed the door open. The howling of the dogs inside their crates was deafening. Ariel peered around Helena. Hunter was nowhere to be seen. But the conditions in which the dogs were living was deplorable.

Horrified, Ariel's stomach rolled. "We have to rescue these dogs. I can't believe that Carly would do this."

"I'll call dispatch," Helena said. "I'll have them alert the humane society."

Ariel couldn't just leave the dogs like this, but her priority had to be finding Hunter. Where was he?

Juneau tried to vocalize something, and the dog's apparent distress broke Ariel's heart. She had no idea what the dog was saying, but she could only guess that he was hurting from the absence of his handler. The same way Ariel was. "I know, boy, we'll find him. I miss Hunter, too."

She more than missed him. She loved him. Deep inside she couldn't deny the truth. Despite his betrayal, despite knowing his stance on love and relationships, she was madly in love with Hunter. She sent up a plea to God that she'd have a chance to tell him.

A Metro police cruiser came screaming down the

drive. Ariel was glad to see it was Officer Everett Brand. She and Helena hurried over and filled him in. He promised to alert the department and to stay until someone came to take care of the dogs.

Helena turned to Ariel. "I'll take you and Juneau to your house. It's the safest place for you both."

Ariel didn't want to be left out of the search for Hunter, but she had no say in the matter. So, with a heavy heart, she climbed into the passenger seat of Helena's SUV with Juneau on her lap. He howled, and Ariel rolled down the window. He stuck his head out as Helena drove away from Carly's.

When they passed the turnoff for the Chugach State Park, Juneau's agitation was more than they could contain within the confines of the cab of Helena's SUV. Helena pulled the vehicle to the side of the road. Once they came to a halt, the canine jumped out the window and ran back toward the entrance to the state park.

"He must've caught Hunter's scent," Helena said. "Follow him!"

The tires threw dirt and snow as Helena made a quick U-turn. Ariel prayed for all she was worth that they reached Hunter in time to prevent whatever Carly had planned.

Hunter came to with a jolt. His eyes opened to a cloudy sky. The sensation of moving made him dizzy. He attempted to sit up, but his body was strapped down. Dropping his chin to see what was going on, he realized he'd been secured to a rescue basket. He craned his neck in an effort to look behind him and could see that Jason and Carly had attached ropes to the basket and were dragging him up a snowy trail. Flattop Mountain loomed ahead of them. They were taking him to the place where Cal Brooks had died and where Ariel had been pushed off the cliff.

"How much farther?" Jason whined. He sounded breathless with the effort of pulling the basket.

Hunter took grim satisfaction in the fact that the much smaller man was struggling.

"Just keep going," Carly snapped. "I had no idea you were such a wimp."

"Hey," Jason said. "I'm helping you, aren't I?"

Hunter spread his fingers wide, gauging how much movement he could get beneath the straps. A little. Hoping he could reach his SUV key fob and the GPS tracker built into the device, he worked at getting his hands to the front pocket of his pants. Hunter glanced back and met Jason's gaze, just as his fingers closed around the knob. Sending a silent prayer of thanks, he deployed the tracker.

"He's awake!" Jason jerked to a stop, forcing Carly to do the same.

Carly rounded the basket to stand at Hunter's feet. "So he is." She looked up toward where they were going and then back at Hunter. A split second later, she grabbed her gun from the pocket of her jacket. "Undo the straps," she instructed Jason. "He can walk the rest of the way."

Jason undid the buckles.

Hunter pushed himself up onto his elbows. His head swam. The world tilted. He gave himself a shake and sat up higher.

"Get him to his feet," Carly snarled. "I don't have all day. I need to get back to the race and be there at the finish."

Jason pushed Hunter's back. "Get up. You heard her."

Forcing himself, Hunter struggled to stand. He got his feet under him but had to put his hands on his thighs and bend over until the world righted.

"Start moving," Carly said. "We'll get the basket on the way back down."

"Carly, what's your plan?" Hunter's words came out a bit slurred. "You're only making matters worse for yourselves."

"Oh, no, not worse for us," she said. "It's gonna be worse for Ariel."

"That's right," Jason said. "Ariel thinks she's too good for me."

"Too good for *us*," Carly reminded him.

"Uh, sure," Jason agreed.

Hunter struggled to understand. "How do you two know each other?" He glanced back to see them look at each other. "You're planning to kill me anyway, so just tell me the truth."

He prayed a rescue would come long before she pulled that trigger.

Carly snickered. "We met at a sled dog event a few months ago and realized we had a common enemy. Ariel."

"I thought you said you didn't like dogs," Hunter said to Jason.

"I wasn't there to watch the dogs," Jason snapped. "I was with the catering staff. Duh."

"Why do you want to hurt Ariel?" Hunter asked Carly. "Jason, I get, because Ariel dumped him. But you? What did she do to you?"

Jason sputtered. "That's not true. I broke up with her."

Ignoring him, Carly's lips twisted with contempt.

"She's been nothing but a pain in my side since I arrived in Anchorage. I have Alaskan Huskies that are just as good as hers. Yet I lost out on selling my most recent litter to people who bought from her instead. Since stealing her prized stud didn't go as planned, I decided with her out of the way, I might be able to acquire some, if not all, of her dogs and expand my operation."

The woman had seriously flawed logic. Ariel's parents would step in and take care of the dogs. Hunter's chest knotted with dread. Best not to point that out or these two might go after Ariel's parents or anyone else who stood in their way. "What do you intend to do to Ariel?"

"It will be ingenious," Jason said. "Carly's got it all figured out. We're gonna push you over the cliff. And then we'll use your gun to kill Ariel."

"Everyone will think you killed her and then threw yourself over the cliff out of guilt," Carly finished.

He didn't point out the error in their plan. First, there was no logical reason why he'd hurt Ariel and second, the medical examiner would know he was dead long before Ariel. Instead, he said, "So you followed Ariel up the mountain and pushed her off the cliff."

"No," Carly said. "But I wish I had."

"Then it was you," Hunter said to Jason.

"No way. I didn't know about that until I saw the nightly news."

"Same here," Carly echoed.

Hunter wasn't sure he believed them, but why would they lie now? "And then you tried to strangle her?"

"Yes, but you got in the way," she said.

Jason snorted.

"You couldn't have done it," Carly sneered at Jason.

"You better watch out," Jason yelled. "Or you might find yourself going over the cliff, too."

Carly waved the gun at him. "Ha. I'm the one who knows how to use a gun."

Concerned the two might start brawling and the gun might go off, Hunter interjected, "You're the one who shot at Ariel."

Narrowing her eyes, Carly said, "Yes. I should've brought my rifle instead of the .32. But I'd heard on the news that the tour guide had been killed with a .32, so I figured if you all thought the same person was shooting at Ariel, I would be in the clear. Now, no more talk. Move it."

As they reached the outcrop, he turned his back to the cliff. Better to make them look him in the eye. "You won't get away with this."

In the distance, a siren echoed through the valley floor. Hunter wanted to cheer, but he wasn't out of danger. He needed to keep these two from doing anything rash until his team reached him.

Hunter couldn't let Carly and Jason off this mountain. He wasn't sure how he would pull it off, but no matter what, he couldn't let them get to Ariel. In that moment, he realized what he had been fighting for so long. He loved her. He'd fallen hopelessly in love with Ariel and wanted to spend the rest of his life with her. But first, he had to figure out a way out of this predicament.

Jason advanced on him.

Hunter braced himself, his heart crying out to God for help, because he feared the moment would come when he'd have to choose between being shot or pushed over the cliff.

* * *

Ariel and Helena and Luna raced after Juneau up the mountain trail, following the footprints in the snow and the deep grooves of something being dragged along the surface. In the distance a siren wailed. But would more officers make a difference? What if Hunter was already injured or dead?

With each passing second, despair threatened to rob Ariel of her strength. Under her breath she prayed for God to show them where to find Hunter before it was too late.

When they came upon the rescue basket abandoned in the middle of the trail, and another set of footprints, Ariel had a jolt of hope that Hunter was still alive.

Helena held a finger to her lips, then whispered, "They can't be too far ahead."

The footprints led toward the outcrop where she'd been sent over the edge. Where all of this had started.

Juneau sniffed the footprints and then dashed ahead with Luna at his side. Ariel and Helena picked up speed.

Voices drifted on the afternoon breeze.

Adrenaline flooding her veins, Ariel grabbed Helena by the arm and crouched down behind a bramble bush. Juneau came bounding back to Ariel, while Luna appeared next to Helena. The trooper motioned she would head off to the right and circle around.

Grabbing Juneau by the collar, Ariel slowly and as stealthily as she could moved forward until she was in a position to see that Jason and Carly had Hunter backed up to the edge of the cliff.

Jason and Carly were working together? Carly had a gun in her hand.

Mind. Blowing. It took all of Ariel's self-control not

to cry out with rage and fear. Juneau lunged forward, but she held him back, afraid Carly would shoot him. Ariel pointed to the ground, hoping Juneau would understand. He folded down onto his belly. She had to figure out a way to save Hunter. Or at least buy enough time for Helena to get into place.

She rose to her feet, intending to distract Jason and Carly. Her gaze collided with Hunter's.

His eyes widened and he gave a subtle shake of his head. To Jason and Carly he said, "You need to reconsider your plan. This won't work. You're going to get caught."

Beside her, Juneau belly-crawled forward, closer and closer to Jason and Carly. Ariel searched for something to use as a distraction and grabbed a large stone. Using all her strength, she lobbed the rock off to the left of Jason. He took the bait, spinning away from Carly and Hunter, looking for the source of the noise.

Carly, however, turned around to face Ariel. She aimed the gun at her. "Well, this will make things easier."

Hunter shouted, "Attack!"

Juneau sprang up like his legs were made of springs and propelled himself at Carly, latching onto her arm. At the same moment, Hunter tackled the woman from behind, sending her flying forward.

Jason whirled around and charged at Ariel. But a streak of gray and white drove at him. Luna's paws landed on Jason's chest and the dog pushed him back. Jason fell onto his backside.

Helena rushed out of the trees. "State Trooper, put your hands up!"

Hunter quickly handcuffed Carly and recited the

vile woman her Miranda rights while Helena did the same with Jason. The two dogs stood guard, baring their teeth. Juneau let out a howl that reverberated across the mountain.

Ariel's legs wouldn't hold her. She sank onto the ground. Then Hunter was at her side. He gathered her into his arms, and as she clung to him, her whole body shook with an overwhelming sense of relief.

And love.

He held her close. "It's okay. We're all okay now."

"Let's get these two down the mountain," Helena said.

Hunter helped Ariel to her feet, then gripped her biceps and looked her in the eye. "Those two will never bother you again, Ariel."

She nodded, thankful that the nightmare with Carly and Jason had ended, and yet what did the future hold? What about Violet?

By the time they got down to the bottom of the mountain, the whole K-9 Unit had assembled along with several Metro PD officers. Colonel Lorenza Gallo stepped forward, directing everyone.

Officer Everett Brand took Carly Winters into custody, placing her into his cruiser, and Officer Gorman followed suit with Jason.

Once the two suspects were headed to jail, Lorenza turned to Hunter. "Did they tell you what happened to Violet James?"

Hunter shook his head with frustration. "Carly and Jason say they had nothing to do with what happened on the mountain. They claim they heard about Ariel's fall on the news, which gave the two of them the idea of trying to do away with her once and for all."

He sent up a silent praise that Carly and Jason hadn't succeeded. His heart still jolted every time he relived that moment when Ariel rose up from behind the bushes. It was a gutsy move that had him terrified that Carly would kill her. But thankfully, his partner, and his coworker, had been heroes, taking down the villains.

The colonel's lips twisted with annoyance. "I was hoping this would all be tied up in a neat bow. And these two would have revealed what happened." She gazed up the mountain in question. "We have to keep working this case, people." She turned around and looked at her team. "All right, everyone back to work. Find Violet James, Lance Wells and Jared Dennis." To Hunter, she said, "I'm glad you're safe. I wouldn't want to lose you."

Hunter tucked her words away, grateful to work for such a great boss.

Lorenza then moved away to talk to Helena. Judging from the expression on his teammate's face, she was pleased with their boss's praise.

Poppy and Maya had taken Ariel off to the side.

Gabriel, Sean, Will and Brayden, along with their respective dogs, crowded around Hunter.

"Man, that was close," Brayden said.

"You're telling me," Hunter replied. "If it weren't for Ariel and Helena." His gaze went to Ariel. Juneau was plastered to her side. After making sure Hunter was intact, the dog had stuck close to Ariel. And that was exactly where Hunter wanted to be.

He looked back at his friends and coworkers. "Would one of you give me and Ariel a ride back to her place?"

"I'll be giving you a ride back," Gabriel said. "But it seems Ariel already has a ride."

Hunter turned to see that Ariel and Juneau were following Poppy to her rig.

He gave a whistle, bringing Juneau back to his side. "If you wouldn't mind, I'd like to stop at my place. A change of clothes is in order." His uniform was sopping wet and muddy and gross, not the way he wanted to look when he confessed to Ariel he loved her.

That night Ariel sat on the back porch with Sasha on her lap. She'd let the dogs out in the fenced yard, and their happy howling as they had fun after their last feeding for the day made her smile. She lamented she hadn't made any money at the race, but she was so thankful she'd been able to save Hunter.

She loved him more than she'd believed possible. When would she see him again? Would it be too brazen of her to call him and ask him to come over?

Doubt swamped her. Not only did he think her capable of doping her dogs, he didn't believe in love. How could they have a future together?

Perhaps it was best for her to suffer her wounded heart alone.

In the twilight of evening, a car turned off the main road onto the snow-packed driveway. Her pulse skipped a beat, then raced through her veins.

Hunter.

His SUV came to a halt. Juneau's plaintive howling reached Ariel, and she smiled. The back compartment opened. Juneau jumped out and raced to her. She held her arms wide, mindful of Sasha sitting on her knees. Juneau skidded to a halt, his rough tongue licking her face.

Her gaze went to Hunter. He walked toward her, looking so handsome in khakis and a leather bomber jacket. His piercing blue eyes held hers. "May I join you?"

She scooted over to make room for him to sit on the back porch. He scrubbed Sasha behind the ears, then took the puppy and set him on the ground. Ariel tucked in her chin. What was this about?

He gathered her hands in his. "I can't believe you saved my life today."

Her anger resurfacing, she shot back, "But you could believe I'd dope my dogs?"

"The minute you explained what the powder was, I realized I was wrong not to come to your defense." He squeezed her hands. "I'm sorry. Please forgive me."

Her anger left in a rush. He was a cop. It was his job to be suspicious, after all. "I understand. I forgive you."

"What you did today was very dangerous."

"What was it you said to me? That I have to trust that God will keep us safe?"

His mouth quirked. "I did say that. And I do believe it. And I believe in you."

She drew back, not sure what to make of his words. "Since when?"

He lifted her hands and kissed her knuckles. "Since the first time I laid eyes on you."

A short laugh escaped her. "Now, I know that's not true. The first time you saw me, I was lying facedown in a bramble bush."

His deep-throated laugh made her giddy. "Okay, maybe not the first time I saw you. But not too long after that. You looked at me with such trust in your eyes. I've never had anyone put that kind of faith in me."

"I do trust you, Hunter. More than you could possibly know." She took a breath. This could be the only opportunity she had to say it. She was going to dig deep and find the courage to take the risk. "I love you. I know that probably scares you. You don't believe in love—"

He put a finger to her lips, cutting her off. "No, Ariel, that doesn't scare me. Not anymore. You taught me that love doesn't have to be a risk. It doesn't have to be scary. Love can be beautiful."

Delight and hope blossomed in her chest. "Do you mean that?"

"I do," he said. "I love you, too, Ariel Potter. And I hope to spend the rest of my life with you, by your side. If you'll have me and Juneau."

Elated beyond measure, she practically shouted, "Of course."

She tugged her hands from his and threw her arms around his neck. "Kiss me," she pleaded.

"I'll kiss you every moment possible," he promised.

And he kissed her.

* * * * *

Maggie K. Black is an award-winning journalist and romantic suspense author with an insatiable love of traveling the world. She has lived in the American South, Europe and the Middle East. She now makes her home in Canada with her history-teacher husband, their two beautiful girls and a small but mighty dog. Maggie enjoys connecting with her readers at maggiekblack.com.

Books by Maggie K. Black

Love Inspired Suspense

Undercover Protection
Surviving the Wilderness

Alaska K-9 Unit

Wilderness Defender
Christmas K-9 Protectors
"Holiday Heist"

Protected Identities

Christmas Witness Protection
Runaway Witness
Christmas Witness Conspiracy

Visit the Author Profile page
at LoveInspired.com for more titles.

WILDERNESS DEFENDER

Maggie K. Black

And the Lord God said,
It is not good that the man should be alone.
—*Genesis* 2:18

To all those who are trying to do it all
and all those stepping in to help others

ONE

Despite the bright blue of the May sky above, a chill cut through the Alaskan air that sent shivers of trepidation running down Trooper Poppy Walsh's spine. Her eyes scanned the empty windows of Glacier Bay National Park's remote cabins. The place was deserted, still awaiting the flocks of tourists who'd arrive in the coming weeks when things really kicked off for the season.

It was the unwelcomed guests who might've been squatting here as they illegally hunted defenseless bear cubs that she and her K-9 partner, Stormy, were here to sniff out. The body of a known poacher had been found shot dead and floating in the water by park troopers. Rumor among the locals was that his fellow poachers had turned on him after they captured a cub and that they were now hunting the park for the baby bear's sibling.

Poppy glanced around the towering spruce and made sure they were alone. Then she reached over and unclipped the Irish wolfhound from her leash. She ran her hand along Stormy's shaggy gray fur, feeling the dog's tension radiating through her fingers. Standing at almost three feet tall on all fours, with a friendly hound-dog face and a protective guardian nature, it took a lot to put the dog on edge. Did Stormy detect something? Or was she just reflecting Poppy's own uneasiness back to her like a mirror?

Poppy prayed and asked God to help her focus. If poachers were hiding out somewhere in the park, that could put tourists' lives in danger, as well as those of the baby animals they captured to sell on the black market. And yet, Poppy's nerves had been frayed ever since the small plane that had brought herself, fellow trooper Will Stryker and their K-9 partners here had taken off from Anchorage. As they'd circled the airstrip of the small town of Gustavus, and she'd looked down to see a scattering of houses give way to a port full of boats, towering trees, majestic glaciers and the roaring Pacific beyond, just one thought had filled her mind—this was where she and Lex Fielding were supposed to go on their honeymoon.

The park ranger had been the reason she'd finally given up her job at Kenai Fjords National Park to become a K-9 trooper. On the night he'd taken her face into his strong hands and asked her to be his wife, her former colleague had told Poppy the deep green of her eyes reminded him of the Glacier Bay's evergreens. He'd promised to bring her here. Just like he'd promised to marry her and to stand by her side for everything life threw at them. Instead, his fear of being anyone's husband or father had apparently wrenched them apart and he'd broken her heart, calling off the wedding just a week before the big day and leaving her with an invisible wound that still ached after all these years. For a moment, Lex's dark serious eyes and rare but generous smile hovered at the edges of her mind. Her chin rose as she shoved thoughts of him away. She was proud of the fact she'd managed to maintain her cool back then... and wouldn't let the memory of Lex impact her now.

The wind rushed past again, rattling the trees and tugging thick sprays of auburn hair from her French braid. Poppy tucked her hair back under her hat. She was a professional, in uniform, with an elite cross-trained poaching and firearms detection K-9 partner by her side. And she had a job to do. No foolish memory of a man who hadn't been ready for commitment was about to shake her focus now. No matter how much she'd once loved him.

Her footsteps strode silently across the mossy ground, moving swiftly from one cabin to the next and letting Stormy take the lead as the wolfhound sniffed for clues. Her phone rang. It was Will, who'd been questioning staff in another part of the park with his K-9 partner about a mile and a half away, where the remnants of drug use had been found. She answered.

"Hey," she said. "Looks like we've still got a cell signal." They'd been warned once they got much farther into the national park cell reception would go dead. "Find anything?"

"Not yet," Will replied. He was a solid trooper, with a knack for handling conflict with humor. But even over the phone, she could hear the tension in his voice. "Have you found anything unusual or out of the ordinary?"

"No, not yet. We've cleared thirteen cabins so far and are approaching the fourteenth now. What kind of unusual should we be on the lookout for?"

Will blew out a breath.

"I don't know exactly," her colleague admitted. "I just have this sense that someone here's not being fully honest with us, about something. I can't tell what. I just know I don't like it."

Stormy growled softly. Poppy glanced down. The dog's posture had straightened, and fur was standing at the back of her neck.

"I've got to go," she said. "Stormy senses something in one of the cabins ahead."

She started toward them slowly. The dog's skill set combined with Poppy's background of working as a wildlife trooper had made them a solid team for investigating illegal hunting and poaching.

"I'm actually done here and heading your way," Will said. Between the shuffle of what sounded like boots on a wooden floor and the jingle of what she guessed were his K-9 partner Scout's dog tags, it sounded like they were already on the move. "I'm going to take one of the park's ATVs."

"Sounds good." She wasn't surprised that he didn't suggest she wait for him. Protocol was that waiting for backup was a judgment call and as Stormy wasn't tracking anyone she didn't expect to find much more than a few bullet cases or maybe some gunpowder. She and Stormy had walked into far worse alone, and Poppy remained endlessly thankful she'd always worked with the kind of folks who didn't treat the male and female troopers any differently in that regard. She'd always been blessed with the people she'd worked with. Even if some, like Lex's former best friend, Johnny Blair, had made some pretty bad life decisions. Alaska was a place where nobody sat around whining and people stepped up to get stuff done. Which is why, even before she'd managed to get the venue and catering deposit back from the canceled wedding that Lex had run out on, she'd already been applying to trooper jobs in Anchorage and packing for a fresh start.

She clenched her jaw. Once again, she was thinking about Lex. *Come on, you're better than that!*

"By the way, there's a park ranger heading your way," Will added. "Says he apparently knows you from back when you worked in Kenai Fjords National Park."

"Okay, thanks." In Alaska, the role of game wardens were played by a specialized type of state trooper, called wildlife troopers. Thankfully, when she'd needed a fresh start, Colonel Lorenza Gallo, one of the first female Alaskan state troopers, had taken her on as part of her incredibly talented and professional K-9 team. Lex might've knocked her down, but thanks to hard work and the kindness of others, she'd definitely landed on her feet.

Stormy growled again and her nose strained toward the next cabin "She's indicating that whatever we're after is in cabin sixteen," Poppy said. "Talk in a bit."

They ended the call and she slid her phone into her jacket pocket. Then she looked down at Stormy. The dog's keen eyes met hers under huge and shaggy brows. There was a floppy, mop-like and almost goofy quality to the huge dog's face that was disarming and friendly. But this was coupled with an intense power, speed and strength that made the dog a formidable foe against hostile people and wild animals alike. "Okay, let's do this. Show me what you've found."

The door swung open at her touch, and the smell of pine filled her senses. Poppy noted that the cabin's main room was simple and empty, with basic wood furniture and two doors ahead. At her signal, Stormy stepped inside and she followed, hearing the floorboards creak beneath their steps. The wolfhound sniffed the air, then signaled toward the second of the closed doors.

Something creaked behind her. The ambush hit swiftly and without warning.

A pair of hands grabbed Poppy by the throat with a tight, pincerlike grip, strangling the air from her lungs and yanking her backward and out of the cabin before she could even reach her weapon. She heard the sound of Stormy barking furiously, a weapon fire and then a door slam, trapping the dog inside the cabin. Desperately, Poppy clawed at the fingers pressing into her windpipe, thrashing against her attacker's grasp and struggling to breathe. Prayers for help surged through her heart. The grip on her throat tightened and darkness swam before her eyes. A male voice swore. Then she felt a second, larger pair of hands grab on to her legs, lifting her up off the ground.

Lex Fielding drove, cutting down the narrow dirt path between the towering trees. Branches slapped the side of his park ranger truck, and rocks spun beneath his wheels. All the while, words cascaded through his mind, clattering and colliding in a mass of disjointed ideas that didn't even begin to come close to what he wanted to say to Poppy. Years ago, he'd had no clue how to explain to the most incredible woman he'd ever known that he didn't think he was ready to get married and have a family. He might not have even had the guts to tell her all his doubts, if she hadn't called him out on it after he'd left a really unfortunate and accidental pocket-dial message on Poppy's voice mail admitting to his mother he wasn't ready to get married.

Not that he'd ever told Poppy that's who the conversation had been with.

He'd have thought, as he'd grown and evolved over the past few years, he'd have come up with something better to say to the woman he'd once loved so fiercely than the tired and hollow clichés now filling his mind. *"It's not you, it's me... You were perfect. I was the problem."* Something about being around Poppy had always made him feel like a better man than he had any right being. Even standing beside her made him feel an inch taller. He just hadn't thought he'd been cut out to be anyone's husband. Something he'd then proved a couple of years later by marrying the wrong woman and surviving a couple of unhappy years together before she'd tragically died in a car crash. Yet, amid all that, God had blessed them with a son—an incredible baby boy named Danny, who was now the center of Lex's world.

He heard the chaos ahead before he could even see it through the thick forest. A dog was barking furiously, voices were shouting, and above it all was a loud and relentless banging sound, like something was trying to break down one of the cabins from the inside.

He whispered a prayer and asked God for wisdom. Hadn't been big on prayer outside of church on Sundays back when he'd been planning on marrying Poppy. But ever since Danny had been born, he'd been relying on it more and more to get through the day.

Then the trees parted, just in time to see the two figures directly in front of him dragging something across the road. His heart stopped.

Not something. *Someone.*

They had Poppy.

He swerved hard, almost clipping his truck's right-side mirror as he came to a stop between two trees. His eyes took in the scene in a glance. Both people were in hunting camouflage, their faces obscured by hats and bandannas with only a slit of eyes showing, but at a glance they seemed to be men. A lanky one had Poppy around the shoulders, with one hand clamped over her mouth. His heavier cohort was trying to keep hold of her feet as she kicked and thrashed against them. Her hat had fallen from her head, sending auburn hair flying loose around her face. And above it all, the sound of banging and howling rose. Sounded like they'd locked her K-9 partner in the cabin and the dog was determined to bust out.

He yanked his weapon, leaped from the truck and aimed the firearm between the larger kidnapper's eyes.

"Let her go!" he shouted. "Now!"

The bigger assailant turned, dropping Poppy's feet. But the thinner one yanked her back against him like a human shield with one hand and pulled a gun with the other. Lex rolled as the man fired, his bullet flying into the bushes behind where Lex had been standing. He crouched up behind a tree and hoped he wouldn't have to take a life, even though he would without hesitation to save Poppy.

Long, tense moments passed.

Lex breathed a prayer, then let off a warning shot, sending it high in the canopy of fir branches above their heads. The men froze, like animals did in his truck's headlights in that perilous moment when he didn't know if they were going to flee or charge.

"Park ranger!" Lex shouted. "Let her go. Now!"

Poppy swung her elbows back, hard and fast, catching the man holding her square in the jaw before he could fire again and knocking his camo hat off, revealing a shiny bald head underneath. He grunted, dropped her and then turned and ran for the trees with his beefy accomplice on his heels. Within seconds they'd disappeared into the trees. She crumpled to the ground.

"Poppy!" Her name flew from his lips as he ran for her and dropped to her side like a baseball player sliding home. His arms wrapped around her, pulling her into his chest as he knelt beside her on the ground. Her eyes fluttered closed. *Please, Lord, let her be okay.* He brushed his hand along her check, his fingertips tangling in her hair as he felt for her pulse. Red welts rose on her neck from her attacker's grasp. He leaned forward, feeling for the reassurance of her labored breath on his cheek.

"It's okay, Poppy," he rasped. "I'm here. It's me, Lex. I've got you. You're safe."

Her eyes snapped open, deep green and devastatingly beautiful. A pink flush brushed her cheeks. Despite every moment he'd spent trying to convince himself his memories of her were just idealized nonsense, she was even fiercer in person than he'd remembered.

"Lex?" she asked. She reached up and pushed back against his chest. He let her go. "What are you—?"

But before she could finish, a deafening crash filled the air.

TWO

His head snapped toward the cabin in time to see the door smash open, crashing onto the ground. A deep, determined and guttural growl filled the air as a huge mass of gray fur flew toward him. A wolf? A bear? All he knew for sure was that it was barreling into him in a fury, snarling its teeth, knocking him back and pinning him on the ground.

"Stormy!" Poppy's voice rose. "Stand down!"

Instantly the beast leaped off him and sat obediently. Catching his breath, Lex sat up and eyed Poppy's ferocious protector. Stormy was like no dog he'd ever seen before. The Irish wolfhound was huge, with a friendly shaggy face that reminded him of Danny's stuffed toys. Stormy's tail thumped and it looked almost like she was smiling. Then the dog's eyebrows quirked, and she whimpered slightly as if apologizing to him.

For a moment, a well of conflicting emotions seemed to churn in the depths of Poppy's eyes. Tension rose up his spine as he braced himself for a well-deserved tirade from woman he hadn't spoken to since he'd broken her heart days before their wedding. Then she blinked hard, and suddenly the look on her face was so professional it was almost as if he was a stranger.

"I'm sorry about that," Poppy said. "She's really very gentle." Tell that to the cabin door he'd have to fix. Poppy ran her hand over the back of the dog's head. "She'd worked up a pretty big head of steam and probably couldn't stop in time. Trust me, if she'd actually tried to take you down, you'd feel it."

Oh, he already felt it plenty. It was like being hit by a small and furry dirt bike. He stumbled to his feet, hesitated and then reached for Poppy's hand, eyeing Stormy to make sure the K-9 was okay with it. The dog didn't blink.

"Are you okay?" he said. The welts on her neck were already fading, but his chest still ached to remember how vicious the kidnapping attempt had been. "It looked pretty rough."

"I'm fine." Poppy got to her feet without taking his hand. "Trust me, I've handled worse."

He didn't doubt it. She scooped her attacker's camo hat up off the ground, waved it under the dog's nose and told the dog to track it. The wolfhound's ears perked. She woofed enthusiastically and took off running through the forest in the direction the men had gone. He heard the sound of branches crashing in her wake.

"My colleague will be here any second with an ATV," she told him. "I'll take it and go after her. Sometimes, when a K-9's chasing down a suspect, it's better to let them have a head start, than slow them down."

"That's one powerful animal you have there," Lex remarked.

"Stormy is a trooper and my partner," she said. There was something about her tone that almost made him

feel reprimanded and he was suddenly reminded of
how hard she'd pushed him to apply to become a state
trooper himself instead of staying "just" a park ranger.
"Irish wolfhounds can run top speed of forty miles an
hour, plus she's more adept at running though terrain
like this than most people. She'll catch those thugs,
unless they've got a vehicle stashed somewhere. If she
finds evidence, she'll protect it until I arrive."

He'd seen K-9 troopers let their dogs go in manhunts
before, and then follow the sound of a suspect shouting
for the dog to let their arm go. Usually they were eager
to surrender when the trooper caught up and ordered
the dog to release them.

"I didn't know you were a K-9 officer," he admitted,
"well, at least not until your partner told me you were the
Trooper Walsh who'd flown out from Anchorage with
him." After all, she had disappeared pretty thoroughly
from his life when he'd called off their engagement.

"Yup." She ran her hands down her legs, and he
couldn't tell if she was trying to wipe the dirt off her
palms, her slacks or both. "Out of Anchorage. We're a
pretty great team."

"I'm really glad," he said quietly. "And congrats.
I know how much you wanted to work with the K-9
unit. Not that you weren't incredible at your other job.
Honestly, you were the best wildlife trooper I'd ever
worked with."

She shot him a sharp glance and Lex hoped he hadn't
just implied he was relieved that she hadn't given up a
career she was amazing at because of him. That was ridiculous. A woman as driven and determined as Poppy
could never have been derailed by a man like him.

"I'm going to go check out the cabin," she said, then

turned and stepped over the remains of the broken door. She scooped her phone up off the floor, dialed a number and put it to her ear. "Will," she said. "It's Poppy."

Lex's eyes scanned the cabin as he listened to Poppy fill her fellow trooper in. Her update was simple, straightforward and professional. The cabin was vacant except for an empty carton of bullets, cigarette butts and candy wrappers in the second bedroom. Whoever had been hiding out here hadn't been there long. He spotted her wide-brimmed hat lying on the floor behind the door. He picked it up and then followed her back out. She ended the call, turned to face him, and he felt his breath catch. How could she still have such an impact on him after all these years? Even disheveled and injured, she was even more beautiful, strong and focused than he remembered.

It was unbelievable to think this woman had almost been his wife.

"He'll be here in seconds by the sound of it," she said. "Then he'll search the cabin more thoroughly with his K-9 partner. Scout's a drug-detecting dog."

He held up her hat, she reached for it and their fingertips brushed on the brim. They lingered there, their hands barely touching. He swallowed hard.

"I'm sorry, by the way," he said. "Even if I can't figure out quite how to say it."

A question lingered in her eyes. "Sorry for what?"

Did she really need to hear him say it? They both knew full well what Lex had done. He'd left her out on a limb to plan their wedding entirely by herself, failed to show up for every significant appointment, from catering to venue, and then only admitted he was having cold feet a week before the wedding when she called him out on it.

"For everything," he said.

She paused for a long moment. Her deep green eyes searched his as if looking for something. Then she looked away, tugged the hat from his hands and put it on firmly.

A two-seated ATV pulled into the clearing. Trooper Will Stryker had dark hair, broad shoulders and the kind of smile that implied he'd also seen his share of pain. His K-9 partner, a black-and-white shaggy border collie, sat on a blanket in a storage basket on the back. Will raised a hand in greeting as Poppy strode over to him.

"Are you okay?" The trooper's eyebrow rose. "Looks like you've been put through the wringer."

"I'm fine," she said. "Mind if I borrow that to go after Stormy?"

"Be my guest." Will hopped off the ATV and signaled for Scout to follow. He nodded to Lex and despite his amiable grin Lex couldn't shake the feeling he was being evaluated. "I hear you two used to work together."

"Actually, we were engaged to be married," Poppy clarified, with a shrug that hit Lex like a punch in the gut. "Didn't work out."

How could she blurt something like that out so casually? Then again, she'd shown practically no emotion when they'd broken up. She hadn't cried, let alone tried to talk him out of calling off the wedding. This woman had been his entire world. Not a day had gone by since he'd regretted breaking her heart.

Hadn't he meant anything to her?

Moments later, Lex and Poppy were driving through the trees, following the bent branches Stormy had left in her wake. Lex hadn't met her eye since Poppy had told Will that they used to be engaged. Had it bothered him that she'd been so blunt about it? Will was a thorough investigator, as were the rest of her team. If any one of them took a look into Lex it wouldn't be long before someone stumbled onto the fact they'd once been planning to get married. Or maybe she'd blurted it out to show Lex what a good job she'd done getting over him, despite how rattled her heart had been when she'd opened her eyes to find his strong arms around her and his dark, handsome face hovering above hers.

Lex's cell phone buzzed. He pulled it out, glanced at the screen and slid it back into his pocket. Then she heard a familiar woof.

"Stormy!" she called.

The dog was standing guard in a clearing over a set of tire tracks. Poppy leaped off the ATV as Lex pulled to a stop. She signaled to her partner and Stormy trotted over.

"Good dog," she said. Stormy butted her head into Poppy's hand, and she ran her fingers over the back of the dog's shaggy head. "It's okay. We'll get them next time."

Lex climbed off the ATV, got out his phone again and took a picture of the tracks.

"I can send these to you for your team," he offered. "I can tell you right now they're no different from the usual ATV tracks we see from trespassers around here. Despite how vast and remote this place is, we have a major problem with people trespassing and illegal hunting." He frowned, deepening the lines between his eyes, and she was reminded of Will's suspicion that they weren't getting the full story. Was Lex keeping something from them? "Not like this, though."

His phone buzzed again; Lex gave it another swift glanced and didn't answer. Then his phone began to ring and he sent it through to voice mail. Who was so intent on reaching him? And why was he ignoring them?

"You want to tell me what that's about?" she asked, gesturing to his phone.

"Don't worry about it," Lex said. "It's just something I need to sort out."

"But is it related to the poachers?" she pressed. "Because if it is and you're withholding information…"

Her voice trailed off as she watched his jaw set firmly.

"Yes, it might be," he said. "And I will fill you in fully. But later. Please, just give me some time. I need to talk to someone first."

Okay, then. She could hardly force him to tell her what she wanted to know any more than she could force any other witness or source on a case. The trooper inside her still wanted to press him for answers. But the woman who'd once loved this man, and expected to spend the rest of her life with him, knew how much Lex hated being pushed into anything and how stubborn it made him when she tried. Usually the only thing that worked to make him open up was to wait until he'd sorted out whatever was going on inside his brain.

Sometimes not even then, she reminded herself. If it hadn't been for the accidental message he'd left on her answering machine she might've never known he had cold feet about marrying her.

But thinking about that is hardly going to help me with this case now, is it?

There was no way Stormy would fit in the storage cage on the back of the ATV like Scout had. So they drove back slowly, while Stormy ran alongside.

"I have a source," Lex said after what felt like an extremely long silence. "He tipped me off to the fact that the two poachers had turned on a third poacher and murdered him, and that a bear cub had been captured for illegal sale. I promised I'd try to keep his name out of it and solve this without involving him, if I could. But I warned him it might not be possible."

His phone rang again and once again he declined the call.

"Is that him?" she asked.

Lex didn't answer. He also didn't meet her gaze. An unsettled feeling climbed up her spine that reminded her too much of the past. Right, so he was definitely hiding something.

"Will suspects someone here is not being fully honest with us," she added. "Are you?"

"Hang on," he said. "I might as well brief you both at once."

She could see the cabin up ahead now. Will and Scout were outside waiting for them. Lex stopped the ATV, they got off and she filled Will in about the tire tracks. He hadn't found anything new in the cabins, either.

"Poppy...uh, Trooper Walsh wondered if there were any significant facts that I might not have filled you in on yet," Lex said, turning to the other man. "As I mentioned to her, I did receive a tip from a local that illegal hunters were poaching bear cubs on one of the glaciers and had killed one of their crew."

"And where did your source get the tip?" Will interjected.

"Claims he overheard someone talking about it at a local hangout," Lex said.

"And is that credible?" Will pressed.

"I believed him." His arms crossed. "Anyway, a colleague and I did an aerial search and spotted a tranquilized mother bear, which we believed to be a black bear. Farther along, we spotted a man's body in the water who turned out to be a known poacher with a long criminal record for illegal hunting and several warrants out in his name. He'd been shot at point-blank range."

This much they'd already known when the team had been called in to investigate from Anchorage, Poppy thought. The fact Lex had a secret source was new, though.

"By the time we returned by boat and retrieved the body, the bear was long gone," Lex continued. "But there was evidence there'd been a second bear cub hiding in a tree nearby. This matched the tip I'd gotten that had said the poachers were after two bear cubs—one of which it seems has now been captured alive to be sold and the other which the poachers are still after."

"Any idea why the poachers turned on each other and killed one of their own?" Poppy asked.

"Money apparently," Lex said. "Greed. Nothing more complicated than one guy just deciding he wanted a bigger piece of the pie."

Poppy thought of the two men who'd attacked her and wondered if that meant one of them would eventually kill the other to keep all the money from the illegal sale for himself.

Will frowned. "No honor among thieves."

Lex ran his hand along the back of his neck.

"There's one more thing," Lex added, "and I'd like you to keep it confidential within your team, please. My source tells me the cub they captured was a blue bear."

Poppy gasped, but her colleague just blinked.

"What's a blue bear?" Will asked.

"Blue bears are also known as glacier bears," Poppy explained. "They're pretty rare and have a silvery gray fur that can look bluish in some lights. They can only be found in Alaska, and people come from all over the world to our national parks in the hopes of seeing one."

She glanced at Lex, wondering if he wanted to add anything; instead, he just nodded as if telling her to keep going. An unfamiliar warmth filled her core. He had always respected her, even when they'd been at their worst.

"They do look a lot like black bears," she added. "Some are only silvery on their underbelly and paws, and there are cases of black bears having blue cubs or vice versa, due to crossbreeding. So, it is completely possible for park wardens to think they'd seen a black mother bear that was tranquilized but that her cubs were blue."

"Right," Lex said. "I hope you can understand why we'd want to keep this news under wraps for now. The news of blue bear cubs would definitely be a huge draw to the national park. But, according to my source, the poachers were as surprised as we are by this and started fighting among themselves when they realized they could get thousands more than they'd expected. They haven't found a buyer yet and want to capture the second cub and sell them together." A muscle ticked in his jaw. "What we don't want to do is put the cubs in further danger or help the poachers jack up the price or attract a wider pool of buyers by publicizing things."

Lex's phone buzzed again. This time he held up a finger and took the call.

"Sorry," he said. "I've got to take this." He took three steps away and held the phone to his ear. "Hey, Mom.

What's up?... Uh-huh... Yup... Okay, I'm on my way. Tell him Daddy will be there soon."

Daddy? The single word seemed to knock the air from Poppy's lungs. *The man who wouldn't start a family with her was now a father?*

Lex turned back; his face had paled, and although he glanced at both her and Will, something made her feel like his words were directed to her alone.

"I've got to go," Lex said. "I have a son. His name is Danny. He's two and my mom thinks she saw someone watching him over the back fence."

THREE

Poppy felt her lips part but no words come out. She'd longed to have a child back when they were engaged and had spent hours agonizing over the fact she desperately wanted to start a family and Lex didn't. Finally, she'd made peace with marrying him, anyway, praying that one day God would change his heart and he'd be ready.

Instead, he'd started a family with someone else.

"Do you think there's a connection between someone spying on your son and the poaching case?" Will asked. Gratitude flooded over her that her colleague was focusing on what mattered even while she was left reeling.

"I expect so," Lex said, and started walking back toward his truck. His voice was grave. "It's too much of a coincidence to be otherwise."

Poppy forced herself to pray for focus. This was about so much more than her own broken heart or the shattered dreams of her past. Stormy's head butted against her leg. She reached down and ran her hand through her partner's soft fur.

"One of us should go with you," Will said.

"It should be me," Poppy announced, heading for the truck. "Stormy is trained in tracking people. If whoever was watching Lex's son left anything behind, Stormy and I can track them."

Lex hesitated a moment and then he nodded. "Yeah, you're right."

He opened the back door of his truck for Stormy to climb inside. It was only then that Poppy noticed the car seat strapped in the back. Stormy curled up into a ball on the seat beside it. Poppy told Will she'd check in with him later and got in the passenger side, and then they were off.

For a long moment, Lex didn't say anything. Neither did she. Instead, she turned her eyes toward the window and watched the trees as they drove past. What could she even say? Lex had known he'd been the only man in the entire world she'd wanted to have a family with when he'd rejected her and called off their wedding. And their past didn't even rank up there in the top three things she had to worry about right now. They drove through the main gates of Glacier Bay National Park and started toward the tiny town of Gustavus.

"I've spent so much time trying to figure out how I'd ever tell you about this," Lex admitted gruffly. "Even now, I have no idea where to start…"

The sound of his voice turned her attention back to his face. He was staring straight ahead. His eyes were locked on the road in front of him and his hands gripped the wheel exactly at ten and two. She hadn't even thought to check for a wedding ring, but now noticed he wasn't wearing one.

"I met Debra through mutual friends about a year and a half after you and I stopped seeing each other." He spoke quickly, like he was giving a necessary briefing of unpleasant information he didn't want to convey.

Not like a man with feelings who had a heart beating in his chest that had ever loved someone. "We fought a lot and she had a lot of personal problems. I thought getting married would fix things. It didn't. Then I thought having a baby would make things better."

His voice trailed off and he sighed. Poppy waited.

"She started traveling to Juneau after Danny was born to see her mother," he continued. "When Danny was six months old, she admitted she thought marrying me had been a mistake. She hated living here and we were separated when she died in a car crash. She'd been driving on a rural road, late at night, in a storm. It looks like either a bear or some other large animal charged at her car and she swerved off the road trying to avoid it. Not her fault. Debra was an anxious driver and it was just one of those tragic accidents that could happen to anyone on these roads. Mom moved out here to help me raise Danny."

He fell quiet again for a long moment.

"I'm sorry," she said eventually, not really knowing what else to say.

"I don't want to sound like I'm putting all the blame on her," he said. "For the failed marriage, I mean. I've spent a lot of time in prayer asking God to forgive me for my shortcomings and examining the mistakes I made so I could become a better man."

There was something about the way he said it that made her think that maybe he hadn't forgiven himself yet.

"She really loved Danny," Lex went on, "and Gustavus isn't an easy place to live. It takes a certain type of person to choose to be happy here. Debra loved it in the summer when the town was full of thousands of tourists. It's a lot harder in the winter, though, when it's dark and cold all day, and only a few hundred people."

He pulled the truck to a stop at the side of the road, then turned and looked at her.

"I don't expect you to understand," Lex said. "But after I got cold feet with you, I was so afraid of making the same mistake twice that I jumped in too fast with Debra and made other mistakes."

For a moment, his eyes lingered on hers. The space between them seemed to shrink.

Was he saying that not marrying her had been a mistake?

He opened the truck door and got out, waving her to follow. She looked up. They were parked outside a large three-story house that looked like a lodge. Cheerful wind chimes hung from the long and covered front porch. A tiny calico kitten, not much bigger than a teacup, was curled up in the large front window and a wooden sign out front welcomed her to the Hope's Nest Bed and Breakfast. Poppy got out, opened the back door and signaled for Stormy to join her. Then she hung back by the truck and watched as Lex hurried up the steps of the sprawling wooden front porch.

The door opened and Lex's mother stepped out, her long gray hair tied back in a bun and a warm smile on her face. A little boy with short and tousled brown hair that seemed to stick up in all possible directions wriggled in her hold, squealing and reaching out for his father as Lex grew closer. Moments later, Lex gathered Danny into his arms, and the toddler snuggled against him as he whispered something into the little boy's ear.

Something tugged painfully in her heart. She'd always suspected that Lex would be a wonderful father. It was another thing to see it with her own eyes.

Lex turned and started down the front steps toward Poppy, with his son in his clutches and his mother in tow.

"Poppy, this is my son, Danny," he said. His smile beamed. "And you remember my mother, Gillian."

"I do." She'd always gotten along so well with Lex's mom that Gillian had even stepped in to help with things like dealing with the wedding venue and arranging the seating plan when Lex hadn't. If Poppy was honest, she'd been surprised Gillian hadn't managed to talk her son into not calling off the wedding. She hesitated for a moment, not quite knowing if she should shake the older woman's hand or hug her. But Gillian opened her arms and stepped forward.

"Welcome, Poppy!" Lex's mother said. Happiness crinkled her eyes as they embraced. "It's so wonderful that you're the one who was sent here to help Lex with this case."

Something about her tone left Poppy wondering if Gillian thought God had sent her.

"Doggy!" Danny squealed, and waved both hands toward Stormy.

Poppy felt a smile cross her lips.

"Her name is Stormy," she said. "She's a very special dog."

"Big doggy!" The toddler's eyes grew wide. "Big and f'uffy."

"Yes," she murmured. "Stormy is very big and fluffy."

Lex chuckled softly and led them around the side of the house. The yard was surrounded by a four-foot-tall fence. Poppy noticed the gate had a solid clasp but wasn't locked.

"Where are you and Stormy staying?" Gillian asked her.

"My colleague, Will Stryker, and I are staying at a motel just outside of town," she said. "It was the only place open that allowed dogs."

"Ugh, that place," Gillian said. Her nose wrinkled, and Poppy wasn't surprised. The motel was pretty run-down and didn't smell all that great, either. They'd be having their team meeting by video chat on a rickety metal folding table later that night. She hadn't even unpacked yet. "Well, you and Will, and your dogs, are very welcome to stay here."

"Thank you," Poppy said. "I really appreciate it."

Not that she was planning on taking Lex's mother up on the offer.

Suddenly finding herself face-to-face with Lex after all these years was already wreaking more than enough havoc on her heart and mind. Staying with him, his mother and adorable little son was more than she could handle.

"He was right over here," Gillian indicated. They crossed the backyard, passing a child's playhouse, swing set and sandbox, and walked over to the fence. "Danny was playing in the sand and I was watching him from the back porch when I saw a large a man in a camo hunting jacket standing right over here. He had a bandanna over this face. I called out to him and he ran."

Sounded just like one of her two kidnappers. Poppy glanced at Lex and watched as he shuddered. She climbed the back fence and directed Stormy to follow. The dog leaped over in a bound and started sniffing the area. But after a few minutes of searching, both she and the dog came up empty. They rejoined her ex and his family on the other side.

"And you're sure he was watching Danny?" Lex asked.

"Sure seemed that way," Gillian said. "I wondered at first if he was an early tourist walking around. But he had his hat pulled pretty low over his head and that bandanna pulled up over his face. If I hadn't known any better, I would've thought it was your friend Johnny. But even though Johnny hasn't been around in a while I'd have hoped he'd have known to just walk up and said hi."

Poppy froze.

Did she mean Johnny Blair? He was back in Lex's life? Lex's friend from childhood had worked with them both at the national park, before he'd been fired for stealing months before the wedding. That on top of a rap sheet full of trouble including selling cigarettes to tourists younger than twenty-one, poaching small animals and hustling tourists at darts and pool. Last she'd heard, the two men were estranged and had fallen out of touch.

Even then, Lex had insisted on dropping by in person to invite Johnny to their wedding when he didn't respond to RSVP to his invitation despite the bad blood with those they'd worked with.

It had been one of the last things she and Lex had fought about. Especially after Lex refused to either confirm or deny that Johnny had been the person he'd been admitting his doubts to on that pocket-dial message that had led to their breakup. Lex said it didn't actually matter who he'd been talking to when he confessed that he sometimes wanted to call off the wedding. But Poppy had suspected that whoever it was had talked Lex into ending it.

She waited until Gillian turned and walked back to the house.

"Johnny's here in Gustavus?" she asked. "What is he doing here? Is that who you've been hiding calls from? Tell me he's not your source."

Lex didn't answer, but one glance in his eyes told her everything she needed to know.

Johnny Blair, the deadbeat former friend with a criminal record who she suspected might've talked Lex into ending their engagement, was also the one who'd told Lex about the blue bear poachers.

Something hardened in Lex's heart as he watched Poppy's lip curl. For all her wonderful qualities, she'd never understood why he'd never given up on Johnny, despite the mistakes he'd made. She didn't get how people who were in a rough place in life needed someone who believed in them and didn't shut them out. Things had always come so easy for her—reaching goals, achieving in school, standing out and getting hired. She'd never known what it was like to struggle with things, let alone need a second chance.

Which might be why Lex had never thought to ask her for one.

His mother had gone into the house, no doubt to put the kettle on and rustle up some cookies. Which gave the two of them time to talk privately.

"Yes," he said. "Johnny moved out here last year when he'd fallen on hard times. We hadn't talked in a while and I was hoping getting away from the temptations in Anchorage would help him restart his life. I tried to get him a job at the park, but it didn't work out." Lex blew out a breath. "He met a woman, who was also new to town, and they hit it off. He got a job doing maintenance for her brother's new air-tourism charter business and stayed to be with her. Johnny said he didn't want trouble, so I promised to keep his name out of it, if I could."

Which Lex might not be able to do anymore now that Poppy had been attacked.

"He's got a criminal record," Poppy reminded him. She didn't even try to hide the disdain in her voice.

"He's a man who's made some mistakes and is trying to get his life back together." Like Lex himself had with the grace of God and the help of people like his mother. Although, thankfully, he had never gotten involved in illegal activity or anything remotely like that. "We're not particularly close now, truth be told. Hadn't seen him in months when he dropped by one night and told me he'd overheard some out-of-towners talking about poaching baby bear cubs down at the local watering hole."

"So a bar?" Poppy asked. "So, he's back to drinking and hustling tourists again?"

She could've at least tried to camouflage the disgust in her voice. Truth was, Johnny had promised Lex up and down for months that he'd stopped drinking or going to places like that. Which is why Lex had been so shocked and disappointed when Johnny had shamefacedly told him that was where he'd gotten his intel. He almost hadn't wanted to believe it.

"It's not an official bar," Lex said. "One of the local guys has a big triple garage out back of his farm, with some picnic tables and a fire pit, that he sort of runs an unlicensed hangout at."

Poppy rolled her eyes. "Perfect."

He fought the urge to try to explain, yet again, why trying to lend a helping hand to old pals like Johnny mattered so much to him. Truth was, back when he and Poppy had been dating in Anchorage, their evenings together had all too often been interrupted by some former friend or another that Lex hadn't spoken to in eons who needed to be bailed out of jail for fighting or given a ride home after getting too drunk to drive. He hadn't minded. Thanks to his mom's strong faith and strict rules while he was growing up, Lex knew he was the token "good guy" from that old bunch people still knew they could call on.

But she didn't get it.

How *could* she? Poppy hadn't gone through hardship like he had. She didn't know what it was like to grow up poor, have her father walk out and be reliant on the kindness of others. Moreover, she had no clue what it was like to barely make it through school and struggle to make ends meet, or to have to put her life back together after it fell apart. So yes, the truth also was that Johnny had been texting and calling repeatedly for the past half hour, and Lex hadn't called him back because he figured it was less important than what was going on with Poppy.

Danny squirmed in his arms to be put down. Lex complied, without even realizing the toddler would make a beeline for Stormy as fast as his little legs would take him.

"Big doggy!" he squealed.

"Danny!" Lex started after him.

But before he could catch the little boy, Poppy waved her hand in a quick and furtive motion. Immediately the dog dropped to the ground, lying on its stomach in front of the little boy. Danny barreled into Stormy, head-butting the dog in greeting and then throwing his arms around her. Stormy licked the boy's cheek gently. Danny giggled and flopped onto the grass beside Stormy, his arms still locked around the dog's neck. "Doggy like me, Daddy! Doggy very silly!"

Lex exhaled.

"Stormy's great with children," Poppy said softly under her breath.

He watched as his tiny son and the huge dog rolled together on the grass.

"Thanks for that signal thing you did that got her to drop and for letting him play with her," he said. "Sorry, I didn't think to ask before setting him down."

"No problem." Something seemed to soften in her gaze as she watched Danny and the wolfhound play together. "You need to let me talk to Johnny," she added. "Regardless of our history, I'm a state trooper, I'm investigating this case and he has information about poaching and a murder."

"I know," Lex acknowledged. "You're right." He'd just been hoping he wouldn't have to ask that of Johnny. His friend didn't trust the authorities and would likely see it as a betrayal. "I agree it has to be done."

"Or Will Stryker could do it," she offered.

"No, it should be you," he said, turning to face her. "I know you think Johnny never liked you, but he always did respect you."

His phone was buzzing and even without glancing

at the screen he knew from the ringtone it was Johnny calling again. There was no time like the present.

He cleared his throat, then answered.

"Hey, Johnny," he said. "Sorry for not calling back sooner. But you'll never guess who I'm standing next to."

"Lex?" The voice was female, breathless, panicked and full of tears.

"Ripley?" Lex asked. Why did Johnny's girlfriend have his phone? "Are you okay? What's going on? Where's Johnny?"

She gasped a sob.

"A man broke into Johnny's house," she said. "He locked me in a cupboard and got Johnny tied up in the kitchen. He's threatening to kill him if he doesn't tell them who he told about the blue bears."

FOUR

Poppy watched as Lex's face paled. He turned and ran back across the yard.

"Stay hidden!" he called into the phone. "Don't make a sound. I'm on my way."

She had no clue who Ripley was or where Lex was running to. But the look on his face told her everything she needed to know. Someone's life was in danger and Lex was determined to save her. Poppy signaled to Stormy and in an instant her K-9 partner was by her side.

"Whatever happens don't hang up," Lex was telling Ripley. In a seamless motion he scooped Danny up with one arm and cradled him to his chest as he sprinted toward the house. Without a word, Gillian stepped back out onto the back porch and Lex slid Danny into her arms.

"Everything okay?" Lex's mother asked.

Lex shook his head. "Johnny and his girlfriend are in trouble."

"Go," Gillian said. "I'll take Danny and go to a friend's house for now until I hear from you. Stay safe."

Countless questions cascaded through Poppy's mind

as she watched Lex take in whatever Ripley was telling him about the situation. Then Lex's dark eyes shot
her a glance that answered the only one that mattered
right now.

"Please come with me," he said. "I need your help."

She nodded and they ran around the house and back
through the gate, with Stormy by her side and Lex one
pace ahead of her. They reached his truck, and he threw
open the passenger side door for her and the back door
for Stormy before hurrying around to the driver's side.

"You need to stay quiet," Lex told Ripley. "I'm going
to put my end of the call on mute so none of what's
going on here comes through the phone. But I'm still
here, I'm still listening and I'm on my way. I promise."

Poppy shut Stormy's door, then hopped in, closed her
own and secured her seat belt. Lex slid the phone into
his truck's hands-free holster and started the engine.

"So, again, Ripley is Johnny's girlfriend?" she asked.

"She is," Lex confirmed. He gripped the steering
wheel so tightly his knuckles were white. His eyes
locked on the road ahead. "She filled me in as much as
she could, which isn't much. Here's what I know. Ripley said a man broke into Johnny's house, tied him up
and threatened to kill him if he didn't tell them who all
he told about the blue bears."

In other words: Lex.

She glanced at Stormy in the rearview mirror. The
dog was sitting alert in the back seat, with her ears
perked and her keen eyes on Poppy, ready to get to work
and leap into action. She wondered what it was like to
have as much unwavering trust in anyone as Stormy
did in her.

"Do we have a description?" she asked.

"No, but she says he was disguised in camo."

Same as the two who'd tried to kidnap her in the national park.

"Ripley says he forced her into the living room cupboard and locked her in," Lex added. "Thankfully she found Johnny's phone in his jacket pocket."

"I'm calling Will," she said, "and getting him to meet us there."

Her colleague's phone went straight through to voice mail. Not surprising, based on how unreliable cell signals could be in the area. She relayed the details and how to find Johnny's place in a phone message as Lex rattled them off to her, and then after she hung up, sent him the same details in a text. Poppy wished she'd been able to reach him and couldn't shake the feeling that Will would've had his own out-of-the-box perspective on things, which would've helped equip her for whatever it was they were about to walk into. She'd always liked to get input from others. Even when she thought it was wrong. Which is why Lex's inability to talk through things back in the day had been so hard.

Come on, think. She closed her eyes. *What would the others on my team notice that I've missed?*

They'd have probably honed in on Johnny's criminal record. Then maybe they'd have pointed out that, just like one of Poppy's attackers, Johnny had always been a beefy guy—something Gillian had just confirmed when she'd said the person on the other side of the fence had looked like him. Because of that coincidence they might've told her to be aware she could now be walking into a setup.

Then again, she'd always thought Johnny genuinely

cared about his estranged friend. Would Johnny really lie to Lex and risk putting his pal's life in danger?

She opened her eyes to see an empty rural road and a sea of trees.

"Does Ripley have a history with police?" she asked.

"I don't know," Lex said. "We've never really spoken. I just know Johnny is very protective of her and she moved here from Juneau with her brother, Nolan, to get away from an ex-boyfriend who treated her badly."

"Why did she call you?" she asked.

"Guessing her brother is off giving some people an aerial tour of the glaciers," Lex said. "His airfield's in a pretty remote area."

"But why *you*?" she pressed.

"There's no local law enforcement in Gustavus," Lex said. "Town actually took a vote and decided against it. We do have 911, but it connects you to the fire department, medical emergency or search and rescue. They're all run by volunteers. Anything park-related falls on us park rangers and for anything major we call in the troopers who fly in from Juneau or Anchorage. Like you." He glanced her way and the faintest hint of a sad grin hovered on the edge of his mouth, then it faded again. "No local government, building permits, bylaws or property taxes, either. Gustavus is an interesting place. But it's not for everyone."

His brow furrowed. They drove past scattered buildings as eight minutes ticked by one slow and drawn-out eternity at a time. Silence had fallen from Ripley's end of the phone. Lex took it off mute.

"Ripley?" he called softly. "I'm on my way and almost there. Are you okay?"

No answer. Just some faint and indistinct scuffling sounds came down the phone line. Poppy's heart clenched.

"Ripley." Lex's tone grew urgent. "Can you hear me?"

"Yeah, I'm here." Ripley's voice was soft and terrified. "I'm locked in the cupboard so I can't get out and I can't hear Johnny or anyone anymore."

Lex exhaled. "Just hang tight. I'll be there soon."

Poppy barely saw the unmarked break in the trees before he turned into it and onto an unpaved track so long and narrow she couldn't tell if it was a road or a driveway. Stormy woofed softly, with just the hint of a growl like the threat of an approaching storm.

"What's that?" Ripley's voice rose.

"My friend's dog," Lex said, his voice both soothing and firm like he was trying to reassure a frightened animal. "Don't worry. She's a really great dog and completely gentle and safe. Now just stay calm and hold on. It's going to be okay."

Suddenly the phone went dead and any remaining hint of color drained from Lex's face.

Prayers poured from his lips, asking God to help them reach Ripley and Johnny in time, and she found herself fighting the urge to reach across the front seat and squeeze his hand.

Suddenly it hit her just how dire the situation was. Out here in the wilderness there was no backup, no law enforcement and no team of police about to sweep in and save the day.

All Lex had was her.

Then she saw the ranch house. It was old and run-down with a sloping roof that was missing a few shingles and yet its structure still implying how majestic a home it had once been. The carcasses of half-built and

unbuilt trucks, boats, motorcycles and trailers littered
the lawn. Clothes fluttered on a long laundry line. Lex
pulled to a stop and jumped out. Poppy checked her
phone, saw no message from Will and then ran around
to the back door and opened it for Stormy. Her partner leaped out and Poppy was amazed anew at how
smoothly and silently she could move for an animal
her size.

She clipped Stormy's leash on her harness and ran
her hand over the soft fur at the back of the dog's neck
and said, "Let's go."

Immediately the dog stretched and rose to her full
height like a mythical wolf preparing for battle. Lex
started toward the house, then crouched low behind a
car chassis. Poppy instinctively grabbed a red T-shirt
off the clothesline as they moved to join him, in case
they needed to get Stormy to track Johnny's scent. Even
without giving the dog the command to search, she felt
the leash tighten slightly with a pressure as subtle as
one dancer guiding the other on the dance floor. She
looked down at Stormy. The dog's snout was pointing
farther down the dirt road away from the house. What
did she sense?

"I don't see anything through the windows and the
curtains are drawn," Lex said, "and I'm not hearing so
much as a floorboard creak, so we've got no idea what's
going on in there. But Ripley said she's hiding in the
living room closet and that they're holding Johnny in
the kitchen. I suggest that I go in through the front door
and you head in around the back."

She resisted the urge to point out that she was the
cop, not him. Despite the fact, she'd encouraged him
several times to apply to become a wilderness trooper,

considering how good he was with animals, calm and
steady under pressure, and skilled at both knowing his
way around a weapon and dealing with life-threatening
adversaries from bears to drunkenly violent tourists.
Stormy tugged the leash slightly harder as if to imply
she had an opinion, too.

Poppy waved the shirt under the K-9's nose and whispered, "Search."

Immediately Stormy straightened, turned toward
the path and woofed.

"What's down there?" Poppy asked.

"An old barn Johnny sometimes uses as a garage
slash workshop," Lex said.

"Well, Stormy thinks we need to head there."

"Okay, we can definitely check that out after the
farmhouse."

"No," Poppy said. "I just gave Stormy a T-shirt off
the clothesline to sniff and she thinks we should go
there instead of the farmhouse."

"No offense intended," Lex said as his eyes met hers.
"But she could be smelling anything off that shirt, and
I think that's the wrong call."

He watched as Poppy's eyes widened. He hadn't actually meant to offend her, but figuring out the right
words to say had never been his strong suit. Poppy had
never shied away from jumping in and taking charge of
things. And it's not like they had time to argue.

"Stormy's not some pet." Her chin rose. "She's a
highly trained state trooper."

"I know that—" he started.

"And if she thinks we need to head down the path,
that's good enough for me."

Lex glanced from Poppy, to the house and then to his phone. It had been barely six minutes since Ripley's call had gone dead and he still had no idea what was going on inside there beyond what she'd told him. He gritted his teeth.

"I get that," he said, "but it's also not like she has X-ray vision and can tell us what's going on in that house."

Something flashed in the green depths of Poppy's eyes, determined and strong, like she was gearing up for a fight. In the months after losing her, he'd started coming to terms with just how much his fear of arguing with her had wrecked and scuttled any hope of a real relationship with her.

Now, it could be an actual matter of life or death.

"Let's just split up," he said. "You and Stormy head down the path and I'll go to the farmhouse."

"But we'll be stronger and more effective together," she protested.

Maybe, but not if they couldn't agree on a plan and just stood around arguing.

"Poppy," Lex said. "You know as well as I do that we were never very good at acting like a team."

He watched as some kind of mental calculation seemed to flicker in her eyes. And realized this might actually be the first time he'd openly disagreed with her on anything instead of either just nodding along or cutting bait just to avoid a fight. Stormy growled, softly, like the tremor of a distant earthquake shaking the ground. Then to his surprise, Poppy nodded.

"Fair enough," she said. "You take the house and we'll follow the scent. Stay safe, Lex."

"You, too."

She turned and ran down the path with her body low

and Stormy just one step ahead of her. In an instant he'd lost sight of them in the trees. He turned toward the house. Doubt trickled down the back of his neck. What if he was wrong and Poppy was right? Either way one of them was heading into danger without the other as backup. He prayed it wasn't her.

He slipped around the side of the house, straining his ears for any hint of activity inside. There was nothing. The back door to the kitchen lay open and his heart sank as he glanced inside. The room was empty, with only a few broken dishes and a single kitchen chair fallen over on its side in the middle of the room to show there'd even been a struggle. He kept praying and pushed the door open, feeling a slight resistance on the handle as if something was holding it back.

The resistance snapped, a twang sounded and instinctively Lex leaped back as something flew past within an inch of his nose and embedded itself in the wall beside him. It was a tranquilizer dart, the kind that poachers used to take out bears and large enough to knock a big person down for a long time and put a smaller one in the hospital. His heart thudded. Someone had boobytrapped Johnny's house.

Had Johnny been worried that someone was after for him? Or had his kidnappers laid a trap for whoever came to rescue him?

"Help!" The voice was female, muffled and seemed to be coming from the living room. "Help me! Please! I'm in here!"

Ripley.

He steeled a breath and cautiously moved through the kitchen to the living room, looking out for other traps as he went.

The living room was empty and dark; the drawn curtains fairly effectively blocked out the light.

He reached the cupboard door. Someone had fastened a crude padlock to its double doors locking it shut.

"Move back," Lex called. "I'm going to break it down!"

He leveled a swift kick at the doors, catching them right above the lock. The cheap wood splintered, the door handles snapped off and the cupboard fell open.

"Lex!" Ripley emerged from behind a shield of coats and outdoor gear. Her long dark hair was tied back in two disheveled braids and makeup ran from her tearstained eyes, making her slender form look years younger than the midtwenties he knew her to be. "I'm so glad you're here!"

A gag lay loose around her neck and as she stepped out into the living room he could see faint welts on her wrists.

"He tied you up and gagged you?" Lex asked.

Ripley nodded. "With bandannas. But I was able to rip them on the edge of Johnny's toolbox, get my hands free and then take off the gag."

And then find Johnny's phone, Lex thought.

"How long have you been in here?" he asked.

"I don't know," she said. "Where's Johnny?"

"I was about to ask you that," Lex said.

Her eyes widened. "I thought someone dragged him into the kitchen."

"Maybe so, but he's not there now."

The front porch creaked. In an instant, Lex threw himself in front of his buddy's girlfriend, pushing Ripley behind him. The door flew open, and two more darts twanged, imbedding themselves in the wooden door as it suddenly shut again. Then the door swung back open again and Lex looked to see the tall, broad-shouldered form of a man standing there silhouetted against the sun.

"Lex," Will said as he stepped into the room, then gave a signal and his border collie partner sprung to his side. "Sorry, I got here as fast as I could. What do you need? Has the scene been secured? Where's Poppy?"

There was something about the man's sharp and focused professionalism that immediately put Lex at ease, while also reminding him of the type of man Lex had always suspected Poppy wanted him to be. Especially after seeing how smoothly Will had dodged the trap.

"The kitchen and living room are secured, but I haven't checked the rest of the house," Lex added. "The back door was also rigged with a tranquilizer dart and I don't know if there are more."

"Do we know why?" Will asked, glancing at the projectile embedded in the door frame.

Lex looked at Ripley. "Do you?"

She shook her head but didn't meet his eye. Okay, so that was something he'd have to question more later.

"When I last saw Poppy and Stormy they were headed to the back of the property," Lex added. "I have to find her."

He needed to. In a way he didn't even understand. It was like his heart was aching to know that Poppy was okay and hadn't walked directly into a trap.

"Ripley, this is Trooper Will Stryker and his K-9 partner, Scout," Lex added, stepping to the side to allow introductions. "Ripley is the one who called me about Johnny Blair's abduction. Johnny was my source about the poaching of the blue bear cubs."

"Please to meet you," Will said. "I'm glad to see you're all right." Lex watched as the trooper stretched out his hand as if to shake Ripley's, but when she hesitated, he pulled it back and simply nodded to her instead. The whole motion had been seamless. "You find Poppy. Scout and I will stay with Ripley and secure the house."

"Sounds good," Lex said. A fleeting thought crossed his mind that Will still might not trust him and was trying to keep him away from Ripley while he took her statement. But in that moment he didn't care. All that mattered was that Poppy was all right. He ran outside and down the path in the direction she and Stormy had disappeared.

The sound of a shotgun exploded ahead of him with what he guessed was buckshot pelting its target. His heartbeat quickened as prayers pounded through his chest with every step. Then he saw Poppy running toward him. Her green eyes were wide in her pale face.

He knew in an instant something was wrong.

"Lex!" His name escaped her lips in a gasp.

His arms opened instinctively, and she crashed into them. She clutched him to her in a tight hug as his own embrace closed around her. There'd always been a mightiness to her hugs. It was like she could see the disjointed pieces of him and was helping him set the glue that held them all together.

Her hugs had made him feel stronger.

"I heard gunshots," he said.

"The garage was rigged with booby traps," she explained. "Both tranquilizer darts and a shotgun."

"House was boobytrapped too," he said. "I don't know if Johnny was expecting trouble or if his kidnapper was trying to kill whoever came to rescue him. You okay?"

"Yeah," she said. "Thankfully Stormy sniffed them out."

He thanked God for Stormy and was about to ask where she was when he caught sight of her over Poppy's shoulder sitting at attention in front of the garage.

Poppy pulled back enough to look in his face.

"Oh, Lex, I'm so sorry—" she began.

"Hey, hey, it's okay."

His hand slid to her cheek and cupped it in his fingers. But her head shook away from his touch.

"It's Johnny." Pained filled Poppy's voice. "Oh, Lex, I'm so sorry. But Johnny's dead."

FIVE

Thunder rumbled in the distance, warning of impending rain. Lex stood alone in the doorway of the dilapidated garage and looked at his buddy's body from a distance, feeling sorrow heavy like a lead weight in his chest. Johnny's large form sat slumped in a sagging lawn chair, with his hands tied behind his back and his head resting over his chest almost as if he was asleep. A single gunshot wound made it clear the death had been instantaneous and he'd probably been killed even before Ripley had managed to get her hands free enough to call him.

Lord, have mercy on him, his family and everyone who loves him. Lex prayed. Johnny had been heading down the wrong path for so very long. Lex wished that he and his old buddy had been closer in the past couple of years, and that he'd been able to do more to help him before it was too late. He hoped Johnny had found the redemption he'd sought in his final moments.

Poppy and Stormy had stayed outside and left him to go in alone to confirm it was Johnny and give him a moment. But as he walked back outside and into the trees, in such a daze he could barely see the world around him, he felt Poppy step beside him. Instinctively his hand reached for hers; she took it and their fingers linked. He stood there, looking up at the clouds building above him and holding Poppy's hand. For a moment he didn't know what words to say or even how to turn and look into her eyes, but somehow just standing there feeling her touch was enough.

"There's nothing you could've done," Poppy whispered.

His hand slipped from hers. Stormy buffeted her head softly against his other side as if she sensed his sadness, too, and wanted to make sure he was okay. He ran his hand over the dog's head.

"I know," he said, not even sure if she was talking about the fact the call had come too late for him to save Johnny or the complicated, two-decades-long friendship he and Johnny had. "We haven't been close in years and every time he disappeared I steeled myself for the fact I might never see him again." He turned toward her. "At least this way I can help ensure his killer is brought to justice."

"And you will," Poppy said as her green eyes met his, unflinching and uncompromising. "I promise you that."

He believed her and he'd forgotten how good it felt to have someone like her by his side.

"Will has secured the house and is taking Ripley's statement," she added. "We've called in troopers from Juneau to airlift Johnny's body to the morgue there for an autopsy. But we didn't know who we should call locally."

"My mother," he said, and watched as she blinked. "As a retired emergency room nurse she's the most qualified medical professional in town. Also, the volunteer firefighters can help secure the area to make sure no one gets in or out."

He paced a few steps back in the direction of the house and ran one hand through his hair, feeling a mental switch flip inside him. Later, he'd mourn the loss of his friend. But right now, he had to turn his feelings off—including the confusing ones being around Poppy stirred up in him—and he started mentally listing the things that needed to happen.

"I'm going to call my mom and explain the situation," he said. "She'll get a trusted friend to watch Danny while she drives out here. You said Will is taking Ripley's statement. I also need to call her brother, Nolan, if no one's informed him yet and let him know what's happened. He runs a small charter airline business and she says he's off flying someone to Juneau today but should be back soon. She lives with him, and while I don't really know him, he's always seemed very protective. You mentioned state troopers from Juneau are coming to take Johnny to the medical examiner's office. What am I forgetting?"

"Nothing," Poppy reassured him. "I also need to call my boss, Colonel Lorenza Gallo, in Anchorage and brief her as the Alaskan K-9 unit officially has jurisdiction of the case. But I'm sure she'll have no problem coordinating with Juneau."

The gray-haired woman with a stylish pixie cut and what he seemed to remember was an affinity for interesting jewelry came to mind. He'd met Lorenza once when, unbeknownst to Poppy, he'd attended an Alaska trooper recruitment event in Anchorage while they were still engaged. Poppy had been pressing him to consider applying to become a wildlife trooper, despite the fact he didn't really have the educational background for it and had never been a big fan of school. Lorenza had been the one who told him he seemed to be really happy as a park ranger, and that he should be in a job that called to him. Poppy's boss had kind of reminded him of his mother.

"Will and I are scheduled to have a video call with my team tonight," Poppy added. "You should give Will an official statement, as well. We need you to go on the record about what Johnny told you, and it's better that Will be the one who takes the statement."

Right, because of their history.

He glanced over at where Stormy now sat, patiently and contentedly waiting for direction.

"You think I should apologize to Stormy for not following her lead?" he asked.

He'd meant it as a feeble joke to lighten the tension, but Poppy's lips didn't even twitch.

"No, there were only two of us, and it made sense to split up." She frowned. "Lex, are you sure you know that none of this is your fault?"

"You're repeating yourself." He shrugged. "You said that before."

"And I want to be doubly certain that you hear me," she said. "The killer was long gone before we got here. You could've run off to the garage the moment we pulled up and it wouldn't have made a difference. Plus, I know better than anyone how hard you've worked to be there for your friends. I was there all those times you ran out of the movies or skipped out on dinner because Johnny or somebody else needed you. I was there when you lent your friends money or vouched for them to get jobs. I also know that you're really good at pushing your emotions down and just getting on with things. I want to make sure you're okay."

She was one to talk. Poppy hadn't even seemed upset when he'd broken off their engagement. Then again, she could probably say the same about him, despite the fact his heart had been breaking. A breeze brushed through the space between them.

"Thank you," he said gruffly. "But I'm fine."

He turned and walked back to the house, pulling out his phone as he went and gritting his teeth.

Maybe she was right. Maybe he wasn't okay and hadn't been for a long while. But if he fell apart now there was no way of knowing what emotions would suddenly come spilling out.

And if that happened, he couldn't afford it to be in front of Poppy.

The sun had dipped lower behind the ominous clouds when Poppy finally finished securing the scene at Johnny's house and was able to take Stormy for a quick jog around the motel where she and Will were staying. A dog Stormy's size would definitely need a second, much longer run than the small gap of time Poppy had before her video team meeting would allow. But she needed the time alone to think and pray.

If she was honest, she'd never really liked Johnny. She'd never particularly cared for any of Lex's friends from childhood. They were reckless, immature, under-employed and content calling on Lex to bail them out instead of taking responsibility for their own mistakes.

But, Lord, I need Your help to make sure my own biases don't cloud my judgment here. I ask You to bless Johnny's family and everyone who loved him. Help my team and me bring his killers to justice. And forgive me for every unkind, unjust and negative thought I ever harbored for him. Cleanse my heart, Lord.

Praying helped, and already her footsteps felt lighter as she saw the motel come back into view, with its rusted metal balconies and uniform orange doors.

She'd admired Lex's loyalty to his friends. Even when helping a friend whose ex had tossed all his belongings out on the lawn in a snowstorm had kept him from making it to their cake tasting or when the check for the reception venue had almost bounced because he'd bailed a friend out. It had been a really attractive quality of Lex's, if she was honest, even when his dedication to his friends had left her to handle too much on her own. And Lex's friends had cared about him, too.

After all, Johnny must've known he was risking his life by telling Lex about the blue bear cubs. Whatever mistakes he'd made, Johnny had died trying to do the right thing.

And that is what she needed to focus on.

She found Will sitting at a picnic table in front of the motel, with his back to the table and his feet out in front of him. Scout was lying under the table, and when Poppy unclipped her K-9 partner's leash, Stormy looked up at her and woofed slightly as if asking Poppy's permission to join Scout.

She patted her side. "Go ahead. If you can fit."

Poppy chuckled slightly as the large dog scrunched herself down low enough to crawl under the table and beside Scout, who patiently moved aside to accommodate her.

Will waved a hand in greeting. "You've got about forty minutes before our team meeting if you want to unpack a bit. It's just going to be a handful of us for now and then we'll have a bigger briefing tomorrow."

Poppy would definitely get changed at least. She'd been wearing the same dirt-streaked uniform all day and knew the colonel wouldn't mind if she showed up for the team meeting out of uniform. Unpacking her stuff into that grimy-looking motel was another thing altogether. She might just leave her belongings in her suitcase.

Sitting down beside Will, she leaned back against the table and stretched her legs out.

"So, how are you feeling?" he asked. She glanced Will's way, but his gaze was fixed on the sky. "Can't imagine it's easy to suddenly come face-to-face with an old boyfriend."

"Ex-fiancé," she corrected him automatically, although she suspected he knew that and was understating it to be diplomatic. "Didn't quite stand me up at the altar, but pretty close. He was missing in action for about all of the wedding prep. Then he accidentally leaves a pocket-dial message on my answering machine, telling someone else he's having serious second thoughts."

"Ouch," Will said.

"Yup," she said. "I called Lex when I got it and asked him point-blank if he wanted to marry me. He hemmed and hawed a bit, then admitted he wasn't feeling it, and that was that. All very nondramatic and civilized."

In fact, she suspected he was surprised at how calmly she'd taken it. And sure, maybe if she had burst into tears and begged him to stay he would've still married her, considering the way he always leaped in to save people in need. But she hadn't wanted to guilt the man she loved into spending the rest of his life with her. She'd wanted him to choose her.

"Did you know Johnny or Ripley at all before this?" Will asked after a long moment.

"Ripley, no," she said. "But I worked with Johnny briefly at Kenai Fjords National Park before he got fired for some small-scale poaching. We were never close. But Lex stayed in touch with him after that and even invited him to the wedding. If I remember correctly, Johnny gave him a really nice pocketknife as an engagement gift that Lex probably still uses."

Although she wouldn't be the slightest bit surprised if Johnny had tried to talk Lex out of marrying her.

"What was your impression of him?" Will's tone was casual, but there was something very professional and investigative about it, too, which she appreciated.

"We didn't get along," she admitted, "but he was also always incredibly polite and respectful to me. He told me once that he'd take a bullet for Lex and that as 'Lex's other half' that was true for me, too." Huh, she'd completely forgotten that until now. Maybe her prayer really was working on her heart. "I think I was too irritated at being called Lex's 'other half' to realize what a big gesture that probably was for him. You know he had a criminal record?"

"Yup," Will said. "Long but petty. Selling cigarettes to people under twenty-one. Driving away from the gas station without paying…"

"Poaching small game," she added, "and hustling tourists at darts and pool. What's your impression of Ripley?"

"Her statement was all over the place, and her timeline doesn't add up," Will said. "But that's not unheard of. My impression is she's very upset and very, very scared. I wouldn't be surprised if it turns out someone was after her and Johnny, and it he boobytrapped his own property. But that's just a guess. Ripley lives with her brother, Nolan. We spoke very briefly when he came to pick her up."

"Lex implied her ex-boyfriend is a nasty piece of work," Poppy offered. "Maybe they were afraid he'd come here and go after her or Johnny."

"Interesting," Will mused. "Now that's worth looking into."

"What's your take on Ripley's brother?" she asked. "Johnny was doing mechanic work for his airline tours business."

"Honestly," Will said, "I wouldn't knock on his door without a warrant. Nolan strikes me as the kind of guy who'd shoot a trespasser first and *then* try to figure out who they were. Condition of his truck implies financial troubles, too." He shrugged. "I was kind of surprised when it turned out he didn't have a criminal record. But maybe there's something there that didn't turn up in a cursory search. He is very protective of his sister and they clearly love each other. Nolan will keep her safe."

Poppy stood and turned to head up to her room. Stormy looked up at her and her eyebrows rose hopefully, as if to say she'd join her if she had to but was hoping Poppy would let her stay with Scout. Poppy chuckled.

"Mind if Stormy hangs out with Scout while I get changed?" she asked.

"No problem," Will said. "Happy to supervise a K-9 playdate. There's a water bowl and hose around the side of the building. I'll make sure she gets something to drink."

Poppy leaned down and ran her hand over Stormy's shaggy head. "Thanks."

Half an hour later, Poppy was no closer to being unpacked, but had changed into her favorite pair of yoga pants and a soft gray T-shirt, with a sweatshirt tied around her waist just in case the temperature dropped. Her long auburn hair, which thankfully had settled from the flaming red of her youth to a color much closer to actual poppies as she'd grown older, now lay damp around her shoulders.

She knocked on the door adjoining her room to Will's.

"It's open," he called.

She slipped through into what the motel had optimistically called the "living room area" of the adjoining "suite." Will sat on the room's only chair in front of a metal folding table with his laptop open in front of him, and Stormy and Scout were curled up nearby on the stained and faded carpet. The room smelled heavily of other people's meals and pets. Will rose to offer her the chair, but she waved him down and instead perched on the arm of the couch behind him. Lex's mother's beautiful and well-maintained bed-and-breakfast brushed the edges of her mind, along with the fact Poppy had turned down Gillian's kind suggestion they all stay there, for fear of being too emotionally compromised by Lex and his adorable son, Danny. She reached her hand down toward Stormy, who licked her fingertips in welcome.

Will pressed a button and a tapestry of faces began to appear in front of them in boxes on the screen. First was her boss, Lorenza, sitting in her office with her senior K-9 husky, Denali, watching the meeting from a dog bed behind her. Poppy had always secretly thought there was something slightly glamorous about her no-nonsense boss, and tonight the pale blue scarf that wrapped around her shoulders and seemed to perfectly offset her silver pixie cut was no exception. Then came troopers Maya Rodriguez and Helena Maddox, who it seemed had gone home for the day and each called in from their respective kitchens. Then finally resident tech guru Eli Partridge, who was still at his desk, his mop of dark brown hair even more unruly than usual.

As happy as she was to see her team members, their images all seemed a bit fuzzier than usual.

"Hey, all." Eli waved at the screen and pushed his glasses up higher on his nose. "I've got most of you all coming through nice and clear. But Will and Poppy's internet connection is really weak. I was hoping to send through some detailed maps and images tomorrow morning I managed to download from a dark web illegal animal auction site that might relate to our bear poaching case, but that'll depend on them getting a better internet connection or us finding a workaround. Anyone else joining us this evening?"

"No, given the late hour I thought we'd just meet as a partial team tonight to go over a potential new development in our missing bride case," Lorenza said, "and have a larger team meeting tomorrow morning at nine."

Poppy met Maya's eyes through the screen. The two troopers had recently worked closely with their colleague, Trooper Hunter McCord, on the troubling and mysterious unsolved case of what had happened to a wedding party who'd gone hiking in the snow-covered trees of Chugach State Park. The tour guide, Cal Brooks, had been found murdered, the maid of honor, Ariel Potter, had been pushed over a cliff and almost died and the pregnant bride, Violet James, was now on the run. Maya and her Malinois, Sarge, had been part of the search party that had found the would-be-groom, Lance Wells, and best man, Jared Dennis. Both men had been pretty banged up and told Maya that Violet had knocked Lance out and shot Jared. Lance also told them that Violet was pregnant with Cal's child, but Ariel, who was now happily engaged to Hunter, was convinced her missing friend was innocent.

"Helena is planning to interview Lance's sister, Tessa, tomorrow," Lorenza said. "I understand you tried to talk to her when you spoke with Lance's parents?"

"I did." Poppy nodded. "But she was out of the country."

It had disappointed her not to be able to interview Lance's sister, especially as Lance's ex-girlfriend had suggested she might be a good person to talk to.

"I've gone over your notes from your other interviews," Helena said. "But I'd appreciate your gut perspective before I talk to her."

Her K-9 partner, Luna, leaned her head on the table beside Helena as if she was interested in hearing Poppy's perspective, too. Helena rubbed her fingers along the Norwegian elkhound's head.

"Lance's parents are definitely looking at their son through rose-colored glasses," Poppy said. "They kept telling me how wonderful he was. I got the impression they thought he could do no wrong." Again, she was thankful she'd taken the time to pray about her current case and ask God to cleanse her of anything clouding her own judgment. "His ex-girlfriend had a much less rosy opinion. She wouldn't tell me what had gone on between her and Lance, only that he'd broken things off when she didn't get an inheritance she was expecting and that she'd caught him lying too many times."

Helena's green eyes widened. "About what?"

"I don't know," Poppy said. "She said they were little white lies mostly. Nothing too serious. But she did tell me we should speak to Lance's sister."

And while she wished she'd been able to interview Tessa herself, she had every confidence that Helena would do an excellent job.

"Say we do determine that Lance isn't that great a guy," Will said. "It takes more than having a lousy personality to prove murder. After all, there are far easier ways to get out of marrying a bridezilla than killing people."

She was sure he meant it as an offhand comment. But Poppy felt her back stiffen just the same.

"A bride accused of being pregnant with another man's child," Maya pointed out.

"Thankfully that brings us to our second break in the case, which is something far more tangible than romantic intrigue," Lorenza added. "Do you want to fill them in, Maya?"

Maya nodded. "Sarge and I found an expensive gold watch belonging to our best man, Jared, at the bottom of the cliff where Ariel was pushed," she said.

Will whistled under his breath. "Well done, Sarge."

Poppy heard Maya's Malinois partner woof off-screen as if in agreement.

"The watch was a gift to him from Lance," Maya added. "He says he lost it."

"But Tala is running forensics on it to see if there's any evidence he was the one who pushed Ariel," Eli added.

And if anyone could find an evidentiary needle in a haystack, forensic scientist Tala Ekho could.

Poppy and Will filled the team in on the poaching case so far, including Johnny's death and Ripley's forcible confinement. Lorenza suggested they reinterview Ripley and also her brother tomorrow, with a special focus on the possible ex-boyfriend angle, and see if any other patrons of the unlicensed "watering hole" had heard anything about the blue bears or poaching. Eli said he'd run a search online for any information he could find out about the sale of the animals.

"One more question," Lorenza said, fixing her eyes on Poppy and Will. "Do you think Johnny told the poacher that he'd tipped Lex off to their plans before he killed him?"

"Yes," Will said automatically.

"No," Poppy declared, just as fast, their voices speaking over each other.

"Interesting," Lorenza said. She leaned back in her chair and looked at the two of them a long moment. She nodded to Will. "Why do you say yes?"

"Looks like death was pretty quick and painless," Will explained. He glanced at Poppy almost apologetically. "There was no sign of serious injuries or that he was really hurt in any way. Which to me implies he cooperated and told them everything they wanted to know."

Lorenza nodded slowly over steepled fingers. Then she gestured at Poppy. "And why do you think Johnny didn't give Lex up?"

Because I just do.

"Hard to explain," Poppy admitted. "But Lex is the kind of man who instills loyalty among those who care about him. Despite their problems, Johnny told me that he loved Lex like a brother and would be willing to take a bullet for him. And to be honest, I believed him. Johnny risked his life to tell Lex about the poachers when he could've just protected himself and kept quiet about it. That has to mean something."

Did it? Or was that just wishful thinking on her part? She pressed her lips together and prayed for wisdom.

"Considering the number of tranquilizer dart traps in the house, and how peacefully Johnny seemed slumped in the chair, I think we should look for evidence that Johnny was tranquilized and out cold when he was killed," she added. Then she glanced at Will. "Although I admit that wouldn't be conclusive either way about which one of us is right."

"It's also possible his kidnapper was interrupted or in a hurry," Will offered, "or that he had some other kind of personal connection to him. We can't jump to conclusions. My hunch could very well be wrong."

"As could mine," Poppy admitted.

A Bible verse from Proverbs 27 sprung suddenly to her mind about how one friend sharpens another like iron sharpens iron. Once again, she found herself thanking God for her team and how working with them strengthened her and made her a better person. Living in a place like Gustavus, cut off from the world, might work for some, but she couldn't imagine ever making that choice. And not just because it would mean giving up being part of the Alaska state trooper's K-9 unit.

After the team said their goodbyes, Poppy took Stormy for a run. Will had offered to come with her if she'd feel more comfortable with company. And she appreciated it, just like she'd appreciated the fact he hadn't pried into her past with Lex. But Scout couldn't begin to keep up with Stormy's speed, and truth was she needed time alone to think. Her footsteps pounded beneath her in a slow and steady jog, with Stormy by her side, the dog grinning at her at intervals as if she was encouraging Poppy to go faster. Every now and then, when the coast was clear of vehicles and homes, Poppy would give her permission to run and then watch as Stormy galloped off into the distance at full tilt, before always inevitably coming right back to her side like a boomerang. If there was a limit to Stormy's seemingly boundless energy, she hadn't found it yet.

Poppy had always enjoyed running, especially at the end of a long workday. She and Lex used to run together at night, and each said exercising together had somehow pushed them to be faster and train harder. Running alone had also helped a lot in those days after Lex had broken her heart. It had given her a way to work through the pain of losing him, pray and cry alone when no one was around to witness it and get her life back on track. And she'd rebuilt her life so much better than she could've ever imagined. First Lorenza had welcomed her into the incredible K-9 team. Then Stormy had tumbled into her orbit like a gigantic, overgrown puppy, so eager to learn and diligent in her training. She couldn't have asked for a better partner.

Thank You, Lord, for the team meeting tonight. It felt good to be reminded of who I am, where I belong and all You've given me. Help us stop those poachers before the second bear cub is captured and the first bear cub is sold. And please bring Johnny's killer to justice.

She hadn't even realized how far she'd run until she saw the beautiful wooden frame of Gillian's bed-and-breakfast looming ahead of her in the darkness. A light was on in the upper floor, over the covered porch, glowing like a lighthouse in the darkness. Instinctively she looked up and saw Lex, silhouetted against the gentle light of what looked like blue-and-white star-shaped wall lamps. She watched as he scooped little Danny up into his arms and spun him around, before cradling the toddler to his chest. It looked like they were laughing.

Poppy looked away as an old familiar ache filled her chest. She'd always been the kind of person who made plans and set goals—and the one dashed dream that had hurt most of all was when Lex had decided he didn't want to have a family with her. She'd always longed to be a wife and mother every bit as strongly as she'd desired her career. And while she didn't resent Lex his happiness, it hurt to be reminded that he'd rejected her and created that family with someone else. Thick drops of rain brushed her skin and thunder rumbled, warning her of the storm that was to come. She stopped and glanced at her watch, surprised to realize it was already eight. Stormy whined softly as if asking to keep going.

"I don't have another sprint in me," Poppy told the dog. "But if you want one last run before we turn around, go for it. I'll wait here for you."

She ran her hand over Stormy's head, then patted her side. The K-9 woofed and bounded off into the darkness. Poppy sat down on a stump, with her back against a fence post and Lex's window out of view. She had pushed herself too far and now would have a long walk back in the rain for her troubles, along with sharing an underwhelming motel room with a huge and soaking-wet shaggy dog.

Lord, help me focus on the task ahead of me and keep my own broken heart from getting in the way.

A motion drew her attention to the bushes at her right. For a moment, she thought it was a wild animal or even her own partner trying to sneak up on her playfully.

She stood slowly and saw the figure of a man half-hidden in the darkness, his masked face staring up at the same window where Lex and his son now stood. The light of a cell phone camera glowed in his hand.

He was filming them.

"Hey!" she shouted, leaping from behind the relative coverage of the bushes, her hand instinctively reaching for the weapon she'd left locked in her motel room. "Stop!"

The masked man turned toward her and snarled. He pocketed the phone, then a knife glinted in his grasp. He leaped at her.

SIX

The sound of a crash outside yanked Lex's attention to the window.

"Bear, Daddy?" Danny asked cheerfully. "Fox?"

He had yet to convince his small son that the parade of wild animals that tried to take up residence in their backyard, including moose, caribou and plain old raccoons, wasn't necessarily a good thing.

"Probably," Lex said, keeping his voice light, despite the warning chill that nudged his spine. He set the boy back down on his bed and raised the toddler safety rails. "I'm going to go check on the animal and come right back to read you a story. Can you pick one out for me?"

"Uh-huh." The toddler nodded enthusiastically.

Lex brushed a kiss over the boy's head and turned. His mother was standing in the doorway. Worry filled her eyes, and he knew without needing to ask she'd heard the noise, too.

"Stay here with him," he said softly. "I'm going to check it out."

He ran down the stairs, taking them two at a time and praying with each step. He burst outside, the house's motion sensor lights flickering on to greet him. Light washed over the lawn to the edges of the road and then he saw them. Two figures were rolling and fighting on the ground, locked in a battle for dominance. A thin masked figure in camouflage was on top, trying in vain to stab the other as she dodged his blows and kicked back furiously.

His heart stopped. It was Poppy. Lex pelted across the grass toward them. The masked figure turned and Poppy struck, catching her attacker hard in the jaw with both feet. He flew back and scrambled down the road into the darkness.

"Poppy!" Lex reached her side, his arms stretched out for her as she grabbed hold of them and pulled herself up. "What's going on? Are you okay?"

"He…he was spying on you and your son."

Her words came out in short, breathless gasps.

An engine sounded, cutting off their words, and he looked up to see a dark van peeling away with the masked figure at the wheel.

For a moment he felt Poppy almost wilt into his arms as if her legs had crumpled beneath her. Then she stepped back and tossed her hair out around her shoulders.

Footsteps sounded like something galloping toward them through the darkness. Instinctively, Lex took a farther step back and raised his hands palm up as Stormy burst through the trees.

"Stormy," Poppy called. "At ease. Everything's okay."

The wolfhound skidded to a stop at Poppy's feet, dropping into a sit. She looked up at Lex, her large tail thumping the ground and her jaw hanging open in a wide grin. So, no hard feelings, then.

"What are you both doing here?" he asked.

"Just getting some exercise before bed," Poppy said. "Didn't realize how far we'd come when we'd hit the bed-and-breakfast. Turns out Gustavus is a pretty small town." She ran her hand over the dog's head. "I stopped to turn around and let Stormy get in a final sprint off-leash when I saw the masked man in fatigues watching you and Danny through the window. I think he was filming you or maybe taking pictures."

The chill that had brushed Lex's spine when he'd heard the noise outside grew colder. First Gillian had seen someone watching Danny over the fence, now this. He reached out for Poppy, somehow wanting the comfort of her hand, but she stepped away from his touch, leaving him unsure if she even noticed.

"Well, I'm glad really you're here," he said. As if on cue, the intermittent drops of rain that had been falling around them broke through the clouds into a full-fledged deluge. He waved his hand toward the house. "Come on. I've got to finish putting Danny to bed, then we can talk and I'll drive you back."

Her chin rose. "It's okay, we can walk."

Yup, Poppy could walk for over half an hour, alone, at night, through the pouring rain, right after battling a masked stranger. Wouldn't surprise him in the slightest if she did.

"I don't doubt you can," he said. "But I'd feel better if you didn't. We need to talk, you need to contact your partner and I'd rather get out of the rain."

He started toward the house, thankful when she and Stormy followed.

"Yeah, you're right," she said. "We should debrief, and we didn't really get much of a chance to talk as the scene wrapped up at Johnny's house. I thought we'd wait until tomorrow, but under the circumstances, we should probably do it sooner than later."

"Absolutely," he replied. "We should talk."

But there was more to it than that. Part of him also just wanted to protect her, to have her close and know she was safe. Was that wrong? They crossed the yard and entered the house. He closed the front door, and for the first time he could remember since moving to Gustavus, he locked it behind him.

"I've got a fire going in the fireplace," he added. "Feel free to sit and dry off a bit. All of the sweatshirts hanging on the pegs by the door are clean if you want to borrow one and change into something dry. And you're welcome to join Danny and me upstairs for story time, if you want."

"Thank you," Poppy said, and as she met his eyes something seemed to hover unspoken in the air between them.

Looking back on his time with her, Lex had never quite been able to believe that someone as beautiful, smart and all around incredible as her had ever been in his life. Now here she was, standing just two feet inside the threshold of his own home, somehow even more amazing in every way than he'd allowed himself to remember. While he had no idea where they even belonged in each other's lives, Poppy had been the one person he'd been close to who he'd never felt needed him. Sure, she might've loved him every bit as fiercely as he'd loved her, but he'd never doubted that she'd do just fine without him. And she had.

"Make yourself comfortable," he told her. "My home is yours."

Suddenly, it was like he was struck by the full weight

of just how much he'd missed her. He longed to gather her close and hold her against his chest as he promised to care for and protect her.

And then he wanted to raise her face to his and kiss her lips.

Instead, he wrenched his gaze away from hers and headed up the stairs to his son, as the weight of everything he'd lost beat down against his heart.

Poppy stood and watched as Lex disappeared up the stairs to the second floor. Part of her wanted to follow him. Instead, she turned and walked into the large living area to her right and paced the space a moment to settle her mind before calling Will. The bed-and-breakfast was an open concept, with huge wood-beamed ceilings. Several smaller living areas were set off by clusters of couches, soft chairs and low tables, with shelves that Lex had made from reclaimed wood that she recognized from his old apartment in Anchorage. A wide kitchen lay to the right of the room, separated from the living area by a marble-topped island and a wooden dining table set for six that looked like it could be expanded to sit double that. Behind the kitchen led a hallway to what seemed to be several guest rooms and a second staircase by the side door leading back upstairs. Framed cross-stitched Bible verses and pictures of Lex, Gillian and little Danny were everywhere.

At some point, Stormy stopped following her, and when Poppy returned to the main living area she found her K-9 partner stretched out in front of a fireplace. The same tiny calico kitten she'd seen in the window earlier now weaved in and out between the wolfhound's giant paws as if looking for a place to settle. Stormy looked up at Poppy under shaggy brows.

"Looks like you've made a friend," she said. The kitten curled up beside Stormy's snout and closed its eyes with a purr far louder than Poppy would've imagined a tiny ball of fluff that small could've mustered. She laughed softly.

"And good for you," she told the kitten, "for being so brave and gutsy to befriend someone a hundred times your size. I like you."

Even if she was feeling anything but brave herself when it came to her own relationship with Lex. She untied her damp sweatshirt from around her waist and rubbed it over her head like a towel. She glanced at herself in the wood-framed mirror over the mantel. Her own wide eyes stared back at her, looking twice as large as usual in her pale face. The youthful flush on her cheeks and unfamiliar fluttering in her chest seemed to belong to a woman who'd lived half the years and heartaches she had. She pulled a dark green zip-up sweatshirt from the pegs by the door, put it on and zipped it up. The achingly familiar scent of Lex filled her senses.

She called Will and he answered on the first ring.

"Everything okay?" he asked. "You've been gone awhile."

After Poppy quickly filled him in on the details of what had happened, he blew out a hard breath.

"Gotta say I'm getting tired of being in a place this far away from law enforcement backup," he said. "I'll make a preliminary report to the team, and you can fill in more details when you're back at your laptop. You want me to come pick you up?"

"Probably in a bit," she replied. "I need to talk to Lex first. He's busy putting his son to bed."

"Call anytime," Will said. "I don't mind if you wake me up."

"Thank you. I really appreciate it."

"And hey," he added. "I'm really sorry if I came down too hard on your point of view or anything in the team meeting earlier."

"Don't be and you didn't," she said. "I really like that we have different opinions. It makes us both better at our jobs."

"Okay, good." Will sighed. "I also felt kind of bad about that offhand comment I made about there being easier ways to get out of a wedding than killing someone. I mean, I had my heart broken once by someone I loved and I know it's no joking matter. I might not be the biggest on opening up about personal stuff, but if you need a friend you can always talk to me."

"Thank you," she said again, feeling a smile spread across her face. "To be honest, I'd completely forgotten you'd said that and I'm trying to keep my personal feelings out of the case right now. But I'm really glad to know that if anything does come up I can talk to you."

"Good," Will replied, and she could hear the smile in his voice. "Hopefully we'll wrap this mess up soon and get back to Anchorage, where you've got a whole team of people who've got your back, too."

Yeah, it had been good to see some of their faces on the video call earlier and she looked forward to seeing even more of them in the morning.

"Thanks for the reminder," she said.

"Anytime."

The call ended and she glanced at Stormy, who was

now snoring softly, still cuddling with her new kitten friend. She left them there asleep and started up the stairs to the second floor. Lex's and Danny's voices wafted down the hallway toward her, and she followed them to the toddler's room. The door was ajar, and she stopped a few paces away from it and listened. By the sound of things Lex was reading a story about a very silly pigeon who kept asking for things he couldn't have. Lex was playing the role of the pigeon in a cartoonish voice while Danny kept telling the pigeon no, in between gales of hysterical giggles.

Her breath caught. The happiness and love that flowed between father and son was so obvious. And the weight of all the times she'd tried and failed to convince Lex that he'd be a good father crashed down around her heart, sending unshed tears to her eyes. She closed them tightly and stopped the tears from falling.

Help me, Lord... I don't want to be jealous or resentful of Lex's happiness. I want to be happy for him. I don't want to feel this sadness in my heart. Please erase my pain so it doesn't impact my actions now.

"Keep go'n, Daddy!" Danny squealed. "More pi'gou!"

She turned and started down the stairs, back to the living room, where she sat on a couch and tried to distract herself with a Victorian suspense novel she found on a side table. Stormy had rearranged herself into a giant circle on the floor, tucking her nose against her tail, and the kitten had curled itself into a new ball inside it. Ten minutes later, she heard Lex's footsteps on the stairs, but didn't look up until she heard his voice.

"Hey, how are you doing?" he asked softly. He sat down on the opposite end of the couch and turned toward her, leaning his back against the arm.

"I'm okay," she said. "How about you?"

He ran his hand over his neck.

"Tired," he admitted. He glanced at Stormy and the kitten, and chuckled. "So looks like someone didn't get the memo about Stormy being a big scary beast."

"What's the kitten's name?" she asked. "I've been talking to it on and off and felt bad I didn't know what to call it."

"His name is Mushroom," Lex said. A grin crossed his face, as if happy for the brief distraction from more serious topics. "Danny named him, although he pronounces it Mu'shoom. It's apparently short for Mushroom Pizza."

Poppy snorted, barely catching the laugh in her hand as it spilled out over her fingers.

"That's a great name for a kitten," she said.

"I agree." Lex's smile grew wider. "I think it's because of the calico pattern, but I'm not quite sure."

And for a long moment they sat there, neither of them saying anything, just listening to the sound of the rain beating against the window and the fire crackling in the hearth. She turned to face him and leaned back against the opposite arm of the chair. Their knees bumped.

"I called Will and briefed him," she said. "We had a short team meeting tonight and will have another longer one tomorrow with the entire team."

"Your entire team is participating in a joint meeting about Johnny's murder and the poaching of blue bear cubs?" he asked.

"Yes and no," she replied. "We try to have regular team meetings with the K-9 unit about the various cases we're working on. We have three main ongoing investigations right now, along with this one."

"What are the other cases?" he asked.

For a moment she wondered if he was just making small talk, until she saw the keen interest shining in his eyes.

"Well, one that's right up your alley is what's been happening at the Family K Reindeer Sanctuary Ranch," she said.

"That's the one run by Addie Kapowski?"

She wasn't surprised he was familiar with it. Lex had always had a close relationship with the various animal sanctuaries around Anchorage.

"Yup," she said. "Addie's niece, Katie, is my boss Lorenza's assistant. A pen of reindeer were let loose recently and all but two were accounted for. Stormy and I were part of the team that found one of them, but the other one is still missing and we can't discount the possibility it was stolen and whoever poached it will be back for more."

Lex frowned. "If there's anything I can do to help with that, let me know."

"Thanks," she said. "I'm sure my team will appreciate that. Also, I'm looking forward to hearing from my colleagues Sean and Gabriel, who are currently searching Chugach State Park for a family of survivalists named the Seavers. The father of the family is the son of our tech guru Eli's godmother. She's dying of cancer and hoping to reconcile with them before it's too late."

"Chugach State Park is also where a bride recently went missing, right?" Lex asked.

Considering the case had made national news she shouldn't be too shocked it reached Gustavus.

"Violet James, yes," she said. "I've been working that case, too."

"Did they ever find any of them? I haven't really followed the case."

"The tour guide, Cal Brooks, was found murdered," she informed him. "The maid of honor, Ariel Potter, was found at the bottom of a cliff with nonfatal injuries. She helped us find the missing reindeer actually and is now engaged to my colleague Hunter McCord. I really like her. The groom, Lance Wells, and the best man, Jared Dennis, were found holed up in a cabin and severely injured. Lance had been hit over the head and Jared was shot. They say it was Violet."

"Who is still missing," Lex confirmed.

"Who is pregnant and believed to be on the run," Poppy said. "Lance claims she was having an affair with the dead tour guide and the baby is Cal's. I'm suspicious of Lance, though, after the mixed messages I got from my interviews and not sure he can be trusted." Then she found Will's words leaving her lips. "After all, there are far easier ways to get out of marrying a bridezilla than trying to kill them."

It was a throwaway line, something meaningless, and she wasn't even sure why she'd said it.

But Lex leaned toward her and grabbed her hands.

"You don't think that's what happened with us, right?" he asked thickly.

"Not really, no," she said, "although I had gotten very caught up in wedding planning—"

"Because you were incredibly organized," Lex interjected. "You were good at all that wedding stuff so I just left you to it."

"I didn't want you to leave me to it." Poppy stood, pulling her hands out of his grasp. Was that what he thought? "I wanted us to work together. I wanted us to be partners. But you said it yourself, just hours ago, that we were never good at being a team. It was like you never wanted to listen when I talked about wedding plans, and every time I made an appointment for something important you canceled on me because somebody else needed you more."

He leaped to his feet, too, and for a long moment they just stood there, face-to-face, just a breath away from each other, and neither of them stepped back.

"I don't understand," Lex said. "You think I called off marrying you because I didn't want to help you with wedding planning?"

"No, of course not," Poppy protested. "I didn't know what to think. How could I? You didn't explain. You just told me you weren't ready to be a husband or father."

"I told you I was having doubts," Lex said. "I was very honest about that."

"But you never explained why you were having doubts about me…or what I could do about it."

"Because I wasn't having doubts about you!" Lex burst out. "You might be the most dedicated and driven person I've ever met in my life, but you still can't fix something that's not your doing. I didn't have a single doubt that you were an incredible, amazing, beautiful woman and any man would give his right arm to be married to you." His voice dropped, his tone growing huskier. "I doubted that I could be what you needed and that I had what it took to be the kind of man you deserved."

Poppy's heart seemed to gasp, sending shivers coursing through her veins. A moment later, she took a deep, fortifying breath and forced herself to have the courage to say the words she needed to say. "Then you went and had a family with somebody else."

"Do you think I was the same man when I had Danny that I was when I gave up on us?" he asked. "Because I wasn't. Losing you broke me into pieces. It destroyed me, blew my life apart, made me reexamine my life and, with God's help, reshaped me into being someone better than I'd ever been before." He stepped closer and their fingertips touched. "Losing you changed me, irrevocably."

"It changed me, too," she whispered.

Thunder crashed outside the window. She looked up into his handsome face and watched as something softened in the depths of his eyes. His mouth opened, and then closed again, as if his brain kept coming up with words he wouldn't let himself speak. Finally, he said, "I'm sorry if I ever made you doubt how much I wanted you to be my wife."

His fingers brushed up her arm until they rested on her cheek. Her hands slid up his back. And they both stood there for a long moment, frozen in a tableau, and Poppy feeling somehow both lost and found at once.

"What are you thinking?" she asked.

Lex broke his gaze as a wistful grin turned at one corner of his mouth. "Honestly?"

"Yes, honestly," she said.

His eyes met hers again. "I'm thinking I missed you."

SEVEN

"I missed you, too," Poppy admitted softly. Then she felt her eyes close as Lex pulled her closer into his chest. Her face tilted up toward his.

"Lex!" Gillian's voice sounded from somewhere behind them as footsteps clattered on the stairs.

She opened her eyes and leaped back, feeling Lex pull away from her equally as fast. They turned and she watched as the older woman appeared in the doorway. And Poppy wasn't sure if she'd just arrived on the main floor, or if she'd seen their embrace and then stepped back and announced her presence to be polite. The cheerful smile that crossed Gillian's face as she entered the room gave nothing away.

"Actually, I was looking for you, Poppy," she said. "I wanted to ask you again if you and your colleague would consider relocating here for your time in Gustavus. We have two large suites on the main floor that would have plenty of room for your K-9 partners. You'd have full use of the kitchen and the fenced-in backyard. And as we don't open again for the season for a few days yet, you'd be free to use our common areas for your meetings. We've also got high-speed internet, plus a photo-quality color printer and fax machine if you need it."

The idea of getting out of the motel was even more appealing now after she'd spent a bit more time there and Eli had said the motel's internet wasn't up to the task for what he needed for the meeting tomorrow. As much as she'd enjoyed taking Stormy for a walk, it was no substitute to having an actual yard she could play in.

"I'll be honest," Gillian added. "I'd feel safer with you here. It's twice in one day we've had a prowler outside our home watching my grandson. And as you know, we don't have an active police force in Gustavus. If you need, I can call your boss and formally request your protection."

"I'm sure she'll agree," Poppy said, "and as for Will, he'll be thrilled to move him and Scout here. Thank you."

In fact, there was no good reason to stay in the motel when they could relocate the operation here. None except the fact she suspected the man who'd once broken her heart had been about to kiss her, and she'd been on the verge of kissing him, too.

Thankfully calling Will gave her an excuse to walk away from the confusing moment she'd almost had with Lex and the distraction of something else to think about.

Within moments her colleague had agreed to relocate. While the continued threat against Lex's son and the realization they'd be better equipped to do their jobs and coordinate with their team from the bed-and-breakfast definitely played into it, she was sure part of him was just happy to be out of the underwhelming surroundings. Since she hadn't unpacked her suitcase yet and had even left it zipped, Will was happy to grab her stuff and bring it over with him and Scout.

Less than half an hour later, he had arrived, and Gillian was showing Poppy to her new digs. The room had high ceilings, with an en-suite bathroom and a large colorful rug more than big enough for Stormy to stretch out on at the end of the large four-poster bed. Lex was standing in the living room with Will as she said a quick good-night to them both, without quite meeting Lex's eye. Then she lay awake, willing her body to sleep and reminding herself of all the reasons why this relocation made the most logical sense, despite what her heart might feel.

She awoke to sun streaming through the window, the scent of coffee, eggs and bacon wafting down the hall from the kitchen and the gentle whine of Stormy standing politely by the bed. The wolfhound's head plonked down on the pillow beside Poppy's at eye level. She rolled over and rubbed Stormy between the ears. Then she got up, got dressed and steeled herself to face whatever the day held.

When she stepped out into the hallway and headed for the living area, a cacophony of ridiculous and happy noises reached her ears, including what sounded like giggling, howling and high-pitched music wailing. What was she listening to? She rounded the corner as Stormy galloped in one step ahead of her, and saw Danny sitting alone in a high chair at the kitchen table facing Will's laptop and laughing wildly.

A few more steps into the room revealed Will was standing by the counter, fixing himself coffee, and Lex was at the stove making scrambled eggs. Each was keeping a watchful eye on whatever Danny was doing.

The tall and blond form of Trooper Sean West sat at a desk, attempting what sounded like "Twinkle Twinkle Little Star" on a harmonica while his K-9 partner, an Akita named Grace, was sing slash howling along. Danny was a rapt audience, oscillating between trying to sing and dissolving into giggles.

Sean's eye met hers through the screen and he grinned.

She waved and he waved back.

"Hey, Poppy!" Sean said. "Sorry, been having a lot of time alone in remote areas recently and been trying to teach myself something new. Still need a lot of practice."

She laughed.

"It's great," she said. "Don't stop on my account."

Her colleague's grin widened.

"Are you good with starting our team meeting in fifteen or twenty?" Sean asked.

She glanced around the kitchen. An array of cereal, bagels, bacon and fruit spread across the kitchen counter, along with the scrambled eggs Lex was fixing.

"No problem," she said.

"Great, I'll let the others know," Sean said. He pushed a button and his face disappeared.

She turned and looked quizzically at Will.

"Am I late?" she asked.

"Sean's early," Will said. "He and Gabriel had a lead he wanted to chase, so he called hoping that we could bump up the call time."

"Big doggy sing, too?" Danny's hopeful voice drew her gaze back to where the toddler sat in his high chair pushing cereal around on the table.

"She doesn't sing," Poppy told him. "But she barks and howls, very loudly."

Danny's little face fell.

"But she does other tricks. Do you want to see?"

The little boy's eyes widened again as he nodded. Wordlessly Lex took the skillet of eggs off the heat, turned the stove off, fixed a cup of coffee and came around the other side of the island to join his son. She hadn't even realized that he'd fixed the coffee for her until he offered it to her and asked, "Half a spoonful of sugar, two splashes of milk, right?"

He'd remembered.

"Perfect," she said. "Thank you."

He set it down on the table in front of her. She picked it up, took a long sip, then called Stormy over to her side, oddly feeling the same nervous flutter in her chest of not wanting to let her audience down that she'd felt when demonstrating Stormy's training to Lorenza.

Immediately, the wolfhound left the ray of sun by the sliding door where she'd been chilling with Scout, walked over and stood in front of her expectedly. Poppy did a quick mental calculation. Standing, the dog's face was almost parallel with her shoulder, and despite the fact the ceiling was probably nine feet, showing off how high the dog could leap was probably best left as an outside trick.

"Okay," she said, "I'm going to give Stormy some instructions and you copy what I do, okay?"

Danny's smile lit his face. "'Kay!"

She slowly walked Stormy through sitting, lying down, rolling and crawling, while Lex helped Danny follow along with the gestures and commands. Gillian appeared in the doorway partway through the demonstration and stood there watching the show. Danny's favorite trick was definitely watching the huge dog sneakily crawling across the floor like a secret agent and had her demonstrate it three times, before Lex chal-

Wilderness Defender

lenged Stormy to see which one of them could crawl the quietest and most stealthily. The dog won. Finally, she took her K-9 partner's favorite ball and hid it behind the bookshelf while Danny covered the dog's eyes with her ears. Stormy dutifully weaved her way around the room sniffing, before sitting in front of the shelf and woofing triumphantly. Danny clapped and cheered.

His grandmother scooped him up into his arms. "Come on, little man. You need to get ready for preschool. I'll be staying as a special helper with you today, too."

Danny waved goodbye to Stormy as he left. The dog trotted to the sliding door and barked hopefully. Poppy let him and Scout out, not even realizing Mushroom had joined them, too, until she skittered past her ankles. She watched for a moment as the three animals jumped and pounced in the air around each other in some elaborate game the three of them all seemed to understand, then she went and helped herself to breakfast.

Ten minutes later, Poppy sat at the kitchen table beside Will, who made a big show of pointing out just how many chair options there were compared to their meeting in the dingy motel the night before. As the team video call reloaded, she could see Lex in the screen's reflection behind them. He was standing at the counter, as if waiting to see if he should go, despite the fact Will had asked him to stay for now. Between Gillian, Danny and Will, she and Lex hadn't been alone in the room once since their awkward moment the night before.

Lord, help me just focus on my job today.

The video call started, and boxes popped up around the screen with Lorenza, Eli and Maya, now joined by Sean, Gabriel Runyon and Brayden Ford, with various

K-9 partners wandering in and out of the shots for pats and to wag their tails at the screen. The only two team members absent were Helena and Hunter. Helena was off interviewing Lance's sister, Tessa, as she'd mentioned the night before. And Hunter was taking some well-deserved time off with his new fiancée, Ariel.

"Anybody else feel like we're all in a 1980s game show when we're on one of these calls?" Eli asked, glancing around the screen. "Will and Poppy, you're coming through much clearer and sharper this morning. So, I'm going to try to load up the graphics I mentioned last night." He started typing furiously.

Lorenza waved to the group, wished everyone a good-morning and started the meeting.

"I'd like to introduce everyone to Park Ranger Lex Fielding," Will said, gesturing behind him. "I hope it's okay that I've included him in this meeting. I think he'll have some good insights on the information Eli's sending through."

"Of course." Lorenza smiled widely. "It's nice to see you again, Lex."

Again?

"I didn't realize you'd ever met," Poppy said.

She glanced at Lex in surprise, but it was Lorenza who answered.

"We met at an Alaskan trooper recruitment event some years back," she said. "As I remember, his fiancée had been encouraging him to consider a career with the troopers. We had a great talk about his skills and interests, and I recommended he stay with the park rangers, as that seemed to be where both his talents and his heart lay. Glad to see you did," she added with a smile, "because it might be good to get your input on some of this, too."

Sean and Gabriel opened by quickly running the team through their attempts to search Chugach State Park for Eli's godmother's survivalist family. Sean explained that while they'd seen no glimpse of the family itself, they had run into two hunters who looked like survivalists. When they'd asked about the Seavers, the hunters had been tightlipped and told them to mind their own business.

"They didn't exactly threaten us," Gabriel added, scratching his Saint Bernard partner, Bear, on the top of his shaggy head. "But it was also implied it would be in our own best interest to stop poking around asking questions. More troubling is that we sidestepped a few fairly nasty traps set in the forest, which we suspect were more for keeping nosy outsiders away than actual hunting."

"What kind of traps?" Lex asked. He moved forward and leaned a palm on the table beside her. "Do you think they were specifically designed for people?"

Poppy sat back and listened as her colleagues described the various traps they'd come across in detail, including trip wires, ropes and various incapacitating weapons. Lex leaned even farther toward the camera, peppering them with very specific questions and then explaining in detail how such snares were constructed and how to avoid them. Poppy could tell that Sean and Gabriel were beyond thankful. She also couldn't help but notice there was that same spark in Lorenza's eyes as she listened to Lex, that her boss got whenever she seemed to be internally celebrating seeing a member of the team excel at their work. Poppy didn't know whether she should be more surprised that Lex had actually gone to an Alaska trooper recruitment event and sought out her mentor for advice—or by the fact he hadn't told her.

As expected, there was no update on the missing bride case as they'd discussed it the night before. She gathered that forensic scientist, Tala Ekho, who wasn't on the call, presumably hadn't finished analyzing the watch that was found at the bottom of the cliff. Although Poppy knew that Lex would've quickly left the room if they had, as he was a civilian and Lorenza would've been unlikely to allow him to be briefed on the case without very good reason.

Then came Eli's briefing on the blue bear poachers.

"So, the bad news is I'm still no closer to figuring out where this black market auction is going to take place," Eli said. His mouth scrunched in a grimace "It's all very vague and encrypted. I never would've even found these posts if we hadn't known about this poaching case from Lex."

Who'd learned about it from Johnny, Poppy thought, who it seemed had lost his life because of it.

"Do we know when it's happening?" Poppy asked.

"It says the day after tomorrow," Eli said.

"Which gives them a pretty small window of time to poach the second bear cub," Poppy pointed out.

And not a lot of time for the team to stop them.

Eli nodded. "But the good news is we've now got pictures."

He clicked a button and a slideshow of images he'd pulled from the dark web postings filled the screen. There sat a blue bear cub sitting cramped and miserable in what looked like a dog carrier.

"What kind of monster would do that to a defense-less animal!" Maya exclaimed off-screen.

"Agreed!" Brayden chimed in. "First we've got reindeer disappearing off Katie's aunt's farm and now this."

Frustration coursed through the trooper's voice like he wanted to step through the screen and rescue the cub himself. Poppy knew how he felt as she stared into the sad bear's eyes.

Lord, please help me find and rescue this poor baby and find his sibling before it's captured.

"Now they claim to have captured a male cub," Eli went on, and it sounded like he was doing his best to push his own emotional reaction at bay, "and that the other cub is female. Here they are together."

The screen clicked and a picture of two much smaller bear cubs filled the screen, with their mother in the background. The mother looked like a black bear, except for a silvery sheen of fur on her stomach and paws, but the two cubs' fur had a distinct silver-blue sheen.

"Yeah, those are definitely blue bears," Lex breathed. "Can you expand the picture at all?"

"On it," Eli said, and the picture grew to show that they were at the water's edge with what looked like a steep rock slope behind them leading up to forest beyond.

"I know where that is!" Lex declared. His finger jabbed in the direction of the screen. "It'll take about two hours to get there, first by truck and then by boat. Although judging by the bear's size this was taken several weeks ago. Still, it's worth checking out."

"Do it," Lorenza said. Her face reappeared on the screen with the rest of the team and her gaze fixed on Poppy. "If the post's timeline is correct, we don't have much time to stop the second cub from being poached. Lex, I assume you can take her there?"

He nodded. "Absolutely."

Poppy tried not to think about the fact this meant they'd be spending more time alone. Stormy was a poacher-detection dog, and she'd spent far more time working in national parks than Will. It made perfect sense for her to be the one to go with Lex.

Still...

"Will," Lorenza continued, "I'd like you to talk to anyone you can who's connected to the watering hole where Johnny supposedly overheard this information. I want to know everyone he talked to, played pool with, threw darts with and sat next to in the past two months. We'll also see what we can pull up from this end about Ripley, her brother, Nolan, and her ex-boyfriend." She glanced to Lex. "Do you happen to know her ex-boyfriend's name?"

"Sorry, no," Lex said. He shook his head and sighed. "I hadn't really been in touch with Johnny for the past few months and he was always very private about his relationships. If anything he was the kind of guy who didn't admit he was in some kind of trouble until it was too late."

The call ended shortly afterward in a flurry of goodbyes, and while Poppy had also been hoping for an update on the missing reindeer case, she looked forward to the next time she could talk to Lorenza's assistant about it, to find out how things were on her aunt's reindeer farm.

Poppy finished her own breakfast, fed Stormy along with Scout and Mushroom, went for a quick walk with her K-9 partner and then got herself ready for the day.

When she left the house and got to the truck, she found Will and Lex talking, and while they wrapped up as she approached, she couldn't shake the feeling they were talking about something seriously.

She wished Will a good day and got into the truck with Stormy, and then Lex headed out. For a long moment, he didn't say anything.

"Everything okay?" she asked eventually. "Things seemed tense with you and Will."

"They were fine," Lex said. His eyes were fixed on the road ahead. "Will just wanted to give me his condolences on Johnny's death and say that he would do everything he could to make sure the poachers were caught and Johnny's killer faced justice."

He paused for a long moment, but she had the hunch he wasn't finished. Eventually he added, "He also wanted to apologize, although I said it wasn't necessary. He said he might've been a little harsh in his assessment of Johnny yesterday, but you'd set him straight."

Now, finally, Lex glanced her way. "He said you told him that Johnny once said he'd take a bullet for me. That was really nice of you to stand up for him that way."

"No problem," she said. "I mean, we still don't know everything that happened between Johnny and the poachers. But I know he really cared about you and I don't think he'd ever knowingly hurt you or your family."

Lex looked straight ahead. "Did Johnny ever tell you he'd take a bullet for you, too, if you married me?"

"He did," she admitted. "I told Will that, as well."

"Even though you never really liked him?" Lex asked.

"I didn't like some of the stuff he did," she admitted.

"I didn't like thinking that his life was going down the drain and maybe taking you with it. I always suspected he told you not to marry me."

"Oh, he did," Lex said. "He tried to talk me out of marrying you more than once. He told me he thought I could do better and I told him he'd got that backward."

They drove through the gate to Glacier Bay National Park. Tall fir trees towered around them on both sides.

"Why didn't you tell me you'd gone to a trooper recruitment event and met my boss?" she asked quietly.

"Because nothing came of it," Lex said. "We had a long talk and she advised me to stay a park ranger—that was it."

There was more to it than that, Poppy suspected, seeing the way Lex's brow was furrowed. But she could also tell by the way he had answered the question he wasn't about to tell her more now.

They drove through the national park, and Lex stopped briefly to check in with colleagues at the ranger's station. Then they went down to a dock, where a small, white park ranger boat was docked. He climbed on board the boat, then hesitated as if he wasn't sure whether or not to reach for her hand. She and Stormy leaped on board.

Lex pulled out his phone.

"You should check for any messages now," he said, "before we get going. Once we get into the glaciers cell signal pretty much disappears. Although I do have both a satellite phone and radio for emergencies."

"Thanks." She got out her phone, checked the screen and didn't see anything out of the usual, just a few follow-up messages from the team meeting earlier.

Then she glanced at Lex. He was staring down at the

phone in his hand, his fingers white and his jaw set so tightly it almost shook.

"Hey, Lex?" She stepped toward him and brushed her hand against his arm. "Everything okay?"

His eyes met hers, fury roiling in their depths.

"I just got a text," he said. "It's from a blocked number."

He held up the phone so she could read.

You saw what happened to your friend. Now you know what happens to people who try to mess with me. This is your final warning. Stay out of my business. Or your son is next.

A coldness seemed to cut through the air as the boat drove through the choppy Pacific waters that had nothing to do with the snowcapped glaciers that hemmed them on either side.

Lex had listened in as Poppy had informed the team of the threatening text and Eli had promised they'd do their best to track it. Both he and Poppy had spoken to Will and made him aware. He'd also called his mother, who'd promised she'd keep Danny surrounded by friends until Lex, Will or Poppy was able to take over watching him. They'd done all they could do. And yet, as they drove through the stunning and picturesque national park, past the roughly hewn rocks, waterfalls, endless trees and towering ice, a deep anguish settled in his heart that seemed to overshadow his ability to even see or appreciate the world around him.

Help me, Lord. First they kill Johnny. Now they threaten my son.

He glanced at the woman standing next to him,

her dark red hair flying in the breeze and tickling her cheeks. She could've stayed in the lower, covered part of the boat where Stormy now dozed. But she'd chosen to stand up by the wheel beside him. Not talking or trying to draw him out in conversation, and instead just being there.

Somehow knowing that was exactly what he needed.

"What do you think of Glacier Bay?" he asked.

"It really is stunning," Poppy said. Wonder filled her voice. "No wonder you wanted to bring me here and show me all this."

Yeah, Lex thought, he really had back when he'd been planning on spending the rest of his life with her. Long before he'd decided that this very small town and huge, glacial national park was where he wanted to escape to in order to start his new life, part of him had always loved it here.

Despite himself he felt an old familiar grin curl on his lips.

"I knew you'd love it," he said.

"You were right," Poppy said. "In fact, the only thing that's stopping me from moving to a place like this myself is my job. Being based in Anchorage allows us to respond to cases all over the state quickly. Out here, we'd have to fly hours everywhere we went. It just wouldn't work."

True. Which is why he'd never even considered it until she'd been gone from his life.

She fell silent again and questions tumbled through his mind as he glanced at the beautiful woman beside him. He'd told her so much about the life he'd lived since he'd last seen her face. But he knew so little about hers. Sure, he knew about her job and could see first-hand how she'd excelled at it. He knew her last name hadn't changed; she'd never mentioned a family and didn't wear a wedding ring. But had she gone on to have any other relationships? Had she ever fallen in love again? And if so, why did the thought bother him so much when he'd clearly gone on to get married and have a family of his own?

Or was having a job she loved enough for her?

"Your team seems pretty amazing," he said.

She smiled. "They are."

"Please thank your colleague Sean for me for spending all that time with Danny," he said. "It was really kind, and Danny had so much fun talking with him."

"I will," Poppy said. "Sean's great with kids. I get the impression sometimes he wishes he had some of his own. I don't know the whole story, but he was married once and it didn't work out. His ex-wife, Ivy, grew up in a survivalist family, which is why he's taken a lead in helping us find the Seavers."

She turned and faced him, sending her hair flying down one side of her face. It was stunning. He took a deep breath.

"I'm a bit surprised you never had kids of your own," he admitted. "I thought there'd be a line of guys a mile long wanting to ask you out."

Poppy shrugged. "Well, if so, nobody told me."

Was she blind? Did she really have no idea how attractive and impressive she was?

"What about Teddy England?" Lex asked. Poppy's nose wrinkled a moment like she was mentally putting a face to the name. "He was a park ranger at Kenai Fjords National Park back when we worked together. He really liked you."

She snorted. "Teddy was an arrogant jerk. Who cares what he thought of me? I was engaged to you."

She was right. He shouldn't have cared that some other man, who'd clearly made no great impression on Poppy, had been interested in his fiancée. He turned his gaze back to watching the horizon and the boat slowed as he neared the inlet.

"You're frowning," Poppy said. "What's up?"

He shrugged. "It's nothing."

"You didn't let me get away with refusing to answer your question yesterday that I wanted to ignore," Poppy said. Her arms crossed over her chest.

"It probably sounds ridiculous now," Lex admitted, "but back when we were engaged Teddy overheard me saying that I wasn't sure I ever wanted kids. He pulled me aside and told me in no uncertain terms that if I wasn't able to give you what you needed, I should step aside and let you be with a man that would."

"Well, that's one the dumbest things I've ever heard," she said. "I'm a person not an object. I make my own choices about what I want and need, not some entitled weirdo at work."

She laughed but irritation flashed in her eyes,

"So, both Teddy and Johnny tried to talk you out of marrying me?" she asked. "Johnny because he thought I wasn't good enough for you, and Teddy who thought you didn't deserve me. I'd ask if there was anyone who didn't try to convince you that marrying me was a bad idea, but instead I'm more curious as to why you cared what anyone else thought as long as we were happy?"

He ran one hand over his face, wishing he had a good answer to that question, but realizing he didn't. She watched his face for one long moment, as if hoping for an answer. Then she turned away, giving up, and went back to join Stormy in the sheltered part of the boat.

Help me, Lord. He never had the courage to say the words he needed to say in the past. Turned out he still didn't now.

Finally, he saw the inlet ahead and slowly steered the boat into shore. He stopped the boat, dropped anchor and then leaped ashore and tied the rope to a huge and ancient tree jutting out of the rock for backup. When he turned to help Poppy, she and Stormy were already scrambling to shore. The dog began to sniff and within seconds she barked.

"Well, looks like we have the right place," Poppy said. She hitched her backpack up higher on her shoulder. Despite the waves of conflicting and confusing emotions that had passed between them on the boat, Poppy was all professional now as she and her K-9 partner traced their way along the shoreline. They found more candy wrappers, potato chip bags and general garbage that lay in between the crevasses, just like they'd found back at the cabin. Even without a word he could see her rancor at seeing how the poachers had littered, as well as her frustration over the fact that it was too muddy to be worth collecting for usable prints. A well-worn patch of mud and grass made it clear the path the poachers had used to climb up and down the glacier.

Stormy barked and indicated toward the slope.

"Go ahead," Poppy told her partner. "Just don't go far."

The dog licked her fingers as she reached to run her hand along the wolfhound's side. Then Stormy turned and galloped up the slope, her long legs moving far faster than either he or Poppy would ever be able to climb.

She glanced at Lex. "I'm going to head up there and join her."

"I'll be up in a second," Lex said. "I just want to take some pictures of the area. I do need to warn you, the glacier is huge. Just because the poachers used this as their entrance point doesn't mean the blue bears are still anywhere near this area."

"Got it." Her eyes lingered on his face for a split second, like she was about to say something more. Then she turned and made her way up the hill after Stormy, until finally she reached the top and he lost sight of her flaming red hair in between the dark green trees.

He let out a long breath and ran both hands over his face. His heart was so heavy from every aspect of the bear poaching case, and even though he knew that right now his small son was safe and being looked after, the lingering fear of the threat made against Danny still hung over him like a pending electrical storm.

And thinking of storms, he had absolutely no idea what to make of the charged moment between him and Poppy on the boat. It was unlike him to blurt out his own insecurities, no matter how incredibly true it had been.

It was also the first time he'd seen with his own eyes how much his getting caught up in other people's opinions of their relationship hurt her. He wasn't quite sure why he'd convinced himself so thoroughly that the fact she hadn't fallen apart when he'd called off the wedding meant she hadn't cared about him as much as he'd loved her.

Maybe he'd just been projecting his own insecurities onto her.

He glanced to the sky and prayed.

Lord, this might be the worst possible time for Poppy to be back in my life. But I'm also really glad she's the one here with me now. I can't imagine facing all this without her. Please, help me be the man You've called me to be, whatever Your plan.

"Lex!" Poppy's terrified voice cut through the air toward him, slightly strangled as if the last syllable of his name had caught in her throat, in a single word telling him everything he needed to know.

She was in danger.

"Hang on, Poppy!" he shouted. "I'm coming!"

He sprinted up the hill, even as his feet slid underneath him on the slick ground, and he had to grasp on to rough brush and rocks for stability. Finally, he reached the top and ran into the thick trees, following a path so narrow it kept threatening to disappear with every step.

Then he saw Poppy standing stock-still, her right hand raised as if telling an unseen Stormy not to move.

A large brown bear towered before her, teeth bared, snarling and poised to strike.

EIGHT

Poppy froze face-to-face with the bear as it loomed over her, its mammoth claws just one swipe away from ending her life.

Years of training in how to handle a bear attack in the wild battled the overwhelming and palpable terror that had swept over her the instant she'd heard it roar. There was bear spray in the side pouch of her backpack. But from where she stood, there was no way to get it without flinching, and that could be deadly. As for the gun at her side, she wouldn't kill the bear unless it was absolutely necessary. Even then, considering how close it was to her, she might not even be able to get off a shot.

Brown bears were the deadliest of all the bears in Alaska.

There were two options to survive and she knew the guidelines better than anyone. Either be large—travel in groups, bang pots and make noise. Or in the worst-case scenario, become small, curl up into a ball and play dead. Neither were options now. She'd been foolish enough to walk through here alone.

Even worse, she'd put her partner in danger.

Poppy glimpsed past the snarling mass of teeth and

claws roaring its intentions to end her, to where Stormy was tensed, crouched low and almost entirely hidden in the woods to her right. She'd had her eyes on the dog when the bear had reared in front of her, and hurriedly given her partner the signal to freeze. She knew the fearless wolfhound would attack the bear without hesitation. But she also knew that Stormy would probably be badly injured if she did.

Her partner might even be killed. Bears had been known to even charge at cars and other vehicles if they felt threatened. Her brave partner was just a pip-squeak in comparison. Poppy's heart beat so hard she could feel it pounding against her chest. She tried to pray, but her mind couldn't get further than, *Help me, God.*

"Poppy, don't move," Lex said from somewhere behind her. His voice was firm and strong, and seemed to cut through the fear welling up inside her. "Just stay calm and stay still. It's going to be okay."

How could he possibly know that? One wrong move on her part, and the bear would strike. And she couldn't save her own life without risking her partner's. She nodded as slightly as she dared, hoping Lex would see the motion and know she'd heard him. The bear growled a deep and guttural roar. Then Poppy heard Lex slowly and quietly walking into danger to stand beside her. Even without turning, she felt him lift the can of bear spray from her backpack. His arm brushed against her side and his fingers linked with hers.

"What are you doing?" she whispered.

"Strength in numbers," Lex said. "We look like a bigger, stronger force together."

The bear didn't move. Neither did Lex. He just stood

there facing the bear, holding her hand and standing his ground.

"We have to protect Stormy," she whispered without even turning to look at him. "I don't want the bear getting her."

Her eyes fixed on her partner's shaggy face.

"I see her," Lex said softly. She heard the faint plastic and metallic clink of the safety cap being flicked off the can. "Now, I need you to take a deep breath, close your eyes and trust me. Okay?"

"Okay." She closed her eyes.

"Lord, help us."

In one swift motion, Lex pulled her into his chest with one hand and cradled her face against him. With the other, he detonated the spray. The bear roared in rage and pain. The thick vaguely acidic smell filled the air. She could feel Lex's heart beating against her chest and heard the sound of something crashing into the woods and felt Lex stepping back.

Then Stormy growled and Poppy opened her eyes to see the bear turn. It had finally realized Stormy was there. The disoriented bear charged on all fours toward Stormy. Snarling, the wolfhound leaped at the approaching animal, teeth bared. Partially blinded, the bear lashed out with a weakened blow that sent Stormy temporarily sprawling into the underbrush, only for Poppy's partner to leap up again, braced and ready for the fight.

The bear hesitated, the turned and lumbered off into the woods. Stormy barked furiously at the departing animal as if warning it not to return. Then she trotted over and butted her head against Poppy's hand. She wasn't even limping, let alone scratched or injured. The wolfhound's eyebrows raised as if asking if she should chase the bear. Poppy laughed. "Stay, Stormy. Good dog. You are such a very good dog."

Then she realized her other hand was still clutching Lex's.

She turned toward him and, as she did, her free hand grabbed ahold of his jacket collar.

"Thank you," she said. "Also, that was the single most reckless and dangerous thing you've ever done. Since when do park rangers run toward brown bears? This wasn't in any of the training I remember."

A cross between a laugh and a relieved sob choked in her throat as she said it. He chuckled softly and dropped the canister of bear spray. His other hand brushed the hair off her face.

"You're welcome," he murmured. "Now, are you okay?"

Suddenly it was as if the tension holding her limbs together gave way and her legs collapsed, almost sending her tumbling to the ground.

"Hey, it's okay, I've got you." He dropped her hand and wrapped both of his arms around the small of her back, pulling her into his chest. Then his right hand ran up the curve of her spine until it rested on her neck. "It's just the sudden jolt of adrenaline wearing off."

Poppy knew that, but it didn't change how good it felt to be held in Lex's arms. She reached her arms up and wrapped them around his neck.

"The bear will be fine, too," he added. "The spray will wear off in no time with no permanent damage."

"I know," she said. "You've never been the kind of person to kill an animal when there was a way you could save it."

"I would've to save your life," he said.

"I know." Just like she knew it might've been even more dangerous for him to fire a gun in a forest that dense where there was the possibility she or Stormy could be hurt. "But you'd be just as likely to wound it and then volunteer at an animal rescue to nurse it back to health."

He chuckled. "True, but hey, my plan worked, didn't it?"

"I said it was reckless," she said. "I never doubted it would work."

"I didn't know if you'd trust me."

"I've *always* trusted you," she told him.

Her face tilted up toward his and his arms tightened around her.

"And I will always be there when you need me," Lex vowed. "No matter where you go and no matter what happens in our lives, if you're ever in danger and you call on me, I will be there for you."

"I know," she admitted.

Before she could say anything more, his lips met hers. Lex kissed her and she kissed him back, both of them holding on to each other as if they'd never been apart.

Stormy growled with that soft rumble, warning her of danger. Poppy pulled back out of Lex's arms and turned to her partner, but not before she saw something like confusion fill Lex's eyes.

"What is it?" she asked her partner. "What do you sense? Show me."

Stormy barked and ran back the way they'd come. She followed, Lex beside her, until they reached the edge of the woods and looked down. A small nondescript speedboat had pulled up beside Lex's park ranger boat.

A thin masked figure in fatigues stood on the deck

of their boat. The second larger one was untying it from the rock where Lex had fastened it.

The poachers were here, and they were stealing their boat.

Lex reached for his weapon, praying he wouldn't have to use it. Open cliffside lay before him, sloping down to the water below with no cover in sight. Both poachers were armed and once he stepped out of the trees he'd be an open target. But letting them steal his boat, leaving them stranded on a remote glacier, wasn't an option.

"Go," Poppy said. "I'll cover you."

Any doubt that she wouldn't never crossed his mind.

He took a deep breath, turned and ran down toward the water, knowing his best advantage was the element of surprise. Lex fired a warning shot in the air. It arched high above the larger man in camo who'd been trying to untie Lex's boat. The man yelped and leaped back.

But the thinner poacher wasn't as easily deterred. He turned from his post on Lex's boat and stepped up onto the side as if preparing to leap down. The poacher raised his weapon and aimed it directly at Lex as he scrambled down the cliff toward them. But he never got the chance to fire, as Poppy took aim. Her bullet rang off the side of the boat and ricocheted safely into the water, far enough away from the poacher so as not to risk hitting him, but close enough to startle him. The poacher slipped and fell off Lex's boat and into the cold Pacific waters. The larger man hesitated as if debating whether to return fire. But then Lex watched the man's face pale and in an instant he knew why, as Stormy leaped to Lex's side, charging down the slope beside him.

The thinner poacher scrambled from the water and

back into his own boat, swearing and bellowing for his partner to follow. The larger poacher turned and ran after him, splashing knee-deep into the water and barely making it into the smaller boat as his partner gunned the engine. In seconds the small speedboat had disappeared from sight.

Lex paused on a narrow ledge and gasped a breath as he felt Poppy reach his side. They kept climbing down the slippery cliffside as quickly as they dared, letting Stormy take the lead.

"The precision of that shot," he said, "considering the distance was incredible."

"Thanks," she said. "I've had a lot of practice."

Lex imagined she had. But there was also a relaxed confidence that hadn't been there before. Back then she'd been so focused on the plans she'd made and guidelines she was following it was as if she believed that if she stuck to them precisely she'd be able to keep anything bad from happening to them. It had made her tense and on edge. He hadn't realized until long after he'd lost her how his impulsive way of canceling plans and dashing off to help his friends had made the situation worse and added to her stress.

Maybe he'd been a little harsh when he'd told her that they'd never been any good at being partners. After all, he hadn't exactly been focused back then on figuring out how to be the partner she needed.

As soon as they were all on board, the rope coiled and the anchor raised, Lex gunned the engine and they took off in the direction the poachers had gone. They searched the surrounding inlet, coves and islands for over an hour and came up empty. While the criminals didn't have too large a head start, there were just too many places a boat that size could hide in the sprawling national park, and the last thing Lex wanted was to be lured out of safe waters into a dangerous game of cat and mouse with a heavily armed foe.

Finally, they had no choice but to give up the hunt.

"The poachers won't return to that inlet," Poppy said. She leaned on the console beside him in the bow of the boat and looked out over the endless gray-blue water spreading out ahead of them. "They probably liked it because it was a secluded way to climb that glacier without too much risk of being noticed. Now that they know we've found that spot, the location is compromised. They'll regroup and find another route to get to the bears."

"I agree," Lex replied. "We can assume mother blue bear and cub won't be back to that inlet there, either, now that we know there's a territorial brown bear in that area. I'm just sorry we failed."

He sighed and ran his hand over the back of his head. Then, as his hand dropped back to his side, he felt Poppy take it and squeeze it hard.

"We didn't fail," she insisted. "If anything, we bought that little bear cub a bit more time and made it harder for the poachers to get her."

"I hope that you're right."

"I know in my heart that I am. And don't worry, Lex, we *will* find a way to stop them. Look, every time my team meets I'm sure we all have in the backs of our minds the knowledge that not every case we face is going to be solved immediately. Some are going to take weeks. Some might take months." She blew out a breath. "And yeah, I have no idea when we're going to find the missing bride or figure out what really happened up on that cliff. I don't know when we're going to help Eli find the Seavers for his godmother or Katie discover who's been poaching reindeer from her aunt's ranch. I just know it's going to happen. Just like I know we're going to stop these poachers."

Silence fell between them again and something caught in his throat that felt even deeper and stronger than the feeling that had surged through him when he'd impulsively held her in his arms and kissed her.

How was I ever blessed enough to have a woman like Poppy love me? How was I ever foolish enough to let her go?

He let the boat slow and just drift gently in the water, feeling like there was something he should say to the incredible woman standing beside him, but not even knowing where to start.

"I'm sorry I left you to arrange our future and plan our wedding on your own," he said. "You just seemed so good at organizing things. I just felt useless, like you didn't need my help. But for what it's worth, I'm sorry."

She blinked and for a long moment didn't reply.

"For the record," she said finally. "I never once doubted that if I was in crisis and really needed you that you'd be there for me. I knew, even after we'd gone our separate ways, that if I was in trouble I could call on you. You're really good at having people's backs."

Then she frowned.

"Is that a bad thing?" he asked.

"I didn't want to have to be in a crisis for you to be there for me," she admitted, a tinge of something almost like defiance filling her voice. "Yes, you were the kind of man who'd rush to help a friend in need. I liked that about you. I even loved that about you. But I needed the kind of man who'd also celebrate my success when I had an amazing day at work or who'd switch off his phone long enough to sit on the couch with me, watch a movie and eat pizza."

He smiled almost ruefully. "I seem to remember us eating a lot of pizza," he said.

But how many times had their dinners and date nights been interrupted by a friend calling his phone or even showing up at the door?

More than he liked to remember.

"I didn't want you to only be there when it counted or when you thought I couldn't handle it," she said. "I wanted all that everyday quality time that comes from sharing life with someone. Even if it meant boring meetings with people explaining how to get a mortgage or how many people could fit in a seating plan. I'm guessing Danny loves spending time with you. Not because he always feels useful or needed, but because he feels loved."

She paused and pulled her hand from his.

"I'm sorry, that's not the best analogy," she added. "After all, he's still a toddler. But maybe a better one is that I really, really love team meetings and hearing my colleagues brief their cases, even if I don't have all the answers or I don't end up doing anything more than sit there and cheer my teammates on while they solve the case."

"Both of those are good analogies in their own way," Lex murmured.

"You care about the same things I care about," Poppy said, and something seemed to break in her voice. "You want to save people's lives, rescue animals and protect the natural world. All I wanted was for us to be a team. I didn't want you discussing your doubts with everyone else and avoiding all the tedious parts of being in a relationship. I loved you and wanted to spend the rest of my life with you, including the hard and boring parts."

His heart caught in his chest. Somehow hearing Poppy say that she'd loved him impacted him every bit as much as it had in the past, even if those feelings were gone. Water flowed beneath them and wind rushed past. Towering islands rose from the depths around the small boat.

"Maybe you were right and it was for the best you called off the wedding," she said quietly. "I don't want to be married to a man who's only there for me when my life's on fire."

"I didn't tell you I'd met your boss and gone to a trooper recruitment event because I felt embarrassed," Lex admitted. "When the woman you admired so much told me I wasn't cut out for the career you loved, I was afraid you'd think less of me. It took a long time for me to really process what I think she was trying to tell me."

"Which was?" Poppy asked, and he was thankful she hadn't questioned why he'd seemingly changed the subject.

"Your boss told me that I shouldn't apply to be a state trooper just because somebody else wanted me to," he said. "She said her hunch was that I tended to follow the lead of other people instead of making decisions for myself. It stung, but she was right. And to be fair, she also said a lot of great things about my skills and abilities, too, which helped."

The dock loomed ahead, and he steered the boat toward it.

"When Johnny first moved to Gustavus he stayed with us," Lex added. "I gave him a set of keys to the bed-and-breakfast, which was mostly symbolic because nobody ever really locks their doors here. When he moved out, I didn't ask for them back and let him know he could return if he ever needed to. Then, when he told me he'd heard about the blue bear poaching down at the watering hole, I asked for them back."

"That's more than fair," she said. "Especially if he was going to dodgy places or hanging out with potentially dangerous people."

"It's not like he was ever going to use them," Lex said. "It was just my way of taking a step and drawing a boundary, of deciding what I did and didn't want around Danny."

He blew out a hard breath.

"Bottom line is, I don't think I made a lot of deliberate choices like that back when we were together," Lex said. "I waited for you to ask for what you needed instead of trying to step up and figure it out for myself. I jumped up and ran whenever my friends called without pausing to even ask if there were other options, like drawing a line and telling them to call someone else, sleep it off, walk or call a cab. Your boss gave me a wakeup call, Poppy. I didn't fight for myself back then. I didn't fight for us."

Her lips parted like she was about to say something more. Then he heard her phone chime and watched as she pulled it out of her jacket pocket. She blinked as she read the message.

"Okay," she said, looking from the screen to his face. "That was Will. He says he's managed to interview what feels like half of Gustavus in the past few hours and has some unexpected news."

"Which is?"

"He'll explain when he sees us." She hesitated. "All I know is he says it looks like Johnny was lying to you."

NINE

They docked the boat and drove back to the house, small talk filling in the spaces between the silence and Lex's spinning mind. Fat and intermittent raindrops had started hitting the windshield again. Stormy was curled up in the back seat of his truck, and the woman who in less than two days had turned his life both inside out and upside down sat beside him on the passenger seat. Poppy's face was turned toward the window. His eyes traced the lines of the back of her neck.

Despite the fact she was sitting just inches away from him, he'd never missed her more.

When they reached the house, they found Will's truck in the driveway and the front door locked. A bit flustered, Lex searched his pocket a moment before coming up with the carabiner of mostly work keys that had his house keys on it, as well. He couldn't remember ever being locked out before and wondered if it had been his mom or Will that had done it.

They found Will in the living room sitting by the fire with Scout lounging at his feet, but they both jumped up when he and Poppy came in. Stormy made a beeline for her water dish and Scout sauntered over to join her.

"Hope it's okay I locked the door," Will said, leaving Lex to wonder if he looked either confused or annoyed. "It's instinctual, and the back door was already locked."

"Probably a smart move," Lex told him. "We should keep the back sliding door locked, too. The windows all have safety latch locks to keep them from being opened more than a few inches. But before this, those were there to keep furry critters from sneaking in." He sighed. Had it really come to this? "Poppy said you've got news."

"I do," Will said. "I do need to brief our boss and told Lorenza I'd call as soon as you got back and Poppy was ready. But I wanted to give you a heads-up about something first."

"Okay." Lex braced himself for whatever the trooper was about to say. "Lay it on me. Poppy says you think Johnny was lying to me?"

"Absolutely everybody I spoke with today agrees that Johnny Blair has not been to the watering hole, touched a drink of alcohol or hustled a game of pool or darts in over four months. So, that can't be where he found out about poaching blue bears."

Lex dropped into a chair, feeling like the wind had been knocked out of him.

"Are you serious?" he asked.

"Yup," Will said. "Trust me, it's hard to get that many different people to lie about the exact same thing without one of them cracking."

"Will is a really tough investigator," Poppy interjected. She sat down on the couch, opposite Lex. "He's naturally suspicious and doesn't fool easily. I'd trust his conclusion.'"

"Thanks," Will said. "I'm going to tell the team that, in my professional opinion, Johnny was telling the truth when he told you he hadn't been to the watering hole in months, and lying through his teeth when he told you that's where he heard about the blue bear cubs being poached." He shrugged his shoulders. "I don't know if that's good news or bad news from your standpoint, but that's what I think and that's what I'm telling the boss. There's more I'm going to brief the team on, but that's the main thing I wanted you to hear from me."

Lex wasn't sure how Poppy knew he needed a few moments to process the news. But she stood and walked over to the kitchen, where the two K-9s had been joined by the kitten and were now all chasing each other around the island, their paws slipping and sliding on the tiles like children on a frozen lake. She let the lot of them outside into the backyard, then went into her room and came out a few moments later in clean jeans and a T-shirt, with her lightly damp hair around her shoulders.

Will set his laptop up at the dining room table and started the video call. As before, Poppy and Will sat at the table in front of the screen, while Lex stood behind them. It was a much smaller group this time. Only Lorenza and Eli joined from the day's earlier meeting, along with a petite woman with shoulder-length auburn hair and a stylish gray business jacket who Poppy introduced as Lorenza's assistant, Katie Kapowski. All three of them shared one screen, with Lorenza in the center and the other two hovering on the edges.

"Nice to meet you," Lex said to Katie. "I've had the pleasure of meeting your aunt and I hope they find whoever has been stealing her reindeer."

Katie smiled. "Thank you."

They listened as Will gave a brief rundown of the results of his interviews in Gustavus today, along with the same conclusion he'd reached that Johnny had been lying through his teeth to Lex when he told him he'd overheard someone talking about the blue bear poachers.

"So, where else could Johnny have learned about the poaching?" Lorenza asked. She leaned back in her chair and crossed her arms. Her keen gaze seemed to fix on Lex's face.

"I don't know," he admitted. "As I mentioned before, we hadn't been close in a while. I do know he was dating Ripley and working at her brother's small tourism charter flight business."

"Well, whatever his source, he wanted to keep it from you," Will said. "Johnny has a record. Is it possible he was contacted by criminal elements from his past wanting his help? Maybe he turned them down and told you, and they killed him for it."

Sadness swelled inside Lex's core. "It's very possible."

"Is it also possible he was working with them and double-crossed them after the first poacher was murdered or for other reasons?" Lorenza asked.

"I don't know," Lex admitted. "I hope not."

He felt Poppy reach her hand back subtly and squeeze his fingers for a moment before letting them go.

"What do we know about the charter airline?" Lorenza prodded.

"It's very small," Poppy said. "Two small planes, one that can carry two passengers and one that can carry four. It caters to tourists with money who want a private tour of the glaciers. Most are wealthy foreigners who fly into his small airport on their personal jets and then take a tour at a much lower altitude with Nolan in his prop plane. Then they leave again without ever coming into Gustavus. The only staff are Nolan, who runs it and flies, Ripley, who does admin, and Johnny, who did mechanical stuff and odd jobs. So, he could've overheard a client talk about poaching the bears and not wanted to risk losing his job."

Lex wasn't sure when Poppy had looked into Johnny's employer, but he wasn't surprised that she had. She'd always been thorough.

"Have you spoken to Nolan?" Lorenza asked.

"The airline was closed when I swung by there this afternoon," Will told her.

"And I just called Ripley from my room a few minutes before this meeting started," Poppy said. "She confirmed what I knew about the airline and told me it was closed today because they only opened when they had customers. She said she'd send me a list of recent clients tomorrow."

Lex thought about the large and thin figures in camo gear who'd tried to steal their boat and an odd thought crossed his mind. Johnny hadn't been covering for his girlfriend, had he? She and her brother couldn't be the poachers?

"Do you think she's lying about Johnny's death and how she got locked in the cupboard?" Lex mused.

"I think she genuinely loved Johnny and she's scared," Poppy said, "but there may well be more she either can't remember or is choosing not to tell us."

"Do they have an alibi for the boat attack today?" Eli asked, leaning into the frame.

"Only each other," Poppy replied. "Ripley says she and Nolan spent the entire day together."

"But neither Ripley nor her brother have any form of

criminal record," Will leaped in, as if anticipating Lorenza's next question. "Ripley's long-term ex-boyfriend, Kevin Wilson, is another story, though. He's been arrested multiple times for aggravated assault, and recently served eighteen months for assaulting Nolan and threatening Ripley. He got out of prison three weeks ago."

"Do we know where he is now?" Lorenza leaned forward.

"Not yet," Will said. "He skipped parole and disappeared."

Lex's mind flashed to the food wrappers in one of the cabins in the national park and his suspicion somebody had been squatting there.

"You're thinking something," Poppy said to Lex. She turned back and looked at him over her shoulder. "The image of you on the screen might be small, but I can still tell when wheels are turning."

"I'm thinking about the fact that before Johnny was murdered, before we discovered the poachers were after blue bears and knew somebody had started stalking my home, I thought we had a problem with squatters camping out in a cabin on the national park," Lex said. "It's possible Kevin came here, looking for Ripley, and was hiding out in the cabins. He could be involved with the poachers."

"We'll look into it," Will announced. "And if Kevin Wilson skipped parole, came to town and is working with the poacher to capture bear cubs, we will find him."

"Anything new online about the bear cub sale?" Poppy asked.

"Not yet." Eli shook his head. "It still lists the sale

as taking place tomorrow. But I'm guessing they don't have the second bear cub, otherwise they'd be posting about it."

On that small shred of hope, the video call meeting ended.

Then conversations about poachers, killers and crime faded into the background as Gillian came home with little Danny, and somehow the house returned to the gentle domestic life of any other afternoon, even with the added guests. Lex played "town" with Danny outside in the backyard sandbox, building houses out of blocks and roads out of sand. Poppy sat by the window on her laptop and watched. After a while, Poppy came out with a small plastic jug of water and helped them add a lake and a river to their town.

Then Gillian called them in for dinner. Lex took Danny to wash the sand off him and made it back to the kitchen in time to help Poppy set the table. They sat down to eat, holding hands as they said grace, with Danny to Lex's one side and Poppy on the other. Conversation darted around the table as they chatted about fishing, hiking, baking and movies, like the topics were shared balloons they were all batting back and forth to keep from touching ground.

Finally, night fell, and he went upstairs and put Danny to bed. When he came back downstairs, he found Poppy, Stormy and the kitten curled up alone in the living room by the fire, just like they had been the night before when he'd come close to kissing her.

"Your mom says to tell you that she's gone to book club," Poppy said, looking up from her laptop. "And Will and Scout are heading to the watering hole, in case any of the locals feel more chatty at night."

So, they were there alone again in his living room, with the weight of the case, their past and the impulsive kiss they'd shared earlier hanging between them.

"Also, I wanted to say thank you for sharing your life with me today," she added. She closed her laptop and set it down on the couch beside her. "It's felt really nice chilling with you and your family this evening."

Yeah, he thought, it had been. More than nice, it felt natural. And it hurt in a way he couldn't put into words to know that in a day or two she'd be leaving again and going back to her life in Anchorage.

The thought of Poppy ever giving it all up to stay in Gustavus was unthinkable. And no one who genuinely cared for her would ever ask her to. Lex took a deep breath and looked down at where she sat, her hair loose around her shoulders and her features highlighted by the fire flickering in the low evening light. If only he knew how to begin to tell her just how much he regretted letting her go, despite all the incredible growth and blessings God had brought into his life during their time apart.

A low and deep rumbling came behind her, like the sound of a glacier about to break off and crash into the water. But it wasn't until Poppy leaped to her feet and turned to her partner that he realized where it was coming from.

Stormy was crouched to spring like she'd been before the bear, the gentle calm of the moment before all but forgotten. Her lips parted in a half snarl.

"Stormy!" Concern washed over Poppy's face. "What's wrong?" The dog woofed urgently. "Show me."

Stormy turned and ran across the living room and up the closest staircase to the second floor. Poppy and

Lex pelted after her, one step behind the dog. Even before they reached the top of the stairs he heard a sound that sent terror pouring down his spine.

His little son was whimpering, a small plaintive and pitiful sound that Danny only made when he was too scared or hurt to scream.

Poppy froze as she reached the top of the stairs, laying her hand on Stormy's collar to make the dog pause, too, while they assessed the threat. He stopped one step behind her. An empty hallway lay ahead of them. Silence surrounded them, punctuated only by the faint sound of the K-9's lingering growl and his own son's tears. He prayed hard, beseeching God for Danny's safety and help in whatever lay ahead. Then, without a sound, Poppy stepped slowly down the empty hallway, Lex one pace behind her, toward his son's bedroom door.

They reached Danny's room. The door flew open ahead of them, smashing against the wall with a deafening crash.

"Daddy!" The sound of Danny's whimpering grew to panicked sobs. "I... Want... Daddy!"

A lanky masked figure in camo fatigues stood in the doorway of Danny's bedroom, his sunken gray eyes as cold as a shark's as they fixed on Lex and Poppy.

In one arm he clenched Lex's son. With the opposite hand he held a gun.

"Don't move!" he said. "Or the kid dies."

The masked man blocked the doorway of Danny's small room. The barrel of the gun was pressed against the boy's side. Fear pooled in the child's eyes. She smelled rain in the air, but it wasn't until the poacher took a step back into the room that she noticed with a start that the window was open about four inches, caught on what looked like a safety lock. How had he possibly gotten in? She had no idea. All that mattered right now was that he was cornered, and he knew it. And he had little Danny in his grasp.

"What do you want?" Poppy asked. She stood in the hallway and faced the man down, keeping her motions just as slow and deliberate in the face of the criminal as she would a wild bear. Vicious killers were always the most dangerous when trapped. She could sense Lex standing stock-still by her left shoulder, his eyes on his son and whispered prayers for Danny's safety on his lips. Poppy's right hand tightened on Stormy's collar, signaling the animal not to move. Her other hand raised slowly to show the man that it was empty.

She willed her mind to block out everything but how she was about to protect the small child and save his life.

If only she had her weapon.

Help. Us. Lord.

"I want you to leave me alone to go about my business," the poacher snarled. He stepped backward, moving deeper into Danny's room. "Someone's been poking their noses around where they don't belong, trying to get in the way of me getting what's mine."

Did he mean Will's questioning? Her own online investigation? Something her team had dug into?

Whatever it was, she was pretty sure he wasn't lying.

"What do you mean?" she asked. She kept her voice low but firm. "What's yours? Do you mean the money you'll get for bear cubs you're trying to capture and sell? Those animals aren't yours."

"You don't get to tell me what's mine!" the poacher

shouted. "So, here's what's going to happen. I'm going to take something that's yours and hold on to your kid as collateral to make sure the bear cub sale goes through with my client tomorrow without interference. Once the buyer has the bear cubs and I have my money, you'll get a call telling you where to pick him up. Turn around right now and walk away."

Fear beat through her heart. She could feel Stormy almost quivering with energy under her hand, coiled to leap into action to protect the little boy. Poppy stared the man down, her tactical mind calculating every piece of information she'd need to save Danny's life—from the man's build, to where he was standing in the room, to the position of the gun, to the way he was clutching Lex's son with one arm.

Her jaw set. "That's not going to happen."

"I'm leaving with this boy right now!" the poacher shouted. "You don't want to face the consequences of stopping me. So turn around and walk away. Now."

Poppy heard the floorboards creak slightly behind her, as if Lex was shifting his stance. They were standing so close and yet she couldn't see his face or know what he wanted her to do. She just hoped he trusted her as much as she trusted him. The gunman shifted Danny around to the other side, as if struggling under just how unwieldy and heavy a squirming toddler was. *Come on, Poppy, think!* The poacher wasn't about to kill Danny here. He wanted the boy alive and unharmed for his collateral plan to work.

So, if he opened fire, it wouldn't be at Danny.

"Now, here's what's going to happen," the masked man said. "You're going to back up down the hallway.

I'm going to walk out of here and you're not going to stop me."

"No." Her voice rose, calm and clear, with an authority that came from somewhere deeper than just herself, from her badge, her team and the legacy of her fellow officers. "Because I'm an Alaska state trooper, this is my K-9 partner and we're not about to let anything happen to Danny. So, set him down gently, drop your weapon and raise your hands now."

He snorted, pulled the gun away from Danny's side and pointed it right between Poppy's eyes. She heard the floorboards creak behind her and then she felt Lex's hand brush against her back for just a fleeting moment and yet filling her with strength. She swallowed her fear. As long as the only weapon in his hand was pointed at her, it wasn't pointed at Danny.

Poppy stroked the back of the dog's neck with her fingertips and felt the tension radiating through her fur. She knew everything inside Stormy wanted to leap into action to rescue Danny. It was her purpose. It was what she was trained for. Stormy wouldn't hesitate to risk her life for the child.

"I would've thought losing Johnny was enough incentive to show you we really meant business," the poacher said. "But apparently you wanted to learn the lesson the hard way."

Poppy let go of the K-9's collar. "Stormy! Attack!"

Snarling, Stormy leaped.

TEN

Stormy reared up on her hind legs and stretched herself to her full, ferocious seven-foot height. The man shouted a swear word in terror and swung toward the K-9. Danny slipped from his kidnapper's grasp, tumbling onto his bed. Poppy leaped for the toddler without hesitation, diving into the room, catching Danny up into her arms and cradling him to her chest. She turned back. Stormy had the poacher down on the floor of the bedroom, her huge paws on his shoulders. The assailant thrashed against the dog, his weapon still in his grasp, their struggle blocking her exit.

The gun fired.

Plaster rained down as the bullet struck the ceiling above their head. Poppy curled herself into a protective ball, shielding Danny with her body.

"I've got Danny!" she shouted. "He's safe!"

The poacher shouted in pain as Stormy's strong jaws clamped onto his arm. A second bullet ripped from the poacher's gun, shattering the window. Glass rained down around them. She and Danny were still caught in the middle, with no way to escape the room and just one stray bullet away from being seriously hurt.

"I can take him down!" Lex shouted.

"Okay," she yelled. "Stormy! Stand down!"

She looked back, cradling Danny's small head into the crook of her neck. Lex's strong shoulders filled the doorway, blocking the kidnapper's path. Stormy sprung back. The perp stumbled to his feet, then as she watched, he turned and threw himself through the broken glass of the second-story window, shoulder first, like a desperate football player trying to block a tackle. He crashed through and into the rain outside.

"Keep my son safe!" Lex shouted.

"I will!" she called. "I promise!"

Without hesitation, Lex ran toward the shattered window and dove through. She looked out. The poacher scrambled and slid across the slippery roof of the covered porch below them. Lex tackled him. The two men struggled for a moment, rolling and battling in the darkness. Then the roof gave way under their weight and they fell through, landing on the lawn in a mass of limbs and broken boards.

The perp recovered first, leaping to his feet and sprinting across the lawn into the blackness of the night beyond. In an instant, Lex was on his feet and running after him. She lost sight of them in the darkness.

Stormy whimpered softly as if asking permission to jump through the second-story window and charge after them.

"Stay," Poppy said, unexpected tears choking her voice. "Good dog."

A moment later she heard an engine roar to life and then a few seconds later a second vehicle, which she recognized as Lex's. So, the poacher was trying to get away and Lex was chasing him. She prayed for his capture.

She ran her hand down Danny's back and gently tousled his hair, thankful he'd stopped crying. Okay, his breathing was strong, there were no obvious bruises or contusions and how hearty his cries were earlier were very good signs. *Thank You, God.* She'd give him a more thorough checkout in a moment, but first she had to get him away from the mess and chaos of the room.

The little boy's tearstained face looked up into hers and suddenly it hit her—Lex had entrusted her with the most important thing in the entire world to him, without even a moment's hesitation.

"Everything's going to be okay," she soothed, looking into Danny's wide and trusting eyes. "You're safe."

She stood slowly, holding him gently and asking God's help to keep the promise she just made to the little boy. She slid her phone out of her pocket and texted Will what had happened and that she was now with the toddler. Will texted her back an instant later that he would inform the team, contact Gillian, try to reach Lex and would head back to join her ASAP. She breathed a sigh of relief, knowing Will had it covered and all she now had to worry about was Danny.

Truly, the most important job of all.

She kept praying while she scooped up all the stuffed animals on the bed, along with Danny's blanket, and cradled them around him like a nest. Then she carried him out of the bedroom, with Stormy by her side, leaving the tossed mess of the room with shards of glass and plaster covering the floor behind. She closed the bedroom door behind her firmly and then looked down at Stormy. The dog peered up at her solemnly under shaggy brows as if Stormy felt the responsibility, too.

She started down the stairs with Danny in her arms

and her K-9 partner by her side. A tiny hand brushed her face.

"Daddy." Danny sniffled. "Want Daddy!"

"I know, I wish your Daddy was here, too," she admitted, "but you and I, and Stormy, are going to go hang out in my room until he gets back."

"And Mu'shoom kitten?" Danny asked hopefully.

If she could figure out where the kitten was hiding, considering she'd probably been frightened by the chaos. "Yes, and Mushroom the kitten, too."

She checked that the front, back and sliding door to the kitchen were all locked, then went into her bedroom suite. She'd barely managed to lock the door when she'd heard a small but persistent scratching sound and opened it to see the kitten shoot past and dive under the bed. Stormy positioned herself against the door, with her head on her paws and her ears perked. *All right, then, the gang's all here.* Poppy locked the door again, climbed up on the bed with Danny and curled up beside him.

"Now," she said, keeping her voice playful and light, "we're going to play a special wiggling game. I'm going to point to different parts of your body and you're going to show me how good you can wriggle it, okay?"

Danny nodded enthusiastically. She breathed a sigh of relief, then sat cross-legged on the bed and methodically started checking the boy for any external or internal injuries. First, she started by having him follow her waving finger with his eyes, to help rule out the possibility of a concussion. Then had him wiggle his feet, kick his legs, waggle his fingers and wave his arms, while he laughed and giggled at the game. She laughed along with him, feeling tears of relief brush her own cheeks. His color and breathing were good, his pulse was strong, he had no bruises or scrapes and nothing was broken.

When she'd run through everything in her mental emergency first-aid checklist, she hugged him tightly and felt the little boy hug her back.

Thank You, God. Just thank You so much.

A gentle knock sounded on the door and Stormy's ears twitched slightly but her body didn't tense. Her heart leaped, hoping it was Lex, but instead Poppy heard Will's voice. "How's it going?"

"Good." She looked down at the little boy in her arms. "Is Lex back?"

"Not yet," Will said. "It's just us for now. Scout and I are going to do a perimeter search and make sure all the exits and entrances are secured."

"See if you can find out how he got in," she told him. "I checked the doors, too. The window was only open a few inches and the porch roof didn't look strong enough to climb up."

"Will do," he said. "You're going to hold tight there?"

She swallowed hard. There were a dozen very important things related specifically to her training as a trooper she could be doing right now, and yet as she felt the small boy nuzzle against her she knew there was nowhere else she'd rather be. "I will."

Danny's small hand brushed the side of her face. "Read story?"

"Yes." Poppy looked down into his big eyes. "That sounds like a wonderful idea." She turned back to the door. "Will? Can you pop up to Danny's room and grab us some of his storybooks?"

Will came back with the books in moments. Poppy

thanked him and locked the door behind him. She checked her phone in vain for texts from Lex, and seeing none, she set her phone down and turned to Danny.

"Okay," she said brightly. "Which one should we read first?"

He grinned. "Pi'gon story!"

Stormy gave up her post at the door and climbed across the bottom of the bed as Poppy tucked her legs up to make room for her. Mushroom slipped out from under the bed, balled up beside Stormy and started purring. Then, finally, Danny curled himself into the crook of Poppy's arm. She leaned forward and brushed a kiss on the top of his head, and she started to read.

She had no idea it was possible for a heart to feel both so light and so heavy at the same time. Was it possible to mourn the marriage and family she never had, while still being thankful for the amazing lives she and Lex had without each other? Could gratitude and grief, joy and pain, coexist inside her heart?

She settled back against the blanket, feeling Danny rise and fall on her chest with each breath. Maybe on some level she'd blamed herself for losing Lex. After all, if she'd been a better partner and done a better job of loving him, he would have stayed, right? And yet, at the same time, if he'd blamed himself for Johnny's life going down the wrong path she'd be the first to point out that no matter how hard and genuinely a person loved someone, they weren't responsible for that other person's choices.

And with those conflicting thoughts swirling inside her, she let her mind both leave the sadness of the past and the anxiety of the future, and exist in the present moment of the stories on the page, the animals snoring by her feet and the precious child in her arms.

* * *

A torrent of rain beat down around Lex's truck, streaming down the windows and clattering on the roof as if trying in vain to drown out his thoughts. He'd been chasing taillights on narrow, rural roads through the dark Alaskan wilderness for almost half an hour, and was no closer to catching the masked gunman. His gas light had been on for at least half of that, warning him that his tank was almost empty, and his windshield wipers were working overtime as they beat furiously against the rain.

The twin lights ahead disappeared as the poacher cut onto a rough road through the trees, then reappeared ahead of Lex as he made the sharp turn after them. It had been like that since they'd left the outskirts of Gustavus—the lights seeming to blink off and then on again, as the truck swerved and weaved, then growing smaller as the truck sped away, then larger as Lex caught up.

He had to catch him. This man had threatened the life of his child, taken the life of his friend and was endangering the lives of rare bear cubs. And yet, after throwing everything he had into the chase, Lex was no closer to catching him.

Lex could feel the steady drag of his truck beneath him, letting him know it was pretty much down to running on fumes. The headlights ahead disappeared in the darkness and this time they didn't return, no matter how fast he drove or how intently he peered through the storm looking for the poacher. Had he taken a turn Lex had missed? Had he recklessly turned off his lights and either kept driving without them or hidden somewhere?

He had no idea. All he knew was that his truck was minutes away from running out of gas and the man he was chasing was gone. But even then, he kept driving, watching minute after minute tick by, until finally he admitted defeat and pulled over to the side of the road.

Lex leaned his head against the steering wheel. Hot tears pressed unshed behind his eyes.

"Help me, Lord, I feel like such a failure," he prayed out loud. "I don't even know who this guy is, how to stop him or what I'm supposed to be doing right now."

Truth was, he felt like he'd never been enough or done enough. As a kid, he'd done his very best to please his father, but that hadn't stopped his dad from losing his temper all the time and then eventually walking out on them, never to be heard from again. Lex had gone all out to help friends like Johnny change their lives, and yet they'd still made terrible decisions. He'd cared about two women and both relationships had failed— the first because he'd felt inferior and bailed on their wedding, and the other because she'd left him. He loved his son with his entire being and yet he hadn't been able to catch the man who'd tried to kidnap him.

"Is all this my fault, God?" he asked. "Did I do something wrong? Because it feels like I've let everybody down and I don't know what You want me to do to fix it."

A song he'd heard once at a summer camp as a kid buzzed through his brain, around and around like a fly, telling him that if he did what was right everything would always work out for him. For the first time in his life, he found himself questioning just how overly simplified that message he'd internalized was.

As he stepped out of the truck into the pouring rain, bowed his head and walked around to the back of his truck, he found something Jesus said in the gospels cross his mind—God sends rain on both the just and the unjust. A grin crossed his face. *Yeah, wasn't that the truth?* He'd lived long enough already to see bad things happen to amazing people, like his mother, and great things happen to people who did terrible things. And, if he was honest, he'd also had some blessings in his life beyond what he ever hoped and deserved.

After all, he knew that Poppy was keeping his son safe right now.

He reached the back of his truck, opened the tailgate and thanked God his emergency gas canister felt heavy when he picked it up and sloshed it. A moment later he found his funnel, too. Other things that Jesus had said crossed his mind as he pulled off the gas cap and poured fresh fuel in the tank. There'd been a story about a man born blind, and while others had been worrying about whose fault the blindness was, Jesus had brushed all that talk away and focused on actually helping the guy.

Maybe that was what he should be focusing on right now, too.

It was a long drive back, prayers and doubts mingling inside him like the raindrops merging into streams on his windshield.

When he got back to the bed-and-breakfast, the front door was locked, but before he could even fish his keys out his mom opened the door. He stepped in out of the downpour. Wordlessly Gillian hugged him.

"He got away, Mom," he said hoarsely. "I tried my best, but I lost him."

"You'll get him next time," his mom reassured him.

And he almost laughed. Yeah, she said that about most things.

They walked into the living room and he was surprised to find it empty. "Where is everyone?"

"Danny's asleep," she said. "Will's upstairs in Danny's room, nailing down a piece of plywood over the broken window and helping me move Danny's bed into my room." She gave her son a hard look as if guessing what he was thinking. "And don't say he should sleep in your room instead, because we both know you won't be sleeping tonight."

Yeah, that was true enough.

"What about the port of entry for the break-in?" he asked.

"Apparently, there was no break-in," she said. "According to Will, looks like whoever tried to kidnap Danny used a house key, unlocked the back door and walked in. He found fresh scratches on the keyhole like someone was trying to unlock it in the dark and a bit of mud tracked in the back door." Gillian shook her head and frowned. "And before you ask, I double-checked my keys right away. They're still in a zip pouch in my purse and haven't been touched."

What could that possibly mean? There were only three sets of keys to the house—his mom's, his and the one he once gave Johnny. But he'd demanded Johnny's keys back when his buddy told him about the blue bears being poached and said he'd been drinking again. Lex reached into his pocket and pulled out his key ring. Sure enough, both sets of keys were still there—his and Johnny's.

Had someone copied a set of their keys? If so, who and when?

"We need to get the locks changed," he said.

"Agreed," Gillian concurred. "I've already been calling around and found someone from the church who can do that for us first thing tomorrow."

"Thank you." He blew out a long breath. "Where's Poppy?"

"With Danny," his mom said. Her lips twisted like she was debating whether or not to say something more. Instead, she waved at Lex to follow her and started down the hallway. She reached the door of Poppy's suite, pressed a finger to her lips to signal for quiet and then eased the door open a crack. He peeked in.

There was Poppy curled up asleep with Danny tucked safely in the crook of her arm, with the toddler's head on her shoulder and her flaming red hair fanned out around them. Lex pressed his hand against his heart, feeling something tighten in his chest. Stormy was stretched out across the end of the bed by their feet with the kitten snuggling against her snout. The wolfhound's eyes opened and silently she looked at him.

"Good dog, Stormy," he whispered, and his voice caught in his throat. "Thank you for protecting my son."

He eased the door closed again. As he turned back, he found his mother's eyes on her face.

"I won't ask if you still have feelings for her," Gillian whispered as they walked away from the door, "because anyone with eyes in their head can see that you do. I'm not even going to ask if you think she'd be a good mother to Danny, because I know she would be. She's a good person who loves hard, works hard and can do anything she puts her mind to."

Her shoulders rose and fell, and he was suddenly

reminded just how much his mother had always genuinely liked Poppy.

"But?" he asked softly.

"But as I told you back when you guys were planning on getting married, I don't like the way you used to get around her," Gillian admitted. "It was like you doubted yourself, shrunk and got smaller. She made you feel inferior."

He shook his head. Yeah, he remembered his mom saying this just before he'd ended things with Poppy and called off their engagement. Although he'd never told Poppy, that conversation had been the one he'd accidentally left on her voice mail and the person he'd been admitting his doubts to was his mother.

"That doesn't make sense," Lex admitted, "because having Poppy by my side made me feel like a better and stronger man than I ever felt without her."

"I know," Gillian said. "But it was like she was a balloon and you thought you were only flying because you were holding on to her string, and since you lost her you've started to grow your own wings. I'd hate to see you lose yourself again now."

He heard a click and turned as the door to Poppy's suite eased open behind them. There she stood, in her stocking feet, with her hair slightly disheveled, a sleeping Danny in her arms and the most beautiful smile he'd ever seen in his life on her face. She looked so happy and so relaxed he was pretty sure she hadn't caught the contents of their conversation.

"Hey." Poppy smiled as she looked from Lex to Gillian and back. Then worry filled her eyes as they searched Lex's face. "He got away?"

He felt himself nod, but it was his mother who spoke first.

"Here," Gillian said, reaching out her hands for Danny. "Let me take him upstairs. I've got his bed made up in my room." She eased the sleeping boy into her arms. "I'll leave you two to talk."

His mother headed upstairs. The bedroom door swung open wider as Stormy pushed her way through. Mushroom darted past and disappeared down the hallway, leaping over the dog's feet. Stormy rubbed her head against Poppy's side. Then the K-9 butted her head against Lex, as well, as if to say hello, then wandered down the hall, leaving just Lex and Poppy.

"I'm sorry I lost him," Lex started. "He got a head start and was a pretty reckless driver."

"Don't worry about it," Poppy said. She ran both hands through her hair. "Happens to the best of us. We'll find him again."

And there was something about the way she said it that was so strong and determined he believed her.

"Thank you for taking care of Danny," he murmured. "I loved spending time with him."

She started to walk past him, down the hallway and back to the living room. But as she passed, his hand reached out and touched her arm. She stopped and turned back.

"I'm sorry if this is speaking out of turn," Lex said, "but when you stopped outside Danny's door last night and didn't come during story time, I wondered if you were avoiding him or felt uncomfortable around him."

"You were right," Poppy admitted. "But only because I felt weak and didn't want it to impact you, or Danny, or this case."

He blinked. Of all the many words that filled his mind when he thought of Poppy, *weak* had never been one of them. He opened his mouth, but couldn't find anything to say.

"I told you," she said, "when you left it tore me open inside. I might not have cried in front of you, sent you a bunch of angry messages or vented about it on social media. But it hurt me so much I haven't been close to anyone like that ever since because I was afraid of being hurt like that again. And I guess I was afraid getting close to your son would make that old wound open up again." Then she smiled. "But I'm glad I got to bond with Danny, because he's absolutely amazing. Thank you for sharing him with me. I'm so happy for you and the life you've built here."

"Poppy..." His hand took hers. "I'm sorry I wasn't stronger back then."

"I'm sorry I wasn't braver," she said softly. "But when I think about Danny, and Stormy, and my team, and the lives we have now, I'm really happy for who we became."

"Me, too," he confided. "I only wish I didn't have to lose you for us to find it."

She squeezed his fingers and he squeezed hers back. They stepped closer together in the darkened hallway until the only thing between them was their joined hands.

The sound of a ringing phone filled the narrow space. But it wasn't until Poppy leaped back and snapped her cell to her ear that he realized it was hers.

"Hello?" she said. "Hey, why are you calling so late?... Oh." Her face paled as she met Lex's eyes. "Okay, we'll be right there. Bye."

She hung up the phone and sighed.

"That was Eli," she told him. "He says, bad news is we're too late and the poachers already have the second bear cub. Good news is they think they've figured out where the poachers are taking the cubs. But we have to act now. Otherwise we'll lose any hope of rescuing the cubs forever."

ELEVEN

"So, turns out some people are more chatty around the watering hole at night," Will said as the three of them stood around the table in the darkened living room and waited for the video call to start. "Not that I know if any of the gossip I turned up helps us in solving the case. But it might give you some insight into what your friend Johnny was going through, Lex, at the very least."

"Thanks," he said, "I appreciate it."

The long drive in the rain, praying after losing sight of the poacher, had helped get his heart and mind right. While there were still a lot of answers Lex didn't have and things he had to figure out—especially in terms of dealing with whatever those invisible threads were that kept tugging him back toward Poppy—he definitely had more peace in his heart about Johnny, and for that he was thankful.

"Go on," he added. "Lay it on me."

"All right," Will said. "Remember I'm dealing in small-town gossip here, not fact. But rumor has it that Ripley's ex-boyfriend, Kevin Wilson, made a beeline here to find her after he got out of jail. Nolan has been complaining to anyone who'd listen that Kevin's been coming by both the house and the airplane charter business, trying to get Ripley back and making trouble. The way Nolan apparently tells it, he chased him off and told him not to come back."

"You sound skeptical of that," Poppy remarked.

"I'm always wary of anyone who paints themselves as the heroic good guy of the story," Will said with a shrug. "But Kevin does have a record for assault, not Nolan."

"Any idea why Kevin went to jail for an assault charge?" Lex asked. "Had to have been pretty major if it wasn't dealt with by probation."

"I can answer that one!" Eli's voice broke through and they glanced to see the tech's face on the screen. "Kevin Wilson has multiple charges for assault and issuing threats, against both Ripley and Nolan. The incident that put him in jail apparently involved smashing Nolan's truck with a baseball bat."

Will whistled under his breath.

"All because he wanted Ripley back?" Poppy asked.

"Looks like it," Eli said. "But looks can be deceiving. Kevin also tried to sue both Nolan and Ripley for lawyer's fees, pressing false charges and lost wages, and it was thrown out."

"That tracks," Will said. "Rumor is Kevin came around the watering hole looking for Ripley and Nolan a week ago, claiming they owed him money for sending him to jail. Maybe Johnny's boobytrapped his house to keep him from breaking in."

Lex looked from Will to Eli on the screen, and then finally at Poppy.

"Then why aren't you hauling this Kevin guy in for questioning?" he asked.

"He alibied out," Will said. "Kevin left town a few hours before Johnny died. Nolan flew him to Juneau personally just to get him out of town. Nolan showed me the flight record proving he was in the air with Kevin when Ripley and Johnny were attacked at the house. From there Kevin hopped on a flight to Anchorage. Nolan's also got both text and phone records showing Kevin's phone calling Nolan and Ripley from Anchorage."

"So, Nolan and Ripley have every reason to hate Kevin and yet they're also his alibi," Poppy said.

"And vice versa," Will noted.

Lex let out a long breath and ran his hand over his head.

"So, we've got nothing," Lex muttered.

Except, as Will said, a window into what Johnny was dealing with. Lex couldn't imagine Johnny dealt well with his girlfriend being harassed by her ex. Johnny was nothing if not loyal and protective.

"Good news is that I finally got the recent client list from Ripley and Nolan," Will added. "Took some persuading as his clients are mostly rich, foreign tourists who like privacy. But we've got people on here from all over Europe, the Persian Gulf and Asia. Any one of which might have been scheming with the poachers to capture the baby bears and then killed Johnny when he caught wind of it."

"Which is a fantastic transition to why I called you for a late-night chat," Eli said, drawing their attention back to the screen. "The whole team will be meeting tomorrow morning and Lorenza is off tonight at a charity event as we speak. But I thought you would want to know now, so she gave me the go-ahead to brief you. I'm sending a package of files through for you to print, so you've got a copy of everything I'm looking at. Long story short, I found a post on the dark web saying both bears will be going up for bid at an illegal animal auction in less than forty-eight hours. They've also apparently got a two-or three-year-old brown bear."

Poppy blew out a hard breath. Nobody in their right mind would try to poach a fully grown bear, no matter how greedy or desperate they were for money. "That doesn't give us a lot of time."

"Less than you'd think," Eli said. "Because also according to dark web chatter the bears are due to be smuggled out of Glacier Bay by boat, to meet up with a ship near Anchorage just before dawn and then from there head out into international waters. We don't know where they'll be headed yet, could be Asia but probably Russia. So, obviously we'll be coordinating with the coast guard on this. Once they've left American waters everything gets a lot more complicated."

And if that happened, Lex knew animal trafficking well enough to know that would probably mean the bears would be gone for good.

Will looked at Poppy. "Guessing that means we'll be heading to Anchorage and coordinating with the coast guard."

"That's not for me to say," Eli said. "But I know the boss wants to talk to you first thing in the morning."

Lex felt Poppy's gaze on his face but didn't dare let himself look her way in case his eyes gave away how he was feeling. The lightness he had felt in his heart earlier now seemed to sink inside him like a stone. So, one way or another, it sounded like Poppy was leaving his life tomorrow.

He didn't notice when Will pushed the button on

the laptop to send things through wirelessly to print, but was thankful when he heard the printer in his office spring to life, because it gave him a reason to turn his back on the conversation and head to the other side of the room. Lex took the sheets Eli had sent off the printer and looked down at the crude posts, with pictures of the sad bear cubs and a description of the terrible fate that awaited them. But somehow his eyes found it hard to focus.

He'd never expected Poppy to suddenly land in his life, let alone thought that she would stay. So why did the thought of her leaving weigh so heavily inside him?

"This doesn't sit right with me," Poppy said, her voice drawing his attention back to the conversation happening around the table. She reached out for the papers in Lex's hands, took them from him and then spread them out. "A poacher goes after Lex's son, tries to kidnap him and says he's taking the kid for collateral until he can sell the bears to his client tomorrow."

"You mean, until the bears are safely on the boat and heading out into international waters," Will clarified.

"No." Poppy shook her head. "That might be what he meant but that's not remotely what he said. He said he was taking Danny until he got his hands on the second bear cub, which he apparently didn't have yet, and sold them both to his buyer." Her emerald eyes met Lex. "Right? Can you back me up on this?"

"I can," Lex said. He grabbed a kitchen chair and sat down beside her, until he was eye level with Will and could see the screen. "My mind was most definitely a mess at the time, but I'm pretty sure she's right about the second cub thing. And I distinctly remember him saying he had a buyer."

"A buyer," Will repeated. "Singular?"

"Yup," Poppy confirmed. "One he was meeting tomorrow."

"Well." Will leaned back in his chair. "That sounds a bit different than an overseas animal auction."

Eli raised his hands, palms up.

"Hey, don't shoot the messenger," he said. "I'm just reporting what the internet is saying. Not that I've verified it's true."

"We know," Poppy told him.

She ran her finger over her lip in a subtle gesture that Lex knew meant she was thinking.

"People do lie," he said after a long moment. "He was kidnapping my son, after all."

"People lie for a reason," Poppy countered. "They do it to get out of trouble or to get some advantage. Why not just tell us he's kidnapping Danny until the boat leaves? Why lie and say he doesn't have the second bear cub yet or that he already has a buyer?"

Lex looked from Will to Eli, waiting for one of them to answer. Instead, Poppy's gaze was fixed on him.

"I don't know," he said, feeling flustered. "Maybe because they still hadn't captured the second bear cub by that point and coming after Danny would keep us from stopping them or act as a distraction."

"But *why*?" she prodded. "Why not just go capture the bear cub? Why come here first?"

"Maybe he tried to grab Danny and when that didn't work he went and captured the bear cub?" Lex suggested. "No, that doesn't make sense. Because he wasn't out of my sight long enough to travel into the park, get to the glaciers, capture a bear, come back and post it online. So, I don't know, maybe he has an accomplice or there's more than one set of poachers? But again, that doesn't make complete sense."

He looked down at the printouts spread on the table. There were some new pictures of the bears, one in a cave and a couple side by side in cages. He frowned. It was like his subconscious was telling him there was something wrong with the pictures but he couldn't place it.

"Either the kidnapper lied, something in the post is false or these were done by two separate people," he added.

He glanced at Poppy's face and suddenly realized the smile that had ignited in her eyes had that same spark as when they used to jog together, urging each other on, making one another faster and stronger.

"Thank you," she said. "My brain gets too caught up on one way of thinking sometimes and hearing you come up with different ideas always helps with that." She looked back at Will and Eli. "Lex is right. Something doesn't mesh here."

Lex glanced back down at the papers in front of them and blinked as he finally realized what he was seeing. No, it couldn't be.

"*Wait*. These two bear cubs are the same bear!" he exclaimed, pointing from one to the other. "They just switched it from one cage to another and took it from a different angle to look like it's two different animals."

Poppy met his eyes and finished his thought. "But they still only have one bear."

Eli shook his head. "Why didn't I see it?"

"Because you're a tech guru, not an animal expert," Poppy said. "I'm sure if they'd added a weird filter you'd have caught it immediately. Was this posted after I reported the attempted kidnapping attempt?"

"Yup," Eli confirmed.

"Then it's still possible we can stop the second bear cub from being poached," she said. "No second bear cub means no boat leaving first thing tomorrow for the animal auction, means more time to find and stop them. Of course, it's always possible they already have a buyer lined up and the auction is a ruse, too." She turned to Lex. "How do we find the second bear cub before they do? Any guesses?"

All eyes turned to him. Right, so everyone was counting on him to figure out the location of a rare baby bear cub in one of the world's largest national parks based on a few pictures where he knew the bears had been, and his own intuition.

He prayed for wisdom. Then he felt Poppy's hand take his and squeeze it.

"You've got this," she said. "And don't worry about getting it wrong. My whole theory about this case might be, as well, and we all get it wrong on this team some-times."

Had she always been so understanding and he'd been too caught up in his own insecurities to see it? Or had she mellowed with time and teamwork? Maybe it didn't matter—they were here now. *Lord, help me see what I need to see.* His eyes scanned the new posts, the print-outs from the day before and a map of Glacier Bay. Then he took a deep breath.

"Okay, this is just an educated guess" he began. "But judging by the shading in this background of this pic-ture here, this cub is near an ice cave." He pointed out each step of his explanation as he went. "Due to the time of year, the location of the bay we found where the poachers were coming ashore and the usual roaming habits of bears, I'm thinking that if the second cub wasn't poached she's likely with the mama bear somewhere near…here."

His finger came to stop on a small inlet about twenty minutes away by boat from where they'd stopped earlier.

"So, Lex and I head there," Poppy said without a moment's hesitation. "We look around and see what we can find."

"Sounds good." Will nodded. "Scout and I will stay here and cover the home front and make sure Gillian and Danny are safe."

"Perfect," Poppy continued. "Worst-case scenario and there's nothing there, everyone will still go ahead with the existing mission as planned to locate, investigate and intercept any potential ship taking the bears overseas for an illegal animal auction. We're just making sure we're covering our bases."

"Hey, I'm not saying we'll find anything," Lex added quickly. "It's just a guess."

"An educated guess, based on your experience, knowledge and expertise," Poppy reminded him. She reached over and squeezed his hand again, this time not letting go as quickly, and as her eyes met his for a split second it felt like they were the only two people in the room. "Whatever we find, I believe in your hunches and think it's worth pursuing."

"Looks like Lorenza's evening plans are being interrupted, after all," Eli chimed in.

"But knowing her, she won't mind a bit," Will said with a chuckle. "But whether the poachers have got a buyer already lined up to buy the bears tomorrow or they're shipping out by boat to an overseas auction in the morning, it sounds like this case is wrapping up within a few hours one way or the other."

Lex took a deep breath as an unexpected pain filled his chest.

In other words, one way or the other, Poppy was leaving his life and going back to Anchorage tomorrow.

As expected, Lorenza wasn't the slightest bit bothered when Poppy called and interrupted her evening and was quick to sign off on their plan to check out the location Lex had identified on the map. It felt good to have her boss believe in her, even when she was chasing a hunch. In fact, Lorenza seemed even more concerned at how tight the timeline was and suggested expanding the mission into a stakeout. Poppy, Lex and Stormy would make their way to the glaciers, locate the area Lex had suggested and hunker down for a few hours somewhere to see if there was any suspicious activity. Then, if there was nothing by sunrise, they'd come back to Gustavus and regroup with a video meeting with the rest of the team.

Poppy napped for a few hours, ate a late dinner and packed some snacks, then got dressed into her rugged outdoor gear and met Lex outside by the truck shortly after 2:30 a.m.

It was a quiet drive through the Alaskan wilderness at night to the national park, punctuated only by the sound of the engine purring, the tires brushing the road beneath them and Stormy's softly wheezing half snores coming from the back seat.

At first Poppy didn't think much of the fact that she and Lex had barely exchanged two words since leaving, and for that matter not really talked much after ending the video call with Eli. After all, she was exhausted and she imagined he was, too, if not more so. Her body ached from being up and moving in the middle of the night on too little sleep, along with the wear and tear of having fought for her life more than once in the past couple days. She felt like she needed to sleep for a week, or at least a solid twelve hours, to rest and recuperate.

Considering the physical strain of what Lex had gone through, she was sure his body was pretty sore, too.

She glanced his way. The darkness of the night around them had deepened his eyes and cast long shadows down the line of his jaw. Lex seemed older than he had in her memories, but more handsome and wiser, too, like his heart and mind had been weathered by the life he'd lived without her.

She turned and looked back out the window, knowing they only had a few hours left in each other's lives and yet not knowing what to say. The sky had cleared, leaving a tapestry of bright stars shining above them.

No, there was more to the weariness inside her than just what her body had gone through. Her heart felt tired and heavy, too, like she'd put all of her painful and complicated feelings for him on ice when he'd broken her heart, but in the past two days they'd all come back demanding to be felt. She had no idea what to say to the amazing, complicated and incredible man sitting beside her and no clue where to even start, so she sat and prayed, and even let her mind drift a little as they drove to the national park.

"I'm fairly confident that we weren't followed," Lex said as they reached the docks. "I took a route that's near impossible to drive without headlights on and tight enough in places that I should've seen running lights."

They got out of the truck and walked down to where the water lay a deep and black roll of velvet at their feet. She shivered into her jacket as her eyes adjusted to the light. They got on board and Lex started up the engine. The boat stayed close to the shore as it cut through the darkened waters, past shadowy islands and glaciers.

As she glanced at him in the dim boat light, she couldn't help but notice the frown lines between his eyes.

"You okay?" she asked eventually. "You look worried."

He shrugged. "I just don't want to let you all down."

"Oh, don't worry, you won't," she said. "You've never let me down."

She'd said the words lightly, hoping to sound reassuring and break the thick tension that seemed to fill the night air. But his frown deepened.

"You weren't disappointed when you found out that I'd gone to an Alaskan trooper's recruitment event and your boss recommended I stick with being a park ranger?" he asked. He still wasn't meeting her gaze.

"No...of course not. Lorenza clearly saw that you're great at what you do. And I think everybody's really thankful you're a park ranger right now—I know I am."

Again, she was trying to sound lighthearted. But still, he didn't smile.

"Look," she said. "Do we need to talk this out? Because I'm sorry if I made you feel like I was disappointed in you or something. I guess I've always been really driven and pushed myself, and maybe that made me push you. But I never meant to make you feel less about it. I loved you and everything about having you in my life. You helped me be better and stronger than I ever was without you."

Again, he didn't answer. It was like he was having some internal argument with himself that he wasn't letting her in on. She prayed that whenever he did choose to open up, God would help her find the right words to say.

Silence fell between them again, and eventually the boat slowed as he pulled into an inlet and brought the boat to shore. Dense trees surrounded them, jagged rocks spread out underneath. They started up the slope on foot in the darkness as stealthily as they could, sticking close together with Lex leading the way and Stormy bringing up the rear. Lex's flashlight swung a low, slow beam across the slippery ground. The rocks by the water's edge gave way to scrub and then dense fir trees.

"See?" He gestured first to scuff marks on the ground and then patches of bark worn off the trees. "Bears have definitely been through this area. Unfortunately, we can't tell if they're the ones we're looking for."

She shuddered, remembering what it had been like to come face-to-face with the brown bear the day before. "Can you at least tell if they're friendly bears or unfriendly ones?"

Finally, she got him to crack a smile.

"Never met a friendly bear in the wild," he said. "Don't think bears are designed to be. Although I've spent time at the wildlife conservation center outside Anchorage. It's really extraordinary how they rehabilitate animals and return them to the wild. There's hope that if we find the first bear cub soon enough, and he's in good enough shape, they'll be able to take care of him and then return him to a full, natural life in the forest again."

And if everything worked out as they hoped right now, the cub's sister might never even be poached.

Finally, he stopped in front of what looked like just another cliffside, seemingly no different than countless others they'd passed. Lex shone his light over it, and she saw the shimmering iridescence of the walls of an ice cave cutting into the rock.

"The bears won't be living in this one," he said. "It's too shallow for their needs. But there are several deeper ones nearby that they might be in and if we stake out here we should be able to hear if anything happens in the surrounding area. And I'm not about to go around knocking on caves looking for sleeping bears inside."

She chuckled. "Probably wise."

One up-close-and-personal bear encounter had been enough for one trip. Carefully they stepped into the cave, set a waterproof tarp down against one wall and sat on it side by side. The cave walls were freezing to the touch. But Stormy lay her huge, fuzzy bulk over their feet, snuggling up against Poppy's legs, filling her with warmth. Lex's flashlight beam ran over the walls and she watched as they glimmered in shades of purple, blue and green. Then he switched the light off and pitch-black filled the space around them.

"Welcome to your first stakeout," Poppy murmured. "Although usually we're in a car or apartment building, nowhere this beautiful."

"Thank you." Lex's voice came from the darkness. "Now what?"

"Now, we wait and make boring small talk," she replied. "Stakeouts are a whole lot of boring suddenly followed by a short burst of excitement."

"Got it," Lex said.

They sat for an hour and then a second one, with whispered chatter in between long lapses of silence. She told him about being partnered with Stormy, the K-9 training they went through together, some of the cases they'd worked on and the unique challenges of living with a dog the size of a small pony. He told her about his marriage to Danny's mom, how Debra's life had been a mess and she'd needed him. He'd married her and then they'd had a baby in the hope it would fix things, but it hadn't. Then she could hear warmth fill his voice as he talked about being a father and how deeply he loved his son. They also reminisced about some of the good times they had together and some of the moments they'd thought were bad times but realized in retrospect weren't as big a deal as they'd thought they were.

After a while, she found her side brushing his and her head touching his shoulder, and finally his arm slipping around her. Eventually they saw the soft gray light of the world lighting outside the cave. She glanced at her watch. It was almost five in the morning.

"We give it one more hour and then we call it a bust and head back," she said.

"You seem very calm about the fact I could be totally wrong about this," Lex asked.

"Because I have complete faith in you," she said, "and nobody's right all the time."

"Yeah, but maybe I don't want to let you down, again."

"Again?" She turned toward him and felt his hand brush her back. "Yes, Lex you ended our relationship

and broke my heart, because you didn't see our marriage working and you thought that's what was best for both of us. But when it came to being a solid, caring and reliable man, you never let me down. Sure you weren't always the best at picking up on minor stuff, but I knew you'd always be there for me if I really needed you." She pressed her lips together a long moment and debated how much more to say. Then again, she'd be leaving his life in a few hours. If she wasn't going to be fully honest with him now, she might never get the opportunity to. "I just never thought you believed in yourself. And I wondered if that's why you were so focused on helping everybody else instead of figuring out what you wanted in life."

He didn't answer for a long moment and she wondered if she'd said something wrong.

"I mean, clearly I was wrong to push you into becoming a trooper," she added quickly, "and maybe you are living your best life working here in Glacier Bay now."

"My mother thought I use to shrink myself to make other people happy because I wanted to avoid conflict," Lex confessed. "She was who I was talking to in that one-sided pocket dial conversation I accidentally left on your phone before we broke up."

Poppy gasped. "Gillian? I thought she liked me!"

"She loved you," Lex said. "She was disappointed when I didn't marry you. But she also knew that I didn't feel good enough for you and that it was keeping me from stepping up and being an equal partner, like you deserved. She said a marriage should feel like a strong partnership of equals, not one person feeling more or less than the other."

She swallowed a painful breath. "I'm so sorry," she choked out. "Did I make you feel that way?"

He reached for her hand and squeezed it a long moment.

"Not really," he said. "Not on purpose. You were just so good at everything. Like, with the wedding, you were so organized and on top of everything. You clearly didn't need my help. I felt like if I did try to get involved I was just going to mess things up, and when I did try to suggest things you'd tell me it was already sorted."

"If I'd known that wedding planning was making you feel that way, I'd have canceled everything and just eloped with you!" Poppy said. "I loved you, Lex. I thought you were the most amazing person I'd ever met and I really wanted to marry you."

"Well, I really loved you and wanted to marry you, too," Lex said. "Truth is, I didn't move out to Gustavus because I was finally stepping up and chasing some big dream. I wanted to get away from everything that reminded me of you."

"Really?" She felt her voice drop.

"Yeah." His voice dropped, too. "You were so incredible, and I just couldn't convince myself I was worthy of you. The fact you went for the K-9 trooper training program the moment we split and got accepted...it made me feel like I'd never catch up."

"A relationship is not a competition." She chuckled softly. "I'm never going to be you and you're never going to be me. I don't have your instinctual heart for those who are suffering. You love people better and stronger than anyone I've ever known. Sure, I might be better at budgeting or spreadsheets, but my life was so much better and richer for having a man with a heart like yours in it."

She leaned forward and felt his forehead brush against hers.

"I could never ask you to give up Stormy, your career and your team to stay here with me," Lex whispered, his voice husky.

"And I could never ask you to be anyone other than who you're called to be, either," Poppy said.

"I wish I knew the right thing to say right now," Lex admitted.

"Yeah, me, too."

Her hands slipped up around his neck, and his fingers brushed her face. For one long moment, she let herself kiss him as he kissed her back. And somehow, despite all the tender embraces they'd shared in the past, this one felt deeper, richer...stronger. It was the kind of kiss shared between two people who'd cared for each other profoundly, missed each other and wished there'd been a way to stay in each other's lives.

Stormy growled, a deep guttural warning sound. The fur stood on end at the back of her neck. Poppy and Lex pulled apart and leaped to their feet.

"What's up, Stormy? What do you sense?" Poppy asked her partner. Her hand slid to Stormy's back. She could feel the tension radiating through her. "Show me."

They followed the K-9 out of the cave, walking single file, pushing their way slowly through the trees in the pale predawn light. For a moment she didn't hear anything.

Then came the wail, high-pitched and terrified. The animal cry was so eerily similar to that of a crying infant that Poppy felt her heart seize in terror as Danny's face filled her mind.

Somewhere, a little baby bear cub was crying out in fear.

"They've got her!" Lex called.

Their footsteps quickened as other sounds greeted their ears. The mama bear was snarling. Voices were shouting and swearing. Then she heard the sound of gunfire and the snarling abruptly stopped.

She prayed she'd reach the baby bear cub in time.

Then the trees parted in front of them and there lying on the ground ahead of them was the mother bear. Her black fur was tinged with a silver-blue around the paws and belly. Red blood soaked her soft fur from the bullet wound in her chest. Poppy grabbed Stormy's collar with one hand as she felt Lex grab her other one. Her heart ached.

"There's nothing we can do," he said and she could hear his own internal pain filling his voice. "She won't make it long enough for us to get her help. And in the meantime a wounded bear can be extremely dangerous."

She blinked back tears. They hadn't been quick enough to save the mama bear. But they would not fail her baby girl...

They pressed onward. Determination and strength radiated through Stormy's tall form, her body strained forward as if wanting to run but holding herself back awaiting Poppy's command. Her ears were perked toward the cacophony of sounds ahead.

The poachers were just steps ahead of them now, and she knew without a doubt that Stormy wouldn't let the little cub down. The K-9 would protect the terrified animal, while Poppy and Lex took the poachers into custody, unmasked them and stopped this travesty once and for all.

A motor roared ahead as they reached a clearing. There was tiny cub trapped in a cage on the back of an ATV. The larger poacher in fatigues sat at the handlebars, with the thinner poacher behind him.

"Go!" the thin man shouted, and the vehicle sped up, leaving Lex and Poppy running behind it.

Poppy pulled her weapon, even as she knew she'd never be able to make the shot at that distance.

"We're never going to outrun them on foot!" Lex shouted.

"No, but Stormy can," Poppy said. She turned to her partner. "Stop them!"

Stormy woofed loudly and charged. Her body sprinted, faster and faster, toward the ATV with the tiny captured bear on the back. Within a moment, she'd pulled alongside them. Her teeth bared as her body leaped. The ATV swerved.

A shot rang out.

Stormy yelped. Her body twisted unnaturally in the air as she fell backward. The ATV drove off into the dawn with the captured cub. The wolfhound collapsed.

Stormy had been shot.

TWELVE

"Stay with me!" Lex shouted to the huge dog as he and Poppy eased Stormy from the back of his truck and into his arms. The dog's eyes were closed, and her breath was labored. Blood soaked through the plaid shirt he'd tied around her leg like a tourniquet. He stumbled up his walkway to the front door, taking the heavy bulk of the dog's full weight into his arms. "You're going to be okay. I promise!"

Stormy whimpered. *Thank You, God!* The wound seemed superficial, as far as bullet wounds went, and the dog was still conscious. Later, he was sure his back and arms would hit him with the full ache and strain of having picked up a dog that heavy off the ground, working with Poppy to carry her through the woods to the boat, speeding as fast as he dared back to the dock and then lifting Stormy again into the truck to drive her home. But for now, there was nothing but adrenaline pumping through his veins.

He would save Stormy. He would not let Poppy down.

He could hear prayers pouring from Poppy's lips for her K-9 partner as she ran beside the dog's head.

His mother threw the front door open before they even reached the porch.

"Will and I got your texts," Gillian said, quickly stepping aside to let them in. "I've got the table prepped and Will is upstairs watching Danny. What do you need?"

"She was shot once, in the right hind leg," he said. "She should be fine. It's just a surface wound. But we've just got to clean the wound and stitch it up or we're looking at infection."

Gillian's portable table, which she used for emergency first-aid house calls, was spread out beside the dining room table. He lay Stormy down on it and looked around. Her medicine bag was on the kitchen island.

"Stay by her head and keep talking to her," he told Poppy as he made a beeline for the sink. "I'm going to wash up. She's going to be fine."

"You're closing the wound yourself?" Poppy asked.

"We have to," he said. He yanked the tap to scalding hot and started to lather his hands. "Our town's usual veterinarian won't be back from visiting his grandchildren in Anchorage for at least a week. And the closest emergency vet is in Juneau. But Mom worked in an emergency room and I've done more than my fair share of emergency animal care as a park ranger."

Then he turned the tap off with his elbow and turned back to Poppy. His heart ached as he saw the depth of worry that pooled in her eyes. Tears glistened on the edges of her lashes.

"Trust me," he said. "I've got this. She's going to be fine."

"I know." A weak smile crossed her lips. "I trust you."

He swallowed hard and prayed he wouldn't let her down.

"What can I do to help?" Poppy asked. She was pacing back and forth so quickly she was practically shaking. "What if Danny wakes up and hears us and it scares him? What should I tell my team? How is this going to affect her ability to be in the K-9 unit?"

"Poppy, listen to me," Lex said softly. Her visible agitation faded, and she stopped walking as he said her name. "You don't need to plan or be in charge of anything right now. You definitely don't need to worry. What I need you to do is be there for Stormy. Stay by her face and keep her calm. Cradle her head, stroke her nose, talk to her and pray for her. Reassure her that she's not alone and that she doesn't need to be scared, because you're there for her, okay?"

Poppy nodded. "Okay."

He took a deep breath, met his mother's eyes and then turned to where Stormy lay on the table.

Help me, Lord. Guide my hands. Then all distractions of the world around him faded as he focused on the task in front of him. It wasn't until after he'd stitched up Stormy's wound and carefully bandaged it again, and his mother had gone upstairs to check on Danny, that the ambient sounds of the world around him came back into focus.

He stepped back and Poppy's hopeful eyes met his.

"It's done," he said, his voice feeling oddly husky in his throat. "She's good. Really good. She might have a limp for a week, but I wouldn't be surprised if she's up and walking in a couple of hours. When you get back to Anchorage be sure to have her checked out by the K-9 vet. Now, come on, help me get her over to the blankets on the floor by the fire."

Poppy nodded and her eyes glistened. When she

opened her mouth as if to speak, no words came out. Gently they carried Stormy over and laid her on the soft nest of blankets on the floor in front of the fire. He went back to the kitchen area to wash his hands and tidy up, and when he returned he found Poppy crouched on the ground beside her partner. She ran her hand gently over the back of Stormy's head. The wolfhound's eyes opened and her tongue licked Poppy's hand, then she closed her eyes again.

"Hey." Will's voice came from the doorway behind them. Lex turned. Poppy's colleague was standing there with his K-9 partner, Scout, by his side.

"Hey!" Poppy replied. She started to get up but Will waved her back down.

"Just wanted to let you know that I just got off the phone with Lorenza," he said. "She wants me to catch an early flight to Juneau to liaise with the team there. They don't know if the ship has left yet for the animal auction or not, but judging by the time you say the second bear was poached, they think we're dealing with a pretty small window of time. She said for you to call her later and she'll arrange a flight out for you and Stormy this afternoon."

"Thanks," Poppy replied.

"How's she doing?" Will asked. Concern filled his face.

"Pretty good," Poppy said, glancing back at her K-9 partner. "Thanks to Lex."

Will nodded and went upstairs, leaving them alone again. Lex crossed the room and sat down on the floor beside Poppy. She leaned back against him, and he wrapped his arms around her shoulders from behind.

"How soon until you think she can fly home?" Poppy asked.

"Few hours," Lex said. "Not long. She really is a tough dog."

"She is." Poppy nodded, and he felt her soft hair against his face.

"I'm sorry we didn't stop the other bear cub from being poached."

She turned and looked over her shoulder at him. Her cheek brushed against his arm. "Are you kidding?" she asked. "You were completely right about the location. If anything, it's my fault for telling Stormy to charge into danger like that, but that's her job. She's a state trooper and is trained to risk her life when duty requires her to. Stormy's far more than just a dog. She's a law enforcement officer."

"I know," Lex said softly.

Just as he knew there was absolutely no way to relieve the unrelenting heaviness inside his heart. Here Poppy was in his arms, her face just inches from his. It would take nothing to lean forward, kiss her lips and pull her closer. But then what? There was little he could say. There was no way he could ever ask her to give up her partner, her career and her team to move here to Gustavus to start a life with him and Danny, no matter how much his heart might want to. There was no possible compromise where she somehow kept her job with the K-9 trooper unit and lived somewhere so remote she'd have to fly hours to every case. And if he gave up his life here to chase after her, wouldn't he just be repeating a new variation of the mistakes he'd made in the past?

"I'm really going to miss you," Poppy whispered.

She closed her eyes and as his hand brushed the side

of her face he felt the soft wetness of tears slipping from underneath her eyelids.

"Me, too," he said.

His heart lurched. He wanted to be her hero, to swing into action and rescue her from the situation they were in. He wanted to go back in time and fix their past heartbreak. He wanted to solve the case, capture the poachers, rescue the glacier bear cubs and rehabilitate them back into the wild himself.

Maybe he'd always wanted to be the one to leap in and rescue her, on some level, and when he didn't need to he didn't know what role he was supposed to play in her life. *A marriage should feel like a strong partnership of equals.* He had no idea what that would even look like.

All he knew is that the longer he stayed there, holding Poppy in his arms and wiping her tears from her eyes, the more likely he was to pull her close, kiss her lips and hand her his damaged heart.

Then they'd both end up hurt again. For both their sakes, he couldn't let that happen.

"I've got to go," he said, easing himself away from her and standing. "I'm sorry, I have to get to work. Glacier Bay National Park opens to tourists for the season in about two weeks and we've still got a lot to do to get it ready. Not to mention we have to manage the press side of the bear cubs being poached."

She looked up at him for a long moment, then she stood and ran her hands through her hair.

"Yeah, you're right," she said. "I'm sorry, I guess I forgot you've got more to your job than just escorting us around and helping out my team."

A forced smile crossed her face and he recognized

it in an instant as the one she used when she was determined to put a bright spin on things instead of falling apart.

"Depending when you get back, I might not be here,"
she added. "I know that Will definitely won't be as
he's leaving momentarily by the sound of things. But
until I talk to Lorenza, I won't know when they're flying me out."

Yeah, she was definitely using that upbeat tone of
voice that meant she'd decided not to be upset. It was
one he wished he'd paid more attention to in the past,
before it was too late.

"I'm probably looking at a ten-or twelve-hour workday today, to be honest," he said, hoping his attempt to
be positive sounded as natural as hers. He shifted his
weight from one foot to another. "There's not much I
can do to help with the case now that the bears have
been poached, and I've got a lot of overtime ahead of
me to catch up on everything. But text or call me to let
me know when you're leaving, okay? And if you happen to still be here tonight when I get back, maybe you
can let me know how things are going with the case?"

Poppy gasped, her attention suddenly diverted before she could answer, and it took a moment to figure
out why. He turned. Stormy was slowly climbing to her
feet. They watched as she rose, gingerly at first, test-
ing whether to put weight on her bandaged hind leg
before deciding against it and standing on three. Her
tail thumped weakly. Prayers of thanksgiving slipped
almost silently from Poppy's lips.

"You're up," Lex said. He reached out his hand and
Stormy licked it gently. "You really are something else.
Even injured you can probably still beat me at crawling."

"I'm sorry." Will's voice came from behind them. "Your mom's on a phone call. And I tried to stop him, but he got away from me."

Lex turned and there stood Danny still in his pajamas, holding the kitten in front of him with both hands.

"Grandma said Stormy hurt," Danny said. "Mu'shoom want help!"

Poppy's hand rose to her lips as if to stifle a cry as Danny crossed the floor carefully holding the kitten.

"No problem," Lex told Will.

The trooper walked over to the kitchen and poured some food in a bowl for Scout and an instant later his K-9 partner bounded down the stairs to join him.

With Lex's guiding hand, Danny set Mushroom down beside Stormy. The wolfhound bent down and sniffed the kitten's head, then slowly she eased herself back to lying down. The kitten curled up against her snout and Stormy's tail thumped slowly in response.

Lex swept Danny up into his arms. "That was very good thinking, buddy."

"Good kitten," Danny said.

"Yes," Poppy replied. "She's not big and strong like Stormy, but she's very good at being a kitten. And you are very good at being you."

Danny nodded enthusiastically and Lex cuddled his son closely.

"I'm going to hug you both now," Poppy said. "This seems like a good time to say goodbye."

She stepped forward and wrapped her arms around both of them at once. For a long moment he felt her there, holding on to both him and his son, before she pulled away.

"I am so happy that I came here to see you and your

daddy," she told Danny brightly. "You are so wonderful and thank you so much for inviting me into your house."

"Stormy come back?" Danny asked.

Lex watched as Poppy's smile wavered slightly, but all she said was, "That is a great idea."

He swallowed a painful breath. "Take care of yourself, Poppy. Don't forget to let me know how Stormy is and that you made it home safe."

"Will do. Bye, Lex."

"Bye, Poppy."

Then he turned, walked out of the room and carried his son upstairs, feeling the hopeless weight of regret in every step.

Poppy exhaled. So, that was that, then. She and Lex had opened another chapter, only to close it, leaving her with the new ache in her heart just as painful as the old one.

Lord, I want to fix this mess, but I don't know how. I've always believed, on some level, that if only I worked hard enough and tried hard enough I could make anything happen. And now? I'm realizing how wrong I was to think I could ever make a relationship with Lex work all on my own. I wish we'd been genuine partners.

"Hey." Will's voice drew her attention back to the room. He was still standing in the kitchen with Scout by the dog bowls. She'd forgotten he was there. "Why don't you go lie down for a bit? I'm guessing you haven't slept. Scout and I can keep an eye on Stormy for you. I've got a can of some really great wet food I save for special occasions in my bag, and I'm sure Scout would be happy to share it with Stormy."

"Thank you," Poppy said, not that she had any confidence her weary heart and body would be able to sleep. "When do you head out?"

"Little over half an hour."

"See you, then." She gave Stormy one more scratch behind the ears, then bent down and kissed the top of her partner's shaggy gray head. Then Poppy went into her room, kicked off the boots she'd forgotten to take off when she'd rushed into the house with a wounded Stormy and lay on top of the bed, fully clothed. Despite what she'd been expecting, she passed out into a deep and dreamless sleep almost immediately, before she could even formulate prayers in her exhausted mind.

Poppy awoke to find the door ajar and Stormy sleeping on the floor beside her bed. She checked her phone and saw with a jolt that over two hours had passed. There was a text from Will telling her that when he'd come to say goodbye, she'd been sleeping so soundly he'd let her be and would see her soon. Another message from Lorenza told her to give her a shout when she woke up, which Poppy guessed meant Will had told her she was napping.

She freshened up and headed out into the living room, Stormy slowly walking on three legs behind her. There she found a note on the kitchen island from Gillian letting her know that she and Danny had gone to see friends, and Lex was at work, but that she'd left Poppy food in the fridge. She glanced at the front door and found it locked.

"Okay, then," she said to Stormy, "guess it's just you and me, partner."

She texted Lorenza that she was awake and free to chat. Moments later her laptop rang with a phone call from Eli. Poppy sat down at the table and Stormy lay beside her and rested her head on Poppy's leg. She answered the call and blinked to see almost the entire K-9 team's smiling faces in boxes on the screen.

"Hi!" she said, running her hands through her hair. Her eyes flickered around the screen.

All of the troopers were there, except for Sean and Gabriel, who she guessed were off searching for the survivalist family, and Will, who she presumed was still in transit. Lorenza's assistant, Katie, was there, too, sharing a screen with tech guru Eli.

"I'm sorry, did I miss a team meeting?" Poppy asked.

"Just a bit," Eli said with a grin.

"But don't worry about it," Lorenza added quickly. "You're allowed to rest, especially after everything you've been through. How's Stormy? Do you think she'll be up to flying back to Anchorage at three?"

Poppy looked over to where her partner lay in a sunbeam by the back window. The wolfhound snored slightly.

"Yeah, I think so," she answered. "She's up and walking already, but she's taking it very slow."

"Wonderful." Lorenza smiled. "Well, wish her the best from all of us and rest assured that we'll have a vet ready to check her out when she gets back."

"Any update on the poached bear cubs or the animal auction ship yet?" Poppy asked.

"Sadly, no," Lorenza said. "But we're expecting Will to check in soon after he coordinates with the coast guard team on the ground in Juneau. And, of course,

Eli is working double-time to try and locate this boat from every possible angle. We'll find those bears and bring them home to Alaska. Meanwhile, Helena was just giving us an update on the missing bride case and her interview with the groom Lance's sister, Tessa."

"Thank you again, Poppy, for giving me your perspective on how your interviews for this case had gone," Helena said. "You were right, there's definitely more there worth looking into and I can see why Lance's exgirlfriend suggested we talk to Tessa to get a different viewpoint than the rosy one his parents were painting."

"So, she backed up Lance's ex-girlfriend's story?" Poppy asked.

"Yes and more so," Helena said. "To hear Tessa tell it, her brother is a raging narcissist and a liar who's really good at fooling people into seeing whatever side of him they want him to see. She says he was never able to fool her because they grew up together so she saw the kind of stuff he pulled and what he got away with."

"Wow," Poppy murmured. "Although, to be honest, I'm not surprised, considering how much Lance's exgirlfriend wanted us to talk to her."

"According to Tessa, anything Lance tells us should be discounted and flipped on its head," Helena added. Then she frowned. "But sibling relationships are complicated. I've got a fraternal twin who's made some bad choices herself."

"All the more reason to bring Lance and his best man, Jared, in for questioning again," Lorenza said. "Anyone got anything else?"

Brayden waved a hand.

"Not sure if it counts as progress," the trooper said, "but another reindeer went missing from the sanctuary."

"Apparently, my aunt blamed one of the farm hands," Katie chimed in. "He got so mad about it that he quit. She's really at her wits' end about who's behind this."

"Do you think Lex would mind if I picked his brain sometime?" Brayden added. "It sounded like he knew a lot about the animal rehabilitation community."

"I'm sure he'd be happy to," Poppy said. She debated mentioning her complicated past with Lex, but wasn't quite sure where to start. She didn't doubt that when she was ready to talk it out with someone her team would be there for her, and for that she was thankful. An odd thought crossed her mind. "Katie, have you tried looking into people you and your aunt have been romantically involved with? It's like what Helena said about how sibling relationships are complicated—romantic relationships are, too."

A light dawned behind Katie's eyes. "It's worth a shot. I'll start working on a list."

"I'll help you," Brayden said.

Motion drew her eyes to the front window. There was someone standing on the porch. Then the doorknob rattled, like someone was trying to let themselves in but couldn't get the door unlocked.

"Hang on," Poppy said, and stood. "I think there's someone at the door."

She muted the call, left her laptop on the living room table, walked to the front entrance and glanced through the curtains. It was Ripley, standing on the porch in a T-shirt, long sweater and pair of plaid pajama-style pants that looked too thin for the spring chill in the air. Her arms were crossed so tightly her hands to be seemed wedged under her arms.

Poppy opened the door.

"Ripley!" she said. "Hi! What are you doing here?" And had she just been trying to let herself in?

"Is Lex home?" Ripley asked. The younger woman's gaze darted to Poppy's face for a moment and then back to the ground, but not before Poppy noticed the raccoon rings of day-old makeup smudged by tears in her eyes.

"No," Poppy said. "But do you want to come in? I was about to make some coffee and you could join me for a late brunch."

Ripley hesitated.

"I can't stay long," she said. "My brother Nolan dropped me off, and he'll be back soon."

"Is everything okay?" Poppy asked.

"No, I mean yeah," Ripley said. "I'm fine. I just wanted to thank Lex for everything and let him know we're leaving town for a bit. I just need to get away for a while."

Poppy believed that last statement, but she wasn't sure about the rest.

"Well, come inside and I'll give Lex a call to let him know you're here," Poppy said and stepped back. "I'm just finishing up a video call with my team, then we can chat while you wait for Lex. Nolan's very welcome to join us too when he gets back."

In fact, she very much hoped he would. It was about time she got to the bottom of what was going on. Ripley unfolded slightly as she stepped into the warmth, and Poppy closed the door behind her. The young woman's hand darted toward her pocket but not before Poppy's keen eyes caught a glimpse of the keychain in her hands.

"Did Johnny give you a set of Lex's house keys?"

Poppy asked. "I thought Lex asked Johnny to give those back."

And apparently he'd made a spare copy before he had. She reached out her hand expectantly with her palm open. The keys shook as Ripley dropped the keys into them.

"Yeah," she said, her eyes darting everywhere but Poppy's face. "He said that Lex was a really good man and that if I was ever in trouble or I needed help I could come here, and Lex would make sure I was okay."

Poppy felt both her heart and mind swirling with questions like two water wheels working together to try and sift lies from truth. Yes, she could see Johnny making a secret copy of Lex's house keys if he thought Ripley was in danger and might need a place to hide. Did that mean that he was also the one who booby-trapped his own house?

She took a deep breath and prayed for wisdom.

"I need to quickly finish my video call," she said. "But then I'm looking forward to talking with you while we wait for Lex. I'm really glad you came over, especially if you were worried about something. You're safe here."

Ripley nodded weakly, then she stood almost hovering in the living room doorway as Poppy picked up her laptop and took it into the bedroom.

"I've got an unexpected visitor," Poppy said to her team as she restarted the call. "Johnny's girlfriend is here. She was actually trying to let herself in with a copy of the keys Lex gave him."

Helena sucked in a sharp breath. "Do you think that's where the guy who broke in and tried to kidnap Danny got his keys from too?"

"I can't rule that out," Poppy said. "She says her

brother dropped her off and will be back to pick her up in a bit. I'm just really thankful she's here. Hopefully, she'll open up to me and we'll finally get some answers."

"If anyone can get through to her you can," Lorenza said.

The video call ended in a flurry of goodbyes from both her team and a scattering of their K-9 partners who made brief appearances on the screens. She dialed Lex's cellphone number, and when he didn't answer left a voicemail message saying Ripley was at the house. Then she headed back into the living room.

Ripley was nowhere to be seen. Stormy looked up at Poppy from where the dog lay on the floor.

Poppy glanced at Stormy. "Where did she go?"

The wolfhound whined softly. A soft thud came from the floor above her, followed by the sound of several somethings clattering on the floor. She turned, ran upstairs and raced down the hall, just in time to see Ripley dashing away down the stairs in the opposite direction. She'd taken her sweatshirt off and was now clutching it to her chest like there was something bundled inside it. A passing glimpse into Gillian's room showed what looked like the contents of the woman's jewelry case strewn across the floor.

She'd been robbing them?

"Ripley!" Poppy shouted. "Stop!"

She pelted after her, down the stairs, as Ripley burst through the back door and out onto the lawn. The door slammed shut behind her, leaving Stormy behind on the other side. Poppy didn't have her weapon on her but could easily outrun and tackle the frailer woman.

"I'm giving you to the count of three!" Poppy shouted. "One, two—"

Ripley stopped so suddenly that Poppy almost barreled into her. The young woman turned and raised her hands, dropping the sweatshirt and sending even more jewelry and a mason jar full of loose coins and bills spilling onto the grass.

"I'm sorry!" Ripley's voice quivered. "I need money. I was hoping Lex would lend me some. But when he wasn't here…"

For a long beat Poppy just stared at her, knowing that Ripley was aware she'd been caught red-handed and asking God's wisdom in what to do next. Yes, she could arrest her and probably still would. But, if she showed the woman mercy, would God use it to open up Ripley's heart? Then Poppy saw the small, round bruises on Ripley's forearms, the telltale signs that someone had grabbed her arms roughly and held on to her too tight.

It was only then she realized she still hadn't called Lex. If only he were here…

"What do you need money for, Ripley?" she asked. "I heard your ex-boyfriend Kevin was back in town saying something about you owing him money. Is he the one who left those bruises on your arms?"

"Like I told everybody, Kevin left town days ago," Ripley said almost mechanically as if repeating something she'd been told to say. "Nolan flew him out of town right before Johnny died."

But those bruises weren't a few days old.

"Was it your brother, Nolan?"

"No!" Ripley's voice rose as something bordering on indignation flashed in her eyes. "Nolan would never hurt me. He's only ever wanted to protect me!"

Fair enough, that much Poppy believed. But during

her time in law enforcement Poppy had seen far too many people make very bad decisions to protect others.

"Is Kevin the one who locked you in the closet and killed Johnny?" she asked, gently.

"I don't know." Ripley's lip quivered "He was masked…"

"But you think it could be," Poppy said. Ripley nodded. "I can't give you money, and I definitely can't let you rob Gillian and Lex. But I want to help you and I'm willing to listen. How about I gather up these things, we go back inside and talk?"

Before she could answer, a large black truck pulled up down the road and stopped beside the house. The man behind the wheel was big, with hands too big and beefy to have left those bruises. A handgun sat on the dashboard just within reach. Between his beard and baseball cap his face was pretty well covered. But something about his form sent a chill down her spine.

Ripley's brother, Nolan, was the large poacher.

But how? Will had been convinced Nolan was protective of Ripley and would never hurt her.

Nolan leaned over and threw the door open for his sister.

"Get in!" he shouted. "We've got to go."

The sound of the man's voice confirmed it. This man was one of the criminals behind everything that had happened and the only one who could help them stop the sale of the bear cubs. She couldn't let him take Ripley and leave. But her weapon was still in her room, Stormy was injured, her team was hours away and she had no backup. She was on her own.

Then an idea struck her.

She reached into her pocket for her phone and hit redial, praying Lex would pick up.

"But, she knows about Kevin," Ripley said. "If we tell her what's happening, maybe she can help us."

"Or maybe we all end up dead." Nolan's eyes narrowed. His hand twitched toward his gun. "This only ends one way. So, Poppy, mind your own business if you know what's good for you. Ripley, get in the truck."

THIRTEEN

Lex's phone was ringing again as he pulled back into his parking space in front of the lodge after a tour of the park's cabins to see which ones were still in need of repair. He turned off the engine, undid his seat belt and glanced at the screen. It was Poppy, again. Lex had let the call go through to voice mail the first time, figuring she was just calling to let him know about her flight home to Anchorage. He'd been mentally kicking himself for letting her go yet again, while also not knowing how he could possibly keep her in his life in any meaningful way, and hearing the sound of her voice was just a little more than he was up for right in that moment.

But now the fact she was calling a second time within a few minutes worried him.

Lord, guide my words and help me be wise in what I say and do. I care about this woman so much. But I only want her in my life and by my side if I can do it right.

He answered on the third ring.

"Hey, Poppy," he said. "How's it going?" She didn't answer. For a moment he heard nothing but background noise of trees rustling, voices too muffled to understand and fabric shuffling. "Hello? Poppy?"

Still nothing. His head shook. Unbelievable, she'd apparently pocket-dialed him. He reached to hang up the phone when he heard Poppy's voice cutting loudly through the sound.

"Ripley," she said. "I don't think you should get into the truck with Nolan. I think we should go back inside the bed-and-breakfast and call Lex."

He froze, his finger still reaching for the button, then he leaned back against the front seat of his truck.

"Poppy? I'm here." He raised his voice. "Can you hear me?"

She didn't answer and he suspected she'd either muted the call or his voice was muffled by her phone being in his pocket.

Nolan's voice rose. "Get in the truck. Now."

"Ripley, listen to me," Poppy said, her voice urgent. "I know Johnny loved you and wouldn't want to see you hurt. It's clear from the bruises on your arm that someone's been rough with you. I'm guessing it was Kevin and that you both have been lying about him leaving town."

Lex knew without a doubt that he was the true audience of her words. His heart ached, knowing she probably didn't even know for certain that he could hear her.

Poppy, I'm here. I'm listening.

"That's enough!" Nolan's voice bellowed.

A gun clicked. Lex's breath froze in his chest. He grabbed his keys, fired up the engine and threw his truck in Reverse.

Hang on, Poppy, I'm coming.

"Ripley, I think Kevin came to town when he got out of jail to cause trouble for you and didn't leave," Poppy's words tumbled over each other quickly, as if she knew she was running out of time to speak them. "I'm guessing he somehow forced your brother into helping him poach baby bears. Maybe he said it would settle the score between you. Or that he'd finally leave Ripley alone if he did. I know he told people you owed him money. You got worried for your brother, or for yourself, and told Johnny who told Lex. But instead Kevin killed Johnny."

"Not another word!" Nolan's voice rose to a roar. "Hands up where I can see them!"

"Lex!" Poppy shouted. "Help! I'm—"

A gun fired. The phone went dead.

"Poppy!" Lex shouted, feeling her name wrenched from somewhere deep inside his heart. "Lord, please, you've got to help me save her!"

He hit Redial as he drove as fast as he dared back through the trees toward Gustavus. Nobody answered. He called his mother and told her Poppy was in trouble, to keep Danny safe and stay with friends. The second he heard her agree he hung up and called Will. The trooper didn't answer. He tried Poppy's line again. It rang through to voice mail.

Lord, help me. I don't know what's going on. I don't know where she is. All I know is that she's in danger and she needs me to save her. I can't let her down.

Finally, he reached his home and swerved into the driveway, barely stopping the engine before he leaped out. The glass on the road in front of his house told him a vehicle window had been shot. Flattened grass indicated there'd been a struggle.

He ran up to the house, threw open the door and ran inside. It was deserted and untouched. Poppy was gone. Then he heard the sound of barking rise around him as, moments later, Stormy scrambled down the hall faster than he'd have dreamed imaginable considering her injury and butted her head against his leg.

"Poppy's gone, isn't she?" He ran his hand along the K-9's head. "Don't worry. We're going to find her."

He found her laptop on the table and turned it on. As the screen came to life, he tried the same password she'd used back when they were dating to stream movies on her television and breathed a prayer of thanks when it worked. Then he took a breath, opened the video chat call and hit the one for Colonel Lorenza Gallo.

Moments later the head of the K-9 unit appeared on screen. She blinked.

"Lex?" she said. "Where's Poppy?"

"She's been kidnapped," he informed her. "By Nolan who also has his sister with him and might have kidnapped her, too. I need help."

Lorenza's face paled.

"I'm sending a team immediately," Lorenza said, her hands moving rapidly over the keyboard. "But they won't get there for over an hour."

Over an *hour*? Poppy might not have that long.

"Where did he take her?" Lorenza asked.

"I don't know!" He tried to sit but found himself jumping right back up again. "The docks, I'm guessing. But I don't know which one or which direction they went to meet up with that boat your team is searching for. There are multiple ways to leave the glaciers and so many places they could hide."

"Think," Lorenza said, her tone so firm it was almost a command. "Poppy's counting on you right now. She's all you've got to direct us where to go."

He felt Stormy's head drop onto his knee. The wolfhound looked up at him and he ran his hand along her back. They were all Poppy had, a wounded K-9 dog and a park ranger who struggled with self-doubt.

"Where is she?" Lorenza's voice cut through his thoughts.

"I told you... I don't know!"

"Take a deep breath," Lorenza said. "Hold it for three seconds. Then let it out and start telling me everything you *do* know."

He took a deep breath in, praying for God's guidance, then let it out again.

"When she called me, she was with Ripley and Nolan," Lex said. "It sounded like Nolan was trying to take Ripley somewhere."

"Did she mention a boat?" Lorenza asked.

"No, just his truck. But she speculated that Kevin somehow forced Nolan into helping him poach the bear. She guessed maybe it was because he thought they owed him money or maybe he promised to leave Ripley alone if he did. She also speculated that Ripley had been the one who'd told Johnny about the bears."

Of course. His former friend was nothing if not loyal and had lied about going to the watering hole to protect the woman he loved. Lex just wished he'd seen it sooner.

"I know all the web traffic says the bear cubs were being moved by boat," Lex added, "but that doesn't make sense considering Nolan owns a small charter airline. I'm guessing Kevin is the one who tried to take Danny hostage. And if he was telling the truth about already having a client lined up to take the cubs, as Poppy suspected, maybe the whole boat business thing online is a red herring. Could be that there is no overseas animal auction and no ship. Which means that it was just a ruse to draw attention away from Nolan's remote airfield."

He closed his eyes a moment and when he opened them again he felt a fresh surge of adrenaline fill his core.

"Nolan had to have taken her to his airfield," he said. "It's just a guess but an educated one based on Poppy's theory that what Danny's kidnapper said was the truth, not the online posting. And that has already turned out to be partially right."

'Good enough for me," Lorenza told him. "I'll send Will back from Juneau, with backup, to meet you there."

"I'm taking Stormy with me," he said. "I know she's limping and can't leap into action, but she's my best hope for sniffing out where they have Poppy stashed if they've hidden her somewhere."

The wolfhound looked up at him and he knew that the K-9 wouldn't have had it any other way.

He just hoped they reached her in time.

Poppy woke up to find her head groggy, what felt like a bandanna blindfolding her eyes and her hands tied together behind her back with plastic zip ties.

Just like she'd found Johnny.

Please, God, help me focus. She was sitting on what felt like a wooden chair. Despite the fact her eyes were blindfolded, the brightness of the light shining through the thin layer of fabric let her know it was still daytime and probably even still late morning. The combination of brain fog and a twinge in her neck told her she'd been sedated with something sharp, probably a dart, but she could also tell it hadn't been that strong. Poppy raised her head and blinked, scrunching her face just enough to catch a glimpse of the world underneath a tiny gap in the bottom of her blindfold. She couldn't see much, not much more than a sliver. But it was enough to tell she was on a concrete floor with crates stacked high on the edges of the room, like in some kind of warehouse. Then she caught a sliver of blue sky to her right.

She was in an airplane hangar.

Help me, Lord, nobody knows I'm here! The entire might of the K-9 trooper unit was focused on checking the harbors, ports and ocean beyond for boats, and here Nolan had taken her to his small private airport.

Sounds reached her ears now, mingling with the beat of her own heart pounding. Multiple voices were talking over each other in a garbled mass of sound. There were at least three men, by the sounds of it, and it sounded like they were arguing over money being exchanged and some kind of big financial deal was going down. There was a low growling too that sent shivers of danger down her spine. Then she heard the plaintive sound of two baby bear cubs crying and realized their sale was happening here and now.

And she was a helpless witness to it—kidnapped, alone and unable to do anything to stop it but pray.

Then she heard another noise coming from behind her. It was a rustling so subtle she could barely make it out above the chaos of noises swirling in front of her. But she heard it nonetheless, a low and soft sound like someone was crawling through crates and tarps across the floor toward her.

No... It couldn't be.

A warm furry head brushed against her bound hands and a wet tongue licked her fingertips.

"Stormy!" She whispered her partner's name so

softly it was almost silent on her lips, but she knew the dog's excellent hearing would pick it up. "Good girl."

What was her injured partner doing here? Let alone crawling across the floor like she'd demonstrated in the bed-and-breakfast to make Danny giggle in what felt like a lifetime ago?

But then she felt the dog shift so that her fingers brushed the K-9 canvas harness that Stormy was now somehow dressed in and felt something cold and hard underneath her fingertips. She eased it out of the harness.

It was a pocketknife. Tears rose in her eyes. *Oh, Lex. You're here, too?* He'd found her, and instead of charging into danger and risking their lives to help her, he'd sent Stormy to arm her.

"Good girl," she whispered again. "Now go and hide! Stormy, hide!"

She pressed her lips together and prayed her partner would obey her command. Then something lurched in her chest as she felt the dog's soft fur leave her touch and heard the sound of Stormy crawling away. She turned the knife slowly in her bound fingertips, pricking her thumb slightly as she released the blade and slid it between the plastic zip ties. Then she began cutting. Relief flooded her limbs as she felt the bonds loosening. Just a couple more moments and she'd be able to snap them free.

A crash sounded somewhere behind her and to her left like a box toppling over.

"What was that?" called the skinny poacher, who she now assumed was Kevin. "Go check it out."

Fear seized her. Was it Stormy? Was it Lex?

She stopped cutting, hid the knife in her hands and

started shaking the chair from left to right, banging the wooden legs on the concrete as loudly as she could to draw all eyes and attention to her.

"She's awake!" Nolan shouted.

"Go get her to stop!" Kevin replied.

Her distraction worked well enough. She heard footsteps pounding toward her.

"Stop that!" Nolan bellowed. "Right now!"

She complied. The poacher's feet stopped just inches to her right, so close she could see his knees and boots through the thin gap at the bottom of the blindfold.

"Listen," Nolan hissed as he leaned closer. "This whole thing is almost done, okay? In just a few more minutes, the buyer will leave with the bears, Kevin will get his money, we'll let you go and we can all go on with our lives."

His voice was so earnest it pained her to think just how much he needed to believe it was true.

"Where's your sister?" she whispered.

"Waiting in the truck," he said.

"Is she free to go or did Kevin insist she was tied up?" Poppy hazarded a guess.

The fact he didn't answer told her everything she needed to know.

"This is just about money," Nolan said. "Kevin won't leave Ripley alone until he gets the money he thinks we owe him for lawyer's fees, bail and losing his business and stuff, from when we called the police on him and he went to jail. You were right, okay? He said if I helped him poach and sell the cubs we'd be even. Then he'd leave Ripley alone and never bother her again."

"You figured if calling the police on him and even sending him to jail didn't keep him away, you'd step up and fix it, right?" Poppy whispered. "I get that. But it won't work. He'll just keep coming back."

"Hey!" Kevin snapped from what sounded like the other side of the hangar. "What are you doing over there? I didn't give you permission to start chatting with her. What's she saying? Tell me what she's telling you!"

Poppy risked sliding the blade of the knife back between her bound wrists again.

"Just shut up, okay?" Nolan whispered. "Or he's going to make me knock you out again and I don't want to."

"Let me go," Poppy whispered back. "I'll save Ripley and protect her. I promise."

Nolan hesitated.

"Change of plans!" Kevin shouted. "The client doesn't want the brown bear. Says it's too big for their little plane. Plus he's worried it's gonna wake up and if we tranq it again, its heart might stop. But he likes the look of Poppy and is willing to pay extra to take her, too. We got the cubs on the plane already and his pilot is all fueled up and ready to go. Help me get the girl on the plane for him quick and then we're done."

Her heart stopped as a quiver of fear sent chills through her core. But she gritted her teeth and prayed.

Lord, give me the strength I need to escape this evil.

"Time for you to choose whether you're going to be a hero or a villain, Nolan," Poppy said. She wrenched her hands apart, her wrist screaming in pain as the bonds snapped. Then, leaping from the chair, she yanked the blindfold down with one hand and clenched the knife in the other.

Sunlight flooded her eyes. Out of her periphery, she saw Kevin dash out the wide and open side of a modest airplane hangar toward what looked like a small but very expensive private plane. She spun toward Nolan.

"I'm Trooper Poppy Walsh of the Alaska K-9 Unit and you're under arrest for poaching, kidnapping, murder and attempted murder. You have the right to remain silent—"

"You kidding me?" He gripped his gun with both hands and pointed it at her face. "I've got a gun aimed at you, and all you've got is a little knife!"

"Yeah," Poppy agreed. "But you're alone and I've got backup."

Somewhere. She couldn't see Lex or hear him. She had no proof that she wasn't alone and that there was no one hiding among the boxes and crates to leap out and save her.

But she knew Lex and that was all she needed to know.

"Now," she said. "Drop your weapon and get down with your hands up."

Nolan hesitated, the small private engine began to purr and Kevin leaned back in and shouted, "Just shoot her in the leg already and we'll drag her!"

Nolan shook his head as if arguing with himself and aimed his weapon at her leg. The sound of a bullet fired, cracking the air. As she watched, Nolan dropped his gun and clutched his shoulder, screaming in pain as the unseen marksman took out his arm before he could even fire.

"Put pressure on it," Lex shouted. He sprinted out from behind a wall of crates with his gun in his hand. "A tourniquet would be great. You'll need a few stitches, but you'll be fine. We're going to go save the bears and your sister."

Poppy yanked the clip from Nolan's weapon. "Then I'm arresting you."

Lex met her eyes and grinned, and she knew without a doubt that she'd give anything to see that strong, determined and charming smile every day for the rest of her life. He reached into his coat's inside pocket and pulled out her badge and weapon. "Thought you might need these."

"Thank you." She took them and then looked past him. "Where's Stormy?"

"My truck." He ran for the door and she matched pace. "It's hidden around the corner. I thought she'd be safest there, so I snuck her back out after she brought the knife to you."

"Thank you," she said. "You know, you could've left her safe at home."

"You kidding? Stormy would've never forgiven me." She chuckled. Yeah, that was true. "Plus, I needed her tracking skills to find you."

They stepped out into the bright Alaskan sunlight, side by side. Poppy scanned the airfield and suddenly realized what Lex had meant about tracking her. Several small buildings, garages, hangars and sheds dotted the expansive plot of land, intersected by three different runways.

Far to their left, the private plane was driving down to the end of a runway preparing to take off, with the blue cubs inside. Nearby the brown bear lay on its side in a wooden storage crate far too flimsy for an animal its size. Its breathing was erratic, the tranquilizers were definitely wearing off and considering what it'd been through that bear would be likely to lash out and attack the first thing it saw the second it could.

Then a panicked scream for help dragged her attention

to the right. Kevin was sitting in the front seat of Nolan's pickup truck, a terrified and bound Ripley beside him on the passenger seat.

"Shut up!" Kevin backhanded her across the face and gunned the engine.

Kevin was kidnapping Ripley. The little blue cubs were about to fly off with the client who'd paid for them to be trafficked. Another suffering and dangerous bear needed their help, as well.

No matter how hard she tried, she couldn't save them all.

She glanced at Lex, and as her eyes met his, she knew it wasn't even a question.

"We've got to stop that monster from taking Ripley," he said.

"Where's your truck?" she asked.

"This way!"

She followed him and they ran for a nearby shed, yanked the door open and sprinted inside. Stormy woofed in greeting from the front seat of Lex's truck, her voice filling the small space.

"I'll drive," Lex said.

"And I'll shoot," Poppy added. She yanked the passenger side door open and slid in beside her dog. "Stormy, get in the back."

The K-9 barked in agreement and complied. Lex gunned the engine and his truck shot out of the building and onto the runway. She glanced in the rearview mirror. The private plane was almost at the end of the runway. Then all it had to do was turn around and come back at speed for takeoff. She watched Lex's eyes follow the same path hers had taken.

Then he gripped the steering wheel tightly with both

hands and fixed his gaze on Nolan's truck, with Kevin and Ripley inside.

"Hold on," he said. "I'm going to speed."

He gunned the engine and chased after the stolen truck, with Ripley still screaming for help inside. Poppy opened her window and braced her weapon to fire as Lex edged the truck closer and closer. Then he swerved sharply to the right, cutting as close to the truck as he dared. She leaned out the window, aimed for the back tire and fired. The rubber exploded with a bang and the truck spun, flying out of control so quickly that Lex had to mash the brakes to keep from driving into it.

Then, with the jarring sound of metal hitting wood, the truck slammed into a towering fir tree almost half its length. Kevin tumbled out and ran.

"I'll get Ripley," she shouted to Lex as he yanked the door open. "Go take Kevin down!"

She allowed herself to watch for one fleeting moment as he sprinted after Kevin, launched at him in a football tackle and brought him to the ground. Poppy told Stormy to stay and ran for the wreck. She crouched down and looked inside. Ripley sat blindfolded and trembling. Her hands were still bound and her body was scratched from the crash.

"Ripley," she said gently. "It's me, Poppy. You're safe. Now let me take your blindfold off and help you out."

She helped ease the blindfold off, thankful to see her eyes were open and showed no sign of head trauma. Poppy then cut her bonds and cautiously helped her climb from the car, thankful there were no major signs of injury. Ripley stepped out of the car and stood on shaky legs.

Poppy glanced back at where Lex had Kevin down

on the ground. Kevin was swearing, thrashing and try-ing in vain to strike out against Lex. But in an instant, he had him pinned. Then Lex flipped the perp over onto his stomach and tied his hands behind his back with a zip tie.

No sooner had Ripley stepped free from the wreck-age than her eyes rose toward the air hangar. "Nolan!"

"Ripley!" Nolan called. Her brother stumbled to-ward her with what looked like the bandanna Poppy had been blindfolded with tied over the bullet wound. "I'm sorry! I'm so, so sorry!"

She stood back and let the siblings run across the tar-mac to each other. Lex marched Kevin over to her. He'd muffled the man's swear words with a gag. Poppy opened the back door of Lex's truck, called Stormy to get out and watched as Lex pushed Kevin inside and locked the door.

Then she turned toward the private plane with the captured bear cubs inside with Lex on her one side and Stormy at the other.

"We need to stop the plane," she said, even as she felt the futility of their situation wash over her. "We can't let them take the bear cubs."

But it was too late. Already they could see the small jet had turned around. Its propellers whirled and flaps rose. She watched as it taxied down the runway ready to lift off.

Her heart sank and her footsteps stopped. She felt Lex grab her hand and squeeze it tightly. She squeezed it back as tears filled her eyes. The plane was leaving. They'd lost. The bears were being flown off by an un-scrupulous criminal and there was nothing they could do about it.

Then a loud crash and terrifying growl filled the air, as the brown bear broke through its cage.

FOURTEEN

Poppy watched as the expensive jet swerved suddenly, trying to avoid the brown bear as it charged. The plane spun wildly, spinning off the runway like a toy top out of control. It smashed into a tree with a deafening crunch, snapping off a wing.

She gasped a breath. The bear turned and lumbered back into the woods. Then she felt Lex tug her fingers, and they ran together across the tarmac to the wrecked aircraft, with Stormy by their side.

The cockpit door flew open.

"Freeze!" Poppy shouted to the two men inside. She raised her badge and weapon. "I'm Trooper Poppy Walsh and you're under arrest."

Beside her Lex was yanking open the back of the plane. Two small bear cubs looked up at him from inside dog crates.

"It's okay, guys," Lex told the frightened cubs softly. "We've got you. You're safe now."

The client, pilot and Kevin were all sitting handcuffed in one end of the airplane hangar, while Nolan and Ripley sat huddled in the other end what felt like moments later, when she saw three rescue helicopters hovering above them. Will leaped out of the first one as it landed, followed by troopers from the Juneau unit. And suddenly, activity was everywhere as she briefed the team, oversaw the arrests and made sure Nolan and Ripley got medical attention before they were placed into custody. The siblings were already pledging to tell law enforcement everything as their statements were being taken. In the midst of all this, Poppy saw Lex signal her to join him away from the crowd.

She walked over.

"I've got to go coordinate with the animal rescue wildlife center about taking the bear cubs," Lex said. "I'm very hopeful they'll be able to be rehabilitated and released back into the wild. But I didn't want to leave without saying goodbye and telling you that everyone's invited back to our place for food later tonight when this wraps up."

She looked around at the crew of law enforcement and medical professionals expertly wrapping up the scene. "I'm sure everyone will appreciate that."

"You okay?" Lex asked. "You seem a bit down when I'd have thought you should be celebrating."

Was she that transparent around him?

"Do you think the brown bear that charged the plane will be okay?" she asked.

"I hope so," Lex said. "But I'll make sure the park rangers try to locate it." Then he frowned. "I just wish we'd been able to save the mama blue bear. It honestly hurts my heart to know that although we saved those little cubs, they're orphans now."

Unexpected tears brushed her eyelids.

"Me, too," she said.

"I think I'm learning that just because an ending

doesn't look the way I hoped it would doesn't mean it's not a happy one." His arm slipped around her shoulders and he pulled her closer to his side in a half hug. "Will I see you back at the house later?"

"I'll be there," she whispered.

He walked away.

But will my own story have a happy ending?

Night had just begun to fall by the time she finally made it back to the bed-and-breakfast. The cozy living space seemed filled to the brim with happy people, including troopers, rescue workers, park rangers and what seemed like the entire town's worth of friends and neighbors. Potluck dishes spilled over every surface. Will had set up a laptop on the mantel and opened a video chat link for the K-9 team so any of them who wanted to pop into the celebration could. Poppy had made small talk, double-checked that Stormy was happily curled up on the floor with Danny and Mushroom, under Gillian's watchful eye, and somehow managed to avoid ever being completely alone with Lex before she flew out with Will later tonight.

She slipped out the sliding glass door and into the backyard, craving a moment alone with her thoughts before she had to pack up and say goodbye. Poppy watched as the sun dipped slowly behind the distant mountains, casting the glaciers in dusty rose and purple hues.

Help my heart, Lord. It feels like You just brought Lex back into my life and now we're going our separate ways again.

She heard the sliding door open behind her and the gentle babble of voices inside the house grew louder for a moment, before it closed again. Then she heard the footsteps of someone walking across the porch, coming down the steps and crossing the grass toward her. Somehow she knew it was Lex, even before she heard him say her name.

"Poppy?" His voice was soft and husky.

She turned around and there he was standing behind her. The dying light cast long shadows down his handsome face. But it was the depth of emotion pooling in his dark brown eyes that made her heartbeat catch in her chest and everything inside her long to throw her arms around his neck and pull him close.

Help me, Lord. How do I say goodbye?

"How's it going?" she asked.

"Pretty good," Lex said. "I have been wondering something, though, and I didn't know how to ask it." He ran his hand over the back of his neck. "At the airfield, when Kevin crashed the truck, you ran for Ripley and I took him down. Was that for operational reasons or because you knew, on some level, I wanted to be the one who took down the guy who killed my friend?"

"Probably a bit of both," Poppy admitted. "As a trooper my top responsibility in that moment was making sure Ripley was okay. But I'm glad you were there to take Kevin down. Two things can be true at once. I've gotten a lot better at thinking I have to do everything by myself. And I think we make a good team."

"So do I," Lex admitted gruffly.

Poppy felt a tired smile cross her face She glanced at Lex and saw a nervous grin brush his lips, too. Then he took a deep breath.

"Which is why I'd like to fly back to Anchorage with you tonight," he said. "Partly because I want to visit Johnny's family to pay my respects and ask if there's anything I can do to help them with the funeral. Also, I've been talking to people I know at the animal rescue sanctuary where the baby blue bear cubs are headed and wanted to see what I could do to help the little guys heal from their adventure and start a new life in the wild. Turns out, they're hiring and want to talk to me about a potential job. As much as I've enjoyed living here, I think it's time for a new adventure." He took her hands and linked his fingers through hers. "And I want you to be a big part of it. If you want to be."

She felt her breath catch. He brought her hands to his lips and brushed a kiss over her knuckles.

"What are you saying, Lex?" she asked.

"That I'm a better man with you than I am alone," Lex said. "You strengthen me and push me, Poppy. You're strong in areas I'm weak and bring out the best in who I want to be. Moving with my mom and Danny back to Anchorage and starting a new life will be challenging. And I don't want to do it without you. In fact, I don't ever want to do anything big without you ever again."

"I don't want to do anything big without you ever again, either," she confessed.

He pulled his hands from hers and wrapped them around her waist as her fingers slid up and linked behind his neck.

"I'm in love with you, Poppy," Lex said. "Head over heels. I always have been. My mother thinks you're amazing and Danny adores having you and Stormy around. You complete my family in a way nobody could."

She felt happy tears shine in her eyes. "I love you, too. I never stopped."

"I'm so glad to hear that," Lex said, and his grin grew

wider than she'd ever seen before. "Because I want to marry you. I want to be your husband and I want you to be my wife and Danny's mom. But more than that, I want to help you plan our new life together. The boring bank meetings, the budgets, the chores—I'm here for all of it."

"I want to marry you, too."

Then his lips met hers for a long moment and he kissed her, lifting her feet up off the ground as he swept her into his embrace. And as the sunset swept the Alaskan sky, Poppy wrapped her arms tightly around the man she knew without a shadow of a doubt that she was going to love forever.

* * * * *